Greetings of the Season
and Other Stories

Barbara Metzger

Untreed
Reads

Greetings of the Season and Other Stories
By Barbara Metzger

Copyright 2014 by Barbara Metzger
Cover Design by Ginny Glass

ISBN-13: 978-1-61187-759-5

Also available in ebook.

Previously published in print:
Greetings of the Season, 1994
The Proof Is in the Pudding, 1996
Three Good Deeds, 1998
Christmas Wish List, 1999
Little Miracles, 2000

Published by Untreed Reads, LLC
506 Kansas Street, San Francisco, CA 94107
http://www.untreedreads.com

Printed in the United States of America

Without limiting the rights under copyright reserved above, no part of this publication may be reproduced, stored in or introduced into a retrieval system, or transmitted, in any form, or by any means (electronic, mechanical, photocopying, recording, or otherwise), without the prior written permission of both the copyright owner and the above publisher of this book.

If you purchased this book without a cover, you should be aware that this book is stolen property. It was reported as "unsold and destroyed" to the publisher and neither the author nor the publisher has received any payment for the "stripped book."

The scanning, uploading, and distribution of this book via the Internet or via any other means without the permission of the publisher is illegal and punishable by law. Please purchase only authorized electronic editions, and do not participate in or encourage electronic piracy of copyrighted materials. Your support of the author's rights is appreciated.

Publisher's Note
This is a work of fiction. Names, characters, places, and incidents either are the product of the author's imagination or are used fictitiously, and any resemblance to actual persons, living or dead, business establishments, events, or locales is entirely coincidental.

The publisher does not have any control over and does not assume any responsibility for author or third-party websites or their content.

Contents

Greetings of the Season

1

"Dashed if I can figure why everyone gets in such a pucker over this Christmas shopping nonsense." Bevin Montford, the Earl of Montravan, paused in the act of putting the last, critical fold in his intricately tied neckcloth. His valet, standing by with a second or—heaven forfend his lordship be struck with a palsy or such—a third starched cravat, held his breath.

"Why, the park was so thin of company this afternoon, you'd think the *ton* had packed up and gone to their country places weeks early," the earl complained to the mirror. "Where was everyone? Traipsing in and out of shops as if the British economy depended on their spending their last farthings."

The earl finally lowered his chin, setting the crease in his neckcloth. Finster, the valet, exhaled. Another perfect Montravan fall. He tenderly draped the reserve linen over the rungs of a chair and reached for his lordship's coat of blue superfine, just a shade darker than the earl's eyes.

"And now here's Coulton, crying off from our dinner engagement," Montravan went on, shrugging his broad shoulders into the garment. No dandy, the earl refused to have his coats cut so tightly that he'd require two footmen to assist. He made sure the lace of his shirt cuffs fell gracefully over his wrists while Finster straightened the coat across his back. "I never thought I'd live to see Johnny Coulton turning down one of Desroucher's meals to go shopping. Haring off to an Italian goldsmith in Islington, no less."

Finster was ready with the clothes brush, making sure no speck of lint had fallen on the coat between his final pressing and his lordship's occupancy. "I understand Lord Coulton is recently engaged," Finster offered, more relaxed now that the more crucial aspects of his employer's toilette were complete.

"What's that to the point? The chit's blond with blue eyes. Sapphires, obviously. Rundell and Bridges ought to be sufficient for the purpose."

"Ah, perhaps Lord Coulton wished to express his affection in a more personal manner."

"More expensive, you mean. Deuce take it, he's already won the girl's hand; there's no need for such extravagance."

"If the viscount is indeed visiting goldsmiths, he might wish to design a bit of jewelry himself to show his joy at the betrothal."

"Claptrap. You've been reading the housekeeper's Minerva Press novels again, haven't you?" The earl turned from the mirror to catch his longtime servant's blush. "Ah, Finster, still a romantic after all these years? I must be a sad trial to you."

"Not at all, my lord," the valet said with a smile, thinking of all the positions he'd been offered and had turned down. There could be no finer gentleman in the *ton* to work for, none more generous and none who appeared more to his valet's credit than the nonpareil earl. Of course, Lord Montravan was a bit high in the instep, his valet admitted to himself, but how not, when he'd been granted birth, wealth, looks, and charm in abundance? No, Lord Montravan's only fault, according to the loyal Finster, was a sad lack of tender emotions. Still, the valet lived in hope. He passed the silver tray that contained the earl's signet ring and watch fob, the thin leather wallet, and the newly washed coins. He also proffered, by way of explaining Lord Coulton's defection, "*L'amour.*"

"Larks in his brainbox, more likely, getting himself into a pother over a trinket for a wench. And those other clunches, the ones who were too frenzied for a hand of cards at White's yesterday, nattering on about where to find the perfect fan, the best chocolates, the most elegant bibelot for madam's curio. Gudgeons, every last one of them, letting their wits go begging over this nonsensical holiday gift giving."

Finster cleared his throat. "Ah, perchance the gentlemen find the difficulty more in the expense than in the selection. The ladies do expect more than a bit of trumpery at this time of year," he hinted.

The earl sighed. "What, dished again, Finster?" He casually tossed a coin to the smaller man, who deftly caught it and tucked it out of sight in one of his black suit's pockets. "You'd think you'd have learned after all these years either to save your shillings or not to fall in love at the Christmas season. What female has caught your eye this week?"

"The new French dresser at Lady Worthington's. Madeleine." Finster whispered the name and kissed his fingertips.

"French, eh?" Montravan tossed another coin, which followed its brother, then shook his head. "Next I suppose you'll be wanting the afternoon off to do your shopping."

"The morning should be sufficient, milord, thank you." Finster smiled. "After milord returns from his ride, naturally."

"Naturally. I suppose I should be thankful my own valet is not abandoning me in favor of the shops." The earl gave a final combing through his black curls with his fingers, setting them into the fashionable windswept style. One curl persisted in falling over his high forehead. He shrugged and left it.

"Though it would be all of a piece with this wretched week. What gets into everyone mid-December that their attics are to let? There must be some brain fever that scrambles perfectly normal minds into this mush of indecision, this urge to outrun the bailiffs, this agony of self-doubt over a bauble or two. Just look at you, the most fastidious person I know." He waved his manicured hand around his own spotless bedchamber, where not a towel remained from his bath, not a soiled garment was in sight, not a loose hair reposed on the Aubusson carpet. "Then comes Christmas shopping. You are ready to desert your post in order to wait for some caper-merchant to deign to assist you in spending your next quarter's salary. Mush, I say. Your brains have turned to mush along with everyone else's."

Finster smiled as he polished the earl's quizzing glass on a cloth he pulled from another pocket. "There is no other way, milord."

"Of course there is," said Montravan, surveying his person through the glass. "Organization, efficiency, an orderly mind— that's all it takes to keep this idiocy in proper perspective. You don't see me chasing my own shadow up and down Bond Street, do you?"

"No, milord, your secretary does that for you."

The earl chose to ignore that home truth. "Humph. The diamond or the black pearl?" he asked, nodding toward the velvet-lined tray holding his stickpins.

Finster surveyed the earl, the muscular thighs encased in black satin, the white marcella waistcoat with silver embroidery. "The ruby, I believe, will be more festive. 'Tis the season, after all."

Montravan frowned. "Blast the season."

Still, he affixed the ruby in his neckcloth, told his man not to wait up for him, and stepped jauntily down the stairs.

Ah, the season. Just a few more weeks and his own perfectly ordered existence would be even more satisfactory. He'd have satisfied his filial duties with a trip to Montravan Hall in Wiltshire and fulfilled his more pressing familial obligations with the selection of his future countess. If Lady Belinda Harleigh proved satisfactory during the visit she and her parents were making to the ancestral pile, Montravan meant to offer for the duke's daughter before the new year. Then he'd be free to return to London and his new mistress. First, of course, was this minor trifle of Christmas shopping to be gone through. The earl consulted the pendulum clock in the marble hallway. Yes, there was an hour before dinner; that should do the trick.

2

The library at Montford House, Grosvenor Square, was larger than Hatchard's Bookstore and likely contained more volumes. Unlike the bookseller's, what it did not contain—and would never contain, if Bevin Montford had any say in the matter—was any gaggles of chattering females or any of those gothicky romances so beloved of polite society and its servants. The library was quite Lord Montravan's favorite room in the house, with its precise shelves of both old tomes and new editions, all neatly cataloged and in their proper order. Situated toward the rear of Montford House so no street noises could intrude, and thickly carpeted to muffle any interior sounds, the library was a quiet haven of dark wood and old leather.

What did intrude, and did offend the earl's usual feeling of contentment in this private place, was the young man standing next to the large desk. Wearing yellow cossack trousers, ear-threatening shirt points, buttons the size of dinner plates, and a puce waistcoat embroidered with cabbage roses, Vincent Winchell was not of an appearance to appeal to the austere earl. Happily Vincent was a better secretary than a fashion plate.

The son of Bevin's mother's bosom bow in Bath, young Winchell had arrived in London with a note from Lady Montravan imploring the earl to do something for dear widowed Bessie's fatherless boy.

Unfortunately dear Bessie's boy had no prospects. He also had no aptitude for the law, the church, or medicine. Bessie, according to Lady Montravan, would go into a decline if her baby took up colors, and likewise if he took one breath of India's insalubrious air. The young cawker's ambition, Vincent revealed upon questioning, was to become a man-about-town. Like the earl.

Trained since birth to the duties and responsibilities of his position, Lord Montravan was not about to feed and house some useless unlicked cub. He had enough pensioners as it was without adopting able-bodied layabouts only eight years his junior. The best solution, of course, was to find the lad a rich wife. But with no fortune, the doors to the polite world were closed to the son of Bessie Winchell of Bath, and with no title, wealthy cits were more likely to offer him a position rather than their daughters. Or they would, Bevin acknowledged, if the chawbacon showed any potential for hard work. Instead, in the fortnight the earl took to think about young Winchell's future, the nodcock had gambled away his pittance and signed himself into debt, come home drunk thrice, and hadn't returned at all once, sending Montford House into a furor. He'd had his nose broken in a taproom brawl and been taken up by the watch until Montravan paid his fines. So Bevin made the pup his secretary.

Three years later the earl was satisfied with his gamble. He had an aide who knew how he liked things done, who didn't look askance when asked to lease a house for his latest light-o'-love or to place a bet at Newmarket. As for Vincent, he had a steady income, a fine address with servants to provide for his every need, ample free time to enjoy London's pleasures—and all for a few hours of paperwork and a promise to stay out of trouble. To the earl's gratification and Vincent's surprise, they even discovered that young Winchell had a knack for pesky details, like Christmas lists.

"I have sent your instructions to Montravan Hall," Vincent now reported, consulting his pages of notes, "along with the proper number of presents for the tenants' children, dolls and hair ribbons for the girls, tops and pocketknives for the boys. I have also sent directions and a bank draft for Boxing Day gifts for the staff, along with last year's distributions. Everything will be arranged before your arrival next week, according to Miss Sinclaire. Mr. Tuttle will oversee the London staff's holiday gratuities."

"Excellent, Vincent. I know I need not concern myself whilst you are in charge." The earl sat behind his desk and lit a cigarillo. "When do you leave for Bath?"

"Oh, not till after you depart, my lord, in case there are any last-minute changes in your plans."

Montravan blew a smoke ring and smiled. "That's a relief. Sometimes I wonder how I got on without you."

"Poorly, I imagine." Vincent ruffled his pages, bringing Bevin's attention back to the matter at hand, and unfortunately back to the multitude of rings on the same hand. The earl winced and looked away.

"Do go on. I surmise you are in a fidge to be off for the evening."

"Drury Lane, my lord. There's a new production of *Othello*."

"And a new farce, with the chorus girls showing their ankles, I hear tell."

"I could not say, my lord." The secretary hurriedly turned and pushed forward a stack of calling cards from the corner of the desk. "I had these printed up special for your holiday messages, if you cared to include a personal note to any of the employees or tenants, and, of course, for your relatives and, ah, close acquaintances." He cleared his throat and scanned another list. "The gifts for those, ah, family and friends are here on the side table, awaiting your final selection."

The earl got up and followed the younger man to the table, where parcels were displayed, two by two, with an elegantly printed name card in front of each pair. Bevin took out his quizzing glass to survey the groupings before once again declaring his secretary invaluable.

"You toddle off now while I scribble my compliments to Lady Montravan and the rest. I'll place my card and the name plaque by the gifts I choose, and you can send them off on the morrow, except, of course, the ones I'll be taking with me to the Hall."

"If you are sure, my lord. I could stay to advise—"

"No, my dear boy, you've done enough. I can surely sign my own name. Have a pleasant evening. Oh, and, Vincent, do remember to give yourself a generous Christmas bonus. You deserve it. Perhaps you'll even purchase a new set of clothes before you give your mother palpitations in those."

"They're all the crack, my lord," Vincent said, bowing his way out of the library. "Bang up to the mark."

"I'm sure they are," the earl whispered to the closing door, feeling considerably older than his thirty-two years.

Bevin returned to the desk and poured himself a glass of sherry from the cut-glass decanter there. He sat and took up a quill—neatly sharpened—and one of the new cards. At least Vincent had learned to restrain his flamboyant taste when it came to his employer's business. The cards merely held Lord Montravan's name and title, under the simple inscription "Greetings of the Season" in raised black letters. The whole was edged in a thin border of holly, with hand-tinted leaves and berries. No gilt edges, thank goodness, or flowing script or flowery prose. The earl nodded, sipped his drink, and began his task, adding a salutation here, a New Year's wish there, knowing his dependents counted on the monetary rewards yet still appreciated the personal touch.

Half a glass of sherry later, Bevin was ready for the challenge of selecting gifts and writing warmer messages. He carried a handful of cards and his glass to the other table, where another inkstand was positioned, another quill perfectly pointed. Raising his glass, he silently toasted the absent, efficient secretary.

For the dowager countess, Vincent had laid out a diamond pendant and a ruby brooch. Montravan chose the brooch. It was larger, gaudier, and more expensive, just the thing to appeal to his flighty mama. Vincent should have been her son, their tastes were that similar. No matter, the earl told himself, Mama's real Christmas present was Lady Belinda Harleigh. Hadn't the dowager been nagging at Bevin since his twenty-first year to find a bride and assure the succession? She must be in alt over the visit of Lady Belinda, ducal parents, handsome dowry, and all. He penned a short message about fulfilling obligations and moved on to his baby sister's gift.

Following the earl's instructions, Vincent had purchased, on approval of course, the set of pearls proper for a young miss about to make her comeout, and a tiara. A gold tiara was totally unsuitable for a chit just out of the schoolroom, of course, even without the diamonds Allissa wanted, but the minx had been begging for one this last age. Allissa was growing into the type of spoiled, grasping featherbrain Bevin most disliked, but he recalled her cherubic infancy and put his card atop the tiara. The pearls could wait for her official presentation in the spring, he decided, when the budding beauty was bound to set London on its ear no matter what she wore. He groaned to think of all the young sprigs haunting Montford House and the idea of having to listen to their petitions for Allissa's hand. Gads, he wasn't that old, was he, that some spotty youth might come quaking into this very library? He downed another swallow of sherry. Mayhap he could get the prattlebox buckled to some country lad before the time, or a beau from Bath, where she and his mother were going after the holidays. Ah, well, at least Miss Sinclaire would not let the rattlepate wear the tiara to any of the country gatherings, so none would know what an expensive bit of fluff she'd be. And in the spring he'd have Lady Belinda to help with the presentation.

For Squire Merton, his mother's faithful cicisbeo, Bevin choose the riding crop over the snuffbox with a hunting scene on the cover. The old fool would only spill the snuff on Montravan's own furniture. Lord Montravan quickly scrawled "Happy hunting" on the card and moved on.

The next grouping was labeled *Miss Corbett*. Ah, Marina, the earl thought fondly, but not so fondly that he was tempted to keep the raven-haired actress on as his mistress. She was exquisite, voluptuous—and boring. She hadn't always been, of course, so he designated the heavily jeweled bracelet as her Christmas present. The extravagance alone would tell her it was also a parting gift, but he added a few words to the card to ensure Marina knew he would not be returning to her when he returned to London after the holidays. Vincent could deliver the package, saving Montravan an unpleasant scene when Marina received her congé. Not that he was a coward, he told himself, just discreet.

And wise. Too wise to leave town without securing the affections, or attentions, at any rate, of the latest highflier to soar over London's demimonde. He tucked his message under the card addressed to Mademoiselle Bibi Duchamps and put both alongside the pair of diamond earbobs, setting the matching necklace aside for another occasion, such as the formalization of their arrangement. Bevin had no doubt there would be such an understanding, not when his note expressed his intentions. Bibi was no fool; she'd wait until Montravan came back before selecting her protector. He was bound to be the highest bidder, even if the earl modestly refused to consider his other attractions. No woman had turned him down yet.

Bevin had never asked a woman to marry him, but he did not expect Lady Belinda Harleigh to refuse him either, if he decided to make the offer. She was an acknowledged beauty, well educated for a woman, and two years beyond that first giddy debutante stage. The *on-dit* was that her father, the duke, was also holding out for the best offer. A wealthy earl was like to be the best, or they would not have accepted his invitation to Wiltshire, where Montravan wanted to see firsthand how Belinda reacted to his home, his tenants, and his ramshackle family. He also wanted to have some private conversation with her, impossible in Town, and at least one tender embrace before deciding to spend the rest of his life with the young woman. Besides, he wanted to get a better look at her mother, to extrapolate the daughter's future.

The Harleighs were not arriving at Montravan until a day or two before the New Year's ball, so a gift for the earl's almost-intended would have to be delivered here in London. The present could not be too expensive and personal, such as jewels or furs, without being a declaration; it could not be too trifling without giving offense. Vincent had done well again, presenting the earl with a choice between an exquisitely filigreed fan and a pearl-studded jewel box. He selected the fan, which Belinda could carry at the ball, indicating her approval of his suit, instead of the jewel box, lest she and her father get the notion he was bound and determined to fill it with the family betrothal ring, now in the vault in Wiltshire. He wrote about looking forward to her visit, then considered the next and last pile of gifts.

Miss Petra Sinclaire. Now there was a problem indeed. The earl went back to his desk and refilled his glass. Then he paced between the desk and the table, undecided. Petra was an employee. She was also an old friend, the orphaned daughter of his old tutor. When Vicar Sinclaire passed on, Bevin had paid for her schooling. Then it was natural for Petra to take up residence at Montravan, where the countess could take her around and find her some likely parti among the local gentry. She had no other connections, no great beauty to attract suitors, and only the modest dowry the earl insisted on providing. Only Petra had not accepted any of the offers and refused to live on charity. She threatened to accept a paid position in London, until Bevin was forced to hire her on as his mother's companion, a position she'd been filling anyway, as well as mentor to his hoydenish sister, surrogate chatelaine of Montravan Hall for the vaporish countess, and general factotum in Bevin's absence. If Vincent was indispensable in London, Petra Sinclaire was the earl's lifeline in Wiltshire. Still, he was determined to see her established in her own household before she was more firmly on the shelf than her five and twenty years dictated. When she accompanied Allissa to London for the Season, Miss Petra Sinclaire was also going to find herself presented to every respectable gentleman Bevin knew, whether she wished it or not. He owed her that much, and more.

Unfortunately he could not express his gratitude for her loyalty and calm good sense in his Christmas gift. It simply wasn't done. He was already paying her the highest wage she would accept, and money would only place her more firmly among the ranks of servitors. He looked at the heap of rejected jewels from his mother's and mistresses' gifts, even the pearls for Allissa's comeout, and had a mad urge to fill the pearl jewel box with the pirate's treasure, for Petra. She was the only one of the bunch deserving of his largesse, the only one without a relative or other protector to satisfy her every whim, the only one not expecting an exorbitant present. And the only one he must not be lavish with.

Vincent had selected carefully: a volume of Scott's ballads, because Petra was of a serious mind, and a set of mother-of-pearl hair combs, which would look well in her long brown hair. Perfectly acceptable, perfectly tasteful, and perfectly awful.

Bevin paced some more, then sat at his desk, thinking that a warmer greeting might better express his appreciation, since his gift could not. He disarranged his hair by threading his fingers through it in thought as he crumpled one card after another. Finally, just as the dinner gong reverberated through the halls, he had a message that met with his approval. He waved the card about to dry the ink, then put it on top of the combs. No, the book.

"Hell and the devil take it!" he swore, putting the combs and the book together and slamming his card and Petra's name on top of both so there was no mistake.

Satisfied, the Earl of Montravan went in to dinner, whistling. This Christmas shopping was child's play.

3

"Christmas gifting should be just for children," Lady Montravan declared. "Gingerbread and shiny pennies and no bother to anyone else. This fustian of bestowing presents on everyone for miles around is too fatiguing for words," she stated from her reclining position on the love seat, a pillow under her feet, a lavender-soaked cloth on her weary brow. The dowager countess credited her enervation to bearing her daughter so late in life. Others, such as her dresser, Travers, blamed it on sheer miserliness. Lady Montravan was so cheeseparing, she wouldn't expand a single groat or an ounce of effort more than she had to. "Besides," she went on now, sighing with exhaustion, "all these gifts take away from the religious celebration." Which cost her nothing except her son's donation to the church.

"Oh, Mama, you cannot mean you wish for a Christmas without presents! Just think of all the treats you'd miss and the surprises you have to look forward to." At seventeen, Allissa Montford was still young enough to shiver with anticipation, tossing her blond curls. Allissa's fair hair was her heritage from the father she barely remembered, while Bevin's coloring came more from his mother, whose own dark hair was now gone to gray—from frailty, the dowager swore.

"Do sit still, Allissa. Your restlessness is agitating my nerves."

"Yes, Mama." Lady Alissa dutifully picked up the fashion journal she'd been studying, but she couldn't drop the subject, not with Christmas just a week or so away. All the cooking going on below-stairs, all the baskets being readied for the tenants, and all the greenery being fetched in for decorations kept her normally high spirits at fever pitch. "Only consider, Mama, Squire Merton is coming for Christmas dinner. He is sure to bring you something pretty, and you know Bev always delights you with his gifts. I'm sure this year will be no different. Except," Allissa said with a giggle, "this year he can buy me extravagant jewelry, too."

"Oh, dear," spoke a quiet voice from the window seat, where the light was better for her embroidery, since too many lamps bothered Lady Montravan's eyes and used too much oil. "You haven't been pestering your brother about a tiara again, have you?"

"Oh, no, I merely wrote to Vincent about it."

Miss Sinclaire clucked her tongue and went back to her needlework. If Lady Montravan did not find fault with Allissa's manners, surely it was not Petra's place to correct the forward chit. Besides, she'd only be wasting her breath. Petra smiled to herself, a smile that softened her rather commonplace features into loveliness, to think that she was growing as stingy with her energy as her employer. She knew what Travers and the others thought of Lady Montravan: that she would let her son's house burn down around her ears without lifting a pudgy, beringed finger, so long as her jewel box and bankbook were safe. Why, the abigail was fond of repeating, before Miss Sinclaire came to the Hall, the place was a shambles and Lady Allissa was running wild through the countryside with none to naysay her. 'Twas doubtful she even knew her letters before Petra took her in hand, the little savage. The staff adored the little hoyden—that was half the problem—but not one of them misdoubted that she'd make micefeet of her reputation ere long.

The tiara was *not* Petra's problem, she tried to convince herself. Bevin couldn't be such a gudgeon as to forget what was suitable for such a young miss. Then again, it would be just like the generous earl to cave in to Allissa's demands, then leave it up to Petra to forbid the peagoose to wear it. And it would be just like Lissa to want to flaunt a diamond tiara at the small local assemblies before her less fortunate friends. At least Bevin would be at Montravan for the New Year's ball. If he wanted to see his little sister make a cake out of herself in front of his ducal guests, or be labeled "coming" by the neighbors, even before her presentation, that was *his* problem. Christmas was Petra's.

"You know, dearest," she hinted, "you might think a bit more of others at this special season."

"Oh, I do, Petra!" Allissa jumped up. "I wonder if Squire Merton will bring me a gift as well as Mama."

"He can well afford it," her fond mother commented, popping another bonbon into her mouth, then sucking on it as if the effort to chew was just too great. "If he ever gets his nose out of the smelly stables and kennels long enough to go shopping. And not in the village, either. There is nothing but pinchbeck stuff in the local shops. He'll send to London if he has any sense."

If the squire had any sense, Petra thought, he wouldn't be hanging around Lady Montravan. The hunting-mad squire was going to see his carefree bachelor days ended, if Petra was any judge, as soon as Bevin brought home his bride. Lady Montravan had declared often enough her refusal to take up residence in Montravan's pawky dower house. And why should she, spending her own jointure on its upkeep, when Merton had a perfectly fine manor house just waiting for a mistress?

The dowager had finally swallowed the sweet, but not the bitter thought of Merton's coming the lickpenny with her present. "He'd better come down handsome, I say, after all the trouble I have gone to for his gift."

The squire's gift was to be the needlepoint pillow with a portrait of his favorite hunter on the cover, the one that Petra was currently embroidering.

Lady Montravan believed that handmade gifts showed greater feeling than mere monetary expenditures. "Why, giving Merton a gift he can jolly well go purchase for himself is foolish beyond permission," the dowager had declared. "And as for buying Bevin a present, la, I am sure the boy has five of everything he could ever want or need. And doxies to provide the rest. Buying gifts for nabobs is like bringing coals to Newcastle."

Still, he was her son, so after much deliberation Lady Montravan decided on a burgundy velvet dressing gown with satin lapels and sash, with his initials embroidered on the chest and the family crest embroidered on the back. By Petra. A lion, a scepter, and a hawk, in gold thread.

"Now that Mama is giving Bev such a marvelous surprise," Allissa had mused to Petra, "I need a really special gift for him, too, to thank him for the tiara."

"What if he gives you something else, something equally nice, just more suitable?"

"Then I'll still want to give him something wonderful, so he feels guilty. My birthday is soon." She twirled a golden lock around her finger, thinking. "Mama says handworked gifts show heart." So Lady Allissa designed a pair of slippers to match the burgundy dressing gown, with a lion on the right shoe, a hawk and a scepter to be embroidered on the left. By Petra.

Miss Sinclaire kept sewing, turning to catch the afternoon light. Lady Montravan was still exhausted from reading Vincent's lists out loud to her companion. "I swear," she said, "this doling out of money to the servants is another ridiculous tradition. Heaven knows we pay them a good enough wage. Why should we have to reward them extra simply for doing their jobs?"

"Because they work harder at Christmastide, with all the extra company and such, my lady," Petra offered. "And so they might have more joy in the season, buying gifts for their loved ones, too."

Allissa looked up from her magazine. "And you know servants can never manage to save any money. Besides, Mama, you shouldn't say such things. Petra is a paid employee, too."

"Nonsense," Lady Montravan stated, without lifting the scented cloth from her eyes to see Petra's blush. "Petra is one of the family. Bevin explained it to you ages ago. We are not paying her a wage to make herself useful; we give her an allowance, the same as we give you one."

Except that Petra could not refuse to make all the arrangements for the ball, the household's celebration, and the arrival of the ducal party. She couldn't say she was too busy to wrap and pack all the baskets for the tenants, and she could not choose to work on her own Christmas gifts instead of embroidering scepters, lions, and hawks! She certainly could not go spend Christmas with her sister and Rosalyn's curate husband at their tiny cottage in Hampshire— no, not even if there was a new niece she had never seen, not with such an important event in the offing, the heir's bringing home a prospective bride.

And as for her allowance, why, Allissa couldn't pass through the nearby village with its two insignificant shops without spending more than Petra's quarterly income. Not that Petra complained, ever. She was nothing to Lord Montravan, no obligation, no relation, no debt of honor, yet he supported her, and handsomely. He even insisted that her clothes money come from the household accounts, not her "allowance." The dowager agreed, not surprising since the bills were on Bevin's tab, and since a well-dressed Miss Sinclaire was a suitable enough companion to send out with Allissa on her rounds of the neighbors, saving Lady Montravan the stress and strain of carriage rides and morning calls. Besides, the dowager liked to show Petra off to the local gentry and her Bath cronies as a symbol of her generosity.

Lady Montravan *was* generous, in her way. She treated Petra like a daughter—just as negligently as she treated Allissa.

*

That night, long after the other ladies were abed, Petra sat up reflecting, not for the first time, on Lord Montravan's generosity.

It was not enough. Her quarterly payments, her life savings, and all the coins she'd managed to squirrel away in a more frugal fashion than even Lady Montravan espoused were not enough for her Christmas shopping. So Miss Sinclaire sat up sewing through the night on her own Christmas gifts.

A gift from the hands was a gift from the heart, she tried to convince herself, echoing Lady Montravan's oft-repeated sentiments. The recipients would appreciate Petra's laboriously worked handkerchiefs more than some store-bought bauble. And pigs would fly. Petra tried to imagine Allissa preferring the lace-edged, monogrammed linen squares to a diamond tiara. Instead she pictured Squire Merton wiping the manure off his boots with his initialed handkerchief.

No matter, she thought, yawning but still setting neat stitches in the bib for her new niece, she could not afford to squander her ready on gifts for people who wanted for nothing. Oh, she set aside coins for the vails for the servants; that was different. And there'd be a coin wrapped in the handkerchief for her sister, and another in the toe of the socks she'd knitted for Rosalyn's struggling husband. But that was all. Not another brass farthing was going to leave her hands, not even if those hands were so needle-pricked, they snagged on her stockings. She looked over at the considerable pile of handkerchiefs. Rosalyn, Cook, and Mrs. Franklin, the housekeeper, were all getting some, as well as Allissa, the squire, and Lady Montravan. And his lordship...

When the tiny stitches blurred in front of her weary eyes, Petra set her sewing aside and stretched her stiff muscles. Then she went to her bureau and reached under her gloves for the old reticule that held her fortune. It was heavy. Pound notes rustled and coins clinked. Petra could almost hear the devil whispering temptations in her ear. If it weren't the middle of the night, she'd take all the money and go buy him the most lavish, stupendous, one-of-a-kind gift she could ever hope to find, something a lot more worthy of the Earl of Montravan than another handkerchief or another embroidered lion, hawk, and scepter.

But it was the middle of the night, and Petra did know that she needed every last pence of her savings if she was going to make her own way in the world. Who knew if Lady Montravan would even write her a reference if she left? Or how long before she found another position, or how much a decent lodging would cost until she found one? Rosalyn and her curate were barely surviving, so Petra could not add to her sister's burden, even if they had room in their tiny cottage.

For certain she could not stay on at Montravan Hall much longer. The earl was bringing home a bride. It was not official yet, but it was all anyone could talk of, and a sure thing, according to the kitchen wagering. She was known to be a peeress with fortune and face, manners and a mind. Lady Belinda Harleigh. Petra said the name over to herself. Belinda. Belinda and Bevin. Perfect.

Lady Belinda would have been brought up to manage a household like Montravan; she'd be an experienced guide for Allissa through the shoals of a London Season; Lady Montravan was already calculating the settlements.

So there was no reason for Petra to stay, nothing here for her except more heartbreak. Could a heart keep breaking eternally, or would it just crumble into dust and blow away?

Petra had loved the earl forever, it seemed. When the wiry thirteen-year-old had ridden over for his Latin lessons and offered a nut brown hobbledehoy six-year-old a ride, she was lost. When he sat by her ailing father, sent her macaroons at school, trusted her with Montravan's running, she loved him the more. Loving Bevin Montford was like loving the hero in a romance novel—from a distance. Bevin was more handsome, more dashing, more caring than any hero—and just as unattainable for a poor vicar's daughter who had to earn her living.

Petra looked over to her wardrobe door, where the burgundy robe hung, the slippers placed neatly on the floor in front, almost as if the earl would walk into her bedroom at any minute. And pigs would not just fly; they'd start teaching astronomy at Oxford. Earls did not look at impoverished nobodies except in charity. And charity was cold comfort indeed when a heart ached for a much warmer touch.

4

White's was fairly thin of company that evening, most of the members having already left town for their far-flung estates or country parties. Some young sprigs were in the dining room, drinking their suppers, and a few of the old gents were snoring in the reading room with newspapers over their faces. After handing his hat and gloves to the footman at the door, Montravan looked into the game room for his own particular cronies, gentlemen past their callow youth but not yet settled into sedentary respectability. They were more Corinthians than Tulips, and generally well breeched enough to pursue avidly the two favorite pastimes of the more raffish section of the aristocracy: wagering and womanizing. Happily there were enough of Lord Montravan's set at the club tonight for a decent hand of whist and congenial conversation. Or so he thought.

After the current war news, talk turned to homely Lady Throckmorton and her handsome footmen, thence to the new bareback rider at Astley's Amphitheatre: her bare legs, her nearly bare chest. Then Lord Coulton came in, rubbing the chill out of his hands.

"Ah, the very gentlemen I was hoping to see," he said, fitting his large frame into a chair near Montravan and the others. "I have just consigned my fate to River Tick and need your heavy purses to bail myself out. Cards, anyone?" A wide grin split his freckled face as he started to deal. The earl called for another bottle.

"'Tis the least I can do for a friend who is so badly dipped," he told his other companions. "Besides, the cognac might dim that avaricious gleam in our Goliath's eye, so we poor Davids have a chance."

For a while the only sounds were softly spoken bids and answers, the slap of cards on the baize, and the clink of glasses. Then the group of younger men strolled in from the dining room, carrying their bottles and glasses. Most sauntered; a few staggered. They took up chairs at a nearby table but immediately started arguing about the stakes. One of the players at Bevin's game glared in their direction, without affecting their raucous noise in the slightest. Finally Viscount Coulton put his cards on the table, stood up to his considerable height, and walked over to the other group.

"Gentlemen, I truly need to win tonight. In order to win, I need to concentrate. In order to concentrate, I need quiet. In order to get that quiet, I'll bash your bloody skulls in." He bowed, smiled his boyish grin, and took up his own seat.

Not only was Lord Coulton larger than any of the young blades, he was Gentleman Jackson's own sparring partner. Furthermore, while the viscount might smile, leaving his intentions in question, the Earl of Montravan had his dark brows lowered in a scowl. No one doubted Montravan's disapproval, and no one wanted to challenge the devil's own temper. The argle-bargle subsided. Two of the Bartholomew babes decided on a hand of piquet, and another came over to observe the earl's game. Nessborough's heir and his chum Rupert Haskell lurched over to where the betting book was kept.

As usual, Lord Montravan figured largely in the current entries.

"Just look at this: Calbert Hodge put twenty pounds on Lady B—H—," Nessborough whispered, loudly enough to rouse the snorers in the next room. "I put down only five." He jerked his head toward the earl. "I wish he'd put us out of our misery before we leave town. I could use the blunt." Haskell curled his lip and didn't even attempt to lower his voice as he asked, "What was the wager, that he'd offer or that she'd accept?"

Nessborough hooted, forgetting to whisper. "No one'd take you up on the last bet, you nodcock. No woman in her right mind would turn down such a title and fortune."

"And the duke wouldn't let her even if she had other inclinations." Haskell spoke bitterly, then downed another glass of liquor. "I need her fortune a sight more than Montravan does, but, no, it's always the rich swells who get everything."

Some of the earl's friends were beginning to look uncomfortable, while Johnny Coulton's florid complexion was turning redder. Bevin took up the cards. "My deal, I believe."

Haskell did not drop the subject. "I'd bet a monkey she wouldn't have him without the blasted title."

Nessborough scratched his head, leaving greasy pomatum on his fingers. "I don't know. There's still the blunt, and the fellow *is* a top-of-the-trees Corinthian. I mean, she ain't like to find a better shot or a better eye for horseflesh. And everyone knows he's a regular prime 'un."

"A veritable paragon," Haskell sneered. "Why, he's—"

Before Haskell could complete the thought, a graceful, manicured hand reached out and slammed the betting book shut. "You are putting me to the blush, gentlemen," Lord Montravan quietly explained in a silky voice with the edge of steel. "I hadn't realized that your lives were so empty, you had to rely on mine for titillation. I *do* wish you'd find a—"

Nessborough recalled a previous engagement. Haskell ordered another bottle, but he did wander over to the piquet table. Montravan returned to his own play, where Lord Coulton was quick to joke about the cards growing cold in Bevin's absence.

Rupert Haskell was such a dirty dish, his own mother didn't invite him home for Christmas. He was mean and dumb at the best of times. Drunk, he was dumber; disappointed, he was meaner. Having suffered a rebuff from Lord Harleigh after three disastrous days at the track, he'd been drinking steadily for the last fourteen hours. Upon muddled reflection he was not about to let some toff on his high horse send him to the corner like a misbehaving schoolboy. He reeled back to the betting book and began flipping pages, mumbling to himself until he reached an interesting entry.

"Ain't that a coincidence?" he asked the room at large. "Here's the Earl of M— again. Lemme see what it says this time." He peered closer at the book, then stood back, attempting a whistle but spraying spit instead. "A golden boy on the golden boy. Too bad his hair ain't blond, Nessborough'd make him out to be some Greek god." He read the wager again. "'A golden boy that the Earl of M— will be first out of the gate with the new French filly.' According to Nessy, there'll be no race." He took another swig and addressed the earl directly: "Unless you're even more of a nonesuch than they say, I suppose that'll leave the beauteous Marina available to us poor mortals."

The card game had stopped, but Coulton had his hand on the earl's shoulder, keeping him in his seat. "Never, to the likes of you," Bevin muttered through gritted teeth.

"That's right, m'pockets are to let."

"Your attics are to let, boy." Sir Cedric laughed from Montravan's other side.

"You going to explain that remark?" Haskell took a belligerent step in Sir Cedric's direction, but Bevin drew his attention again. He cleared his throat and said, "What my friend means is that you are dicked in the nob if you think the lady would entertain you at any price. Miss Corbett is too refined in her ways. She never lets slime cross her threshold."

"Slime? You're saying your doxy's too good for the likes of me?" Haskell shouted.

Never raising his voice, the earl answered: "No, I am saying the lady is under my protection, and I'll have your liver and lights if you so much as mention her name again."

"Why, you—"

Haskell lunged toward the seated nobleman, but the piquet players grabbed him by the coattails and wrestled him into a chair. One of the vigilant footmen immediately came by with a dice cup and suggested a game.

Some other late-arriving members wandered into the card room, attracted by the yells. A few stayed to bet on the first roll, surrounding Haskell and his chums with a hum of conversation.

Having tossed down their cards in preparation for battle, Montravan and his friends declared the game over and undecided. Before dealing out the new hands, Bevin turned to Lord Coulton. "I take it you've found the perfect gift for Miss Framingham at last, Johnny, since you're suddenly so badly dipped."

"The fairest for the fair," the viscount said with one of his ready grins. "And likely paid three times too much for the gewgaw."

"It's worth it, to have you returned to our ranks. Now you can come with me to Tatt's tomorrow. I hear Adderly's chestnuts are going on the block."

Lord Coulton shook his head. "Sorry, old chap. Elizabeth's was the easy one. Now I have to find something for my four sisters and my mother, to say nothing of the governor. When I think of all the ready I'll have to spout, I could thrash that muckworm Haskell. I was winning that last round, I know it. If I don't win this next one, I'll be handing m'sisters vouchers."

Sir Cedric groaned. "Don't remind me. My wife will comb my hair with a footstool if her sister's husband is more openhanded or original." No one disagreed with him, knowing how Lady Margaret had her spouse so thoroughly cowed, which was why he was so often to be found at White's. "Whatever happened to the days of shiny apples and a ha'penny?"

"Gone the way of perukes and farthingales." The earl finally unclenched his jaw and relaxed back in his seat. "My friends, you make too much of a simple thing."

"Simple for you, Bev. You're as rich as Golden Ball."

Montravan gestured toward the dice game. "You're sounding like that rum touch over there. Money isn't everything. You'd be dithering over baubles at half the cost."

"I suppose you've got all of your shopping done, eh, Bev?" Lord Coulton asked, winking at Sir Cedric.

"But of course." The earl tried not to sound too smug, but his blue eyes crinkled at the corners.

"Dashed if I know how you do it," Sir Cedric complained. "'Something thoughtful,' she says. Balderdash, I say! Blister me if I can figure where to start."

"Come on, Bev," Lord Coulton urged, "give us poor sods some hints. The dowager cannot be an easy one to shop for, and you've got a sister the same age as one of mine."

Lord Montravan steepled his fingers in front of him and closed his eyes in serious contemplation. Then: "Very well. There are two basic steps. First, make a list. Second, hand the list to the brightest, most efficient and reliable person on your staff."

They all laughed, until Haskell's slurred voice rose above the room's chatter. "Tha'sh right, Montravan. Says so right here." No one had noticed him stagger away from the dice table. Now everyone turned to stare in his direction, back at the betting book. "Says you have the most effemin—no, efficient secretary in all of London."

"Oh, take a damper, man," Sir Cedric called, while Lord Coulton mumbled, "We're in for it now." The earl looked to his friends, who were desperately trying to get his attention, asking about his stable's latest acquisition or inviting him into the adjoining room for a late supper. Then he looked back at Haskell, who was rocking back and forth on his heels, his mouth trailing saliva, his clothing rumpled and soiled. Bevin casually leaned back in his chair until the front legs tipped up, and just as casually he drawled, "Found another bone to chew, have you, Towser?"

Someone's laughter was stopped midsnicker by the earl's one raised black brow. He fixed his unflinching gaze back on Haskell, who was too castaway to realize his days at White's were numbered, if not his days on earth.

"Leave it be, Bev," Lord Coulton appealed to his friend. "The dirty dish ain't worth soiling your hands over. You can see he's just an unlicked cub who can't hold his liquor and is spoiling for a fight."

"Then perhaps you'd care to explain that bet, Johnny." The viscount looked away. "No? I thought not. I myself always believed Vincent Winchell was a prince among secretaries, but I never thought anyone would lay blunt on his capabilities, did you, Johnny?"

"It's just a foolish joke, Bev, blown out of proportion by this addlepated tosspot. Let it go."

"Perhaps the makebate would care to explain the joke to me, for you can see I am not laughing." He tipped his chair forward again. "You, Haskell, suppose you tell me the point of that entry you're so fond of."

"The point, your stiff-rumped lordship, is what everyone knows. Your blooming secretary is so efficient, it's a wonder he doesn't wipe your nose. And he's so efficient, he even beds your women for you! Your bits o' muslin may not share their favors with poor gentlemen like me, but it seems they can give 'em away free to—"

Haskell swallowed his next words, along with his two front teeth.

"He is no gentleman" was all Lord Montravan said as he wiped his hands on a napkin, while footmen carried Haskell's prone form from the room. Then Bevin turned to Lord Coulton. "Is it true, Johnny?"

The viscount couldn't meet his friend's eyes. "I don't know, Bev. I heard rumors, that's all. Don't even know who put it in the book— there were no initials—so I didn't think it was worth mentioning."

His nose wasn't worth mentioning either, after Lord Montravan's right fist connected with it.

5

The first thing Bevin did on his return to Montford House was collect the pearl-decorated jewel box from the library. He placed one of his holiday calling cards under the lid, then thrust the box into the hands of Tuttle, the butler at Montford House since before the wheel was invented.

"Here, Tuttle, since you insist on waiting up for me, make yourself useful. Wrap it."

The white-haired servant blinked at the box on his outstretched, gloved palm. He couldn't look more surprised than if a particularly hairy spider had suddenly landed there. "Wrap it, my lord?"

"Yes, blast it, wrap it. It is a gift. You know, paper and ribbons, that sort of poppycock. Then rouse one of the footmen and have him deliver it to Miss Elizabeth Framingham."

"Miss Framingham?"

"B'gad, are you going deaf on me, Tuttle? Yes, Miss Elizabeth Framingham, who resides three houses away, in case you have forgotten. Lord Coulton's fiancée. The footman is to say that it comes with my most sincere apologies."

"But...but, my lord, it is the middle of the night."

"I didn't say he should deliver it to the young lady in her bedchamber, dash it. In fact, I *forbid* him to deliver it to her bedroom altogether. He's to leave it with the butler or night guard or whatever, as long as she gets it first thing in the morning. Is that clear?"

As clear as the air over London town. Tuttle nodded.

"Oh, and fetch me some ice."

"Ice, my lord?"

"Ice. These are the 1800s, man, and it's winter. Somewhere in London there must be an icehouse. I need some upstairs in a bowl. And the good cognac."

Now the stately majordomo was really shocked. Master Bevin wished to chill the Bouvelieu? Never. Tuttle carried up the ice in a silver bucket and hot coffee in a silver urn. More of the latter than the former.

Lord Montravan sprawled on a chair before the fire, his shoes kicked off, his coat lying in a heap near the wardrobe, his cravat draped over a bedpost, and his right hand soaking in a bowl of cold water.

Life was hard, he lamented. A fellow just couldn't trust anyone. Not his best friend, not his faithful servant, not his mistress. Bevin was glad he didn't have a dog; it would most likely bite him. He couldn't even trust the old family retainer to bring him a brandy, and the bellpull was so confoundedly far away. What good was coffee going to be in keeping infection from the cut Haskell's teeth had opened across Bevin's knuckles? What good was coffee going to be in dulling the pain of betrayal?

Hell and damnation, Vincent and Marina. Unless... No, it couldn't, be. That peacocking twit of a nobody *couldn't* be tupping Bibi Duchamps while he, the Earl of Montford, was still trying to fix her interest. Life couldn't be that hard, could it?

No. There was still some softness in the world, some tender honor a man could trust. His mother? If she never played his father false, it was because she was too lazy. His sister? Allissa was growing into another avaricious, manipulative harpy. But there was Petra, sweet and pure. Petra, who had never let him down, never went back on her word.

Bevin laughed at himself. He hadn't seen Petra since the summer. For all he knew she'd have some local swain just waiting for the earl's arrival to declare himself. Hell, Petra was only a woman; there was no justification for putting her on a pedestal. For all Bevin knew she already had some gent's slippers under her bed.

✴

The next morning did not start until nearly noon. Finster took one look at his master, asleep in the chair, and called for the sawbones. That worthy poked and prodded, only to declare that perhaps the knuckles were broken, perhaps not. As if Lord Montravan could not have figured that out for himself. At least the cabbagehead put basilicum powder in the open cuts and wrapped the hand—in enough linen to shroud a mummy.

He couldn't tie his own neckcloth. He spilled coffee on the one Finster had fashioned, trying to breakfast left-handed, and had to have the thing done again. At last, in an even more foul mood, the earl was ready to confront his secretary.

According to Tuttle, Mr. Vincent was in the library wrapping gifts. This last was said with a sniff, indicative of the butler's opinion of such a lowly occupation. Vincent obviously did not mind, for he was whistling in a welter of silver paper, tissue, and bright ribbon. Nothing was quite as bright as his parrot-embroidered waistcoat. Montravan paused in the doorway to let his aesthetic sense acclimate itself gradually.

"Good morning, my lord," Vincent called cheerfully. "I'll be finished here in just a bit unless you needed me for something immediately. I heard you had the doctor in to see about your hand, so I wanted to get this done in case you had any additional chores for me. I hope it's nothing serious, whatever happened."

"Marina," Montravan stated, striding farther into the room and skipping all preliminaries.

Vincent's mouth hung open. "Miss Corbett did that to you? Good grief, what did she do? I mean, pardon me, my lord. None of my affair, of course."

"Precisely!" Bevin was across the library's expanse, almost nose to nose with the younger man, and was about to take Vincent by the ridiculously high shirt collar and shake him as a terrier would a rat. Except that he couldn't bend his swollen, throbbing fingers in their wrapping. "Blast! Have you been seeing Marina, sirrah?"

"My lord?" Vincent took a step back, dropping the scissors. Then he seemed to reconsider, what with his employer running amok right in front of him. Picking the scissors off the table, he cut a length of ribbon.

"Answer me, damn you! Have you been seeing Marina?"

Vincent's hand started to shake. "I saw her last night in the play. Remember, I told you I was going?"

"And otherwise?"

"I don't know what you mean, my lord. I took her home that night last week when you had to attend the reception at Carleton House. Recall, you asked me to?"

"And did you see her in?"

Vincent squared his padded shoulders. "Naturally. You charged me with her escort. And she asked me to have a glass of wine," he said with a tinge of defiance. "She is a very gracious lady."

"And what about Bibi Duchamps?"

The bow Vincent was tying became knotted around his finger. "Drat." He tossed the ribbon aside and cut a new one, not half the length needed to go around the box he was wrapping. Sweat was starting to bead on his forehead. "I...ah...have seen Mademoiselle Duchamps only once, outside of the opera house."

The earl was seated at his desk, hefting the weight of the silver letter opener in his left hand. Vincent swallowed audibly and continued: "The one time when you had me send her flowers after her debut."

"Send. I said *send* her flowers, not bring her flowers, you lobcock!"

"I...ah...thought she'd be more impressed that way. 'Twould show your interest more personally than having the flower seller's boy just drop off another bouquet."

Bevin scowled; Vincent trembled.

"I swear, my lord, I have done nothing without your direction or your interests at heart. Neither lady has cause for complaint at my conduct."

"Well, somebody does. Something you've done has given rise to the most damnable rumors, and that's a fact."

"That's impossible. No one saw us. That is…ah…what rumors, my lord?"

"No one saw you and…? Great Scott! Belinda? You've been sniffing around my intended?" the earl thundered.

"No, no," Vincent cried. "That's not how it was. I never intended…that is, Lady Belinda is… You see, it was the invitation."

"No, you miserable mawworm, I do not see. What bloody invitation?" The papers on the earl's desk went flying, from the gale winds of his rage.

"The…the one to the house party for New Year's," Vincent stuttered. "I thought I should deliver it in person, like the flowers. Only no one was home except Lady Belinda. The footman mustn't have realized, for he showed me into the music room, where she was practicing. I would have given the invitation over and left immediately, I swear. Young lady with no chaperon and all, I knew it wasn't seemly."

"Then why the hell didn't you?"

"Lady Belinda asked me to stay, to tell her about the house party, who else was invited, what activities were planned, that type of thing. I suppose she wanted to know what to pack. I never even *thought* of…of…"

"Yes, I know what you never thought of: what every young man spends every waking hour trying not to think of. Go on."

"It was the mouse, you see. This mouse ran across the room, and Lady Belinda started to scream and jumped up on the sofa. I jumped up, too, thinking she might fall, and I accidentally dislodged one of the sofa pillows. Did I say we were sitting on the sofa? Well, the pillow hit the mouse and must have stunned the poor thing, because there it was, just lying there, with Lady Belinda starting to turn greenish, so I scooped it up with the coal scuttle and tossed the little blighter out the window."

"Lancelot to the rescue," Montravan commented dryly.

"I thought I'd done a neat job of it myself. But then—"

"Ah. The denouement. I am all aflutter to hear the outcome. Do go on," he urged, rising. "'But then?'"

"I promise you I never meant to… Lady Belinda was thanking me, and I was looking around for some brandy or something, a restorative, don't you know."

"For you, the lady, or the mouse?" Bevin asked sarcastically, knowing full well what was coming.

"Then suddenly she was in my arms, and it seemed only natural, and she didn't tell me to stop, and suddenly we were back on the couch."

"And then?"

"And then the butler came in. But Belinda swore he'd never tell a soul. And…and I am terribly sorry, my lord."

"Sorry? You're sorry you were caught making love to the woman I am going to marry?" Bevin pounded the desktop in fury, then had to catch himself on the edge of the table as the pain made him almost light-headed enough to faint.

Words failed Vincent. He could only hang his head, staring at the elaborate buckles on his shoes.

When Bevin caught his breath, he corrected himself. "No, Lady Belinda is the woman I *was* going to marry. I'd never have the jade now. By Jupiter, did she think she'd play me false with my own secretary? My God!"

"It wasn't like that, my lord! Belinda is a lady! We didn't… That is, the butler…"

"No? Were you waiting for after the wedding to plant horns on me? Should I be thankful? Or were you going to take up with

36

Marina where I left off once *Lady* Belinda and I were leg-shackled? Or was it Bibi whilst I was honeymooning?"

Montravan sank wearily back into his seat. "No, don't answer. I wouldn't believe anything you'd say." He toyed with the letter opener again, making Vincent anxiously measure the distance to the door while his lordship pondered his fate.

"I would thrash you to within an inch of your life, you know," Bevin told the other man, speaking conversationally now, "were my hand not already knocked to flinders. Instead I'll give you until dark to gather your things and get out. If I see you after, or if anything but your own possessions is missing tomorrow, there is no answering for the consequences, for I still have my left hand, by Jupiter. You'll have no references out of me, not that it makes much difference; your name is already a byword in town. No sane man would ever hire you, not if he had a wife, daughter, or mistress."

The earl reached into a desk drawer and pulled out a purse, which he tossed onto the table amid the ribbons and wrappings. Standing, he said, "Go as far as this takes you and don't come back. Consider it an early Christmas gift. Greetings of the season, you bastard."

*

Vincent hadn't wanted to be a secretary anymore anyway, he told himself after the library door slammed behind the earl. He wanted to be a gigolo. Now he had the wherewithal. He lifted the purse, thinking. He'd need a new name, of course. Perhaps a mustache for a disguise. Yes, a military-style mustache, with sideburns, maybe even a hussar uniform. Women couldn't resist a man in uniform, especially if he had a slight limp or a scar for sympathy's sake. Besides, he would look a handsome devil in the scarlet regimentals, if he had to say so himself. Who'd ever check the rosters for a retired captain? No, a major.

The future was not dim at all, but the present certainly had a shadow over it. This was no way to treat a chap after all those years of faithful service, booting him out on his ear the week before Christmas. Vincent poured himself a healthy dose of the earl's brandy. He *had* done a deuced fine job for old sobersides. He really was quite good at all the details that made Montravan's life much simpler, and he never left a task uncompleted. Vincent simply hated to leave a job undone, so he finished wrapping the earl's gifts, then regretfully locked the unchosen jewelry et cetera away in the earl's desk. He carefully printed each recipient's address on the outer wrapping, matching direction to gift, and just as carefully switched all of the cards.

He handed three to a footman to be delivered that very day in London. Then Vincent ordered a groom to set out for Montravan Hall immediately with the rest of the parcels, saying that the earl might delay his departure because of the accident to his hand and wished to make sure the presents reached his family in time.

Now Vincent was ready to go upstairs and pack.

And greetings of the season to you, too, my lord.

6

Lord, what was he to do now? Bevin could only think of things he *couldn't* do. He couldn't write to the Harleighs claiming their visit had to be canceled due to an influenza epidemic or such. They'd be sure to twig that faradiddle. Besides, he couldn't write at all with his hand all swollen, and he had no blasted secretary to write for him! And Bevin couldn't let Miss Harleigh's name be bandied around town—he was a gentleman, after all—as would be sure to happen if he suddenly claimed an emergency at his Scottish property. He'd be lucky if Harleigh didn't get a hint of the current gossip and come demanding an explanation.

If not, Belinda and her family would be off for the ducal seat in Dorset in a day or two; from there they'd travel on to Montravan Hall to wait for the earl's offer, an offer that he couldn't, wouldn't make. Zeus, what a house party that should be! What a damnable coil.

And he couldn't stay drunk for the rest of the century either. His innards were already protesting. Besides, he had to hire a new secretary. An old, ugly secretary. Vincent had seen to the Christmas gifts, heaven be praised, but there was new mail every day that needed answering: invitations, bills, and personal letters, to say nothing of the household accounts and all of the correspondence appurtenant to Montravan's vast and varied holdings. The first man the agency sent over was so old, he could have transcribed the Ten Commandments. Bevin was afraid he'd expire before the sennight.

The second smelled so bad, the earl knew he couldn't share the library with this man, much less his personal life.

When the third man spoke, he whistled through ill-fitting false teeth, and the fourth took a coughing fit and nearly fell off the chair. Bevin felt guilty over not hiring one of the decrepit oldsters, but he sent each home with hackney fare after a snack in the kitchen.

And he canceled his previous specifications for prospective employees, this time requesting a middle-aged misogynist. The first man smelled of lavender, and the second man lisped.

What about a scribe who was happily married? the hiring agent wanted to know. Bevin doubted that there was such a thing, but he said he would consider the applicants, who would have to be paid more, living out. Mr. Browne blanched at the idea of handling love-nest leases, and Mr. Faraday was newly wed; he couldn't leave his bride alone in the evenings. Stedly had shifty eyes and four sons who were willing to do any manner of work, most likely including purse snatching and housebreaking. The earl made sure Tuttle escorted this last applicant out the door.

"Damn and blast," Lord Montravan exclaimed when Tuttle returned, this time alone. "This should be Vincent's job."

"Ahem." Tuttle stood in the doorway of the library, looking more disapproving than ever.

"Whatever it is, I don't want to hear it. There must be hundreds of other employment services, or I can put an advertisement in the newspapers."

Tuttle cleared his throat again. "If I might be so bold, my lord, may I suggest you ask Miss Sinclaire?"

"What, ask Petra to move into Montford House and become my secretary? Have your wits gone begging altogether, old man? You mustn't go senile on me quite yet, Tuttle. I couldn't face having to hire a new butler, too."

"What I meant, my lord," Tuttle continued as if Lord Montravan had not spoken, "was that Miss Sinclaire most probably knows of some likely lad from Wiltshire, a young man on the scholarship lists at Oxford that you support, or perhaps one of the tenants' sons returning from the war. You must already have their gratitude and loyalty, and knowing their families have roots in your holdings should keep the young men from overstepping the boundaries."

"Tuttle, you are brilliant!"

"Thank you, my lord. I find that younger men are easier to deal with, more comfortable about taking advice."

"I am convinced, Tuttle. Petra will know just the right man, and if not, her brother-in-law, the curate, might. He's not that long out of university." Lord Montravan was delighted. His problem was as good as solved, once he dumped it into Petra's lap. Not that he was ungrateful, nor that he thought Petra would consider his difficulty another burden. Petra would see the situation as a welcome opportunity to help some worthy lad. She was just like that. And he'd make it up to her. Why, he'd find her the finest gentleman in town to wed, not one of his own rakish friends.

"That's what I'll do, Tuttle. I might even travel to the Hall a day or two early. There's nothing pressing here, after all, so close to the holidays." And it just might be politic to stay out of Johnny Coulton's proximity for a while, and to give the gabble-grinders a chance to find another juicy morsel. Devil take it, soon enough after New Year's they'd be talking about the ring that was not on Belinda's hand. Perhaps, the earl mused when Tuttle went to advise the agency that no more applicants would be interviewed, he could stay on at Montravan after his mother and sister left for Bath, sit by the fire, read books, ride around the countryside, and talk to Petra. He was tired of this drinking, wagering, and wenching. Then again, Petra would travel to Bath with the others, and Bibi would be waiting for him here in London. Country pursuits palled so quickly. Still, the sooner he left, the sooner he'd have a competent secretary. He almost rang for Vincent to make all the arrangements. Hell and confound it!

Then Tuttle came back wearing a censorious frown and bearing a letter on a silver salver. The smell of jasmine wafted halfway across the room, identifying the sender even before Montravan recognized the curling script on the address. He waited for Tuttle to remove his condemnatory but curious phiz before slitting the wafer to see what Marina had to say.

"What the bloody hell?"

The second reading made no more sense than the first. Marina was effusively grateful for his gift and his note. What had he written? Montravan tried to recall. Something like "Thank you for our past association and the pleasant times, and best Wishes in your future relations." How could that send her in alt unless she was happy to be shut of him? But, no, she wrote that she couldn't wait to see him, just knew he'd be calling on her after the theater tonight since they had so much to discuss. For the life of him, Montravan couldn't think of one thing a cove discussed with his discarded mistress.

He went anyway. He was too much the gentleman to keep a lady waiting, and too curious. Marina met him at the door of the neat row house in Kensington and instantly threw her arms around him. One of those arms wore the multigemmed bracelet he had picked as her Christmas-cum-parting gift, and it looked even more garish by the candlelight. Marina must have liked it, because she wore a diaphanous red robe with matching multicolored ruffles at the hem. That gown, what there was of it above the ruffles, could have made the devil blush. She also must have liked the bracelet, he deduced, from the enthusiasm of her greeting. "Darling," she gushed, "I cannot wait."

With her lush curves pressed against him, Bevin's body was stirred despite his loftier intentions. "I can't wait either," he whispered in her ear, trying to free his arm to remove his coat.

"No, silly, I mean I cannot wait for the wedding."

"The wedding?" Those two words had more effect on Britain's population than any number of cold baths. He took a step back. "What wedding?"

"Why, ours, of course. Your card made me the happiest of women, darling. I mean, you could have knocked me over with a feather. I never would have guessed. I never dared let myself hope."

Bevin wiped at a nonexistent smudge on the sleeve of his bottle green coat. "Ah, what exactly did the card say, my sweet? I cannot seem to recall."

Marina chewed on her lower lip in a well-rehearsed seductive pout. "Now isn't that just like a man, forgetting something so

8888

important. The card is already tucked into my Bible, but I swear I'll remember the exact words to my dying day. I always did have a mind for memorizing, you know. That's real helpful in the theater. Anyway, 'Greetings of the season,' it said, only that was inscribed. And then: 'To a real lady, with respect and affection,'" she quoted with enough timbre for Lady Macbeth. "And then you wrote, ""'Ware, I hear wedding bells in your future.'"

Which was, of course, the note he'd written to Petra, concerning her Season with Allissa on the Marriage Mart. Oh, God.

"I never thought you'd do it," Marina was going on, "so starchy you always seemed and all. The other girls said you were too toplofty by half, and here you've gone and proved them wrong in the most wonderful way. Respect and affection," she intoned as if they were her passport into heaven, "and a real lady. Just think, Mary Corby, a real lady. And not just a plain lady. I'll be a countess."

When hell froze over. Obviously there had been a horrible mistake. Obviously there was going to be a horrible scene.

Bevin could feel a droplet of sweat trickle down between his shoulder blades. He despised disordered freaks and disputations, so he damned the decamped secretary for the hundredth time. The chawbacon must have been so rattled at being found out that he mixed the cards by mistake. If Vincent wasn't already dismissed, he'd be turned off for the atrocious lapse. "May he rot in purgatory for the rest of eternity."

"My lord?"

Bevin took a deep breath. Following the hunting maxims of riding quickly over rough ground and throwing one's heart over the hurdle, he opened his mouth to speak, but all that came out was the whoosh of the same deep breath.

"Darling?" Marina—Mary—was ready to soothe his agitation the way she knew best.

Oh, no. Montravan couldn't let himself get distracted. Fully aroused, he might promise anything. He put more distance between her ample charms and his traitorous body. "No, my dear Marina, er, Mary. There isn't going to be any wedding, at least not yours and mine. I am afraid there's been an error with the cards."

Then he was afraid there'd be a visit from the watch, the constable, and the local magistrate, so piercing were her shrieks, so loud was the sound of shattering bric-a-brac and furniture bouncing off walls.

Marina threw everything at him but the sofa, which was too heavy, and the bracelet, which was too valuable. She was too downy to act the fool twice in one day.

Montravan tried to appease her with cash, which was a foredoomed effort, since what he had in his pocket couldn't possibly compare to what he had in the bank, all of which would have been hers along with that title. "But, Marina, you must have known the Earl of Montravan couldn't marry a wh—an actress."

"Stranger things have happened," she insisted, emphasizing her point with a china shepherdess that missed his head by scant inches.

Not in his family, not in his lifetime, Bevin vowed, but was wise enough to keep that thought to himself. He gave up trying to placate the raging woman when she dashed for her little kitchen and returned with a carving knife. The heretofore dauntless earl daunted himself right out the window onto a bare-branched rosebush.

Shredding his inexpressibles away from the prickers, Bevin had time to think about the second half of the disaster. If Marina had Petra's note, then come Christmas morning, Petra would be receiving that tripe about past attachments and future plans. Petra was needle-witted enough to recognize the note for what it was— and what type of woman it was meant for—but she was a trump. She'd not fly into the boughs like some others. He'd explain about the mix-up, they'd have a good laugh, and that would be the end of it, except that he'd look the fool in Petra's eyes. No, things never need come to such a pass that he had to explain about errant secretaries and discarded mistresses to an innocent girl. He'd simply travel to Montravan a bit earlier, as he'd planned anyway, intercept the gifts, and write a new card to his mother's companion. No one would ever be the wiser, except Bevin, who had instantly learned not to leave everything up to the servants.

7

White's was more a habit than a destination. Bevin's fuddled brain just took him there, not in hopes of having a convivial evening—it was too late for convivial, convenient, or comfortable—but just a way to pass this wretched night until he could set out for Montravan Hall in the morning.

The majordomo kept his usual imperturbable expression, but some of the members visibly started to see the earl's condition. The black look on his face kept any from commenting, however. A few of his usual associates, in fact, suddenly started yawning with the need to make an early night of it, with their own journeys to the country soon to commence.

Bevin walked through the rooms until he spotted his friend Coulton, who looked as if an ale barrel had rolled across his face. The earl winced but gamely took a seat next to the viscount. Johnny raised his quizzing glass and painstakingly surveyed the porcelain shards on Bevin's shoulder, the pillow feathers in his hair, and the scratches on his cheek, scratches the earl was only now beginning to feel.

The viscount held out a clean handkerchief. "I'd beat you to a pulp, my erstwhile friend, but it appears someone has been there before me."

"No one up to your weight, so go ahead, take your shot. You're entitled." Bevin held up his bandaged hand. "I won't put up much of a fight."

Coulton nodded toward the bandage. "My nose do that?"

"Your nose or Haskell's teeth. Makes no nevermind which. You've got my apologies, for what they are worth."

"'Twas a flush hit."

Bevin lifted one corner of his mouth. "That it was." He waited to see if the big man smiled back, or if it was to be pistols for two and breakfast for one, unless Johnny decided on more immediate, brutal, and bloody retribution. Bevin was debating whether he should throw the first blow or just go down quietly, when the Duke of Harleigh walked into the room, leaning on his cane.

Bevin stood to offer his gouty grace a seat, pleased that Coulton's revenge would at least be postponed by the presence of the august peer. The duke looked at Montravan, then through Montravan, and limped on to greet an acquaintance at the next table without even a nod for Montravan.

The cut was direct, and right in front of half of White's members. Now that was sure to set the cat among the pigeons. A few of the gambling men were already scrambling for the betting book to change their wagers. The earl shrugged. He wasn't the one whose daughter was playing fast and loose with the servants.

"Not too popular tonight, are we?" Johnny asked, with more than a tinge of satisfaction.

Bevin waved his unbandaged hand. "His Grace must have heard of last night's debacle. He doesn't like gossip."

"Gammon. His Grace wouldn't turn his back on an eligible parti like you if your name was as black as Byron's. You must have done something beyond the pale for him to cut you that way."

"I merely dismissed his daughter's—ah, that is, I had to discharge Vincent. I believe the duke thought he was a coming lad with political possibilities," he temporized, "so His Grace might disagree with my decision. He is welcome to hire the blackguard."

"It sounds like you have some fence-mending to do before Harleigh and his family travel to Montravan Hall."

"No, I have never been good at manual labor. I think I'll let these fences stay broken."

"But the chickens might fly the coop," Johnny hinted.

"And that would be a shame," Bevin answered with a grin. "A veritable shame."

Lord Coulton gestured toward the betting book. "Then I can lay my blunt on the banty cock staying out of the parson's cook pot?"

"From the, er, rooster's mouth. If it will make your fortune, bet the farm. That particular little game pullet will never take up residence in my coop, the saints be praised."

"From your noticeable lack of regret, I take it that your heart was not involved." Newly affianced and deeply in love, Lord Coulton looked at his friend in pity. "Then you are better out of it."

"My thinking entirely. Of course, now I'll have to explain to Mama why I am not filling my nursery posthaste, and then I'll have to go through the whole tedious business of finding another suitably well-born bride. But I'll have to attend some of those debutante affairs with m'sister Allissa, at any rate, so I can kill two birds with one stone."

"Still in the barnyard?" Coulton shook his head regretfully. "There are other reasons for taking a wife, you know, besides begetting an heir."

"Of course, there's marrying for money. Luckily I don't need a large dowry, so my choices will be that much wider."

"I would have offered for Elizabeth if she were penniless and a cit," Lord Coulton insisted.

"My dear romantic friend, you wouldn't even have *met* Elizabeth if she did not have entry to Almack's and the fashionable dos. You'd not have looked twice at her if she dressed in twice-turned gowns or dropped her aitches." Bevin suddenly recalled—with help from the additional color suffusing his friend's face—that he did not wish to antagonize the large man any more than he already had. "But, of course, Elizabeth is a gem who would possess the same beauty of soul no matter her social standing. You're a lucky devil, Johnny."

The angry blotches faded, except for the viscount's nose, of course, and his freckles. "And now you are free to find such a treasure for yourself, if you aren't blinded by that fustian of finding a 'suitable' bride."

"I take it Elizabeth has forgiven me, then?"

Coulton lifted his glass in silent toast. "She thinks I should have mentioned the rumors to you."

"A prize indeed. I'll keep your words in mind, after my narrow escape," the earl said, getting up to leave before Coulton had yet another change of heart. There was no reason to tempt fate.

And speaking of tempting fate, Bevin considered confronting the duke on his way out of the club, then gave himself a mental shake. He mightn't understand Harleigh's actions, but if they meant that dreaded house party was canceled, the duke could turn his back on Bevin five times a day for the next ten years.

*

The duke's behavior made more sense when Bevin reached Montford House and Tuttle presented him with a wad of tissue on a silver salver.

"This was delivered earlier from Harleigh House," the butler informed him.

Bevin eyed the misshapen lump with suspicion. "Was there any message?"

"I believe the item is self-explanatory," Tuttle said with a sniff of disapproval. "But there is a note."

Montravan gingerly pushed aside some of the paper to find a gilt-edged card with a border of angels playing improbable musical instruments like floating pianofortes, and inscribed with the message: *May the heavenly host make joyous music for you at this season of gladness.* At least Vincent hadn't committed that travesty. On the back of the card was written: *Her Grace, the Duchess of Harleigh, regrets that she and her family are unable to accept your invitation.* Short and simple, no flimsy excuses. But why? Dash it, *he* was the one who should have cried off; he was the wronged party, wasn't he?

Perhaps Belinda hadn't thought his gift was substantial enough for the almost betrothal, for surely that had to be the gold filigree fan returned in its crumpled wrappings. Odd, Vincent's taste was usually impeccable, and Bevin had thought the fan a charming token. Belinda must have thought otherwise, for each and every one of the delicate spokes was snapped in half. A trifle excessive, Bevin thought, for an unappreciated gift. Why, he accepted Petra's embroidered handkerchiefs every year with all the graciousness at his command, even though he had a drawerful by now. He didn't rip them up just because he rarely had the need to blow his nose. She went to the considerable effort to create the blasted things, just as he—or Vincent—had selected the fan expressly for Lady Belinda. That made three insults from the duke's family in one night, still without explanation.

Bevin was contemplating the ruined fan when Tuttle lifted a few shreds of silver paper and a bow to reveal his employer's own calling card, the one with its holly edge and simple message of season's greetings. This, too, was decimated, torn into halves and then smaller bits, but not so small that Bevin could not piece the thing together enough to read: *With fond thoughts of our past shared pleasures, and best wishes for better luck in your future relations.*

Marina's message. So the one for Petra and the one for his ex-mistress did not simply cross each other's paths. *All* of the cards were somehow confused.

This was so unlike the methodical Vincent with his attention to detail that the mingle-mangle had to be deliberate, the bounder. And what an unintentional favor he'd done, Bevin thought, freeing him of unwanted houseguests and an even more unwanted fiancée. The earl went up to bed, freer of dreary thoughts than he'd been in an age, he realized, or at least since he'd contemplated making Lady Belinda his wife.

As Finster was helping him remove his boots, however, Bevin suddenly recalled that the gifts to his entire family, gifts that the dastardly scribe had already sent on ahead, might also have mismatched greetings, not just Petra's. One of the boots and Finster went flying across the room. "The devil take it!" Heaven only knew what a mare's nest that would stir up!

Bevin still had a few days' leeway before his acquisitive sister would dare open the box to find her tiara, so he wasn't really worried. As long as he got to the Hall before Christmas Eve, with enough time to spare to rewrap the gifts, he'd be safe. And if he left tomorrow as planned, he'd have time to speak with Petra about finding a new secretary, too, before the festivities began. There, the dibs were in tune again, despite that gallowsbait, and the earl could finally rest easy, except for having his hand so swaddled, Finster had to button his nightshirt.

In the middle of the night Montravan woke with a start. Zounds! He'd forgotten all about Bibi! How in the world could he have forgotten that she might have another's message? He desperately tried to remember what he'd written and to whom, but he'd just dashed the things off, never suspecting anyone else but the so-discreet Vincent would ever see them. Now he'd have to wait until late afternoon to go make amends to the alluring demirep. He couldn't very well call on a woman at three in the morning, even if she was a Cyprian. She wasn't *his* Cyprian yet, and might never be if Vincent took it into his vengeful mind to wreak more havoc on his late employer. What if the cad had written his own message? What was to stop him from doing more than switching the cards, now that Montravan's bullet couldn't reach him?

Blast, he couldn't even call on the woman until after luncheon. Birds of paradise never strutted their plumes until the sun was well up. And what the bloody hell was Bibi's card supposed to read anyway?

Certainly not *Here's what you wanted, you greedy little hoyden. Next time I'll warm your backside instead.* That was meant for his sister Allissa and her tiara.

Bibi was not open to explanation or apologies. Bevin's ears were ringing to her screams of "I'm not that kind of woman," and his cheeks were stinging from the resounding slaps she'd administered.

She'd thrown the earbobs back at him, too, being either more highly principled or less intelligent than Marina. She had also kept him waiting for two hours, so it was too late to set out for Wiltshire that day.

8

He still had plenty of time to reach the Hall by Christmas Eve. That was the latest Bevin could be, for every year his sister cajoled the countess into letting her open the gifts that night after church, instead of waiting till the next morning. The dowager never held out much resistance to Allissa's wheedling, since she was equally impatient to rip into her own pile of packages.

When Montravan confidently figured his travel time, though, he had not taken into account the damage to his hand. The blasted thing couldn't be trusted to tool the ribbons of his curricle's spirited matched bays, and going on horseback the whole way holding the reins in his awkward left hand sounded cold and painful. Besides, Finster was full of dire warnings about splintered knucklebones grinding away at each other and the muscles around them until the fingers never moved again. Worse, according to Finster, a fragment of the broken bone could work itself loose and travel with the blood flow until it pierced his lungs.

So the prodigal son was going to return home in style: the coach and team, with driver and postilions and outriders, and the painted crest on the door with all those rubbishing lions and hawks.

But Bevin also forgot that Vincent was no longer around to make all the travel arrangements. Therefore blood cattle weren't waiting at the changes, just the usual posthouse breakdowns. The tolls had not been paid in advance, nor had suitable accommodations been booked. With so many other travelers abroad at the holiday season, oftentimes Bevin was lucky to get a bed at all, without having to share with Finster. The sheets were unaired; the food was deplorable and served in the public areas, since the private rooms had been reserved ages ago. Lord Montravan was not that much of a snob that he minded breaking his bread with sheep drovers; he did object to the dogs, though.

The trip was taking so long—and Bevin's patience was wearing so thin—that he decided to hire a horse for the last stages, bone slivers be damned. If he didn't get to Montravan Hall in time, he might as well be dead anyway.

The nags for hire at that last inn were an unprepossessing lot at best, but Bevin was considered a notable judge of horseflesh, so he picked the likeliest steed, a rangy black gelding with an intelligent look. The horse was so intelligent, he had definite ideas on where he wished to spend Christmas Eve. He waited a mile past that inn to express these sentiments, and Bevin was not turning back. The contest of wills over who chose which road left Bevin's left hand numb and the seat of his breeches caked with mud. He never let loose of the reins, consummate horseman that he was, and finally convinced the hard-mouthed brute to give the stables at Montravan a look-see.

Then the gelding cast a shoe, out of spite, Bevin was sure. The nearest village was a mere five miles down the road, according to the driver of a passing high-perch phaeton who not only didn't slow to give the directions, but also managed to splash a more liberal amount of mud on the earl's caped coat. The five miles afoot were cold, hungry, and at least *seven*, Bevin swore.

And the blacksmith was away at his daughter's in Skellington, two miles east.

There were no horses to be let in the little village, although the tavern proprietor thought old Jed Turner might lend his ass, now that farm chores were slacking off. Instead a boy was dispatched to fetch the blacksmith home with the promise of a generous reward. Bevin hadn't figured on handing over the ready every time he stopped either, since Vincent had always seen to all charges in advance. At this rate the earl would soon be forced to sleep in empty barns and eat winter-dry berries as cold and hard as that dastard's heart.

He sipped at his ale in the tavern for the time it took for Duncan the smith to get back, making each tankard last as long as possible, then had to stand the man a round to warm his innards. Bevin thought Duncan would warm up faster by heating the forge, but he refrained from pointing that out to a man who dwarfed Johnny Coulton in height and Prinny in girth. Duncan was, moreover, Bevin's only way of getting that black bone rattler back on the road, so he ordered another glass.

Johnny Coulton moved quickly for a big man. Duncan moved slowly, even for a big man. He walked slowly, readied his fires slowly, and took forever to shape one blasted horseshoe. And all the time he wanted to talk, about his daughter, about the state of the nation, about his craft. He even insisted, while the iron was heating, on the earl's trying his hand at the job. Bevin reluctantly bent a nail into a circle, just to show the smith that all noblemen weren't effete wastrels. Then he wiped the sweat off his brow with his throbbing hand.

The black didn't cooperate, naturally. They had to send to the tavern for two more men to hold the brute, which of course necessitated Montravan's standing them a round, too. By the time Bevin was back in the saddle, the gelding was well rested indeed. With a short memory for everything but his own barn, the black was more unruly than ever. By the time his lordship had the beast headed in the right direction, darkness had started falling. So had the snow.

*

It was Christmas Eve, and it was snowing. He wasn't coming. Most likely he had changed his plans and decided to spend Christmas with his new in-laws. More likely he couldn't bear to be parted from his bride-to-be, Petra thought irritably. That was entirely understandable, she told herself, not understanding in the least how he could leave Montravan Hall at sixes and sevens without him.

There was no head of the household to bring in the Yule log, no lord of the manor to greet the villagers who came trudging through the snow to carol for their benefactor. There was no Earl of Montravan to sit in the front pew at church, and no neighborhood nabob to pledge a new roof for the school. There was no dutiful son to soothe the dowager's nerves, and no loving brother to tease Allissa out of the sullens. And there was no smile for Petra.

Then his carriage arrived with Finster and the baggage. The countess swore Bevin was lying dead in a ditch somewhere and called for her hartshorn and vinaigrette.

"Don't be goosish, Mama," Allissa said helpfully. "Bevin is never so cow-handed as that. Be sure he's decided to spend his last nights of unfettered bachelorhood in the arms of some tavern doxy."

"What do you know of doxies, missy?" her mother demanded.

"I know a man's mistress gets nicer presents than his family." Allissa had been eyeing the stack of packages neatly gathered on a piecrust table in the drawing room all week. The devious little minx might just have opened her presents and resealed them, Petra considered, except that Allissa was still on tenterhooks, working herself into a frenzy of excitement and despair when she had to wait.

The dowager was also sadly out of curl. The snow might keep her guests away, Cook's lovely goose might be overcooked if that rattlepate son of hers didn't get here in time, and the package Squire Merton placed on the piecrust table was much too large to be the ring Lady Montravan had hoped for. Besides, her companion had *two* presents from the dowager's own son, while Lady Montravan had only one. True, one of Petra's gifts appeared to be a book—from the size, shape, feel, and nonrattle of the package—but Lady Montravan was known to enjoy a good novel, too. Petra was a good enough girl in her way, the dowager admitted, but it was outside of enough that her firstborn was not only taking a bride to supplant his mother in his affections, but was also showing preference for a charity case.

So Lady Montravan had been more querulous than ever, demanding more and more of Petra's time, right on top of all the holiday preparations...and an outbreak of measles in the village.

Petra had done what she could, working with the earl's steward to make sure there was enough firewood to go around and spending hours in the kitchens herself to ensure the afflicted families had proper nourishment without overburdening Montravan's already busy cooking staff. She tried to find time to visit the homes of the stricken families, singing carols to the restless, feverish children, cutting paper stars to win a weak, spotted smile.

If only it were as easy to put Allissa in better spirits. The girl was anxious about meeting the new sister-in-law who was going to be responsible for Allissa's own presentation. She was in a fidge over attending her first New Year's ball, and she was near hysterics over that dratted inappropriate tiara. The present from Bevin *could* be the headpiece. The box was big enough, Allissa remarked at least twice a day. Petra decided Bevin should be drawn and quartered for sending those packages so early and putting them all through this adolescent agony.

Petra distrusted Allissa's hectic, glassy-eyed look and tried to get the younger girl to rest.

"Oh, do stop treating me like a child, Petra," Allissa snapped. "I am not the one snoring away or yawning over my sewing."

No, Squire Merton was the one having a catnap near the fire, and Petra was the one who was yawning, from being up since dawn. But Petra had had the measles, and no one, typically, could recall if Allissa had. That was something else Petra had to worry about.

A small hint to the dowager that perhaps the roads were getting slippery was enough to cancel the trip to church. Lady Montravan was delighted not to move from her sofa into the cold night, so she declared that they would do better to await Bevin here, or word of his demise.

They took turns reading the Nativity from the Bible, listening to the clock tick and the squire snore.

"Please, Mama," Allissa begged for the nth time, "can we please open the presents? Bevin is obviously not coming, and I *am* growing a trifle weary." She peeped at Petra through lowered eyelashes in an effort to enlist the other's sympathy. "You know I'll never get to sleep tonight with so much anticipation fluttering my nerves, and I do so want to be in looks tomorrow. You always say a woman needs her rest to be her best. Why, if I am too fatigued," she added slyly, "I just might grow ill or something." Petra tried not to stare at the slight blotch on Allissa's cheek. If she didn't notice it, perhaps the spot would vanish. Perhaps it was merely a blemish, and if the chit did indeed get to her bed, it would be gone by morning.

"I am sure Lord Montravan would not want us to be disappointed," she said. "Maybe we could open the other gifts first, since Finster is certain his lordship will arrive momentarily."

Lady Montravan was convinced. If that lobcock Willoughby Merton hadn't come through with a ring, she'd have to rearrange tomorrow's dinner seating. Sir Fortescue was invited, as well as old Redford from the Grange. Redford had one foot in the grave, but...

She jabbed the squire awake with the tip of her lorgnette. "We're opening the presents now, Willoughby, since we'll likely be out searching for Montravan all night." As if she or Allissa would go riding out with lanterns. Or sit up past the unwrappings.

"What's that? Montravan's lost? Downy fellow like that, I'd wager a monkey he's found a snug nest for the night." The squire's wink let them all know he didn't believe it would be any hot brick keeping Bevin warm that evening. Petra's heart sank lower. Everyone knew the man was a rake, so why should it bother her now, when it was Miss Harleigh's problem? She sighed, drawing the dowager's attention.

"We may as well start with Petra's gifts," Lady Montravan decreed. No surprises there, and no one could accuse her of hurrying the proceedings out of vulgar curiosity or greed.

They all opened their handkerchiefs to the usual polite, unexcited mouthings. They all tossed Petra's hours of effort aside to reach for the next offering.

Allissa and Lady Montravan exchanged their gifts then, each receiving an elaborate new ensemble for the New Year's ball: gown, gloves, shoes and shawl. Cost had been of no concern, since they put the charges on Bevin's account.

"Oh, thank you, Mama," Allissa enthused, holding up the gown of spangled satin in the exact color blue as her eyes. "It's just what I wanted. However did you guess?" she asked for the squire's benefit, since he was the only one not along for the shopping and fittings.

Lady Montravan had to hold up her own new lavender sarcenet, with turban to match, complimenting Lissa on her exquisite taste. Then it was Petra's turn to open Lady Montravan's present. Petra was actually surprised to see the exquisite dress length of gold velvet, until she noted the slight water stain near the edge. The color would bring out the gold in her brown hair, Petra knew, and might even give some life to her brown eyes and honeyed complexion. Of course, there was hardly time to make up a gown by the New Year's ball, which Lady Montravan *might* have taken into consideration, but Petra expressed her honest delight enthusiastically enough to gratify the dowager's self-esteem as a gentlewoman of genuine generosity.

Allissa gave Petra a matching stole, which coincidentally also matched a stole Petra knew the chit had two of. No matter, Petra vowed, she'd be as finely gowned as any lady at the ball, even if she had to stay awake for the next six nights to do it. Why, she might even outshine Lady Belinda Harleigh. And the barnyard animals might speak at Christmas Eve. At least she wouldn't be ashamed at the ball, appearing as the poor hanger-on in made-over dresses.

Squire Merton adored his embroidered pillow. "Can't think of a more thoughtful gift, m'dear." He even had a tear in his eye as he kissed the dowager's pudgy fingers. She puffed out her chest until he got up, corsets creaking, to go buss Petra heartily on the cheek. "And I bet I know whom to thank for the effort. Why, it's Skipjack to the life. Just think, he'll be on my sofa forever."

Just think, Petra thought, she'd be in Lady Montravan's black books forever, too. It was a good thing she had already decided to leave after the new year.

While he was up, the squire fetched his own gifts to the ladies. Petra and Allissa each received a pair of York tan riding gloves, which Petra truly needed and appreciated, thanking the squire for his consideration. Allissa made barely polite responses, then waved a glove to tease Pug into a game.

Lady Montravan opened the box from her portly gallant and lifted out a fox tippet, complete with glass eyes. While the squire related every detail of the poor creature's gory demise, Lady Montravan was turning it this way and that, searching the box and tissue for the ring. "How nice," she said, tossing the object of at least seven hunts aside, knocking over a glass of restorative sherry. She mopped at the spill with Petra's handkerchief, then threw the soiled lace-edged linen to the floor.

"We might as well open Montravan's presents," she grumbled. "He's not coming."

"Don't you think we ought to wait for his lordship?" Petra suggested.

"No, I do not, miss, and I still make some of the decisions around here. I am worn out with the tension of worry and must seek my bed soon. If that rakeshame is so inconsiderate as to be late, then he cannot expect me to ruin my health. Allissa, bring the gifts. I'll start."

No one dared contradict the countess in such a mood, not even Allissa, who merely whined at her mother to hurry; she'd go next.

Lady Montravan unwrapped a magnificent ruby brooch. "Oh, the dear boy," she cooed, holding the pin to the lavender gown to judge the effect. Then she reached for the enclosed card just as a commotion was heard in the hall.

"'Greetings of the season,'" Lady Montravan started reading when a disheveled, dirty earl tore into the room.

"Mama, don't!" he shouted. Too late.

"'Looking forward to seeing you with your esteemed parents,'" she continued, puzzled. Then she shrieked. "He wants me dead! It's not enough that he's sending me to that dreary dower house; now he wants me in the vault with my ancestors! My heart! My heavens!" And she swooned dead away, there on the sofa.

9

"There's been a dreadful mistake," Lord Montravan tried to say into the ensuing chaos, but no one paid him any attention after Petra's first tentative smile. The butler was shouting for her ladyship's maid and the housekeeper, while Petra was scrambling under the sofa for the smelling salts. Squire Merton poured out another glass of restorative—and swallowed it down. Then he started coughing and bellowing for something decent a fellow could drink at a time of crisis. Footmen were sent running in all directions, and Allissa was gulping back sobs of frustration, saying that she'd never get her tiara at this rate and if her older brother was in such a hateful mood.

"That was despicable," she raged at him. "You know how Mama's nerves are so easily overset. And at Christmas, and your coming late! How could you write such a thing?"

"I didn't, brat, so stubble it," he began, looking on helplessly as a maid started burning feathers under Lady Montravan's nose.

Allissa snatched the card off the table and thrust it at Bevin. "It's your handwriting, isn't it?"

Petra glanced up from her place at the side of the reviving, moaning countess. Those were indeed Bevin's heavy, slanting strokes on the holly-bordered card.

"Yes, but the messages—" he began again, his words lost anew to Lady Montravan's groans and clutchings of her heart.

Her mama being alert and her usual stridently complaining self, Allissa now felt free to gather up the box with her name on it while no one was watching. Petra glanced over, frowning, just as the younger girl ripped the wrappings apart. The earl had bought Allissa a tiara after all, but Petra was relieved to see the circlet was of delicate gold, with no ornate tracery and no diamonds. The coronet would look sweet with flowers woven through it, entirely in keeping with a young miss's debut.

"It's for babies!" the young miss wailed when she saw there were no diamonds. Then she reached for the enclosure at the bottom of the box.

"No!" Bevin shouted, leaving off patting his mother's hand and reassuring her of his continued devotion and affection, that the message was meant for Lady Belinda, who would not, after all, be... He jumped up and tried to seize the card, but Allissa danced out of his grasp. He couldn't very well wrestle with her over it, so, heart sinking, he watched as his spoiled sister's face grew redder and redder, just as it used to before she threw herself on the floor in a tantrum. Someone should have saved them all the trouble by drowning her then, he thought, when she began to scream.

"'Happy hunting'! How dare you, Bevin Montford! As if I'm going to the Marriage Mart just to snare the most eligible parti! Is that all you think of me, that no man will ask for me, but I have to go...go *hunting* for a husband? Just because you fell into the parson's mousetrap, you think all women are sneaky and devious, don't you? You are mean and nasty, Bevin Montford! Nasty, nasty, nasty, and you always have been, making me have those horrid governesses, and making me wait to go to London."

Allissa was sobbing in earnest now, totally beyond reason or control.

Petra left Lady Montravan's side to take Allissa into her arms. The girl felt warm, likely from her overheated emotional storm, Petra hoped.

Bevin was raking his fingers through his already mussed hair. "I didn't write that to you, Lissa, I swear. I wrote that for Squire Merton. Now where the devil has he gone off to?"

The squire had unobtrusively unwrapped his own gift, thinking to make a courteous thank you and a genteel early departure, seeing the dustup at Montravan Hall. The riding crop was a handsome one, but the earl's note gave Merton pause: *Greetings of the season, from a son who knows his duty.* Montravan was assuring his mother that he would fulfill his responsibilities to his name, that he was bringing

66

home a fitting bride for her approval. However, Merton shook his head over the earl's meaning. Could the lad be thinking he'd been dallying too long with the dowager? Blast, could Montravan be aware of those intimate encounters in the conservatory? That dutiful son bit could mean Montravan might call a fellow out for not coming up to scratch. The earl was certainly hot-to-hand enough, and more than skilled enough to have Merton's knees knocking together. The squire decided to see about a new hunter—in Ireland. Tonight. He crept out the side door while Bevin was raging about riding the devil's own horse through a blizzard just to get to this madhouse.

Petra scowled at him, so he subsided, content to fill a glass with the brandy the butler had brought for Merton. She tried again to soothe the girl in her arms: "Allissa, dear, do try to calm yourself. I am sure there is an explanation. You are only upsetting your mother and making yourself ill."

"And likely giving Merton a disgust of us," Montravan added, aggravated that his mother's likeliest suitor had shabbed off. "So cut line. You're only blue-deviled that you didn't get the diamonds you wanted. Why, a seventeen-year-old schoolgirl with spots could only look nohow in diamonds and—"

"Spots?" Allissa screamed. Lady Montravan echoed with a hysterical "Spots?" and fainted again.

"Damnation!" swore Lord Montravan, and "Welcome home, my lord," said Petra.

*

Later, after the physician had gone and both invalids were well dosed with laudanum and in the competent hands of their maids, Petra sought out Lord Montravan in the drawing room. Bevin had had a bath and a snack in his room and was immaculately dressed in dove gray pantaloons and black coat, his hair still damp from its recent washing. Petra still wore her second-best gown, somewhat rumpled from her exertions, and her hair was coming undone, but she intended merely to stay a moment. She couldn't think it was altogether proper for her to be alone with such a handsome, virile man, even if he was her employer. Her reputation might suffer; her already tortured feelings certainly would.

"The physician thinks that the dowager is merely overset," she reported. "A good night's rest should restore her to normal."

Bevin muttered something about that being bad enough, which Petra ignored. She went on: "He feels that Allissa's case should be a mild one if she is kept quiet, which will not be easy, once she realizes she'll miss her first real ball."

Bevin nodded. "There will be others. I'm sure if I promise her an early visit to London, she'll be more resigned. And there must be some gaudy, trumpery bit of something in the village I can buy to win her back to humor, since she was not so fond of her present."

"The presents!" Petra recalled. "You never had yours." She quickly moved to the piecrust table and brought three packages back to where Bevin stood staring into the fire.

"I can wait, my dear. I daresay I have all the patience in this family."

But he looked as if he needed some cheering right now, Petra thought, noting how the flickering flames showed the lines of weariness on his face. "But the countess will not rise till just before church, and then the vicar and local families will arrive for nuncheon."

"Very well," he said, indicating she should take a seat, so he might sit and open the gifts. Her handkerchiefs were duly appreciated, one placed carefully in his pocket. And the robe and slippers were exclaimed over to such an extent that Petra was soon blushing. Bevin got up and poured out a glass of Madeira for each of them, then raised his in a toast. "You are the best thing that ever happened to this family, Petra. I do not know what we have done to deserve you, but I thank heaven you've taken us in hand."

Embarrassed, Petra sipped her drink. "I have done nothing, my lord."

"Nothing?" He held up the robe with its intricate work. "You call this nothing? Or the way you were such a pillar of strength through that bumblebroth tonight? You've even forgiven me for ruining Christmas by making sure I have my gifts."

Petra did not pretend to misunderstand. "However did you come to make such a mull of things, my lord? That is not like you in the least."

"Not like Vincent, you mean." He sank back into the chair opposite hers with a heartfelt sigh. "I swear I know what hell is like. I feel as if I've been visiting there for the last three days."

He proceeded to tell her about the gossip in the clubs and about confronting his secretary. Then he described the horror of the mixed-up notes, with his "lady friend" receiving Petra's note of appreciation and Lady Belinda receiving Marina's congé.

"I realize this is all horribly improper, my discussing such things with you, but I knew you, at least, wouldn't fly into a pelter."

Instead Petra was giggling uncontrollably, especially when she realized Miss Harleigh would not be coming, that there would be no engagement. Her heart was so lightened, she practically danced across the room to return with the last parcel from the table, the one addressed to Miss Petra Sinclaire.

"I didn't get to open my gift, my lord," she said merrily, mischievously.

"Oh, Lord! Let me take the card out at least!" he begged. "And you might as well be calling me Bevin as you were used to, after witnessing my fall from grace."

"Not at all, my lord. You have not tarnished your image in my eyes, merely restored yourself to the ranks of us poor humans. The last time I saw you take a misstep was when you were conjugating Latin verbs with my father." She peeled away the tissue around the hair combs and exclaimed over their loveliness. "Oh, they are just the thing to go with my new dress, my lord." Then she unwrapped the book and raised shining eyes to his. "Except how can I finish sewing my gown when I'll be wanting to read this?"

"I'll read it out loud while you stitch," he offered unexpectedly, surprising himself as well as Petra.

"That's quite the kindest thing of all," she said with a catch in her voice, imagining nights such as this, by the fire. No, she dare not dream.

"Then be kind in return," Bevin was saying into her reverie, "and give me back the card."

She grinned, showing sudden dimples he'd never noticed, and shook her head, freeing even more soft brown curls to rest against her glowing cheeks.

"Minx," he muttered appreciatively, racking his brain to think what message was left unaccounted for. It must be the one for Bibi, meant to go with the earbobs. What was the blasted message? He groaned.

Petra read the card, then lowered her head, her shoulders shaking. Rising, Bevin rushed to kneel by her side. "Please don't cry, my dear! You know I didn't mean it for you, whatever it says!" She kept on making whimpery sounds. "It cannot be that bad, Petra."

"Bad? It's wonderful!" When she raised her head, he could see tears glistening on her lashes. "I can figure out about the hair combs, but I am not sure about this," and she held up the book before going off into whoops of laughter. "'Th-thinking of you in m-my arms,'" she tried to read through her giggles, "'w-wearing just these.'"

Soon the usually somber earl was laughing so hard, his sides hurt, and he had to wipe his own eyes with one of the fine new handkerchiefs. Then he tenderly wiped Petra's cheeks with the same cloth.

"I've been a fool," he said, staying next to her, taking her hand in his.

"You certainly have," she agreed, "putting all your faith in that bounder."

"No, I mean about so many other things. My friend Johnny tried to tell me, and I never really understood. I was looking for a suitable bride, when I should have been looking for a woman who suited me."

"Lady Belinda?"

Bevin waved that away. "I hardly knew her, beyond her social standing. I know now that I should have sought a woman who can laugh with me, understand my failings, and share my concerns."

"Yes, I think that's important for a happy marriage."

"I never realized I already had all those things in my grasp. That is, I did realize, but I never understood I could have it all. I'm not doing this well, am I?"

"I'm not quite sure what it is you *are* doing, my lord."

"Bevin." He got up to pace, while she nearly shredded the handkerchief she'd labored over so long. "I had time on the long ride here to think, and all I thought of was how much I wanted to see you, be with you. Do you think you might ever consider…? That is, after you've had a proper Season, and a chance to look over the crop of bachelors, and a proper courtship—"

"Never."

He kept his back to her. "That's it, then. I'm sorry, Petra, if I have embarrassed you. I never meant—"

"No, I mean I will never wait that long."

In two long strides he was next to her again, with his arms on her shoulders. "Do you mean that, sweetheart, do you really mean you might come to love me?"

"Silly, I've loved you forever."

The kiss that followed left them both shaken. Petra never knew a kiss could do such amazing things to one's insides—and outsides and upside-down sides—and Bevin never knew how desire could be so incredibly intensified by affection. It was the earl who found the willpower to set Petra away from him, at least a handbreadth.

When he found his voice, he gasped, "I can see there is going to be nothing proper about this courtship after all."

"My lo—Bevin, I need to know, will you do *that* with other women? I mean, I know about your *chéries amours*, but I don't think I could bear it, after…"

Bevin stroked the back of his hand along her cheek. "After that kiss I don't think I'll even want to look at another woman. I cannot hide my past from you, but I do mean to be a faithful husband. Do you know, when I thought about Belinda and Vincent, I realized I didn't truly care, except for my pride, of course, and the idea of having to worry about the paternity of my children. That's when I realized I wouldn't be happy with that kind of society marriage, where both spouses go their own way. I want a wife who will love me enough to mind if I stray."

"I'll mind! Why, I'll…I'll darken your daylights if you look at another woman."

"And if you so much as smile at another man, I'll call him out!"

So they sealed that accord with another kiss, which ended at the rug in front of the hearth, perilously close to the fire.

"Blast, I depended on you to be level-headed," Bevin complained, lifting her in his arms back to the sofa. Petra only grinned, so he kissed the tip of her nose. "This is no way for a gentleman to behave, and us not even formally engaged. Luckily I can remedy that." He reached into his pocket for a small box. "It's the family betrothal ring, from the vault. I was hoping, you see. I can have one made that will be more to your taste, but will you wear this for me, for now?"

"Not for now, forever."

As Bevin slipped it onto her finger, he murmured, "Merry Christmas, my love," but instead of the kiss he expected in return, Petra jumped up and ran from the room.

"I'll be right back," she said.

Bevin took the moment to straighten his clothing and vow to keep his passions under control—and pray for an early wedding. Petra was an innocent, a lady—and back within the circle of his arms before he could think of how many cold baths he'd have to take.

"I wanted to give you a special Christmas gift," she whispered, "to mark the occasion."

"But you've given me so much, two handkerchiefs and your love. What more could a man need or want?"

Petra smiled at his teasing and held out her hand. "Here, it's my father's watch. I want you to have it."

He took the gold watch on its chain and raised her hand to his lips. "I know how much this must mean to you, and I shall cherish it always as the second-finest Christmas gift I've ever received."

"After the embroidered robe?"

"After your love, my precious peagoose. But wait, I have another gift for you, too."

"But the ring and the book and the combs... It's so much."

"The ring is an heirloom, the book is in every bookseller's, and you must know Vincent selected the combs. I want to give you something all your own." Bevin was searching through his pockets, damning his valet for being so meticulous. At last his fingers touched the object he was seeking, and he drew out a small black circle, a horseshoe nail twisted into a ring, rust showing in spots, uneven welding in others. He proudly placed this ring on her finger, right above the diamond-and-emerald Montravan betrothal ring. "This one I made myself. Greetings of the season, sweetheart."

And every season.

The Proof Is in the Pudding

1

"Faugh," declared Sir Otis Ogden from his place at the head of the long table. "'Tis a waste of good spirits, I say."

Since Sir Otis considered any spirits not flowing directly down his shriveled gullet a waste, his wife Johna did not bother raising her voice to be heard across the mahogany expanse. Lady Ogden's younger sister, Phillipa, though, seated somewhere in the middle of the table behind an arrangement of pine boughs, holly leaves, and red apples, clapped her hands when the butler and two footmen carried in the flaming pudding on its silver platter. Drenched in brandy, the traditional holiday dessert flared blue and gold and scarlet in the dimmed dining parlor.

"It's beautiful," Phillipa whispered. "It's…it's Christmas."

"It's poppycock," Sir Otis spit, spewing wine down his shirtfront. The claret stains added a festive touch to the remnants of turbot in oyster sauce, roast goose, and asparagus already decorating the aged knight's neckcloth. If his young wife had thought to sweeten Sir Otis's disposition by serving a fine meal, festooning his dreary house with ribbon and holly, entertaining him with carols in Phillipa's pretty voice and her own pianoforte accompaniment, she was wrong. Again. All the sugar in the gingerbread men, in the marzipan angels, in the candied fruits—all the sugar that got baked, boiled, and blended for a hundred holiday feasts—was not going to improve the curmudgeon's nature. As for peace, goodwill, and Christmas feeling, Sir Otis was feeling bilious.

"Next thing you'll be doing is setting the blasted house on fire," he muttered. "Just my luck to marry a damned arsonist. Fires in every hearth, a fortune in candles gone up in smoke, now you're setting torches to my food. Hell and tarnation, if you had any fire in your blood mayhaps I'd have me an heir."

The servants pretended deafness, a not infrequent malady in this household, while Johna supervised the cutting of the pudding. Her face might be as red as the maroon velvet gown she wore and her lips might be pinched into a thin line, but Johna would not let the old glump ruin Phillipa's Christmas. He'd already ruined Johna's hopes for a happy life with a man who could love her. That was enough.

Obviously, this was not a marriage made in heaven. It was, in fact, a business transaction conducted in a smoke-filled gambling hall, over a table of unpaid and unpayable gaming debts.

Slavery being illegal, Johna's father, Baron Hutchison, sold his elder daughter into matrimony. Johna was eighteen at the time, a raven-haired beauty with her dead mother's blue eyes and levelheadedness. She might have made a splash in the Marriage Market if Hutchison could have dowered her, dressed her, and dropped her into the *ton* under some dragon's watchful eye. But the dissolute baron could barely feed his daughters, much less get them entree into the *belle monde*. Gambling, drinking, and poor management of his properties, all had combined to keep Hutchison one short step away from debtor's prison.

Sir Otis Ogden was his only hope—and the holder of most of his notes. If Lord Hutchison was barely skirting the fringes of society, Sir Otis was beyond the pale. He'd been able to purchase a knighthood but not respectability. A cardsharper, a moneylender, a fleecer of green lambs fresh from the country, his reputation did not bear scrutiny. His lusting after a young girl did.

So Lord Hutchison got his debts paid and a handsome settlement besides. If his conscience needed more soothing than the sound of rustling bank notes, he convinced himself that Johna would be a widow sooner rather than later, considering Ogden was ten years older than himself, to say nothing of the rough company the man kept. Odds were she'd still be young enough to attract another husband, and wealthy enough to provide for her dear papa in his dotage. He promptly gambled away his windfall, got tossed out of some foul dive into the snow, caught an inflammation of the lungs, and died—before seeing another shilling of his senescent son-in-law's blunt. Which only went to prove that Hutchison never had been lucky at playing the odds.

Sir Otis got his bride, but not quite what he expected of the marriage either. No female of such tarnished pedigree could advance his social standing, no matter how beautiful she was. And no female could put the wind back in his sail, no matter how young she was. After a few sweat-covered attempts at conjugal consummation, Sir Otis gave it up, along with hopes for an heir. No society belle, no son, just a damned expensive piece of goods, that's what his money had bought him. So he fired his housekeeper and two maids.

Of them all, Johna was perhaps the least disappointed in her marriage, especially once the grunting and groping were over. She hadn't expected much, after all, just a better life for her sister and herself. She could have refused the match, could have hired herself out as a governess or companion, but she wouldn't leave fifteen-year-old Phillipa alone in Berkshire. Hutchison Manor's roof was falling in, the staff had left for positions that actually paid a salary, and who knew what misguided notion Papa would get into his muddled head next?

Sir Otis agreed to take in the spotty schoolgirl sister, though, so the marriage contract was finalized. Now, three years later, the sisters weren't hungry and they weren't in the poorhouse. They were, however, bonded servants. The bonds might be those of holy matrimony, but the results were the same. Johna kept house in London for Sir Otis and did half the cooking, mending, and cleaning. Phillipa worked alongside the maids, dusting and washing. She wasn't spotty anymore, and she wasn't a schoolgirl. She was eighteen, the very age at which Johna had been wed. Prejudiced or not, Johna thought her sister was lovely with her brown ringlets and softly rounded form, in contrast to her own straight black hair and tall, willowy frame which Sir Otis, for one, found boyish. Too, Phillipa was an unspoiled, uncomplaining treasure of a girl. She'd make some man a fine wife since, perforce, she knew all about managing a gentleman's household. The problem was, there were no gentlemen.

Sir Otis didn't entertain at home and never invited the two young women to accompany him on his evenings out. In fact, he barely allowed them to leave his house, determined not to share what he couldn't enjoy. Be damned, he thought, if he'd have any dandified nodcocks strutting around his chicken coop. If they could get out of the Albemarle Street residence, Sir Otis and duties permitting, the girls knew no one in London and had barely the fee for the lending library between them. Their few treats depended on what Johna could squeeze out of the nipcheese household budget. The generous allowance her father had negotiated for Johna was going, according to Sir Otis, to pay for the maintenance of Hutchison Manor, to settle the baron's last debts, and to keep the girls in modest home-sewn gowns so they didn't shame him.

'Twould take the devil in lace drawers to shame the old reprobate, thought Johna. And 'twould take the heavenly host to please him. For sure her lovely Christmas dinner hadn't. Johna had hoped to get Sir Otis in a mellow mood, to beg permission to take Phillipa to Bath for the winter. Social standards were less rigorous there, she'd heard, and the place was reportedly full of young army officers, widowers, and second sons. Well, she still had her Christmas wish. While stirring the pudding last month, she'd wished that Sir Otis would relent enough to provide dear Phillipa with a dowry and a future. Meanwhile, Johna was not going to permit the miserable old muckworm to ruin her sister's joy in the holiday season. She'd been working on this Christmas pudding since early fall, just for Phillipa. First she'd let everyone from the scullery maid to the stableboy help stir the pudding and make their wishes—while the master was out, of course. Then she'd divided the mixture into four boiling bags to steam for hours, then hung them out to set and age, just as in her grandmother's old recipe. According to the faded household book, one was for family, one for company, one for the servants, and one for charity. Since there was no company, Johna had traded the extra pudding for the special tokens she'd hidden that morning in the family's dessert, the one that had been soaking in rum for the past week.

As she carefully cut the pudding in precise sections, Johna asked, "Do you remember Mama's little charms, Phillipa? The ones she used to hide in the Christmas pudding?"

Phillipa clapped her hands again, beaming around the centerpiece. "Never say you found them, Jo. I can't wait to see. Oh, hurry, do."

"What's that you two are nattering on about now?" Sir Otis demanded. "Mealymouthed chits talk barely loud enough to be heard."

The footmen passed the plates while Johna tried to soothe her husband. "It's just an old tradition, like making wishes when you stir the batter."

"Balderdash. Tommyrot. More nonsense to fill a gudgeon's empty head." He stuck his spoon into the dish before him.

"Look, Jo, I got the ring! That means I'm going to be married within the year!"

Johna smiled. Of course Phillipa had found the ring, right where Johna'd planted it. She dug around in her own portion and came up with a coin.

"What's this blasted jibber-jabber?" Sir Otis shouted around a mouthful of pudding. "Is this food or some tomfool parlor game?"

"It's just for fun—" Johna started to explain, and Phillipa chimed in with, "It's part of the Christmas magic. I got the ring, and Jo got the coin. That means she's going to come into great wealth this year."

Sir Otis took another heaping spoonful into his mouth, then banged his fist on the table and thundered, "You mean you stuck a coi—A ch—"

Phillipa answered: "Not a real coin, sir, a special token. Besides the ring and the coin, there's the shoe that means a long journey, and the key that portends a wonderful opportunity. What else, Jo?"

But Johna was watching her husband down the length of the table. She was frozen in her seat, horrified, as Sir Otis went "Ch—

ch—" a few more times, his face turning purplish, before he fell over, right into his dish of pudding.

Sir Otis had gotten the shoe.

*

Six months of mourning was all the respect Johna was willing to accord her departed husband, and that was five months more than the dastard deserved. No improvements had been made at Hutchison Manor, no outstanding debts had been marked paid. And Sir Otis's own private papers showed exorbitant interest rates on loans, dealings in smuggled goods, a strongbox full of nefarious and underhanded dealings. Johna relocked the box and hid it deep in her clothespress, wondering if a man could be more despicable dead than alive.

Not when he'd left her a fortune to rival Golden Ball's, he couldn't. Not when he'd *left*, by heaven's grace. Johna was twenty-one, rich, and free. There was no one to issue orders, no one to criticize her looks or behavior, no one to tell her what to do. Sir Otis's solicitor threatened to challenge her in court: a young woman needed a guardian, a trustee. Johna threatened to find another man of affairs to handle her finances. Mr. Bigelow withdrew his complaints.

For six months the Widow Ogden could not go to the theater or the opera or even the assemblies in Bath, not without permanently destroying her reputation. But she could spend her husband's ill-gotten wealth, smiling with every bank draft she wrote. Johna refurbished the London residence top to bottom, with enough servants that she had a maid just to tidy the other maids' rooms. She hired a manager for the Berkshire property, and made sure he had ample funds to restore the manor house to a glory never seen in her lifetime. She set up a bank fund for Phillipa's dowry that made Mr. Bigelow's hand shake. And then she called in the dressmakers.

By the end of June they were ready. Johna wore pale grays, silvers, the smoky lavenders of half-mourning that became her better than any colors she might have chosen, while the fashionable high waists emphasized her slender elegance. Phillipa's gowns were pretty pastel muslins, trailing ribbons and rosettes. The fabrics were the finest to be had, the styles absolutely à la mode.

The Prince Regent went to Brighton for the summer and the cream of society followed. So did the Hutchison sisters. They rented a lovely house on the Steyne, frolicked in the sea, rode the little donkeys, and partook of every public concert, every promenade, every open-air pastry shop. To no avail.

Johna made no secret of her widowhood or her wealth, and made sure to mention Phillipa's dowry in the hired staff's hearing. To no avail.

They were noticed, of course, as two beautiful young women would be noticed anywhere, but not by the right people. The only persons who approached them, who tried to scrape up an acquaintance, were half-pay officers, basket-scrambling fortune-hunters, or outright rakes. The Regent's set seemed to consist of an inordinate amount of all three, plus a contingent of bored, blasé snobs. Acknowledging any of their suggestive smiles, accepting a rum-touch as escort, being at home to a here-and-thereian, would have put paid to Johna's hopes of seeing her sister creditably established. She knew what they all had in mind for a wealthy widow and she wasn't having any of it. Not yet.

By the end of summer, back in London, they were no closer to Johna's goal of seeing her sister dance at Almack's. Johna had overestimated the value of her father's title and underestimated the stench of Sir Otis's. She thought of hiring one of those well-connected ladies of the *ton* who, for a fee, acted as chaperone, social mentor, matchmaker. If they were so well-connected, though, Johna couldn't help wondering, why did they need to hire out their services? Besides, she couldn't bear putting herself under the thumb of some prune-faced dragon. Not yet.

Johna wasn't giving up her reputation, her independence, or her dreams for her sister's future. Not yet. Instead she called in her markers.

2

Duty and dignity. Those were words a man could live by. A dainty morsel like the Black Widow was a delight a man would cheerfully die for. Merle Spenser, Viscount Selcrest, tapped Johna's thick vellum note against his booted leg as he sat in his library, thinking. And smiling.

Oh, the viscount had noticed the stunning widow in Brighton, all right. A man would have to be deader than that dirty dish Ogden not to notice her. Like every other man in Brighton, Selcrest had even tried to strike up a conversation with the dasher, at the library one day, at the jeweler's on another occasion. Both times she'd turned her fine-boned shoulder and ignored him with a faint tilt to her rose-petal lips. His grandmother the duchess couldn't have depressed his pretensions more elegantly or with more finality. The chit had style.

She also had a younger sister in tow, a pretty bit of fluff and frill. The reluctant consensus among the sporting gentlemen in Prinny's circle was that the widow wouldn't be entertaining any proposals—honest or otherwise—while chaperoning the girl. Even before Selcrest entered the lists, enough money to pay half the Regent's debts had been wagered and lost on which lucky swell would capture this so-ripe plum. Odds changed when the well-breeched, well-favored viscount took the field, only to go down in ignoble defeat.

And now, that same speedily dispatched challenger to the widow's supposed virtue wondered, what had changed her mind? Had she sent the sister back to school or off to the country? Or had she finally realized she'd never reach respectability, not with the baggage she carried? Marrying a disreputable old man for his money and then, rumor had it, killing him to get it sooner was not a high recommendation. There were at least four loose screws in Brighton who needed her blunt badly enough to marry Johna, Lady Ogden, despite the *on-dits*. She hadn't given them the time of day either. And she hadn't sent for them in London.

Viscount Selcrest had a broad chest. It swelled a tad broader as he called for another tub and shave—his second of the day. His only problem, as he sat in his sandalwood-scented bath, was the wording of her message: Could he please call at his earliest convenience, on a family matter. A female like Lady Otis Ogden had nothing to do with his family. Not ever.

Duty and dignity meant everything to the viscount. Granted he hadn't gotten around to marrying and filling his nursery but, 'struth, he was only twenty-eight and did have his brother Denton to ensure the succession. Other than that minor detail, he tried to lead an exemplary life, guarding the family honor as zealously as he protected his property and dependents. Perhaps because of his own unfortunate beginnings, Merle firmly believed that his sons had as much right to inherit a good name as a good income. The viscount was a conscientious landlord, a dedicated member of Parliament, and a devoted son to his widowed mother. He wasn't a gambler, a drunkard, or a womanizer—not by the measure of the day, at least. That's where discretion mattered.

And that was why the viscount stepped down from his curricle two blocks from the address on Albemarle Street and handed the reins to his tiger. "Keep walking them around the square. I'll find you when I have concluded my business."

Contrary to his preconceptions, Merle was impressed with the widow's home. The entry was light and airy, furnished in the best of taste with priceless Chinese vases filled with flowers and a Turner scene he'd love to own. The liveried footmen were properly deferential as they accepted his hat and gloves, and the be-wigged butler's backbone was as starched as his shirtpoints as he announced that, yes, milady was receiving.

Here was another surprise: she wasn't receiving him alone. The sister sat on the sofa beside the widow, sharing the latest issue of *La Belle Assemblee*. A pretty little filly, Merle noticed in passing. Too bad she came from such a dicey stable. While the widow asked his preference for refreshment and gave directions to the butler,

Selcrest made a mental list of suitable chaps to match the gel to, one of his local squire's sons out in Suffolk, or a distant cousin in the Horse Guards who needed a rich bride-price to further his career. The chit's future settled to his satisfaction—and his convenience—Merle turned his attention to the widow. "Yes, the weather is cool for this season," he agreed, thinking that she was even more lovely than he remembered. She wore a gray-striped cambric gown with a black shawl draped casually over her shoulders. With her black hair and magnolia skin, she looked good enough to undress.

The poker-backed butler returned with a tea cart and two maids. While they were busy positioning the plates of poppy seed cake, macaroons, and raspberry tarts, Johna took time to observe her guest. She congratulated herself on picking just the right name from Sir Otis's strongbox. Lord Selcrest was as polished as a fine diamond, hard-planed yet vibrant with an inner glow. He had the self-assurance of a born nobleman and more than a tinge of the haughtiness she'd noted in Brighton. And yes, he still had that raffish smile, as if his brown eyes could see beneath her clothes. Johna tugged her shawl closer. "Do you take lemon in your tea? Sugar?"

"Just sugar, please. One lump."

Johna busied herself pouring and stirring and passing plates until all three of them were served and the butler and maids were dismissed. "Phillipa, dearest, perhaps his lordship would enjoy some music while we chat," she suggested, indicating the pianoforte at the far end of the well-appointed room.

Phillipa obediently took her cup and a third raspberry tart and sweetly asked if he had any favorite pieces.

Other than raspberry tarts, Selcrest wanted to say, he favored elegant widows, so she should play anything long and loud. "I'm sure whatever you select will be charming, Miss Hutchison." When she moved off, with still another tart, the viscount resumed his seat on the cane-back chair, nudging it slightly nearer the sofa, the widow, and the platter of pastries. "A lovely girl, ma'am. And you have a fine cook."

Johna smiled. "And you're likely wishing them both to perdition right now."

"What, am I that transparent, my lady? I had hoped to make your acquaintance in Brighton, so naturally I was delighted at your invitation to call. I was hoping we could come to some agreement."

Merle was hoping he hadn't rushed his fences despite her candor, so he was relieved when the widow said, "Good. I am hopeful of that myself." Then, before he could inch his chair a bit nearer, she surprised him yet again with, "Did you know my husband, Lord Selcrest?"

"Why, no, I never had the, ah, pleasure." He'd sooner eat nails than go near a Captain Sharp like Ogden.

"But you knew of him, surely?"

"Yes, but—"

"I was going through some of his papers and came upon this note." She pulled a paper from the journal at her side and handed it to him. "I believe it to be your brother's. Am I correct?"

There it was, as big as life, *Denton Spenser*. The amount scrawled under the unmistakable IOU was bigger than life. Bigger than Den's yearly income, for sure. The viscount was staggered by the sum. He knew his scapegrace brother was running with a rackety crowd, but to fall into the clutches of a makebate like Otis Ogden? And not consult Merle, or ask his help? That was a crushing disappointment when he'd striven so hard to be head of the family. Then his lordship realized an even larger disappointment. "So you didn't invite me here to…"

"To throw myself at your feet, to ask you to make a scarlet woman out of me, to beg your protection against the cold, cruel world? To—"

"Enough! I beg your pardon if I have offended you with unwarranted assumptions." Thunderation, Merle could feel his cheeks growing warm, the first time a woman had confounded him in years.

"But you don't think they are unwarranted, do you? Everyone believes Sir Otis's wealthy young widow must be a trollop, so naturally you supposed I'd be amenable to your suggestions."

The bitterness in her voice was unanswerable, and the sadness. He reached for another raspberry tart rather than look her in the eyes with a lie. When the silence became uncomfortable, even with the Bach in the background, the viscount smoothed Denton's note on his thigh. If the widow was too virtuous to join the muslin company, what was she doing taking over her husband's loan-sharking? Merle's compassion for her plight died aborning. He'd redeem the vowel, of course. Devil take him if he'd let some harpy get her talons into his little brother.

As if reading his mind, or his sneer, Johna quietly explained, "When I found the voucher I did not write to Mr. Spenser. I had heard that he is always pockets to let and I did not want to send such a young man to the moneylenders."

Selcrest acknowledged her meager benevolence with a curt nod. "I don't carry that much of the ready. Will a check do?"

"I do not want the money, my lord." She waved one delicate hand at the room, the house, and all its splendor. "I have more than enough wealth for my needs. I do, however, require something that only you can provide."

Now this was more the thing, Merle thought. She wasn't calling in the chit, she was begging a favor. After which minor feat of dragon-slaying, the damsel would likely fall into his arms in gratitude. "I am at your service," he said with that lopsided smile that left no doubt as to what service he'd like to render.

"What I'd like" — she paused while the viscount helped himself to the last raspberry tart — "is an introduction to your mother."

"My mo—" The notion so startled the viscount that he swallowed wrong. He coughed, or choked, or perhaps laughed.

In any other household, a gentleman might be gently slapped on the back or politely offered a drink of water. Not in this household, not now. Johna leaped to her feet, upsetting her teacup. "Oh no, not again! Pippy, come quickly!"

And then, before Lord Selcrest could swallow the rest of the tart so he could speak up, young Miss Hutchison had rushed over and grabbed his arms over his head, shouting at her sister to remember what Dr. Browne had advised, too late. Her sister did remember, the whole nightmare of her husband's sudden departure. So she drew back her fist and with all her might belted the viscount in the stomach, right below the ribs.

In the ordinary course of events, her fist would have bounced off his lordship's rigid muscles. He worked out with Gentleman Jackson and fenced with Monsieur Lamartine. But he wasn't sparring or parrying; he was sitting in an attractive female's parlor, eating raspberry tarts. The impact of Johna's fist sent the air straight out of him. It also sent the cane-back chair toppling over, with Merle in it, so his head struck the floor right where the thick carpet ended.

"My stars, Jo, you've killed him!"

Johna was on the floor beside the viscount, loosening his neckcloth, shaking his shoulders, and drenching him with tears. "You can't die! Oh, please wake up, my lord. Please please please." And she took to slapping his face. Merle was seeing a dozen Lady Ogdens and feeling a million slaps on his aching head. So he made a grab for her hands, which pulled her off balance and onto his chest. So he kissed her, which seemed like the right thing to do at the time. It certainly made his head feel better.

Johna pulled out of his arms with a gasp. Whether from relief that he was alive, humiliation at her actions, or indignation at his, Johna was incensed. She hauled back that same deadly right and punched the viscount in the jaw. It seemed like the right thing to do at the time, and made her feel a great deal better. Of course it bounced Merle's head on the hardwood floor again.

This time when he awoke Lady Johna was sending her sister to fetch the brandy decanter, thank God. Merle slowly managed to drag himself to a sitting position while Phillipa poured a wavery stream into the tilting glass Johna held, their hands were shaking so badly. The viscount reached out to take the glass before they spilled the whole bottle, only to see the elegant widow down the shot in one swallow.

He had to laugh. "Mama's going to love you."

"Then you'll do it? You'll help?"

Phillipa handed him another glass. "He has to help; we saved his life."

"Saved my life? Bloody hell, you damn near killed me."

"You took liberties," was all Johna said as she helped him to his feet and onto the sofa.

"It was a dying man's last wish."

"Fustian."

He smiled. "Have you never heard of the kiss of life? It worked."

"Rubbish."

"But lovely rubbish, if I remember correctly. Of course I wasn't in any position to truly appreciate your efforts at reviving me. Perhaps you'd care to—"

"I was *not* trying to revive you. That is, I was, but not then." To hide her blushes Johna crossed to the bellpull.

Within minutes her efficient staff had the mess cleaned up and the brandy decanter refilled. The viscount had a full glass in his hand, a slab of raw meat on his jaw, and a sack of ice on his head. He also had his brother's note of hand, rescued from the debris. "I owe you for this, if not my life."

Johna reached for the marker and ripped it up. "No, I was wrong to hold that over you. I know what my husband was. He likely cheated your brother, the same way he cheated Papa. I was desperate, my lord."

"For my mother's approval?"

Johna gazed toward the pianoforte where Phillipa had resumed her playing. "I want my sister to have the chance I never did. She cannot help being Sir Otis Ogden's sister-in-law, any more than I could help being Papa's daughter. She deserves a decent husband, a true gentleman the likes of which we are not liable to come upon on our own, nor back in Berkshire. I found your brother's voucher, but he is too young to lend any kind of countenance. And your escort..."

Merle finished for her "Would have been damning."

Johna shrugged. "If you showed interest in Phillipa, no other gentleman would pay her attention, and if you paid me particular notice, they'd all assume I was your mistress. Either way, Phillipa would not get to meet any decent, worthy candidates for her hand and dowry. We have no female relations, no connections for all the three years we've spent in London. Your mother is known to be...eccentric. I've heard that she keeps rabbits in the drawing room and plays cards with her butler, but she is still good *ton*. She could lend us that veneer of respectability we so dreadfully need."

"Higbee has been with us forever," was Selcrest's only comment. He leaned back to think, sipping his brandy. To call his mother an eccentric was like calling the Thames wet. It didn't half describe the thing. Mama was downright attics-to-let. The reason Merle clung so firmly to his dignity was because he found so little of it at home. He'd had to fight his way through boarding school because it was public knowledge that he'd been born a scant six months after his parents' wedding. A premature birth, hell; to this day he didn't know if he was the rightful heir or the butler's son! Mama would only answer that she was always faithful to the love of her life.

The rabbits were the least of his embarrassments, just another passing fancy like the seances in the munitions room and the mud baths in the backyard. Merle would not let it happen again, his name becoming a fixture in the *on-dits* columns. He spent his days keeping his mother from her wilder extravagances, like flying her own hot air balloon. When the viscount wasn't scrambling to keep his mother from the brink of social and physical disaster, he was pulling his brother out of scrapes. He was not about to sacrifice years of holding them to the straight and narrow for the sake of these two outcasts.

Selcrest no longer believed that Lady Ogden had killed her husband. That was something, at least. If she weren't quite the innocent her sister was, neither did she seem quite the mercenary baggage he'd assumed. Testing the waters, he asked, "Were there other outstanding loans among your husband's papers?"

She nodded. "I'll burn them tonight. I never intended to ask anyone for money."

Were favors just as bad? Merle's head was aching too much to decide and, deuce take it, the widow was too alluring to let slip away into rural obscurity. "I'll put it to Mama. I'll ask her to help sponsor you and your sister into polite society. But on one condition: if you cause one poor reflection on my mother's good name, one misstep or least hint of impropriety, the deal is off. I'd rather pay my brother's debt in cash, with interest, than let you stir the scandalbroth. Are we agreed?"

"Agreed," she said, holding out her hand.

Merle was about to turn the slender wrist over and kiss her palm, or her fingers, or perhaps the pulse beating through the blue veins. But she wasn't finished: "My sister and I are entirely capable of behaving like ladies." Her eyes narrowed and her chin rose an inch. "Are you agreeing to act like a gentleman?"

Merle looked at that fragile hand and rubbed his aching jaw. He decided a firm handshake was the safer course. "Agreed."

3

"Coo-ee, gov, wot 'appened to you?" The viscount's tiger looked back down Albemarle Street for the gang of thugs that had attacked his master, perhaps a runaway carriage. But the midday sun was still shining on the quiet street. "I thought you was makin' a mornin' call, not goin' to a mill."

"Stubble it." Lord Selcrest took up the reins and flicked his whip over the horses' heads, forcing the tiger to scramble onto the back of the curricle, lest he be left behind. Merle drove around to the stable mews rather than getting down at the front door of Selcrest House as usual. He thought he could go in the back door, through the service entrance near the kitchens, without disturbing the household.

Unfortunately, one of the maids saw him and swooned dead away. Another started screaming, which brought his high-strung Welsh housekeeper, with the kitchen's largest meat cleaver. What next? Merle thought as he tried to wrest the blade away before Mrs. Reese injured herself. The cooks and scullery maids were shrieking by now, knocking over buckets, barrels, and bowls of ingredients in their hysteria.

Of course Merle's mother came to see what all the commotion was about. She loved a good riot, so joined Higbee the butler under the heavy pantry table. Once they'd placed their wagers, the dowager chirped into the mayhem: "Did you have a nice day, Merry dear?"

*

Once the viscount was cleaned up, and after Higbee had reassured Lady Selcrest that the stains on her son's neckcloth were raspberry preserves, not blood, she wanted to know all the details. So did Higbee. Merle didn't waste his time telling the old man to go polish the silver or something. Higbee wouldn't do it anyway. Selcrest thought with envy of Lady Ogden's so-correct butler. Then he tried to decide just which of the morning's details he ought to relate to his fond parent. He didn't think his mother would be impressed to hear what a handy set of fives the widow possessed. So instead of explaining how he got the purple bruise on his chin, or what the sticking plaster was doing on his head, the viscount asked: "Do you know the Hutchison family, Mother?"

Lady Selcrest knew everyone. If she didn't, Higbee could find them in Debrett's *Peerage.* "The Devon or the Berkshire Hutchisons?"

"Berkshire. The mother was a Whittaker, I believe."

"Ah, *those* Hutchisons." Lady Selcrest was intrigued. Her dry-as-dust eldest son came home looking like he'd been in a dockside tavern brawl, and mentioned two young females of questionable virtue. Maybe there was hope for the boy after all.

"I know there's been a deal of conjecture about them, but they're not as unacceptable as painted. The younger is a sweet little charmer, all round and rosy, the usual accomplishments. Handsome dowry, I understand."

"And the elder? She's the poor girl who was forced to marry that awful Ogden person, isn't she? It wouldn't have happened had her mother lived, of course. I understand Hutchison fell apart after that. It's no excuse. The varlet should be boiled in oil for what he did to his own daughter."

Higbee was standing by the door. "Lord Hutchison is dead, my lady."

Lady Selcrest smiled over at him. "That's right, he is. Thank you, Higbee."

Merle gnashed his teeth. "Do you think you might give the sisters the occasional invite?"

"Do you mean for tea, dear? Of course, if they are friends of yours."

"Well, I was thinking more in the order of dinner, an evening at the theater, a ride with you in the park." Selcrest brushed at a gray rabbit hair on his burgundy coat sleeve. "We're not friends, precisely. I, that is, we, stand somewhat in their debt. I thought to repay the obligation by helping them find their feet in the social waters."

A debt? This was getting better and better. If there was one thing Lady Selcrest liked more than aggravating her son by creating a stir, it was matchmaking. So far, she'd had lamentably few successes. "Let me think. Whittaker's eldest gel married a Babcock, and so did my brother's wife's aster. Not the same Babcock, of course, but yes, I think we can claim a connection that might explain your chicks under my wing."

"They're not my—"

Higbee cleared his throat. "Ahem. Lady Margaret Spenser was godmother to Clementine Whittaker, Baroness Hutchison."

"Great-aunt Margaret?"

"The same. I am sure Lady Margaret would expect you to look after her loved ones."

"If she hadn't died two decades before they were born," the viscount muttered, but his mother was delighted.

"Higbee, you are a genius. Merle, raise his salary." The man already earned more than the Prime Minister, but Merle nodded, to get back to the issue at hand. "So you think we can do it? Bring Lady Ogden and her sister into fashion?"

"It's quite a challenge, but not beyond my powers, of course. Don't you agree, Higbee?"

"If anyone can reclaim two fallen sparrows, my lady, it is your gracious self."

The viscountess was almost purring. The viscount was almost puking. He got up to leave, but his mother called him back. "I cannot perform miracles, Merle. If your protégées are hopeless rustics or of dubious character, the venture is doomed to failure. I doubt that even I could foist milkmaids, fortune-hunters, or Haymarket ware on the *ton*."

"That's what most of the young misses at Almack's are, Mother, which is why your efforts at matchmaking always fail. Great-aunt Margaret's grand-goddaughters will fit right in."

"Ahem. May I suggest that my lady invite the two young females to tea before undertaking a public appearance? That way we might be certain of their suitability before committing the Selcrest name to their advancement."

"Excellent, Higbee! What would I do without you?" Most likely find a lonely old duke or an eligible earl to marry, but Merle wasn't that lucky.

*

"What do you mean, Mama says we have to show a united front of family approval?" Denton was proving more difficult to convince than Lady Selcrest, after the viscount managed to track down his errant brother in the billiards room. "Do the pretty with two harum-scarum females I've never met? Not for the price of that new hunter I saw at Tattersall's."

Merle reset the balls and waited for his brother to take aim. "How about for the price of your gaming debt to Otis Ogden?"

The balls scattered wildly, two landing on the floor. "My, ah, debt?"

"What, did you think a sum like that would never come to light?"

"But the man is dead!"

"So you thought you didn't have to pay?" Merle had retrieved the balls and his own cue stick. He was calmly, methodically, sending his shots into the appropriate pockets. "I wonder, if I should die, would you feel you didn't have to pay the coal-hauler or the vintner? Perhaps I had better be thinking harder about my successor." Merle set his stick aside, leaving Denton an almost impossible shot.

Denton threw his stick down and faced his brother. "Dash it, this was different. I think the wine was tampered with."

"Most likely it was. If you were fool enough to enter a snakepit like the Black Parrot, you should have expected to be stung in some fashion. Marked decks, uphill dice, or footpads in the alley when you left, should you have been unfortunate enough to win."

"Exactly. But the fellows were going, so I went along."

"And gambled away your patrimony and part of mine. It's a debt of honor, you cloth-head. Play and pay. If you thought you were cheated, you should have called the blackguards out."

"They would have killed me."

"And I still might if you won't help launch those two females. We owe them."

"But, Merle, come-out balls and afternoon teas?" Denton shuddered. "I'd rather face Bonaparte's cannons." His face brightened. "In fact, you can reconsider and purchase my commission. That way you won't have to keep bailing me out of these scrapes. I might even bring some glory to the family name, as you're always lecturing about."

"I don't lecture and I'm not going to send you off to get blown apart in some act of bacon-brained bravado. You are still my heir."

"I know the solution then. Why don't you marry Miss Hutchison and beget your own heir? You said her mother was of decent lineage. That way her place in society would be guaranteed and I could go off to the Peninsula, instead of to perdition at Almack's."

The viscount was tossing a billiard ball from hand to hand. He stopped. "What, marry a chit from the infantry? I don't recall Nurse dropping you on your head, but someone must have. She's a sweet child, but I'd be bored within a week."

"Then marry the widow."

Merle placed the ball in the exact center of the table. "What, take Otis Ogden's leavings? Pigs will fly first."

*

The tea went well, Selcrest thought. He was relieved to note that the sisters were dressed in modish modesty, curtsied to the proper depths, and didn't sit mumchance like so many fledglings he'd seen, intimidated by their betters. He carefully suppressed the notion that Lady Ogden did not consider the Selcrests her betters. Restored to her cool elegance, she was remarkably unfazed by his mother's current penchant for Gypsy attire, the peasant blouse, tiered skirts with billowy red petticoats, and chains of coins and hoops. Merle even thought she sounded sincere when she commented, "How gay you look, my lady," as she took her seat. One would think the female used her fan daily to sweep rabbit pellets off damask chairs. No, he did not think the Hutchison sisters would embarrass his mother. The alternative was more likely, however. Merle refused to consider the possibility that Selcrest House and its inhabitants mightn't pass muster, nor why the idea so distressed him. He ought to be feeling relieved that Lady Ogden might show them her heels. He wasn't. Deuce take it, she was exquisite. If his mother could get the sister fired off in this fall's Little Season, the widow just might be more amenable to dalliance before the *ton* left town for the holidays. Merle daydreamed of how he'd like his Christmas present unwrapped, while the ladies furthered their acquaintance.

Lady Selcrest was charmed. She declared that, had she known young women could be so enchanting, she'd have had daughters instead of sons. The younger girl read the viscountess's favorite Gothic romance novels and the older one played cards. What could be more accommodating? Lady Selcrest delightedly announced that she couldn't wait to introduce the girls to her circle of friends, to arrange parties in their honor, to take them shopping with her. Her stiff-rumped son may have cringed at this last item, Lady Selcrest observed, but Johna didn't. Excellent female. She'd do, especially if Selcrest continued to watch the beautiful widow like a fox eyeing a particularly plump partridge. He was practically drooling, the gudgeon. Lady Selcrest had only to make sure that the bird stayed just out of reach until the clunch was well and truly caught. She'd have a grandchild before the cat could lick its ear, and before Higbee won their wager.

After showing the Hutchison sisters to the door, Higbee pronounced them prettily behaved misses. "Not at all above themselves like some of the gentry." He shot a meaningful glance at his employer. "And most of the nobility." Higbee's money was still on Selcrest's bedding the lass, not wedding her.

Happily unaware of the machinations at Selcrest House, Johna was happy with the tea, with the meeting, with the arrangement. Their new benefactress was definitely an Original, which could only work in their favor. And, to Johna's relief, Lady Selcrest's son minded his manners in his mama's presence. Johna still remembered the tingle of Selcrest's arms enfolding her, the thrill of his warm lips on hers, the cad. He'd promised to keep his distance, and seemed to be keeping his vow, the cad. No matter, Phillipa was going to have her Season.

*

Any fool could have predicted a success. Money, looks, and the Selcrest cachet could easily whitewash a checkered past when the females were also personable and eager to please. Besides, the dowager and her butler weren't the only ones to notice the sparks flying between Selcrest and the Black Widow. White's betting book required a new page. Every hostess wanted to provide this latest spectator sport at her do. Invitations started trickling into Albemarle Street, then turned into a veritable deluge of requests for the ladies' presence at routs and ridottos and rides in the park, balls and breakfasts, and balloon ascensions. They even received vouchers to Almack's, that pinnacle of social aspiration. Handsome, intelligent, and wealthy gentlemen left cards from daybreak to dinner, and the floral deliveries left scant room for them to sit down in the few scattered moments when the sisters were home to receive callers. The gentlemen were short and tall, dark and fair. They were peacocks and poets, soldiers and sportsmen, students and statesmen. Surely among them Phillipa could find one man to make her happy.

Everything was perfect, just as Johna had planned, except for one minor detail: Phillipa had already fallen in love.

4

"I won't have it, Selcrest, do you hear me?"

"Everyone in the cursed ballroom can hear you, dash it. You're creating a scene. Do you want to ruin your sister's chances after we've all worked so hard?"

Johna and the viscount were one of the few couples waltzing at Almack's. The patronesses did not approve of younger girls indulging in the wicked dance. Married ladies and widows, however, were considered experienced enough not to be led into indiscretion by a man's hand on their waist. Hah! Selcrest had been waiting all night in hopes of just such an opportunity. Instead of melting in his arms, though, his partner was boiling mad. Instead of the gossamer butterfly he'd hoped to whirl around the dance floor till her senses were disordered, he held a buzzing, stinging wasp. Deuce take it, she looked like she wanted to box his ears. "Smile, confound it, everyone is watching."

"Not everyone," she replied through clenched teeth, her mouth fixed in a grin that would have done Grimaldi proud. "Half of them have run off to change their bets. What do you mean, not dancing all night and then singling me out for a waltz?"

"I meant to honor my mother's guest with a dance, that's all. It would have been discourteous, else."

"Fustian, you were hiding in the card room all night because you were afraid to face me earlier. Now you've set the cat among the pigeons, and after you were the one preaching discretion and decorum. You have to know what the gabble-grinders will make of this."

"They'll make note that I had one dance with the most beautiful woman in the room." Or they would, he thought, if she weren't as rigid as the carved figurehead on a ship.

Specifically intending to avoid bringing attention, to avoid giving credence to any rumors, Selcrest had left for the card room after escorting his party through the receiving line of curious doyennes, dowagers, and dragons that made up Almack's patronesses. What harm could one dance do though, he'd thought, especially if he also stood up for a *contra danse* or such with Phillipa? The more he thought, the more that one dance with Lady Ogden took on the aspect of a drink of water to a man parched by the desert sun. He lost three hands in a row to Lord Carville, thinking of holding her in his arms. Then he'd heard the strains of a waltz. They would have had to tie him to the mast, like Odysseus, to keep him away from the widow in silver tissue with its black border and scattered sequins.

Johna almost relented to savor the compliment and the feel of Selcrest's firm touch on her skin through the thin layers of her gown's fabric. Almost. But the viscount twirled her about so that she was facing the gilt chairs set along the edge of the dance floor. Phillipa was quite properly sitting out the waltz at Lady Selcrest's side, surrounded by her usual coterie of beaux, with the Hon. Denton Spenser standing behind her chair—with his hand on her shoulder!

"Two dances they've had. Two. And now this...this blatant public display! If your gallows-bait of a brother thinks to force me into countenancing such a connection, he's even more of a fool than I thought, and that's saying a lot." She'd stopped dancing in the middle of her diatribe, so other couples were bumping into them.

"That's saying too much about my brother, madam, and too much for this company, dash it." He dragged her off the floor so fast her slippers almost left skid marks on the highly polished surface.

*

By the time he found a secluded alcove in the fishbowl of Almack's, Johna was panting and smoke was almost pouring out of her ears. She stamped her foot, only accidentally stomping on Selcrest's instep. "I didn't go to all this effort just to see my sister wasted on a half-breeched basket-scrambler."

"Smile, damn it."

"Smile? When my only relation in this entire world is about to ruin her life after I married that awful old man just to provide her the chance for something better?"

Merle stepped in front of her, his back partially shielding them from the avid watchers. "Do you think I want this any more than you do? My brother aligned with a—"

Johna crossed her arms over her chest. "Go ahead and say it, sirrah."

"With a female too young to know her own mind, is what I was going to say."

"Oh, but Phillipa assures me she does. We've met every sprig and noble spawn on the town, bucks and beaux and all manner of gentlemen. She won't look at any of them, and it's almost November."

"And Denton's never been serious about a female before. He's actually stopped complaining about having to attend those tedious picnics and afternoon dancing-lesson parties. I thought he was sick."

"Lovesick, more like, the moonling. You have to do something!"

"Me? You're the one who let the chit read those romance novels. Just what do you expect me to do about your sister's infatuation?"

"End it! Let Denton join the army. He's been wanting to this age and more. In fact, if you didn't keep him on such a tight rein, he wouldn't have tried slipping his lead in the first place. The nodcock even confessed to me that he believed you would buy his commission if he caused enough aggravation."

"He *is* a fool."

Johna unthinkingly took Merle's hand in earnest entreaty. "Let him go, sir. Let him grow up, make something of himself besides the Viscount Selcrest's brother. Separated, they'll get over this silly calf-love. My sister will find a young gentleman who won't gamble away her dowry or break his neck on some untried hunter."

"Confound it, my brother is not the villain you make him out to be. He is merely full of the usual high spirits, sowing his wild oats."

"Let him sow them in Spain where they might do some good ending this stupid war!"

Merle suddenly realized he'd been staring at the skimpy bodice of the widow's gown as her chest heaved with her passionate plea. Worse, he'd been holding Johna's hand for the last few minutes, in front of half the *ton*. He couldn't decide whether to drop it like a hot coal, or bring it to his lips. Gads, his wits went begging every time he was near the impossible creature! For sure his backbone turned to porridge in her blue-eyed gaze because he heard himself say, "Very well, I'll ask around about commissions in a decent regiment."

"Good." Johna patted his hand. "See that you do, or I will purchase the ninnyhammer's colors myself."

*

The more she thought about it, the more Johna liked the idea. Perhaps the Selcrest coffers weren't as deep as rumored. Perhaps the viscount saw Phillipa's dowry as good riddance to his expensive brother. Perhaps he would have kissed her hand if they'd been less in the public eye. Great heaven, she had to get disentangled from the entire family! Denton was not a bad sort, at heart. He was just young and unsettled—and his handsome brother was unsettling.

Why couldn't Phillipa have thrown her bonnet at any other man in London? Johna would have seen her wed and gone home to Berkshire in two shakes, with no temptations, no lingering regrets. If her sister married Denton, Johna would be thrown into the viscount's company for the rest of her life, and thrown into a bumblebroth every time he gave her that seductive smile. By heaven, she would *not* be seduced! Johna didn't even want to be married again, not after the first time. Marriage wasn't the remotest possibility, of course, for Selcrest would never lower himself to marry her, the arrant egotist, so his uppity lordship could just go to the devil—and take his brother with him.

Johna couldn't make arrangements with the devil, but she could with the War Office, if that was how one went about starting a young man on an army career. Her solicitor would know the procedure and the expense. It was time she paid a call on Mr. Bigelow anyway, concerning her own expenses. The Season had been more costly than she'd figured, what with both sisters needing new gowns for every occasion and changing ensembles four times a day. Johna had also purchased a fashionable barouche for drives in the park, which meant she then needed the most elegant and thus extravagantly priced pair of matched bays at Tattersall's. The horses required an additional driver, more grooms, and higher stable fees. There was also the lavish ball in Phillipa's honor that Johna and Lady Selcrest were planning for late in the Season, just before everyone left town for Christmas at their country estates. With even the highest sticklers sending their acceptances, Johna's respectability and Phillipa's eligibility were finally being recognized. Johna meant to give them a party they wouldn't forget.

Between her outlays here in London and the staggering sums her manager at Hutchison Manor deemed crucial for the estate's recovery, Johna was noticing her bank accounts dwindle. They seemed to be shrinking at an ever faster rate.

*

"That's because you are earning less income, my lady," Bigelow explained, as if Johna couldn't figure that out for herself by comparing one month's statement with the next. She didn't care for the patronizing little man, but supposed one solicitor was as prosy and prejudiced against her gender as the next. Johna only wished he'd get on with it, instead of dragging out ledgers and bank slips.

She had left Phillipa behind, not wishing to discuss army business in her sister's hearing, nor financial matters. Lady Selcrest had agreed to chaperone a group of young people on a visit to the British Museum this morning if Johna didn't get back in time. The dowager was a delightful companion, their social savior, and a fond chaperone. Fond of whom, though, was Johna's concern. The widow didn't want Denton and her sister disappearing behind any marble statue. Everyone knew what those old Greek and Roman gods were up to, by Zeus. So Johna was in a hurry.

"Please, Mr. Bigelow, just get to the heart of the matter. I know how much I am spending, and it should be well within my income without disturbing the capital. Suddenly it is not. I wish to know why."

"You do? Ah, of course you do." Bigelow closed the ledger and picked up a quill and a penknife. He concentrated on his new task until Johna cleared her throat. "Actually, my lady, it's quite simple. Without your husband's touch, some of his investments have not been earning the same profit."

"Which investments might that be, sir? The consols pay a fixed rate, the shipping ventures were for speculation, and we sold the foundry at great profit to those steam-engine people."

A tremor in Bigelow's hand caused the penknife to gouge a furrow in his desktop. "It's the gaming parlor that's losing money."

"Excuse me, I thought you just said gaming parlor." The solicitor coughed. "Why yes, and very profitable it used to be, with Sir Otis at the helm. Made his fortune that way, he did."

Johna sat forward on her seat. "A gambling den? I own a gambling den?" All she could think of was Selcrest's hearing this news. He'd have her tossed out of the *belle monde* so fast her new horses couldn't keep up. No scandals, he'd said. No improprieties. The only thing more improper than owning a gaming hell was owning a bordello. Johna might as well tie her garters on Bond Street as let it be known that she was financing her sister's debut with the profits of such a place. Lud, how did she get into this coil?

"Mr. Bigelow, how is it that you let me be ignorant of this fact, when I specifically mentioned that I wished everything aboveboard?"

"Ahem. I, ah, didn't want to bother your head with too many details. New widow and all. It was an emotional time, and I was trying to spare you more agonizing decisions. And you mentioned costly renovations and repairs. I was right: you did need the additional income."

"I wonder how much additional income *you* were earning from this arrangement that you let it continue." Johna was seething by now, that this greedy little man with his thinning hair and trembling fingers, this toad, might lose her everything.

Bigelow could hardly pick up the pen. "But, but that was my percentage, for handling the bookkeeping for the Black Parrot."

"The Black Parrot? That's known to be one of the worst hellholes in London, where young men are regularly cheated out of their fortunes and estates."

"Not always. They were often permitted to mortgage them back, on loans. That was how your husband made such a profit."

"That was how he destroyed my father, charging blood money! I will shut down that cesspool before one more life is ruined."

"Oh, but you can't. The proprietor holds a lease."

"I don't care if he holds a gun to your head, I shall not own a havey-cavey establishment."

Bigelow was starting to develop a twitch in his right eye. "Perhaps Marcel will be able to purchase the building from you. He used to cook for Sir Otis, you know, excellent French cuisine. I had the pleasure of dining with Sir Otis on a number of occasions. Marcel wanted to go into business for himself, so Sir Otis helped finance a gentlemen's club, with supper and a card room. Then it seemed that the gambling became more profitable than the cooking. And the money-lending was most profitable of all. Unfortunately Marcel doesn't seem to have the touch for that. Blancmange, yes.

Interest rates, no. I do not know how much Marcel will be able to pay you for the building and for your share of the business."

"I will not sell it. I will shut it down. Today. Get your coat."

He had to wear it open. Buttons were beyond his shaking grasp.

5

The lawyer was shivering, and not just from the cold. He didn't dare reach into his pocket for the silver flask of comfort, not with those blue eyes fixed so accusingly on him. The widow was worse than the old codger, Bigelow thought. Ogden had been greedy; this female was righteous. One was predictable; the other made no sense whatsoever to the self-serving solicitor. Well, if the lady couldn't see where her best interests lay, Bigelow could. That was his job, after all, protecting his clients from risky ventures. Charging into the Black Parrot like Joan of Arc, intent on displacing a corrupt cook, wasn't just risky. It was suicidal.

As he scurried out of his office, therefore, Bigelow managed to whisper an urgent message into his clerk's ear: "Find Viscount Selcrest. Tell him his lady is at the Black Parrot." Bigelow had heard the rumors and believed them to be true. No man could *not* be interested in this black-haired beauty who was an heiress besides. And passionate, to judge from her outrage. A downy cove like the viscount would know how to take the female in hand, out of a gent's business.

Who knew when Selcrest would get there, though? Marcel had a true Gallic temper—and a criminal past. Trust a makebate like Ogden to latch onto a convict no one else would hire. They said he'd stabbed his former employer because the man complained his roast was too well done. Then again, perhaps Marcel and the widow could compare recipes, like what was in that pudding she served Ogden. The devil take it, Bigelow would rather stand between a wolf and its next meal than get between these two. His father was right: he should have chosen the military instead of the law. He'd have lived longer. Bigelow kept shaking.

So did Johna. Was she out of her mind, she asked herself, going into the bowels of London with no more protection than her spastic solicitor? She'd been concerned about gossip when she sent her coach home, along with the driver, the footman, and the maid who would have noted her destination. Johna insisted Bigelow hire a hackney, to protect her reputation. Lud, she should have worried about her life. This section of town was dark and dirty, filled with the reek of poverty. No one would know where she was going so no one would know if she ever got there.

Johna wished she had a pistol. She wished she knew how to use a pistol. She vowed to learn tomorrow, if she lived that long. No, she'd look on the bright side: it was still morning. Surely villains waited for dark to go about their evil business. After luncheon, for certain. Johna could get this imminent catastrophe averted and still be home in time for the jaunt to the museum, or a fit of apoplexy, whichever came first.

The hired coach pulled to a stop at the entrance to a shadowed alley. "Oi'll bide 'ere an 'arf an 'our, then ye're on yer own," the jarvey told them, shaking his head at their foolhardy errand. He spit over the side of the carriage to punctuate his disdain for corkbrained Cits like Bigelow, bringing his gentry mort to a dive like this.

Bigelow gestured toward the painted board on the corner building. "Are you sure you want to do this, my lady?"

The black parrot on the sign looked more like a vulture to Johna. "What happens to this place if I die?"

Bigelow had his hand on the carriage door, rattling it. "Then it becomes your heir's property, of course. According to the will you drew up, your sister's."

Nothing could have put courage into Johna's steps faster than being reminded of the threat to Phillipa's well-being. "Never!" She got down, holding her skirts away from the foulness in the street. She let Bigelow take her arm up the four grimy steps to the black wood door that had a parrot's head for a knocker.

"Should we knock?" Johna was sure her knees were already knocking. "Is there a footman?" Was there a certain etiquette involved in evicting an unknown, unwanted tenant?

Mr. Bigelow just pushed the door open and led her inside. It took a few moments for Johna's eyes to adjust from the dismal gray of the street to the more dismal gray of the interior. She almost gagged on the stench of rancid smoke, unwashed bodies, and cheap perfume. "I own this horrible place?"

The Black Parrot had its head tucked under its flea-bitten wing this early in the day. There were very few patrons, a handful of huddled men Johna didn't recognize, thankfully, looking as if they hadn't gone home for the night, for many nights. Two or three women sat or sprawled in the corners. One snored. Johna decided she wouldn't examine the women too closely.

"Dealers," Mr. Bigelow whispered, mopping his brow, hoping she wouldn't ask what they dealt in. "I'll go find Marcel."

What, and leave her here? "I'll go with you."

"You cannot go upstairs!" Bigelow squeaked. "That is, perhaps the man is in his office. We'll look there first." He led her down an even darker corridor where damp-stained paintings of nude females hung unevenly on the paneled walls. Thank goodness for mildew, Johna thought for the first time in her tidy life.

The office was better lighted, so Marcel could count the piles of coins in front of him. He looked up with a snarl, a hyena defending its carrion booty. "*Qu'est-ce que c'est?*" He stood when he recognized the lawyer, unfolding to spindly height.

The man was so emaciated, his cooking must be dreadful, Johna thought. And he was so dirty, filth under his nails, oil pasting his hair to his scalp, that she wouldn't have let him in her kitchen to clean the stove. Bigelow made the introductions.

Marcel turned to Johna with an unctuously ingratiating smile, blackened teeth and all. "Ah, but you find me unprepared. If I had known of your visit, I would have made my *specialité* mousse a la Marcel." He kissed his dirty fingertips, then waved them around the nearly empty room. "Instead I do not have even the chore to offer you."

"He means 'chair,'" Bigelow interpreted. At Johna's nod of encouragement, he went on: "And this isn't a social call. Lady Ogden wants to close down the Black Parrot and sell the building."

Having explained their mission, the solicitor spotted an unfinished glass of wine on Marcel's desk. If the Frenchman was drinking it, the stuff couldn't be dangerous. Bigelow gulped it down, almost wishing it were drugged.

Marcel was still being polite, although he did not offer her any of the wine. "Then I am sorry you made this visit for nothing, Madame Ogden. But you cannot close the Black Parrot, *n'est-ce-pas?* Your husband and I, we have the partnership."

"My husband is dead. The partnership is dissolved. Besides, I thought it was a lease."

Marcel shrugged. "Lease, partnership, my *Anglais* is not so good. *Tant pis.* Either way, you cannot be throwing me up. Out? *Oui,* throwing me out. You tell her, Monsieur Bigelow. It is a matter of law, no?"

Bigelow was feeling better. He'd feel better still if Marcel weren't towering over him, so he backed toward a dark corner of the office, pretending to read the titles on the bookcase shelf. "I tried to explain."

Johna had faced the Almack's patronesses. One filthy French felon was not going to faze her. She did take a step backward, though, so she wasn't having to crane her neck upward, and so she did not have to inhale Marcel's foul breath. "What Mr. Bigelow tried to explain was that the usual money was not being paid to my account. That sounds very much as if the terms of the agreement are invalidated."

"Ah, the money. Now I see. Marcel has a bad month, and madame grows impatient to buy another trumpet."

"Trinket? No, you don't see. I would not keep this...this insult to decency open for any amount of money, and there is nothing you can do about it. Are you going to take me to court? Do you think your operations will stand the light of day?"

"Bah, you will not make me try. You would not want your connection here to be made public."

Bigelow choked. For once Johna didn't care, she was so angry. Let the man suffocate on his own guilt. "Are you threatening to expose me? I'd rather it be known that I was trying to rid myself of this hellhole than that I condoned it! The club is closed as of immediately. You and your slime will be gone by the end of the week. The building is now for sale. *Le Parrot Noir c'est fini.*"

"Your accent, feh! And your demands, they are like cockroaches in the kitchen. You sweep them away or step on them"—he made a damp, sucking sound—"or you add them to the stew."

Johna's stomach turned at the thought. "No wonder you couldn't make a go of this place as a supper club."

"*Tiens,* now you insult Marcel's cooking?"

Bigelow groaned.

"I don't care if you cook bat blood for Beelzebub! You will *not* do it here!"

With a guttural roar, Marcel lunged. Before Johna could step back, his hands were at her throat, squeezing. "What, do you think Marcel takes orders from some murdering English whore? I'll teach you to stick your nose in my business, *chérie.* I cut it off, eh, so you don't have to smell Marcel's bad breast. Close my rooms? I close your mouth—for good."

Johna was struggling mightily, kicking out at his legs, trying to connect her flailing fists with the Frenchman's head. The dastard's arms were so wretchedly long, though, that she wasn't reaching. A red haze was beginning to cloud her eyes, and she could barely hear Mr. Bigelow's hysterical shouting. She started clawing at Marcel's hands at her throat, digging her nails into his fingers.

"*Chien!* I'll see you in hell. When you get there, say *bonjour* to your murdered—"

Marcel's next words were abbreviated, stoppered by the fist in his mouth.

Merle didn't know why Johna was here. He couldn't begin to imagine, but he'd shake that out of her later, after he took apart this ape who dared to lay his foul hands on her.

Marcel shoved Johna away from him, into a wall, so he could face this new challenger. *"Mon Dieu,* the Black Widow has a new *chevalier.* You chose better this time, *chérie,* but this one won't stick his fork in the wall so easily. Marcel will help, no?"

"No!" Johna croaked. "He's not my—"

The men were trading punches. Selcrest had the strength and the science, but Marcel had the reach.

One of the viscount's eyes was swelling shut, but Marcel kept spitting blood and teeth out of his mouth. When Selcrest's next punch connected with the Frenchman's nose and flattened it against his face, Marcel had enough.

The cook was cadaverously thin but he was strong, and he was a dirty fighter. A knife appeared in his hand. Johna screamed. Selcrest backed out of range. Hadn't he played this role before, the day he met the impossible female? He shook his head to clear it.

"Que mal you didn't get a ring from this one," Marcel mumbled through battered lips. "You'd be a richer widow tomorrow."

Mr. Bigelow peeked over the desk he was hiding behind to see what was happening. He saw Marcel's back and he saw Marcel's knife shifting from the Frenchman's right hand to his left. So he picked up the desk chair—the only chair in the room—and brought it down on Marcel's head. The fight was over.

Johna snatched up the knife and waved it under Marcel's streaming nose where he lay on the stained carpet. "If you're not gone by tomorrow morning, or if you ever bother us again, his lordship will...will have your guts for garters."

Selcrest raised his eyebrows but he nodded, taking the knife from her hand. "Count on it, you miserable scum." He turned toward Bigelow. "I don't know your name, sir, but I am in your debt." They shook hands, then the viscount softly inquired, "Are you quite finished here, my lady?"

Johna ignored the dripping sarcasm. "I do believe that I have made my position clear to Monsieur Marcel. Mr. Bigelow, I shall be leaving with his lordship. You shall find a buyer for this hellish place tomorrow or you shall find a new client. I do not care what pittance you accept, just get rid of it."

*

"Is your throat very sore, Jo?" Somewhere between the Black Parrot and her place by his side on the curricle's seat she'd become Jo to him.

"N-not terribly, Merle."

"That's good. And it's also good that my hands are busy with the reins."

"It is?"

"Oh, yes, or I'd strangle you too."

6

"How could you be so blasted stupid?" Selcrest yelled as soon as they were alone in Johna's drawing room. He'd held as tight a rein on his temper as on the horses during the drive back to Albemarle Street. Then came the interminable wait for the servants to bring tea—with honey for her bruised throat—and brandy for his bruised nerves. Selcrest's mood wasn't improved by the sideways glances he received from the footmen and maidservants. Nor by the niffy-naffy butler's inquiry: "Another steak, milord, for your eye?"

He couldn't see out of it, so the thing must be deuced ugly. He'd worry later how the devil he was going to get past his mother and Higbee this time. Right now his swollen phiz couldn't be half as ugly as the red welts he could see on Johna's slender neck. Ugly? Those marks turned his stomach inside out. Hell and damnation, he should have butchered the bastard who did this to her. Merle kept pacing, trying to keep his blood from boiling. "Dash it all, woman, what were you thinking, going to a place like that? And going alone?"

"I thought I was doing the right thing," Johna managed to whisper through trembling lips. Turning her head to watch him walk from her sofa to the mantel to the window and back was making her neck ache even more. "And Mr. Bigelow was with me."

"The pinchbeck pettifogger who got you into the mess in the first place? The man's a tosspot if I ever saw one." Merle took another sip, frowning into his glass of spirits as he remembered the solicitor's quaking hand. He slammed the glass down onto the mantel and resumed his circuit. "And a scurvy lot of help he was, hiding under the desk. I didn't even know he was there until he crowned that maniac. And you tell me what's right about a lady traipsing through London's worst stews. Nothing, that's what! If you had a problem, why the hell didn't you come to me, Johna? My mother is looking out for you. That makes you my responsibility!"

"No, your mother has done a world of good for my sister and myself. That's enough. You are not obliged to do anything more, certainly not act as guardian to us, or trustee. And I suppose I didn't think my actions through," she conceded. "I was so disgusted, I just wanted to get the deed done." Johna was close to tears from the pain, from the shock, from the anger she read in his one-eyed scowl and relentless pacing.

"I know you are furious with me for landing you in such a hobble. And I know I broke our agreement that there would be no scandalous behavior. So what now? Will you wash your hands of us or denounce me to your mother's friends? I've blotted my copybook, but poor Phillipa doesn't deserve to be ostracized. That's what will happen, you know, if you...if you turn your back on us."

Merle strode over to the sofa and bent down so he could look her in the eye. Hers were damp; one of his was swollen shut. "Are you that big a peagoose, or do you think me that much a snob? Can't you see that I don't give a rap about the scandal, Jo? My God, you could have been killed."

"Oh, and you too, coming to save me. I'd never have forgiven myself. And your poor eye." She was crying in earnest now, so it was only natural for Merle to take her in his arms for comforting. She fit so perfectly, it was only natural for him to kiss away her tears. And then her fears. "It's all right, sweetheart. Everyone is safe now. Nothing is going to happen to you or your sister. I won't let it."

Amazing how a kiss could cure a sore throat and a stiff neck and shattered composure. Johna sighed.

"What, did I hurt you?" He jumped back. "I never meant—Lud, only a ham-handed cad would paw at you at a time like this. I beg your pardon, my lady."

Johna sighed again, in contentment. "You do care."

"Care? I..." It was obviously a new and troubling concept for the viscount. He tried to fix Johna's disarranged hair, tucking a black lock behind her ear. It felt like silk running through his fingers. Care? Oh, Lud. "I care that my mother would be devastated if anything befell her protégée."

Johna touched his cheek and smiled. "You care. I know you do."

Merle turned his head and kissed her palm. "I care enough that if you ever give me such a fright again, I'll thrash you within an inch of your life."

So she sent for him that night, when Marcel tried to burn down the Black Parrot.

*

If Marcel was going to lose his investment, so was Ogden's widow. He waited till early evening, before the club was officially open for business, then tossed some Blue Ruin at the heavy, faded draperies that kept the gaming parlor shielded from the street. But the pervading dampness and years of leaks made the fabric hard to burn. That and Marcel had used the watered gin. So he went back to the kitchen.

There was so much grease on every surface, so many dirty rags, he had no trouble getting a good fire going, before he got going. Marcel left a message on the front door, right under the parrot's beak: "Ogden's widow owns these asses."

So the constables knew right where to come, to report the fire. "He must have meant ashes, ma'am." Johna sent a note to Bigelow, another to the viscount. Merle was easily found at Selcrest House, at home like Johna was, hiding his bruises. She could cover the marks with a high-necked gown or scarf, not unreasonable with the November chill. There wasn't much Selcrest could do with a swollen, empurpled orb, except lie. He'd already told his mother and Higbee that a sparring partner at Jackson's had landed a flush hit, but he couldn't tell that to the chaps who'd been at the boxing parlor that morning. A riding accident? Footpads? Neither reflected well on Lord Selcrest, so he stayed in, waiting for the morrow when the swelling would go down and cosmetics should cover most of the violent colors. Perhaps by then he'd come to his senses, too. He arrived within minutes of receiving Johna's message. "You are not going, period."

"It's my business. I have to go."

"You called on me for help, dash it, now let me help."

"I asked for your help, as you demanded this afternoon. Help, not supervision. The constables said some of the occupants in the building were injured, although there were no fatalities, thank goodness. I couldn't have borne that, someone dying because Marcel hated me so much. But I own the building, therefore it is my duty to see that the people in it get care. I can make sure they are taken to the hospital if they need it, or found a place to spend the night."

"What, you are worried about the dregs of humanity who live and work at a place like the Black Parrot? I admire your sense of duty, but that rabble can find their own way around the back alleys and gin mills. It's too dangerous for you to go. Didn't you learn anything this afternoon?"

"The constables said Marcel was likely halfway to France by now. His note was practically a confession of guilt, so he wouldn't chance being caught and hung."

"One cockle-headed cook isn't half as dangerous as the rest of the neighborhood. You saw it at its best, by daylight. By night every kind of slime crawls out from under their rocks to prey on unwary strays. You're not going, and that's final."

*

The fire wasn't even smoldering when they arrived. Most of the crowds dispersed when the constables from the sheriff's office joined the Watch, the fire inspector, and two runners from Bow Street. A small knot of women surrounding Mr. Bigelow were passing a bottle of rum, for their tiny coal-filled brazier wasn't putting out nearly enough heat in the raw night.

Bigelow separated himself from the group when he recognized the viscount's curricle. He carried a lantern over to the open carriage, where Selcrest's tiger had gone to the horses' heads to keep them calm amid the threatening cloud of smoke. Bigelow waited for the viscount to help Lady Johna down. "According to the fire inspector, the structure appears sound. He won't know for sure until daylight, of course, but the interior is pretty well demolished." He shook his head. "No one will buy the place now. Costs too much to renovate these old buildings."

Johna was staring at the handful of women who were inching closer. The shape of one in particular caught her eye. "That's fine, I'm not selling. I'll turn it into a home for unwed mothers instead. It will be a memorial to my husband."

"But...but Sir Otis would have hated the idea!"

"Yes, I know. That must mean it's a worthy cause. The Otis Ogden Hospital and Foundling Home."

Selcrest patted her hand, which he was holding firmly by his side. "And I'll help finance the renovations."

One of the women, the one who had put the idea in Johna's head in the first place, called out, "That's the ticket, lovey, then I'll have somewheres to go."

"That's all right for Mimi, for later," the oldest of the drooping females said, "but what about the rest of us, lady, for tonight?"

All of the women came forward now. They ranged from younger than Phillipa to tired middle age. The card-dealers had soot-darkened faces, some with tear streaks running down their cheeks.

"Is anyone hurt?" Johna asked.

"Lorraine found some salve in the pantry," Mimi told her. "It works fine."

Lorraine was also the spokesperson for the others. "Marcel took everything with him, without leaving our fair share. All our clothes and such is burned and ruined. We ain't got nothing, and nowhere to go."

Johna started to say, "I have roo—" when the viscount's arm clamped down on hers.

"No!"

"Then perhaps you could give them shelter until other arrangements can be made. Surely there's more than enough space to spare at—"

"No," Merle hissed in Johna's ear. "Think of your sister!"

"I am. I wouldn't want her left out in the cold." Selcrest dragged her a few steps away from the others. "Deuce take it, Jo, they're prostitutes!"

"Not dealers?"

"They might cut the deck for an occasional hand, but that's not their purpose for being here, or for all those little rooms upstairs."

"They still need help." Obviously, Johna was going to have to do it herself; his lordship couldn't lower himself to expend his pity on these unfortunate females who had to put up with the likes of Sir Otis on a nightly basis. She shook his arm off.

While she was thinking what was best to do, another one of the women peered in the viscount's direction, clutching a thin blanket around her shoulders. "Silky, is that you?"

"Silky?"

Everyone turned to stare at Lord Selcrest: Johna and the lightskirts, Bigelow and the minions of the law, two would-be customers at the Black Parrot, three passersby, and his own tiger. The only ones not gawking at him were the horses.

Lorraine pinched the speaker's arm. "Hush up, Kitty."

But Kitty waved the bottle of rum in the air and giggled. "At least I didn't call him Shorty." She giggled again. "Or Speedy."

Two of the other tarts and one of the Runners thought this was hysterical. So did Johna. The great and noble, high-and-mighty, stuffed-shirt lordship had feet of clay after all! And he'd just fallen off his pedestal. She joined the others' laughter.

At least no one could see Merle's scarlet blush. He grabbed Johna's arm and none too gently turned her toward his curricle. "You wait in the carriage. I'll make arrangements for your new friends."

When Selcrest came back to take the reins from his tiger, he told the grinning servant, "If one word of this night's work gets out, I'll make a rug out of you." After he settled next to Johna on the narrow seat and gave the horses the signal to start, Merle stared straight ahead. "Don't ask. You don't know those females, you never saw them. And if you don't stop giggling, I'll leave you here with them."

*

Merle wanted his family—and Johna's—to leave for his country estate on the instant. They'd avoid any gossip, have an extra week or two to prepare for the holidays, and put Johna out of harm's way in case that thatchgallows Frenchman tried more mischief. The paperwork was completed for Denton's commission, so there was nothing holding them in London.

"Nothing? What, did you forget that I am throwing a ball in two weeks? The acceptances are in, the food is ordered, the orchestra—"

"Confound it, Jo, it isn't safe! The man is a Bedlamite, setting fire to places where people live."

"Then I'll hire some extra watchmen. And thank you for the invitation"—it was actually more of a summons—"but Phillipa and I intend to spend Christmas in Berkshire."

"I think your sister will have something to say about that. If Denton is shipping out in the New Year, don't you think you should let them spend Christmas together with Mother at Seacrest?"

"Perhaps Phillipa could go by herself. Your mother is adequate chaperone, of course. It's time I saw how the renovations are going to Hutchison Manor."

"What, go off by yourself to have Christmas alone in a moldering old pile under construction? Are you dicked in the nob?"

No, she was just afraid to spend any more time in the viscount's presence.

7

Johna opened the ball with Selcrest as her partner. Let the tongues wag, Johna had decided, she was going to enjoy her last night among the ton. In three days, Selcrest was escorting all of them to Suffolk. Johna had agreed, in return for Phillipa and Denton agreeing not to become engaged before they left London. An understanding between them was obvious. Phillipa, glowing like a sunbeam in her primrose gown, danced with the handsome young officer, so proud in his scarlet regimentals. Johna couldn't deny them their last few weeks together.

She was adamant, though, about not having a formal announcement. That way, for one thing, Phillipa could change her mind, or Denton could. The looks they shared, the adoring gazes, the thread that seemed to connect them even when others were present, didn't make such an occurrence likely, no matter how long he was off fighting. But, too, Phillipa would not be plunged back into mourning if, heaven forbid, Denton did not return from the war. Johna prayed nothing would happen to break her sister's heart.

It was too late for her own. Going to Merle's home in Suffolk was what she wanted to do, of course, but what she positively knew she shouldn't do. The more she saw of Selcrest now, the more she'd hurt later. There was no later for them.

Johna saw the way Merle resigned himself to his mother's foibles, the way he fretted over his brother's welfare. He'd even hired a squad of Bow Street Runners to watch over her and her household. His own mother might call Selcrest a twiddlepoop for his fastidious decorum, but Johna knew better. The man was genuinely kind. He wouldn't mean to break Johna's heart, but he would. He wasn't going off to die for his country; he just wasn't going to offer for her. When she and Phillipa went home to Berkshire after Christmas, Phillipa would wait for Denton to come back. Johna would wait for Merle to come to his senses. One sister had hope; the other, none.

Johna was sure he liked her and cared for her, beyond feeling responsible for her well-being. Even Sir Otis had a favorite pointer in his kennel. Selcrest might just be coming to love her. Lud knew he was attracted to her, and had been right from last summer in Brighton. He would never be happy with all her fits and starts, however, the legacy from her husband and father. It would be torturing him with another Original like his mother. Johna wouldn't have a spouse like her own parent, so she couldn't blame him, but no matter what she did, scandal was always a hairsbreadth away, it seemed.

But, oh, it felt good to be in his arms for this dance! Later she'd remember the dreams she'd had, dreams that had all fallen short. Her sister'd had her pick of all the eligibles—and had chosen a hot-spurred second son. Johna'd fought for her legitimate place in society—and found it was not worth holding when she couldn't hold this man. Where she thought she'd never marry again, now she felt she'd never be whole again.

She was glad that the ball was a success, at least. There'd been thirty to dinner earlier, and that too had been superb, with compliments to her on the menu, the service, the urns of flowers everywhere. The company enjoyed the extra remove or two that she hadn't recalled ordering, so she did not fret over the meal. She'd been too nervous to do more than nibble at anything herself. Perhaps Cook had trouble with the preparations or ingredients and had to make substitutions. Johna well knew that good cooking had to be a flexible art form.

*

That dinner was about as flexible as cooking could be: eel in aspic—and arsenic; carrots with caramel sauce and castor oil; ipecac in the poached perch; mouse poison in the mousse.

Mousse? Johna assumed Gunther's had made an error. She'd never have ordered such a dessert, not after— No, she wouldn't think about it!

Unfortunately Lord and Lady Throckmorton couldn't stay after dinner for the ball; his gout was acting up. Princess Lieven and the dyspeptic Russian ambassador left early too. Everyone else stayed to greet the rest of Johna's nearly two hundred guests. Her ball was not quite a squeeze, there still being room to sit or stand, but it was definitely a success. Long after the receiving line had been dispersed so that Johna could open the dancing, the butler was still announcing names. Every title, every prominent honorific, was a sonorous declaration of Johna's social standing. The only one missing was the Prince Regent himself. That would have put the seal on Johna's triumph, but she couldn't have everything, she allowed.

Everyone was eating and drinking, laughing and gossiping. The talk was mostly about Johna and Selcrest, not Johna and the Black Parrot. Speculation reached a new high when he stood by her side after the opening set, greeting latecomers instead of fleeing to the card room. He had to know they were feeding the rumor mills, so she didn't bother to mention the lapse, not when it seemed the most natural thing in the world to have him next to her.

Then one of Phillipa's friends got sick. Johna had to escort the girl to the ladies' retiring room where her own maid could tend the chit until her mother could be found.

"Too much excitement, don't you know," that lady declared. "Silly twits starve themselves, then sneak off to the punch bowl. They'll learn," she added as another green-tinged female entered the room. Johna went back down to find Selcrest waiting at the foot of the stairs, with his mother accepting farewells in Johna's stead as another couple left. "Lady Cheyne's not feeling at all the thing," she told Johna. "An interesting condition, I'd guess."

It might be interesting, but she wasn't alone in the condition. More gentlemen were visiting the necessary out back, more ladies were needing to lie down. More guests were leaving, with regrets.

"Won't you stay for supper, Lord Alvanley?"

"Sorry, another function to attend. Press of invitations, don't you know." That and the pressing pain in his midsection.

"Did you happen to have the truffled grouse at dinner, Jo?" Selcrest asked as they bade another guest good-bye at the door to the ballroom.

"No, I was too tense to eat anything. Why? Did you?"

"No, I never cared much for it. It's always been one of Denton's favorites, though."

"Yes, that's what Phillipa said, so I put it on the menu." She was looking around, searching through the thinning crowds. "Oh dear, I don't see either one of them. And they promised not to go off alone."

"Don't worry, Denton is out in your garden, wishing he were already in Spain eating army food. And I believe one of the footmen carried Phillipa up to her room."

"And you think the grouse was tainted? Good heavens, how could such a thing happen?"

"It happens all the time, cream gone rancid, oysters out of season." Selcrest was patting her hand for reassurance, but he was frowning, scanning the row of gilded chairs where the chaperones and companions sat. They were almost all nodding off to sleep or fallen over in their seats. "But not all of these people were at dinner. I don't understand what's going on."

Neither did Johna, when they returned to the hallway and she saw her head footman, not the butler, handing guests their hats and canes and cloaks. "Where is Jenkins, William? It's not like him to be away from the door."

"Mr. Jenkins took ill, milady. Just sort of keeled over, he did, right into a potted fern. But I can manage things here, and the new cook says he's got the late supper in hand, so there's nothing to worry about, ma'am."

"Nothing to worry about when my guests are falling like— What new cook?"

The footman looked at her as if she'd sprouted another nose. "The cook who arrived this morning, saying you sent for him when his cousin Alphonse came down with the influenza."

"That explains the changes in the menu, but I never sent for anyone—and Alphonse doesn't have a cousin!" Johna and the viscount looked at each other and simultaneously shouted, "Marcel!"

"Damn, I had all those Runners and guards trying to protect you from someone who was already here!" Merle turned to leave her. "I'll gather them up and go find that hell-spawn. This time he's not getting away."

"Wait! We have to tell everyone not to eat any more of the food!"

"I don't think you have to tell them."

Guests were filing past Johna and the viscount with barely courteous farewells. It was not quite a panic, more a hurried exodus. Then Johna heard some mutterings about the Black Widow. "Oh, my Lord, they think I've poisoned them!"

Someone heard the word "poison." There was a stampede for the door.

*

Marcel was having a grand time. He meant to destroy Lady Otis, not necessarily kill her guests, but if they died, *c'est la vie.* Or *la morte.* Revenge was sweet, and so was the syrup of poppies he'd been pouring into the champagne bottles as fast as that so-proper butler ordered them opened. Marcel had seen how Jenkins tasted each bottle before letting the footmen serve it. Jenkins didn't have his nose in the ear now.

Marcel should have left, but he was having too much fun watching all the servants scurry around for basins and bowls and clean towels. When he heard Selcrest shout, "To me, men, secure the kitchen," he didn't bother trying to flee. He'd seen all the guards outside. Instead he pulled a pistol from under his apron.

As soon as Selcrest came through the door, Marcel fired. The distance was too great and Marcel's aim too uncertain for the ball to find its intended target, but it did hit a stack of dirty dishes, sending food scraps and china fragments in every direction.

"Stop," Marcel ordered, "or I shoot again. This time I don't muss."

This time Selcrest was so close that Marcel couldn't miss, if he had another shot. He fired. Nothing happened. The Frenchman stared at the gun. "I told that oaf I wanted a reporter!"

A slim, bespectacled fellow with a pad and pencil stood up. "That's what you wanted, a repeater? You, monsieur, are a jackass. But I thank you. What a story I got. 'Bellyache at the Ball'? 'Misery on Albemarle Street'?"

Now Selcrest had two maggots to dispose of. The reporter was in his way, so he tossed him aside first.

Johna was right behind him, wielding a heavy skillet from the cookstove. "You ruined my ball! You poisoned half the haut monde, and you shot at us! I'll see you in—"

Marcel made a grab for her. Perhaps he intended to take Johna hostage, or just to finish the job he'd started earlier. But he forgot about the broken crockery and splattered foodstuffs all over the floor. So he slipped and skidded, right to her feet—so Johna bashed him over the head with the iron skillet. Runners and hired guards and footmen and grooms from the stable, armed with pitchforks, rushed into the kitchen. In short order they had Marcel trussed like the Christmas goose, ready to be dragged off to Newgate. In all the commotion, the reporter made his escape.

*

"It will be in all the papers." Johna whimpered into her lemonade—made with her own hands from fresh ingredients.

Merle was beside her, dusting cobwebs from his once-elegant evening attire. He'd been down in the wine cellars unearthing unopened, unadulterated, vintages to serve the few remaining guests. "Yes, but such a juicy tidbit would have made the *on-dits* columns anyway, with so many prominent people involved. It likely would have been mentioned with the criminal proceedings, too. Now, at least, if that reporter does his job, everyone will know that you had nothing to do with the whole mingle-mangle."

"They'll also know I had something to do with Marcel. It will all come out now, the entire sorry mess. My reputation will be destroyed. They'll hold me responsible, anyway, those old tabbies. You know they will."

"So what? You're still the same person, so your friends will understand. And remember, no one was seriously injured. Bow Street found all sorts of bottles and packets, but just small amounts of various poisons. You'll have to throw away anything that dirty dish might have touched, but other than that, you are quite lucky, my dear."

"Lucky?" That wasn't the word Johna would have used.

"Indeed, with a great deal to be thankful for."

"You should be thankful I don't still have the skillet in my hands."

Merle laughed. "Truly, Jo, you can be thankful the Prince didn't come. Poisoning him would be treason."

8

They'd all recover, the diners, the drinkers, and the denizens of Albemarle Street. Cook was found tied and gagged behind the tavern he frequented, and Jenkins submitted his resignation, for such a lapse in good butling.

Lady Selcrest chose to be amused. "The polite world can use a good purge now and again. They'll get over it by the spring Season. You wait and see, you'll be welcomed back to London with open arms." Open or shut, Johna wasn't coming back. She'd stay on in Berkshire and raise roses and rabbits, like Lady Selcrest. No, she'd get herself a little dog and name it Sunshine, so she'd have a ray of brightness in her long, empty days.

For now, she couldn't wait to be gone. The knocker was already off the door; they were just waiting for Phillipa to regain her energy before leaving for Selcrest's Suffolk estate. A month in his company, though, might prove more torturous than staying to face the censure of society.

He hated her, that's all she could think. Why else would he leave for the country without them? Selcrest had left her alone to write the hundred notes of apology, to face the hundred curious columnists wanting to see the scene of the crime. At least Jenkins agreed to stay on to keep the onlookers at bay.

Selcrest said he had to go get things ready, as if the man didn't have an army of servants to see to his every comfort and that of whatever guests he might invite. Selcrest said Denton would be escort enough, as if the silly mooncalf had eyes for anyone else but Phillipa. Selcrest said he was looking forward to having Johna at his family home— Hah! Johna didn't believe a word the two-faced peer said. He'd been bumped and bruised, almost stabbed, almost shot, and almost poisoned—all on account of her. Now his name was on everyone's tongue again, connected to a lurid, ludicrous, hideous hobble. He hated her, and she couldn't blame him.

*

Everything had to be perfect for his brave girl, Merle decided. No gossip, no danger, no worries over people liking her. If he had his way, she'd never have another worry in this world. Then again, if Selcrest had his way, she'd be in his room, in his bed, in his arms this very minute, so he had to leave London. He'd leave her some shred of reputation while he still had some self-control. A week wasn't long—just two lifetimes.

Everything was perfect, Johna thought. Perhaps his lordship had needed the time in Suffolk after all, for she'd never seen a lovelier place. Seacrest was constructed of mellow brick, comfortably nestled among sprawling gardens and stands of wood, evergreens and holly instead of crouching like a fortress on a bare hill, as so many other great houses did. The house itself was immense, but all one style, having been totally rebuilt in the last century, after a fire. Somehow Johna didn't find the place overwhelming, although Hutchison Manor would have fit in the front hall.

Maybe she felt so welcome because he was there, or because Christmas was there. Every sight and smell of the season was present except for the snow, and Selcrest apologized for that, but thought they might have some soon. If anyone could organize the weather, Johna thought, he could.

There were pine boughs and holly and red velvet ribbons, clove-studded apples and scented candles and hanging balls of mistletoe that Phillipa and Denton just happened to find, no matter how often Johna moved them. There were minced meat pies and gingerbread, mulled cider and lamb's wool punch. Every tradition, every special festive delicacy, was done just right, for her.

"Oh, we never bother doing up the whole pile," Lady Selcrest told Johna before disappearing after Higbee to see about releasing her pets from their traveling boxes. "Just the occasional ribbon or wreath if the maids remember to fix them."

Even more telling—and more touching—to Johna was how Merle didn't appear to be ashamed of her. He invited all of his neighbors in, both high and low, although most of them would have heard of the London debacle. The viscount proudly introduced her to all of them, even taking her with him on his rounds of the estate to meet his tenants, where he knew the name of every child and half the watchdogs. Mounted on a pretty mare from his excellent stables, Johna felt welcome. He let her feel useful, too, helping fill Christmas baskets for his dependents, helping to wrap dolls and toy soldiers for all those children. Her only complaint was that he wouldn't let her near the kitchens. It was her holiday, he argued, but she had to wonder.

Phillipa and Denton, meanwhile, were gone for hours on long walks, sightseeing rides, paying calls on the young people in the vicinity. Rules were more relaxed in the country, Lady Selcrest assured Johna, who was so used to worrying about her sister's reputation. In the evenings when there were no guests they all sang the old carols. Then Phillipa and Denton whispered in the corner of the drawing room while the others—and Higbee—played cards.

Lady Selcrest took to retiring early and taking naps in the afternoon. "Too much gadding about," she declared. "You won't mind organizing the Christmas dinner, will you, Johna dear? We usually have twenty or thirty guests, sometimes dancing after. Do whatever you wish. Talk to Frye. He's the underbutler who stays here when Higbee goes with us to London. The man needs a bit more experience, and I need Higbee with me. There's a new breed of rabbit I want to research. Wouldn't think of bothering Selcrest to escort me."

Frye was well up to the task of planning a small function, but deferred all decisions to Johna. Then the housekeeper took to consulting her, with Lady Selcrest generally unavailable or uninterested. The gardeners needed to know which plants to bring up from the conservatory, and Mrs. Tibbetts, the wondrously English cook, sought her preferences for the menu. And the rest of the menus, not just the Christmas dinner? Johna agreed to look them over too.

Johna adored the house and its people, the tenants, and the neighbors, and she was pleased to be of service to Lady Selcrest for all that woman had done for them. She just couldn't understand, however, how it came about that everyone considered her, a disreputable widow, as chatelaine of Seacrest. Embarrassed, afraid she was causing him more aggravation still, Johna went to the viscount. She didn't want him thinking her encroaching or a managing type of female.

"But you are, managing the place, that is, and everyone knows it. Capably too, I might add."

They were in his curricle, driving to the next town so Johna could complete her Christmas shopping, now that she had so many new friends among the staff and neighbors. "Silly goose, you've already given us so much just by coming," Merle told her, warming Johna to the tips of her boot-clad toes, despite the freezing temperature. "I cannot tell you how much I appreciate all the help you've been to my mother."

"It's my pleasure to relieve her of any chores, you know that. Lady Selcrest seems less careworn these past days, don't you think?"

"Yes, with your help. I thought she was upset about Denton's leaving. I suppose she's resigned herself now."

"And Phillipa, too. She doesn't have that grim look anymore. You were right about not separating them. She's had this time to learn to be brave."

*

Johna admired her sister's fortitude. She didn't know if she could face losing the man she loved without falling to pieces. She was having enough trouble facing the man she loved, period, knowing their time was limited. If Johna weren't so busy, she told herself, she just might go into a decline.

Phillipa was being noble, her loving sister thought, hiding her distress for Denton's sake. She smiled as they all drove home from church services on Christmas Eve, and laughed as they exchanged gifts over the wassail cups. Phillipa was delighted with the ermine-lined cape from Johna, and the pearl earbobs from Lady Selcrest to go with the pearl ring Denton gave her. In return she gave Denton a fob watch with her portrait on the inside of the case, and gave Johna the new paint set she wanted. Selcrest gave Johna a gold pin—in the shape of a parrot.

They all laughed then, that Merle thought Johna needed a reminder. He liked his book and the handkerchiefs painstakingly monogrammed by both sisters with his family insignia; Lady Selcrest was pleased with the Oriental jade hare. Everyone agreed, however, that the dowager's gifts were their favorites: scarves and mittens knitted from her rabbits' fur.

Then they sang carols, led by Phillipa's lovely soprano voice as Johna played the pianoforte. They all watched Lord Selcrest light the Yule log from last year's sliver, and joined in when Higbee led the traditional servants' toast to their master's health and the prosperity of the family in the coming year. More carols, more toasts, hugs all around, then it was time to go to bed before a busy Christmas Day. After a final embrace of her sister, with calls of "Peace and joy to you," still echoing in her head, Johna left Phillipa and Denton to make their good nights. It was Christmas, after all.

While Johna brushed her hair, waiting to hear her sister's footsteps in the room next door, she thought again how cheerful Phillipa was being, how brave.

She kept on thinking that right up to Christmas Day, at lunchtime, to be exact.

Johna was up early on Christmas morning, with many last-minute details to oversee. Then she and all the servants attended service in the family chapel. Merle read the nativity, as heads of households did this morning throughout the land. Johna thought Phillipa and Denton must have decided to attend the village church, after all. Lady Selcrest would still be abed, resting for the evening's festivities.

Then it was lunchtime, and Phillipa still had not returned. That's when Johna discovered that the peagoose had been brave enough to elope on Christmas Eve.

There was a note. Denton had been offered a better position as aide-de-camp, it seemed, but in the American campaign. It was much farther away than the Peninsula, but Denton liked the idea of seeing the New World, perhaps carving a niche for them there once the conflict was resolved. Phillipa couldn't bear to be parted from him for so long, she wrote, and so had to go along. They'd be married by special license, by the captain of their sailing ship.

Folded inside the note was the little ring from last year's pudding. "Now my wish can come true," Phillipa wrote. "I pray that yours, can too."

"I can't even go after them to try to dissuade her," Johna cried into Selcrest's neckcloth. "They've been gone so long, and they were alone last night. Her reputation is already ruined. And I thought she was being so good, putting on a cheerful face for us."

"She was. It couldn't have been easy for her to leave you." He handed her one of his new handkerchiefs.

"I only wanted the best for her."

"And Denton will see that she gets it, I swear. But now you have to be the courageous one, my dear, for there is more bad news."

She stepped back and blew her nose. "More? My only sister has gone off to some barbaric place with your madcap brother. He'll go away to war and she'll be all alone."

"She won't be alone." He took a note out of his own pocket. "My mother is with them."

"Oh, I'm glad! That is, I'm sorry, Merle. But whyever would your mother decide to go to America in the middle of winter? I mean, even for your mother..."

"Higbee went too."

"Ah." There was a world of understanding in that "Ah," understanding how upset Selcrest must be, and how happy his mother and her longtime beau would be in the Colonies with no titles, no prejudices to keep them apart.

"Yes, they've also got a special license, thank goodness. In fact, Mother enclosed a third one, for us."

"Us?" There was no understanding in that syllable whatsoever.

"Well, yes, Mother knew what she was doing. You see, she was chaperoning your sister last night, but no one was chaperoning us. Your reputation is damaged far worse than Phillipa's. You've been hopelessly compromised with no chance of finding a respectable duenna for tonight either. That's what I meant about needing to be brave."

"What's bravery got to do with it? You could move in with one of your tenants for the night, or my maid and I could go to an inn."

"What, on Christmas?" He pried the little ring from her stiff fingers. "You've got the ring, I've got the license. Shall we?"

"Shall we what, Merle?"

"Get married, of course. That was Mother's intention all along, naturally, befriending you, having you take over the household, leaving us in the lurch like this so you are hopelessly compromised past redemption."

"That's fustian! You're forgetting that my name is already so tarnished my own mother wouldn't receive me. I can go on home tomorrow with no one the wiser to this latest coil except for your servants."

"And the thirty or so guests coming for dinner in three hours."

"Oh no! I have to leave, now!" Johna made a dash for the doorway, but Selcrest grabbed for her hand.

"What, and leave me to face all of them? Besides, where would you go? There's an easier way, Jo. Would it be so bad, being the new Lady Selcrest?"

"You don't wish to marry me, Merle. I cannot let your sense of duty force you into such an impossible situation."

He let go of her hand. "You're refusing me, then?"

There hadn't been a single word of love. Not even affection. "I have to."

Selcrest was studying his fingertips. "Old Lady Wilburham is coming to dinner. I'll ask her to spend the night. She's half-deaf, but will satisfy the conventions. Everyone will be too busy exclaiming over Mother and Denton to notice any irregularity. We can talk more about this later, after the guests leave."

But the guests never came.

9

"It's me, I know it. They aren't coming because of me." Johna was wearing out the velvet of her new crimson gown, rubbing it between nervous fingers. The goose was hot, the wine was cool, and no one was there except her and the viscount. Not even old Lady Wilburham. Her sister leaving, the love of her life offering a marriage of convenience, now this fiasco of a holiday feast—this had to be the worst Christmas ever, if one discounted last Christmas and Sir Otis's demise. No, this was worse. "You see, marriage to me would cost you all your friends. We're not even married and they won't come to dinner. You'd be throwing out food every day."

Selcrest poured her a glass of sherry. "Don't be a peagoose. You have nothing to do with it."

"What then? Are your neighbors staying away because they disapprove so strongly of your mother's elopement?"

Merle drank the glass himself. "That's even more foolish. Mother's friends knew about her and Higbee for years. They'd come to laugh and drink a toast to her happiness."

"Then it's me. They're all afraid I did the cooking! I told you word would reach Suffolk. Now you see I was right: I would ruin your life too. You wouldn't dare show your face in London."

Merle put his arm around her, but she didn't relax against him. "And that's not going to work either."

"Silly goose, I only want to show you the view." With his arm still on her shoulder, he turned her to the window and pulled the heavy drapes open. "I bet you've been too busy all day to look outside."

Johna looked, and saw nothing but white. The trees were covered, the lawns, everything.

"It's been snowing all day, a regular blizzard. I hope Mother and Denton made it to their ship before the roads became impassable. But that's why no one is going to come out on such a night, especially when they all have to travel at least three or four miles."

"You said it was going to snow."

"I said a lot of foolish things. But come, get your coat and boots and a heavy muffler. We're going for a ride to see your Christmas surprise. I meant to take you earlier, but there was too much upset and confusion."

"But it's nearly dark, and you said carriages couldn't get through."

"Carriages can't, but sleighs can. And it's not so far away, on Selcrest lands. Besides, you wouldn't want all that food to go to waste, would you?"

So they bundled up in their warmest hats and Lady Selcrest's new mittens, with hot bricks at their feet and heavy blankets over their laps. The rest of the sleigh was filled with baskets and boxes of roast goose and ham, a baron of beef, pies and punch and marzipan angels. The sturdy farm horses pulled the sleigh effortlessly, bells jingling, ribbons streaming from their harnesses.

The countryside was like a Christmas painting. No, Johna thought, it was like a magical glass snow globe that someone had shaken, with swirls and shadows and stars peeking through the clouds. She was sorry when they arrived so soon at a stone building set off the path. The structure was small but solidly built, with lights pouring from all three stories and an enormous wreath on the door.

"What is this place, Merle?"

"I'm not quite certain yet," he said, lifting her out of the sleigh. "The Otis Ogden Home for Unwed Mothers? Hutchison Hospital? You'll have to decide. I was hoping you'd select Lady Selcrest's Girls' School."

The door was opened and Johna could see Lorraine and Kitty and a much expanded Mimi shepherding a flock of nightgowned moppets up the stairs, laughing and singing Christmas carols.

"You did this, for me?" she asked, standing in the hallway.

"Don't you know I would do anything for you, my lady?" He unwrapped the muffler from around her neck. "But I did have help. Do you remember those gambling chits you were going to burn? Those chaps were so pleased to be out of Sir Otis's clutches that they all decided to contribute to the maintenance of this place."

"With a little persuasion?" Her heart was so full, Johna could have wept, if she weren't surrounded by the children and the women. They were all talking at once, exclaiming over the baskets of food, explaining how they were learning to sew and cook and read—with real teachers, too. They could go into service or make good housewives, Mimi said, eyeing the viscount's tiger, who was helping unpack the sleigh.

"So you better let him make an honest woman out of you, my lady," Lorraine teased with a wink and a nod. "We're counting on you for references, don't you know."

*

"One more surprise," Merle told her when they were back at his home. By chance and by Merle's maneuvering, she was standing under the mistletoe bough. So he kissed her. It was but a moment's work to warm their cold lips, faster than the wassail could have done.

Johna's thoughts went flying like the snow in the glass globe; they always did when he kissed her. And her toes were tingling. Eventually she recalled herself enough to say, "No, you've done enough. Truly, that house for the girls is the best present I could ever receive."

"Then this one is for me." He left, to return in a minute with a silver tray on which reposed a magnificent Christmas pudding.

"Oh, no, I never want to taste another spoonful of pudding!"

"You'll like this one, I swear. I didn't cook it but I prepared it myself, just for you." Merle was having trouble, cutting the pudding. The knife kept hitting things.

"What in the world, did you put in that pudding?"

He handed her the knife. "Here, you try slicing it."

So Johna pressed down with the blade, and a ring fell out, then another. With her next cut, more tumbled onto the plate or rolled to the floor with the nuts and candied fruits. Rings and tiny keys and little boats and coins and crumbs—but mostly rings.

"And this one goes with them." Merle reached in his pocket for a velvet pouch, and removed a diamond-and-ruby ring. "Will you marry me, my dearest Johna, and make me the happiest of men? I'm not asking out of duty or to fulfill any notion of propriety. You've given me the gift of knowing there are so many things that are more important than maintaining my dignity. Your love is the most important of all, the finest Christmas present I can imagine."

Her hands full of rings and raisins, Johna couldn't reach out for him, but she could say, "Then Merry Christmas, Merle, for I have loved you for ages, ever since I saved you from choking to death."

Selcrest didn't care how sticky she was, or how she still persisted in her rattle-pated rescue. He took her in his arms, crumbs and all. "I do love you, Jo. More than I can ever say." And he placed the ring—the ruby-and-diamond one—on her finger. "According to your sister, tradition says that the girl who finds the ring in her pudding will marry within the year. What would you say to within the week?"

"I'll marry you tomorrow, Merle, on one condition."

"Anything, my love."

"Tell me why Kitty called you Silky."

"Now that, my precious, I can only show you." He picked her up and headed for the stairs. "What was that little key for anyway? A grand opportunity, was it?"

*

Christmas Pudding
(makes 4)

2 cups raisins, halved and stoned

1 tablespoon orange peel, grated, plus 1/3 cup juice

2 cups sultanas, halved and stoned, or figs

rum for soaking (optional)

1/2 pound beef suet, finely chopped

11/2 cups currants, washed and dried

4 cups bread crumbs

1 1/2 cups candied fruit peel and candied cherries

2 cups flour

1 cup brown sugar

1 cup almonds, blanched and shredded, or mixed nuts

1 teaspoon allspice, grated

1 teaspoon salt

1/2 of one nutmeg, grated

1 green apple, peeled, cored and chopped

6 eggs, well beaten

1 cup brandy

1 carrot, grated

More rum for soaking (optional)

1 tablespoon lemon rind, grated, plus 1/4 cup juice

1/2 cup brandy for flaming (optional)

Soak the fruits in rum, at least one month in advance. This makes them plump, as in plum pudding.

Mix the fruits and dry ingredients well. Separately, mix the eggs, juice, and brandy, and add to the mixture, stirring thoroughly. Everyone in the household can take a turn stirring and making their pudding wishes. Let the whole thing stand, covered and cool, overnight.

Divide the mix into four greased pudding basins, molds, or bowls, covered with foil, or tie into boiling bags. Place the puddings into large pots of water and bring to a boil. Cover the pot, reduce the heat, and steam the puddings for 8 hours. (Make sure the water doesn't boil away.)

Remove and cool, then cover and store in a cool, dry place, for a month.

One week before serving, soak the puddings in rum if you wish. Just before serving, steam the puddings again, 1-2 hours, before unmolding. This is when coins, tokens, and such can be pressed into the pudding.

To set on fire, warm the brandy and light it, then pour over the puddings.

Three Good Deeds

1

No noise is louder to the ears of a boy than the sound of a window shattering when he is left holding the cricket bat. Unless, of course, the unfortunate pane of glass happens to have been in a church. At least this one was not a centuries-old stained-glass work of art. That noise would have made the crack of doom sound like a snowflake landing.

The boy could have run, as the other local lads had, disappearing through the village streets like so many leaves fading into the forest floor. This boy's sense of honor kept him in place outside the tiny chapel. Honor kept him there, as well as his bright red hair, which would make him visible for miles. Besides, he'd just left the vicar's study, his Latin lessons not ten minutes past. So he stayed, waiting, and his two brothers stayed with him.

"Oh, dear." The Reverend Mr. Davenport had been working on his Christmas sermon. That is, he'd been thinking of working on his Christmas sermon, which meant he'd been dozing when the glass shattered. He wheezed himself out of his comfortable chair and into his coat and muffler against the December chill, then joined the three boys outside in staring at the jagged edges of the window. "Oh, dear Lord in Heaven, and the bishop is coming."

'I did it, Vicar," confessed ten-year-old Martin, the eldest of the Greene siblings.

"No, sir, I hit the ball." The middle boy, Jasper, adjusted the spectacles on his nose. "Mama told me not to play with my glasses on, and I couldn't see where I was aiming."

Benjamin, the baby of the bunch at five years of age, was not to be left out. "I made them let me bat, Mr. Davenport. Honest, I did."

"Oh, dear." The vicar huffed into the scarf around his neck. "What's to be done? Whatever is to be done? We'll have to go inside to discuss this; yes, we will." He turned to trudge back into his warm office, where Martin had so recently been reading his assigned passage of Vergil, and Jasper had struggled with Caesar through the Gallic wars. Little Benjamin had practiced his letters with first declension nouns. Now Benjy was the first to voice the dismal thoughts of all three boys.

"Do you think he'll cane us?" he whispered as the Greene trio followed in the vicar's wake, like felons to the gibbet.

"He didn't last time, when we left the gate open and Maude Binkum's cow got in and ate his roses." Still, Jasper handed the bat over to his older brother.

"No, but he told Mama, and she was that upset she cried." As one, the three slowed their steps, falling farther behind the vicar and their fate.

"Oh, dear, oh, dear," Mr. Davenport kept repeating as he lowered himself back into his study chair. "I'll have to call in the sexton and send him off to the glazier's with measurements, and hire a carpenter, and oh, my, I don't know what else. Paint, I suppose, if they have to take the frame out, and caulking. Oh, and I so wanted St. Jerome's to look perfect for the bishop. We cannot very well ask him for the funds for an extension when we don't care for our little church now."

"We'll pay for the repairs, sir," Martin offered, emptying his pockets. His brothers did likewise. Soon a collection of stones and string and colored chalk rested on the vicar's desk, with a few coins buried in their midst. Mr. Davenport used his penknife to poke through the pile, separating two shillings and some copper pennies from the rest.

"We've been saving for Mama's Christmas present," Jasper confided.

Martin nodded. "We were going to buy her a dress length of velvet."

"Red velvet," Benjy put in, "so she'll have something pretty to wear to the duke's dinner for the bishop."

The vicar shook his head, whether at the alarming thought of Sabina Greene in red velvet, her with the same flaming hair as her three sons, or the unlikelihood of the young widow's being invited to Espinham Castle for the festivities. "It is not enough, boys. Glass is expensive, and the workmen need their wages."

The youngsters looked to one another, but it was Martin who spoke. "We'll work, sir, we'll do anything, so long as you don't tell our mother."

"No, no. The dear woman has enough in her budget without this. Why, I feel bad already, taking her money in exchange for your lessons, but she insists."

"We'll give up the lessons!" Benjy volunteered.

"No, that won't do. Perhaps I should go to the duke and ask him for the funds."

"No! Please don't," three desperate voices chorused.

"You can beat us, or...or take our pony, Chocolate. Just don't go to the duke." They all recalled the incident last spring involving a ram and a ewe and the Duke of Espinwall's garden party. His Grace had demanded Mama's presence, then thundered at her for a day, it seemed, leaving Mrs. Greene pale and shaking, weeping for a sennight. No, they would sell Benjy as a chimney sweep before they let the duke berate their mother again.

"Let me think, let me think," the vicar muttered, rubbing the penknife along his whiskered jaw. "I can take some money from the roof fund, and replace that with a bit of the choir robe budget. And, yes, I do believe you three can work to repay the cost. His Grace has generously offered the dead wood in Espy Forest to the poor of the parish, if we come and get it, of course." The vicar did not mention what he thought of such generosity. The fallen limbs would keep the poor warm this winter, no matter how cold the duke's heart. "You can go along with Wilfred Snavely and his son to gather the firewood, so the job will get done that much sooner and the parish can save a few pence there."

The boys grinned. "We'll pick up every twig, sir! In fact, we can climb the trees and knock down broken branches. Old Wilfred's too big to climb trees, and Young Wilfred's too lazy. And Chocolate can help carry, so you won't have to pay them so much to use their donkey." Martin slapped Jasper on the shoulder, and Benjamin bounced up and down.

"Ahem. That's not all, boys."

Three similar freckled faces turned pale again.

"No, you cannot learn to believe that money alone fixes wrongs. That would be a poor lesson indeed. Why, they say that two rights don't even mend a wrong, so we'll try for three, shall we?"

"Three, sir?" The boys looked to each other in confusion.

"Aye, lads. Three rights to make up for the broken window. Three good deeds to repay the parish for the aggravation of having you three rapscallions loose among us."

"We don't understand, Mr. Davenport," Martin spoke for all of them. "Just what is it you would have us do?"

"I don't know, lad. Use your heads for once. It might be a good exercise. Look around and see who needs help this holiday season. And I don't mean using your pennies to buy candy for the needy children, or getting money from your dear mother to give to the poor. That's too easy. And helping each other with your homework assignments and chores won't count either. I mean you should perform three selfless acts, ones that aren't just for your own benefit, and do it anonymously, too. That means no one is to know who helped them," he added for Benjy's sake, "because this is not about winning praise for yourselves. It is about helping the Lord at His busy season. You look around the village and see who is unhappy and what you can do to ease their souls. And make sure you complete your three good deeds before Christmas, mind you, or I'll have to go to your mother after all, or the duke. Do you understand?"

The boys understood they'd be carrying firewood to stoke furnaces in hell if the duke got hold of them, so they nodded, but they weren't entirely sure they did comprehend the vicar's penance, nor what to do about it. So that night, when they were gathered around their mother for the evening story, Benjy asked, "Mama, who is the most unhappy person you know?"

Sabina squeezed her youngest, there in the old worn leather chair at her right side. Jasper sat on her left, and Martin was perched on the stool by her feet. "Unhappy, dear? Why, I don't think I know anyone who is unhappy. Mrs. Cotter could use more milk for her children, but Jed Hanks said he'd lend her a cow. And Mr. Jordan at the inn is worried about his son off with the army, so we must remember to add young Tom to our prayers, along with the other brave soldiers."

"Gads, I hope Mr. Davenport doesn't expect us to end the war," Jasper whispered to his older brother, at which Sabina's brows came together.

"Now what is this about?"

"Oh, the vicar was just practicing his sermon," Martin quickly told her. "Something about windows to the soul, I think. What did you hear, Jas?"

"He definitely mentioned windows, all right. And...branches of knowledge. Isn't that right, Martin?"

Sabina shook her head. "Mr. Davenport must be preparing for Christmas Eve, hoping to impress the bishop if the children's pageant and the chorale don't sway His Eminence enough to loosen his purse strings." She only hoped the vicar didn't put everyone to sleep.

Seeing her frown, and worrying more over their thorny dilemma than over the bishop's visit, Benjy asked, "You're not unhappy, Mama, are you?"

Speaking of purse strings, Sabina would have been a lot happier if she did not have to worry about her finances all the time. She managed on her tiny income, but without the luxuries, nay, the comforts she wished she could provide for her children, especially with Christmas coming. But her late husband's clutch-fisted man of affairs had no idea of how much three boys ate, or how quickly they outgrew their clothes. Still, she made do. "No, darling, I am not unhappy. How could I be, when I have the three finest sons a woman could wish?"

"Even if we are not rich?"

"Especially. Money doesn't bring happiness, darling. Just look at the duke. He never has to worry about paying the butcher or the wine merchant, so he overindulges himself right into the gout. Then he is even more discontented."

"But why is the duke so unhappy, Mama? He has the finest stable in the shire." Martin couldn't imagine anyone with such prime horseflesh not being delighted with his lot in life.

His Grace of Espinwall was the meanest, most ill-tempered old curmudgeon of Sabina's acquaintance. She believed he must have been born raging at the midwife, and he'd likely die swearing at St. Peter for interrupting his schedule. Sabina couldn't say that to her sons, of course, especially not if the vicar was trying to instruct them about goodness and mercy, along with their Latin. "Well, I suppose he is so downcast because his wife has passed on and his son never comes to visit. Think how wretched I would be without you and your brothers. Espinwall has that whole enormous castle to himself, with no one to talk to except his servants. Perhaps he is lonely." And perhaps pigs had wings.

"Why doesn't his son come?"

Sabina fingered the locket at her throat. "They had a disagreement a long time ago, before any of you were born. And I suppose both have too much pride to mend the rift now. Viscount Royce makes his life in London, and his father stays in the country, so they never have a chance to reconcile their differences."

Benjy nodded somberly, but Jasper and Martin winked at each other. "What about Reverend Davenport, Mama?" Jasper asked before Sabina could resume her reading or announce bedtime. "Do you think he is happy?"

Sabina laughed. "Oh, Mr. Davenport frets himself to flinders, but I believe he enjoys worrying over all of us. I always thought he'd be better off with a wife to look after some of the parish duties for him and see that he gets a proper meal, but he hired Mrs. Hinkle to keep house for him, most likely with your Latin lesson fees, so I am even more pleased that he agreed to take you on."

Jasper nudged Martin with his foot, and the older boy nodded, already making plans. "Someone else in the village must need our prayers, don't you think, Mama?"

"Well, I suppose you could ask God to look after everyone in Chipping Espy, darling. That would be lovely, and wouldn't leave anyone out."

"What about Miss Gaines?" Benjy wanted to know. "Should we pray for her, too?"

"She doesn't even go to church, you noddy!" Jasper ridiculed. "You can't pray for a—"

His mother clamped her hand over his mouth. "Of course you may pray for Miss Gaines, Benjamin. She is one of God's creatures, too."

"And she needs it more, 'cause she has no friends. No one ever calls on her. Do you think that makes her unhappy?"

"How should Mama know, cloth-head? Miss Gaines ain't respectable. Besides, that toff from London used to come visit every few weeks. Ty Marshall says—"

"I do not think we need to hear what Ty Marshall has to say about Miss Gaines, Martin. In fact," Mrs. Greene quickly added, "it must be time for bed." She jumped up, nearly tumbling Benjamin out of the chair in her efforts to head off any more awkward questions. Giving each boy a kiss on the forehead, she said, "Good night, my darlings. Sleep well. And please try to remember to wear your old clothes tomorrow, and to be more careful near the briers. I am so proud of you for volunteering to help bring in the firewood for the poor families, I could burst. What would I ever do without my good boys?"

Sabina Greene's good boys stayed up for hours, plotting and planning. The next morning, before they went off to the vicarage for their lessons, the three redheads detoured to the posting office, where they parted with one of their hoarded coins to see a letter delivered. They were not entirely sure of the complete address for the missive they'd spent half the night composing, but another tuppence convinced the post rider to discover Viscount Royce's direction. "Th'fella can't be that hard to locate," the rider declared, pocketing his fee. "Famous rakehell, ain't he?"

2

Connor Hamilton, Viscount Royce, rode as if the hounds of hell were snapping at his stallion's heels. Why he was in such a hurry, cutting across fields and taking barely remembered shortcuts through the home woods, he was not sure. The demons that were urging him on were nothing to the devils that waited ahead.

He hadn't wanted to come. He hadn't wanted to see his father. Despite the lack of affection between them, Connor certainly had no desire to see the old dastard stick his spoon in the wall. He didn't want to be duke, didn't want to live in Espinham Castle, with its foolish turrets and crenelations, arrow slits and drafty halls with rows of armor, where he and his best friend had played for hours. He did not want to rule Espinham's acres of fields and spinneys and ponds and forests, where he and his best friend had rambled. Most of all, he never wanted to see that best friend again. *Friend, hah!* The jade had married someone else as soon as his back was turned! By George, Connor didn't even want to be in the same county as Sabina Martindale. No, Sabina Greene.

He'd managed to avoid her for years—eleven, to be exact. She did not attend his mother's funeral; she was lying in, he was told at the time. And he did not attend her husband's. He'd thought of sending his condolences, but that would have been the height of hypocrisy. Connor wasn't the least bit sorry the old lecher was dead, nor that Sabina was left alone with a passel of brats to raise. She'd made her bargain, hadn't she?

Now the duke was dying, but the memories never would. Hell, even the urchins gathering kindling in the woods reminded him of Sabina's bright hair and ready laughter, blast her to hell!

He tossed Conquistador's reins to a slack-jawed groom and pushed through the carved front doors. "Am I on time?" he shouted to the startled butler who hurried to see what manner of caller dared to open the massive castle doors by himself.

"On time?" The duke kept regular hours at Espinham Castle. Always had, always would. Watson glanced at the huge clock that stood in the entryway. It was barely five. "Dinner is not till six, my lord."

"Who cares about food at a time like this? Has the vicar come?"

"Tuesday, my lord." Watson hurried to catch the viscount's riding coat, hat, and gloves before the younger man tore up the wide, winding stairs. He shook his head at the retreating figure. "Same as always. That's His Grace's cribbage night."

Connor was already on the floor above, headed past the hanging tapestries and the battle axes on the wall, toward the modern wing of the castle. He burst into the duke's suite without knocking.

The duke had been enjoying a preprandial sherry and a salacious French novel in the privacy of his bedroom, where neither his busybody butler nor his meddling manservant could say him nay. His gouty foot was propped on an extra pillow on the immense ducal bed; his shirt collar was open, awaiting a fresh neckcloth. His Grace looked up at the commotion in his sitting room, prepared to tear the hide off any servant who dared interrupt his afternoon's repose.

There stood his son. In all his dirt, with a trail of mud behind him and the smell of horse wafting ahead of him, and a scowl on his face. The duke's glass tipped, dribbling sherry down his chin and onto his shirt. He dabbed at his mouth with his sleeve, then recalled the French novel and tried to stuff it under the bedclothes, which dislodged his foot off its pillow, which sent pain shooting through him. He shouted in agony.

"Oh, my God, it's as bad as I feared! Thank goodness I got here in time!" The viscount strode to the bed and reached for his father's hand. "I came as soon as I heard."

When the pain subsided, Espinwall asked, "Uh, Royce, just what was it that you heard?"

"Why, that you were ailing, of course. Or did you think to keep it from me? That would be just like you, I suppose, dying all alone so your son could feel remorse for the rest of his life. Thank goodness your physician had the sense to send for me."

The duke took a moment to think. "You came to Espinham because you thought I was sickly—is that right?"

Connor's blue eyes narrowed. The duke's handclasp was surprisingly firm, and his eyes were as clear as the viscount's own. His Grace had always been a heavyset, robust man, and he hadn't lost a smidgen of heft that Connor could see. He took his hand back. "You don't look ill to me."

The duke gasped and clutched at his chest. He moaned a bit, too.

"Oh, Lud, I'm sorry. I shouldn't have burst in here like this, shouldn't have upset you or doubted the doctor. Would you rather I leave?"

For answer, the duke held out his hand, pleadingly. "Please...stay," he whispered.

"Of course, Father. Just tell me what I can do for you. Shall I send for your man? The doctor?" All Connor could see in the way of medication was a decanter of sherry. Perhaps it was too late for anything else but solace for the pain. He poured a glass and held it to his father's lips. "What do you need?"

Groaning again, His Grace mumbled what sounded like air. Connor started fanning him with the French novel. "There, catch your breath."

The duke pushed the book aside. "I said, 'heir,' you dolt, not 'air.' I don't want to die without the succession assured."

Connor left the bedside to get help. His father was obviously delirious. The viscount shouted for the duke's man, then demanded he send for Dr. Goodbody immediately.

"But, my lord, His Grace's physician is Mr. Kennilworth, same as always."

"He must have consulted another doctor when the condition worsened. We'll track the man down later. Just get someone here, now!" He went back to the bedside.

"I thought you'd left," the duke whimpered, hanging onto Connor's coat sleeve.

"No, I won't go anywhere as long as you need me."

"And you'll look after Espinham and everything after I'm gone? You won't disappear back into London's stews?"

"You're not going anywhere," the viscount insisted, trying to keep his voice steady through the lump in his throat.

"Of course I am, you gudgeon. Everyone dies eventually, even youngsters like you, going off to wars and duels and madcap curricle races. Then where will the estate be? In the hands of some humgudgeon upstart fourth cousin, that's where."

"It won't happen, Father, I swear."

"You do? Heavens be praised! Now I can die in peace!"

"You're not dying," Connor insisted, but his father was already babbling about grandsons.

"Why, you could even marry that Martindale woman. She's a widow now, you know."

Connor took a step back from the bed. "What? You absolutely forbade me to marry her! That's why I went away in the first place."

The duke waved one hand in the air. "That was then, when she was my librarian's daughter, barely gentry. This is now. You haven't found anyone else to marry in all these years, and she's a proven breeder. Three sons, by George, and you have none."

"I wouldn't marry Sabina Greene if she were the last woman on earth."

The duke gasped and fell back on the pillows, his hand over his heart again. "Damn if you're not as perverse as ever. When I say nay, you say aye. When I say you can, you say you cannot. Thunderation, boy, I demand it!"

"And you are as pigheaded as always. I do not dance to your tune, sir, and never shall."

"Then I'll never get to dance at your wedding, will I?" The duke wiped a tear, or something, from the corner of his eye. "And I'll never live to dandle grandsons on my knee. Is that too much for an old man to ask?"

*

The Greene boys, meanwhile, ran to intercept Reverend Davenport. They'd followed the viscount and his flying stallion to the Espinham stables, where the grooms always let them watch the horses. They were there when messengers were sent for the physician and the solicitor and the vicar.

"We've killed the duke!" Martin cried.

"The groom says the shock of seeing his son sent him into heart palpitations. Or apoplexy," Jasper explained. "We were only trying to help, the way you said we should."

"We thought the duke was lonely," Benjy added. "Now, if His Grace isn't dead, he'll kill us for sure,"

"Oh, dear."

So the reverend Mr. Davenport had to take the viscount aside and explain about the three poor fatherless children who were trying to do three good deeds for Christmas.

"Those redheaded urchins in the woods?"

"Yes, my lord, they are also doing charity work in atonement for a broken, window. They are good boys at heart, and their mother tries her best. I thought this would teach them better values than a birching would."

The viscount shoved a paper under the vicar's nose. "You've taught them to be criminals instead! They've forged Dr. Goodbody's name, whoever the deuce he is."

The vicar studied the paper, recognizing Martin's handwriting instantly. "No, my lord, it is signed 'Dr. Goodboy,' not Dr.

Goodbody. They must have thought that the end justified the means. After all, you are here, and the duke is pleased to see you."

"Pleased? He dashed near had a heart attack! He's too frail for such a shock."

"Frail? His Grace?" The vicar wondered if Lord Royce was the one suffering a brain fever. "The duke is the healthiest man I know, except for the gout."

"He has the gout?" Connor asked, only slightly embarrassed to be unaware of his own father's condition.

"Of course he does. That's why you found him abed at all. He stayed too long at Squire Marsden's last night, washing down Mrs. Marsden's lobster patties with the latest shipment from the Gentlemen Traders. Otherwise, he'd be out exercising one of those brutish horses of his."

Now that sounded more in keeping with Connor's memory. "So he's not dying?"

"Oh, dear me, I pray not. The bishop is coming to visit our little church in Chipping Espy for Christmas Eve services, and your father has invited him to stay for dinner. My lord, do you recall the pennant that is flown over Espinham Castle when the duke is in residence?"

"Of course I do. It's my family's emblem. The lion rampant on a field of blue."

"To be sure. Well, one of the footmen is assigned the task of placing a white cloth over one of the lion's paws when His Grace is having a bad day. That way everyone in the neighborhood knows when to stay away."

"Deuce take it—then I changed all my plans, nearly broke my neck and almost lamed my horse trying to get here, for nothing!"

"I wouldn't say nothing, my lord, if you and your father are reconciled. Why, the Greene children might have done a good deed after all."

Connor was having none of it. "I'll murder them, by Zeus. That will be my own good deed, ridding the world of those sneaky, scheming little bastards before they grow into embezzlers or extortionists."

The vicar pretended not to hear. "Of course, I cannot condone their methods, but their intentions were—"

"Their intentions were to feather their own nest! Well, my father will not succeed in backing me into a corner, and neither will three future felons—nor their conniving mother!"

3

"I will not marry you, madam, and that is final."

Sabina was sitting with her mending, an endless task with three small boys, when the madman barged into her wee parlor, shouting. She took a firmer grip on her scissors. It wasn't much of a weapon with which to defend her sleeping babies, but the raving Bedlamite was between her and the fireplace poker.

Molly, the young parlormaid, was twisting her apron in her hands and wailing, "He wouldn't stop, ma'am, no matter what I said about the late hour and you not receiving. And he wouldn't let me announce him proper, like you taught me. What should I do?"

By now Sabina'd had a better look at the intruder, and decided he was better-looking than ever. His shoulders were broader under his well-cut coat, and his blond hair was styled in a fashionable crop. His eyes were the same angelic blue, but now they had tiny lines around them. Well, so did hers. A person could not live a score and a half of years without gathering some tokens of passing time. Of course her lines were from laughter and his were from depraved dissipation. And Sabina couldn't care for the new, sardonic sneer to his lip as he surveyed her with equal intensity. Oh, how she wished she wasn't wearing such a faded frock and such a dowdy widow's cap—not that she had any better in her wardrobe. And she really should have replaced the worn draperies ages ago. Most of all she wished she wasn't wearing her locket. Perhaps he wouldn't notice, she hoped, and, while she was wishing, perhaps a great wind would swoop down and scoop him away. For whatever else Connor Hamilton was doing here, he was sure to disrupt her life.

"Ma'am? Had I ought to run to the castle and get help?"

"No, Molly. I don't think help will be coming from that direction. Nor heaven, I suppose," she added with a sigh.

The poor girl appeared confused, and Sabina couldn't blame her. She wondered if she was dreaming herself, or in the throes of some dire nightmare. "You may go to bed, Molly. I'll show our caller out."

Molly was uncertain about leaving her mistress alone with such a large, loud gentleman, until Connor tossed her a coin. "Go on, girl. I am not going to strangle your mistress, much as I might wish to."

"Should I be fetching the tea things, then, ma'am?"

Sabina had risen to her feet by now, to face him on his own level. Or to run. She took a step toward the door. "No, Viscount Royce will not be staying that long."

Molly's eyes widened. "Lord Royce? Him what's in all the London scandal columns? I'll be right outside the door, ma'am, iffen you should need me."

Sabina smothered the urge to smooth her hair or kick the boys' jackstraws under the sofa. And whatever made her think he'd be less formidable if she was standing up? He was casually leaning against the mantel; her knees were quaking. She'd forgotten how tall he was, that was all, Sabina told herself as she collapsed back into her chair. She would *not* invite him to sit. In fact, she refused to let herself be intimidated in her own home, certainly not by this...this loose screw.

"Very well, Con—Lord Royce. You have five minutes. What do you want?"

He crossed his arms over his broad chest and glared at her. "I want you to call off your brats. I don't know when you and my father grew as close as inkle-weavers, but the plot you two hatched won't wash, no matter how many crimes you encourage your hell-born babes to commit."

Brats? Hell-born babes? Her precious darlings? Sabina jumped to her feet, hands on hips. "Whatever wits you might once have had have obviously gone begging, Connor Hamilton. I've heard a life of debauchery can do that. As for your father and myself, why, we have not had one halfway polite conversation since you left nearly twelve years ago. He barely nodded to me at Squire's house last night. If we were on the least of speaking terms, he could have warned me that the prodigal son was returning."

"He didn't know. But someone did." He raised his voice even louder. "Someone arranged the whole thing."

"And you think it was I, or my sons?"

"There was a note."

"Good grief. I can barely get them to practice their penmanship! How dare you accuse my boys of...of plotting against you? I cannot even begin to imagine how you might have seen them."

The vicar had sworn Sabina was ignorant of the forged letter, and her indignation seemed genuine. Connor decided he'd have words with the iniquitous infants himself on the morrow. "I've seen enough of their handiwork to know they should be away at school instead of getting up to mischief."

"They are too young."

"They are too old to be tied to their mother's apron strings, especially the eldest. But like your father, you are keeping them around so you won't be alone. You'll make them into weak, puling cowards, afraid to leave your side, just as your father did to you."

He might say what he would about her, Sabina thought, but criticize her children? *Never!* "And you are mean and judgmental, just like *your* father. You dare come here to my own house to accuse my sons of heaven knows what, then declare they should be sent to some barbaric boarding school—and you don't even know them! You have become another Espinwall, a vile-tempered tyrant. And you shout just as loudly as the duke. If you wake my sons I shall skewer you with my darning needle."

"I am not shouting," he bellowed, causing the china shepherdess on the mantel to rattle only slightly. "And I am not like my father."

"No? It would be just like His Grace to appear, uninvited, at any house in Chipping Espy, and expect to be received. As though we lesser folk were not entitled to our privacy or our rest."

Connor shrugged. What else could he do, admit he was in the wrong? Hardly. "I did not come here to discuss the duke," he said stiffly. "Except that my father has the notion to see me wed. To you." A mouthful of lemons could not produce a more sour expression on Viscount Royce's face. "I came to tell you that it won't do. I will never marry you, Sabina Greene."

"You will not marry me? Well, I do not recall asking. And let me tell you, my high-and-mighty lordship, that I wouldn't have you if you begged on bended knee. Nay, if you came crawling through broken glass. What, should I take up with a rake, a libertine, a womanizer? A fine example a wastrel like you would be for my sons, if you weren't killed in some war or a duel. And what kind of father would you be to them? A clamorous, cantankerous clunch who'd chase them off, as yours did. Why you...you'd likely have little Benjy running away to be a cabin boy in the navy and I'd never see him again!" Sabina realized she was shredding one of Jasper's mended shirts in her hands, so she used it to dab at the tears that were streaming down her cheeks.

"You still look like a roasted pig when you cry," Connor told her, taking out a fine lawn handkerchief. "All pink and puffy. And your nose is shiny."

"I am not crying," she sniffed.

Connor raised one eyebrow, but did not comment as he gently blotted the moisture from her eyes. "You seem to have lost your freckles, anyway. What was it that finally did the trick? Lemon juice? Denmark lotion?"

"I merely stopped traipsing about the countryside without a bonnet. I am a mother now, a respectable matron, not a ramshackle miss."

Connor had loved her freckles, all one hundred and seventy-nine of them. And he'd loved the girl who raced at his side through meadows of flowers. He turned away so she wouldn't see his pain at the memories, and he wouldn't see her tears. Damn, he knew he shouldn't have come back. Eleven years, and he was still mesmerized by the little witch. Looking anywhere but at her, Connor inspected the sitting room. At first he'd seen only Sabina; now he noticed the pinchpenny parlor. His eyes took in the bare spots of the carpet, the chairs with more pillows than upholstery, the chipped vase holding a bedraggled sprig of ivy.

"You could have had a better life, Sabina."

Sabina took a deep breath, knowing they were to have an eleven-year-old argument, one she'd heard a million times in her head. "I could not leave my father, Connor, and you should not have asked me to. He was sickly; I was all he had."

"I wasn't asking you to leave forever, dash it, Sabina, only long enough to get to Gretna Green and back."

"You didn't ask me; you gave me an ultimatum. Either I flee with you to the border, or you'd go off without me. You could have waited."

"What for? An elopement was the only way. You know my father would never have given us permission to wed."

"He was right. I was far beneath you."

"I was willing to chance it. You were the coward who was unwilling to face society's censure."

"Society had nothing to do with it, Connor. That's your world, not mine."

"Your little society here in the countryside, then. You were quick enough to marry a man twice your age for the security of staying here."

"What was I to do? You left and never sent a word!"

"Thunderation, Sabina, I was with the army in Spain, fighting for my country. There was no way to—"

"You were there to spite your father, you nodcock."

"I had funds of my own to purchase my commission. I did not need his approval."

"The only heir to the Duke of Espinwall? They say Wellington demanded your resignation himself, when His Grace protested."

"I sold out when I was injured, damn it! And this isn't about me, Sabina, it's about your marrying that old man before I got back."

"Don't you understand? I would have been alone, with no way to live. When my father died, his pension would end. There was nothing put aside for me, not even a roof over my head. Before he passed on, Father begged me to wed Mr. Greene so I'd be cared for. I agreed so that he could die in peace."

"So now you're a widow, with no one to look after you."

"Married to you, I could have been a widow thrice a year, if that were possible, with the life you've led."

"Who's to say what path I would have chosen if you were with me? You cannot know that we would have been unhappy."

"Connor, we were children! You were an irresponsible, daredevil boy then, and what are you now? I've been raising my sons, at least. You've been raising Cain."

Viscount Royce was pacing now, with barely enough room for five long strides in any direction. "Your opinion of me is gratifying, Mrs. Greene, especially coming from one who has never been out of Chipping Espy."

"I do not need to travel to London to hear the gossip. Besides, if you weren't a here-and-thereian, a care-for-naught, you'd be in Chipping Espy yourself, looking after the people who depend on you."

"No one depends on me, madam, and that is the way it should be. The duke is not in the ground yet."

"But he is too cross and choleric to reassure his tenants. Why, you don't even understand how the people you've known all your life live in fear of him, and more fear of his passing. It's positively medleval, but the countryside depends on your family for its very life. What if the next duke brings in sheep, or raises the rents, or forbids fishing in his streams? What if he shuts down the racing stud and no more wealthy gentlemen come to purchase horses? What if he never resides at the castle at all, and the army of servants is dismissed? How will the village survive, Connor, and do you care?"

"Of course I care. That does not mean I need to be here holding the blacksmith's bellows and the pig farmer's pitchfork. Espinham has overseers, accountants, and land agents. No one has to worry."

Sabina shot him a look of pure disgust. "It is you who has no need to worry; your inheritance is secure. You can do whatever you like, go wherever you wish. The rest of us have no such luxury. Hired stewards have no loyalty to the land, Connor, or to the people."

"What would you have me do, then?" He'd already promised the duke to stay around, but he wanted to hear what Sabina had to say about his remaining in the vicinity.

"I'd have you be a son to your father. Help him manage the estate but, more important, assure the succession. That's what you were born to do, Viscount Royce, and I shouldn't be the one to have to remind you."

"You are not the first today, madam," he said through clenched jaws, heading toward the door. "But I shall not be forced into leg-shackles by any man, woman, or child, dying or otherwise. I suppose we shall continue to disagree about a son's duty to his parent. Or a daughter's to hers. Good night, Mrs. Greene. I am sorry to have disturbed your pleasant evening." He turned before leaving. "And I always liked your freckles."

4

The viscount stayed on, as he had promised his father. And he stayed away from Sabina Greene, as he had promised himself. He also stayed away from discussing any controversial topics, in deference to his father's health. If the duke mentioned marriage and Sabina again in the same breath, Connor feared it just might be Espinwall's last, and not because of that counterfeit cough the cad contrived for his son's edification now and again. By mutual, if tacit, agreement, they did not speak of politics, the viscount's way of life, the succession, or the duke's miraculous recovery. There were some very long silences at the castle. Thank goodness for horses, a subject dear to both men's hearts.

To fill the awkward moments, the duke took to inviting company to tea or dinner, for cards or conversation. He entertained the neighborhood's first families, and any nobility or gentry or gentleman farmers near enough to travel to Chipping Espy. His Grace even invited a few of the wealthier merchant class who had bought property in the area. They all had one thing in common—daughters of marriageable age. Thank goodness for horses, which enabled Connor to put as much distance between himself and the company as possible.

Contrary to most people's surmise, Viscount Royce was interested in good land management. He'd attended enough country house parties to accumulate farming techniques from every corner of the kingdom. He was knowledgeable and, now that his father seemed willing to turn over some of the reins, he was eager to bring modem improvements to Espinham. First, Connor had to survey the farms and fields. The more his father trotted young females past him, the more thorough his inspection. Returning from one of his long rides, he decided to while away another hour by scouting out a Yule log. Christmas was only a few weeks away now, and his father's old friend, the bishop, was to spend the holiday eve at the castle. The kitchens were already working overtime, and the housekeeping staff was recleaning spotless corners of unused rooms.

When he was a lad, bringing in the Yule log was a celebration in itself. Lighting the log in the castle's massive hearth was a tradition for the entire household, family, servants, and guests. They'd all gathered around as his father lit a sliver saved from last year's wood, then handed it to him to light the new. Everyone had toasted the prosperity of the house, the continuity of succeeding generations. Hell and tarnation, Connor cursed. Even his recollections were turning into nags. He spurred Conquistador along the path through the home woods, more interested in losing his memories than in finding a log to burn for the twelve days of Christmas.

Some kind of melee was going on in the clearing, he could hear. So Connor headed in that direction until he could see a group of boys, fighting. Now, he wasn't one to interfere in a good bout of fisticuffs nor a squabble among young hotheads, but this was different. Young Wilfred Snavely, who was nearly a man grown, had a much younger, slighter lad on the ground, and he was rubbing the other's nose in the dirt. Old Wilfred was shouting encouragement while he held off a still smaller boy who was kicking and clawing to go to his brother's aid. A third red-haired sprig, the smallest of the lot, was dangling by his coat collar from a protruding tree branch, screaming for all he was worth.

"You cost me da a day's pay," Young Wilfred was shouting as he pushed the boy's face deeper into the ground. "You rich boys what can do charity work for nothin'."

"That's right, son, make 'im pay!" Snavely called out, cuffing the boy in his hands across the cheek to shut him up. The littlest lad had ripped his coat to get down, and ran toward his fallen sibling, but Old Wilfred grabbed him by his shirt front this time.

"I say it stinks," Young Wilfred taunted. "An' you stink, Martin Greene. Fartin' Martin, that oughta be your name. Go on an' say it, or you can eat some more dirt." He raised the boy's head so he could speak, and Connor could see blood streaming from Martin's nose. The other two Greene boys were bellowing, and one managed to bite Old Wilfred's fingers that were holding his arm. Snavely cracked the two boys' heads together.

"Enough!" Connor shouted, leaping off his horse. He didn't see a scuffle. He didn't see bullies tormenting helpless infants. What he saw was Sabina's face. My God, he thought, her children are being hurt! He would have gone to the aid of any outnumbered, out-muscled soldiers, but these, these were Sabina's life. A tiny voice whispered inside that they could have been *his* boys, his own flesh and his own blood pouring onto the ground. "Enough, I said, you bastards." Snavely did not release the little boys quickly enough to suit Connor, so he planted the man a facer that would have made Gentleman Jackson take note. It made Snavely keel over backward. Then the viscount grabbed Young Wilfred by the scruff of his dirty neck, lifted him off Martin Greene and shook him until he could hear his teeth rattle. "If you or your miserable father ever lays one finger on any of these boys again—one finger, mind you!—I'll have you thrown off my land, arrested for trespassing, and transported. After I tear you to pieces. Is that understood?"

Young Wilfred nodded. The viscount was holding his neck too tightly for him to speak. The father was stirring, so Lord Royce called over, "Do you understand me, Snavely, or do I have to show you again?" He received a grunt in return. "Then get out of here before I change my mind, and take this offal with you." Connor shoved Junior toward a donkey cart that stood nearby, overloaded with wood. Snavely Senior staggered aboard, then snapped his whip at the poor ass and was gone.

Blast, Connor swore to himself, looking around the clearing at the tattered, battered boys. Now he supposed he'd have to take the miserable maggots home to their mother. And she was sure to blame him for not protecting her progeny on his property. Damn!

The oldest boy's nose was still streaming, and Connor thought his lip was split, too, but it was hard to tell through all the blood and mud. The viscount hoisted him onto Conquistador's saddle, where he could hold Martin's head back to stop the bleeding before

Sabina saw the lad. The other two boys mounted double on their pony. The middle boy, Jasper, he learned, was developing a magnificently colored black eye. The youngest, Benjamin, was delegated to steer the pony, since Jasper's spectacles were broken and he could barely see the mare's ears, much less the path home. Benjy was missing all four of his front teeth, which made his excited babble nigh unintelligible, so Connor couldn't tell if that was a recent loss or a previous condition. The infant's clothing hung about him in shreds, so Connor wrapped his own coat around him, before mounting his stallion and leading the little caravan home to their mother. He thought of taking the halflings to the castle first, to clean them up, but the sun was sinking and Sabina would worry if they were late. Besides, the castle was filled with simpering young females who were sure to swoon at the first sight of blood. With any luck, he could sneak them into Sabina's kitchen before she caught a glimpse of them.

As luck would have it, Sabina was in her kitchen, ironing, a task Lord Royce had never seen a well-born woman perform. As he'd predicted, the first words out of her mouth were, "My stars, what have you done to them?"

"Drawn and quartered the lot of them. What else do you expect from the ogre of Espinham?" he asked wryly as he half carried Martin to one of the worn chairs drawn around a battered oak table. The boy's nose had started bleeding again from the walk to the kitchen door. Connor tilted Martin's head back, over the chair rung. "Deuce take it, Sabina, he's had his cork drawn, is all. You've seen worse, so don't turn missish on me now."

By this time, all three boys were nattering at her with the news of the fight, how the viscount had rescued them and threatened to have the Snavelys transported, and how Martin got to ride the stallion, but the others were promised a turn, too.

"And his lordship is going to teach us how to defend ourselves."

"He has boxed with the Gentleman himself, Mama. Isn't that marvelous?"

"And the viscount says that if the other chap is already fighting dirty, it's all right to kick him in the—"

"Quiet!" Connor shouted over the din, winning instant silence in the small kitchen. "Your mother's head is already spinning. What we need is some hot water and clean cloths, not all this racket. Where is the maid?"

"She's gone to market," Sabina replied, clearing the table of her clean linens and reaching into the laundry basket for towels. She filled a kettle with water at the sink and went to put it on the stove. Without thinking—and without the protective cloth she'd been using—Sabina picked up the flatiron that was heating there, to make room for the kettle. She screamed, which had all the boys and Connor at her side. Benjamin started whimpering. "It's nothing, boys," she reassured them. "I'll be fine. I'll just put some lard on it."

"No!" Connor yelled. "What you want is cold water, not grease to sear the skin worse." He picked up the kettle and poured it over her burned hand, and over her floor and her clean sheets.

"Now see what you've done," she cried, pulling her hand from his clasp. "Let me tend to my boys first."

"Deuce take it woman, I've seen burns fester and turn to blood poisoning. This one is already blistering, by Zeus. That's a lot more serious than a bit of spilled claret. Now sit down, Sabina, before you fall down! I'll take care of the brats."

Before she could protest further, he shoved her into a chair, with her arm resting on a clean pillow slip. In short order, he had the two youngest boys running to fetch soap and salve, bandages and brandy. While the water was heating to mop up Martin, Connor found a glass and poured Sabina a drink. He poured himself one, too, swallowed it, and had another. "Gads, the war in Spain was nothing to this!"

Sabina watched, numb with shock, pain, and simple amazement, as London's premier rake tenderly dabbed at Martin's face and chin, until her son reappeared from the muck. "His nose doesn't appear broken," Connor reported, to her relief. The viscount had Benjy and Jasper lined up for inspection and repairs, then ordered them all into fresh clothes while he brewed the tea. He added a bit of brandy to the pot, too. "So they'll sleep better," he told her. "Otherwise the excitement would have them up all night, and they'll feel every bump and bruise. And you'll need your rest, too." When the boys returned and had their tea, and Connor felt fortified enough himself, he gingerly spread some ointment Sabina had over her hand. The whole palm was burned, with the flatiron's handle imprinted on her soft skin. "Damn," he cursed as she drew in a breath. "I'm so sorry, Sabina."

"Why should you be sorry for my own stupidity?"

"Do you mean there is some evil in this world I am not responsible for? I was beginning to wonder."

She smiled at him, and now he had to take a deep breath. "Let's get this bandaged, shall we?" he said, trying to ignore the warmth he felt spread through him from the touch of her warm skin, the contact of her knees brushing his as he worked on the burn. And Sabina wasn't indifferent either, for her cheeks were as red as her hair. Or perhaps that was merely the brandy. He cleared his throat. "You'll have to keep this bandaged until it heals, and you won't be able to use your hand much, you know. Will you be able to manage? I could send a maid or two from the—"

"Oh, no. Molly will be back shortly, and the boys are quite helpful, really."

"But, Mama, how are you going to play the church organ for Christmas?" one of the helpful lads asked. "The bishop is coming!"

5

"Oh, dear. Oh, dear." The vicar was predictably upset at the Greene boys' news that their mother would not be able to play the church organ. "And the bishop does so love a musical service. He has always sworn that music brings one closer to heaven. I was hoping to bring him closer to releasing the funds for our extension."

"What if we could find someone else to play the organ for you instead?" Jasper asked, peering at the cleric through one cracked lens.

The vicar looked at the middle boy, then winced at the lurid colors of his eye. Mr. Davenport had carefully avoided asking about the split lip, swollen nose, broken spectacles, and missing teeth: What he didn't know was better all around, he felt. "Another proficient performer in this town? Why, if you could find one, that would be more than a good deed, my lad. That would be a miracle."

"What if this organist wasn't a usual churchgoer, sir? Would that matter?"

"Such talent can only be a gift from God—that's what the bishop said. So I would welcome Beelzebub himself, if he could play the *Messiah.* But—"

"And it is all right for us to invite this person to come play for you?"

"Of course, of course, but there is no one, lad, no one at all. Perhaps the choir can be encouraged to sing louder." He waved them off, so despondent he forgot to give their homework assignments.

Once they were away from the manse, the other boys turned on Jasper. "Why did you say we'd find him an organist? We'll never, and then he'll make us do more good deeds."

"I know someone who can play," Jasper claimed. "Miss Viola Gaines."

Martin opened his cut lip again, laughing. "She can't play the church organ!"

"I heard her playing the pianoforte one day when Vicar kept you on after lessons."

"Is she as good as Mama?"

"Almost," Jasper answered loyally. "And she's almost as pretty."

"She smells almost as nice," Benjamin added. "I helped her get her cat out of a tree once, and she gave me a biscuit."

"She dresses better than Mama," Jasper said, and no one could contradict him. They all sighed, wishing they had some way to earn enough to buy their mother that length of velvet.

"But just because she can play the pianoforte doesn't mean she can play the organ," Martin reasoned.

"There's still ten days before Christmas Eve. Mama can teach her. She taught Georgina Marsden to play *Greensleeves*, and Georgie's just a dumb girl."

Martin was beginning to permit himself to be convinced. "But Miss Viola never goes to church. Why should she do it for us?"

"She'll do it if the vicar asks her special."

"I'm not writing any more letters," Martin announced. "Two jaw-me-dead lectures were enough. 'Sides, we made up Dr. Goodboy; copying the signature of a man of God has to be a sin."

"You don't have to write another letter, 'cause Mr. Davenport said we could invite her, plain and simple, he did. Only he didn't know her name."

"And if that doesn't work," Martin said eagerly, "we can get Benjy to cry. That always works with Mama." Benjy was way ahead of them. "And she and the vicar can get married! Then we'll have all our good deeds done!"

Even serious-minded Jasper had to laugh. "The vicar isn't going to marry Miss Viola, noddy! She's a Bird of Paradise. I heard Squire Marsden say so once."

"So what? Mr. Davenport is always going on about paradise, too, isn't he?"

*

While the boys were at their lessons, or so he supposed, Connor called at Sabina's cottage. He told himself it was just polite to see how she was going on, and to deliver in person the tin of soothing salve.

"You shouldn't have bothered your kitchen staff at a time like this," Sabina said when she answered his knock on her door. "They must be frantic with the Christmas preparations and the company coming."

"Actually, I didn't bother the cooks at all. I had my head groom mix up the stuff from a recipe I had in Spain. It won't smell as good as the kitchen's, but ought to help heal the burn faster."

After such a kind gesture, Sabina had to invite Connor in, as much as she wished to keep her distance. She gestured him to follow her to the little parlor, which was strewn with fabric, trims, sewing supplies, and a sheepskin.

"Dash it, Sabina, not using your hand would help more than any ointment. What the devil are you doing, anyway?"

She gathered some of the material into a pile to make room for him to sit. "It's the costumes for the children's Christmas pageant. I thought that, since we will not have organ music, perhaps I can improve on the Nativity."

"With your hand bandaged? I suppose you're still cooking and cleaning besides."

"Oh, no. Molly is doing everything. She's in the kitchen right now making gingerbread while the boys are away." She would not let on that the gingerbread was going to be almost the only Christmas delicacy for her sons. With new clothes to replace those damaged in the altercation and new spectacles for Jasper, her meager stock of coins would be nearly spent.

"Is she making gingerbread men?" Connor asked, his blue eyes lighting up. "With currant eyes?"

"Of course," Sabina said with a laugh, remembering how much he'd always loved the treat. "They'll be ready in an hour or so. You could come back then for a taste."

"Or I could wait here…?"

Sabina bit her lip, not knowing how to answer. The man was definitely not healthy for her equilibrium, but, oh, how sweetly he smiled at her now, flashing a well-remembered dimple in his right cheek. She nodded, then picked up some gold braid to pin on one of the Magis' robes. She was awkward in his presence, and the bandage didn't help. The pins kept falling.

"Why are you the one doing this?" the viscount demanded as he retrieved them from the floor at Sabina's feet, then took the fabric from her and proceeded to fasten the braid on, all higgledy-piggledy, but on. "Surely one of the other women in the congregation could help."

"Who? The village women are too busy with their cooking and cleaning and helping their husbands at work. The farm wives have animals and gardens to tend. And the vicar has no wife, Mrs. Marsden has the rheumatics in her fingers, and the castle has no lady bountiful to oversee the needs of the community. I at least have help with the chores."

This last, pointed reminder destroyed Connor's good humor and determination not to argue with her again. Besides, he was pricking himself with every pin he put in. "Thunderation, Sabina, do you have to take on the responsibility for the whole town now?"

"I find that more estimable than not taking responsibility for anything, even one's own actions, my lord. The life you've led…and you are pinning the trim to your coat sleeve."

"Blast!" He tossed the wretched mess aside. "I have a seamstress at the castle who does nothing all day that I can see. I shall send her down with a wagon this afternoon to pick up this whole jumble, and your instructions. And no argumentation for once, miss, if you please. Now let me see your hand. It would be just like you to put the medicine on an injured rabbit rather than use it for yourself."

He sat on the floor next to her chair and unwrapped the bandage. While he worked, he told her some of his plans for the castle and its holdings. He thought he might start a small hand-weaving guild, or a pottery to employ more local residents. And he'd see a dam built along the stream, so the workers' cottages wouldn't flood come spring. Sabina thought he ought to move the whole lot to higher ground and start anew, since some of the houses were no more than ramshackle huts. Soon they were talking like old times, passing comments back and forth, building on each other's ideas and opinions. If he could have wrapped a mummy in the time he spent rebandaging her hand, Sabina did not complain.

This was madness though, she told herself. He was bored in the country without his opera dancers and actresses, that was all. That was why he was spending time with his estate managers...and with her. Connor was flirting with her, she decided, trying to seduce her with his newfound respectability. Then he'd leave. He always did.

"Oh, I forgot," he was saying, reaching into his pocket. "I brought a pair of spectacles a guest left behind at the castle. I don't know if they'll do for Jasper until you can have another set made up, but these were going to waste."

Sabina smiled. "Between the boxing lessons and your offer to let the boys ride Espinham's cattle, they already think you are top of the trees. Pulling new spectacles out of thin air should convince them you can walk on water."

And their hearts would be broken when he left, too. "You...you won't disappoint them, will you?"

"What? Go back on my word? Such an accusation would be cause for a duel among gentlemen, by Jupiter. I have been waiting until their bruises are healed, is all. But, thunderation, do you really believe me to have so little honor as to lie to innocent children? I keep my promises, madam."

Except for the ones that hung between them: *I'll love you forever. I'll be back.*

Connor got up from the floor and strode to the mantel, where he stared at the framed miniature of Jessup Greene. "Did you love him, Sabina?"

Sabina could have taken umbrage at his familiarity, but she felt she owed him an honest answer. "I...I respected him. He was kind."

"Kind? Is that all you can say about the man who fathered your children?"

She shrugged. What more was there to say, except that Mr. Greene was not used to children, not used to women having thoughts, and not used to his steady, bachelor life being continuously disrupted. She'd always wondered what he thought would happen, taking a young wife. And she still resented his giving the trustees absolute control over her finances, as though she could not balance her bank accounts. "I did not know him well. He kept himself apart. But I was not unhappy," she quickly added. "And I had my sons. Other women fare much worse in their marriages of convenience."

"Yet you wore my locket."

Sabina's hands flew to her throat, where the locket usually rested on its chain. She'd removed it after Connor's first visit, hoping he hadn't recognized the only piece of jewelry she had on, other than her wedding ring. Silly notion, that. "I don't have much jewelry," she tried to explain. "Mr. Greene was a frugal man."

"So he was a nip-farthing besides a lecher. But to wear another man's token, Sabina?"

"He believed it had come from my mother. I saw no reason to disabuse him of the thought. And, very well, if you must know, I wore the locket to remind me of those other times. Days when I was neither caretaker for my father or for my children, nor a necessary inconvenience to my husband. I wore the locket to remind me that once, very briefly, I was loved for myself, and in love with the world. It was a magical time."

"Just like Christmas."

She ignored him. "And I took it off because I am not that girl anymore." And because she did not want him to think she'd been wearing the willow for him all these years. She'd never say that, though, so she told him, "I have a rich, full life, with people who love me and need me. That's enough."

But was it? she asked herself. Had it ever been enough? Could it ever be again, when he was gone? Sabina had no answers.

6

Viola Gaines almost burst her stays, laughing, when the little boys asked her to play the church organ. What a chuckle the girls back in London would have over this. But she wasn't back in the city; she was in a tiny, respectable town, and she was bored with her own company. Besides, Viola was used to being the center of attraction, not being treated as if she had the pox. What she had was the lease to this cottage from her last protector, and no desire to go back to her old way of life. So why shouldn't she perform at Christmas, especially if that prim and proper young Widow Greene was sending her boys over to second the vicar's invite? Miss Gaines had played for merchant princes and members of Parliament. What was a bishop or two? Viola was fairly confident she could master the pipe organ, too.

Viola did not need a great deal of convincing. Neither did the vicar—he needed smelling salts. Oh, dear.

When Mr. Davenport found his breath again to speak, he addressed the three red-haired imps grinning up at him, instead of the woman by the door. "What trouble have you wretched children gotten into now?"

"Remember how you said you'd welcome Beelzebub himself if he'd play the organ?" Jasper asked. "We couldn't get the devil, but we did get Miss Viola."

The next worst thing to the vicar's thinking. "Oh, my. Can she play?"

"Like an angel," Martin told him. "Like the one you sent us to find."

"Like an angel in Paradise," Benjy chirped. "It's a miracle, isn't it?"

'Twould be a miracle if lightning didn't strike the little church during Christmas Eve services. And bring the rotting roof right down on the bishop's bald head.

*

With two good deeds accomplished, the boys were stymied. They couldn't think of anyone else who needed their help, and Christmas was coming. Bad enough their mother was injured; her holiday would be ruined beyond hope if the vicar told her about the broken window. She'd feel obliged to pay for the replacement, and the trustees would never deem that a necessary expense, the old nipcheeses. Heaven only knew where she'd get the money.

"Maybe we could teach Chocolate to count like that horse at the fair last summer." Benjy was taking his turn riding the old pony while his brothers walked alongside. They were on their way to Espinham Forest to finish gathering the deadwood for the poor. "Everyone paid tuppence to see him add."

"We can hardly teach you to count, gudgeon. How are we going to teach Chocolate?"

"The viscount is richer'n Golden Ball," Jasper pointed out. "I heard Molly telling the egg man."

"So? We can't ask him to lend us the money, 'cause we couldn't pay him back. That's not honorable."

They each got to thinking on the rest of the walk, about good deeds, good incomes, and their good-as-gold mother. No one wanted to be the first to voice the obvious connection, for fear the others would only laugh.

There was no laughter when they reached the meadow, where Wilfred Snavely was supposed to have his donkey cart ready for loading. Wilfred and his son were there, and the cart, but the donkey had fallen over, dead. Old Wilfred and Young Wilfred were cursing and shouting at the beast, cracking the whip over her head, but she was beyond caring. The Snavelys cared, for they'd have to pull the cart all the way back to the village themselves. And the donkey foal, nuzzling its dead mother, cared. The baby donkey was braying for all it was worth, trying to waken its mother. Young

Wilfred kicked out at the thigh-high creature, which ran, still shrilling its distress, into the woods.

"Good riddance to it," the elder Snavely snarled. "Damned noisy nuisance'll be no use to me for over a year, eating its ugly head off at my expense. Bad enough I'll have to come back with the cart and a winch to haul the mother off. I ain't feeding and cleaning up after some useless creature. I already got my boy for that." He cuffed his son on the ear and laughed.

"You mean you're just going to leave the baby out here alone?" Martin wanted to know.

"At night?" Benjy asked, jumping off Chocolate. "In the dark?"

"With nothing to eat or drink?" Jasper peered into the woods.

Snavely eyed Chocolate, and the empty traces of his laden cart. He calculated the odds of the viscount killing him if he took the boys' pony, then shook his head. It was a sure bet. "Makes no difference. The beastie'll be dead by morning anyway less'n it learns to eat grass quick-like. Ain't weaned yet, and I ain't wet-nursing no ass."

Jasper said, "We'll take him, Mr. Snavely."

Both of his brothers turned to him. "We will?"

"We can't just let him die, can we?"

Benjy shook his head. So did Martin, after a momentary hesitation. "We'll take him home with us, then. Mama will know what to do for him."

"If not, Viscount Royce is sure to. He knows everything about horses, and donkeys can't be all that different."

"Hold on, Carrot-top. Afore you go making plans for the spawn, what are you going to give me for it?"

Martin tried to be reasonable. "Why should we pay you for something you were throwing away? If you wanted the baby, you'd put it in the cart and take it home with you."

"'Sides, you said it was going to die," Jasper added.

Snavely scratched his armpit. "But the little bugger just might surprise us all and learn to eat grass and stuff. It's mine till it dies or I say different, understand? So how about we makes us a bargain, eh? How about if I trade you the asslet for use of your pony there? It'll just be for a few days so I can deliver the wood for the reverend, and get the jenny out of here. His Grace won't like no dead animal littering his property."

Benjy started sniffling, and Jasper said, "He'll never give Chocolate back, I know it."

Martin eyed the heavily loaded wagon, the whip in Snavely's dirty hand, and the dead donkey. "No, sir. We can't let you have Chocolate, even for a day. Our Mama wouldn't let us, even if we wanted to. But we can find the viscount and tell him how you beat your poor donkey to death and left its baby in his woods. He was calling on us this afternoon, wasn't he, Jas?"

"Viscount Royce said he was bringing Mama some medicine. They're old friends, don't you know, Mama and Viscount Royce," Jasper contributed, deciding it couldn't hurt to invoke their powerful protector's name a few times.

"The jenny died of old age, and don't you go spreading no tales, hear? And the viscount's too busy to get himself in a swivet over no orphan ass, so we'll leave him out of this. Iffen you won't lend your pony, I figure I'll have Young Wilfred go put the spat out of its misery. You got the axe there, son?"

"We've got some money. You can have all we've got," Martin offered in a rush.

Snavely rubbed his chin. "Well, that's more like. You brats cost me' some wages, so it's only right you hand over some blunt. How much've you got?"

The boys did not have enough for a church window, and not enough for a dress length, but it seemed they had just the right amount for a useless, dying baby ass. Snavely took all of the boys' coins, along with Jasper's pocketknife and Martin's handkerchief, which was of finer fabric than any he owned. And if you held the thing upside down, the embroidered *M* could be a *W* for Wilfred.

"Better'n nothing, I guess," he said. "Enjoy your purchase, brats, while you can." He gestured to his son to hoist the wagon pole, and they started off, leaving three pale-faced boys in the meadow, with no coins, and no little donkey, either.

The boys dove into the woods where they'd seen the baby run. Jasper tripped over a protruding root and landed in a mud puddle. Benjamin thought he'd climb a tree to get a better view, and tore his pants. Martin listened quietly till he heard the baby's whickers, then he located the beastie where it was all tangled in briers, panting. He took off his jacket, remembering Mama's laments over their clothes, and pushed through the prickers to free the infant. His shirt, of course, was torn to shreds, but he got the donkey. The small creature was shivering, so he wrapped his jacket around it and tugged it back to the clearing.

Chocolate took offense at the baby's nuzzling attempt to find milk, and was not having any hoofed creature ride on her back, either. The baby was too heavy for the boys to carry, and protested too much anyway, so all three removed their belts, cinched them together to make a collar and lead, and half carried, half dragged the donkey along the path toward home.

With such slow going, they had time to reflect on their new acquisition.

"Do you think this counts as a good deed?" Jasper wanted to know.

"We couldn't let them kill him!" Benjy wailed.

Having looked beneath the donkey, Martin reported that Baby, as they were calling the donkey to encourage it along the trail, was a girl. "And the reverend always said we are all God's creatures, big and small."

The three boys looked at the sorry specimen, all big ears and sad brown eyes and skinny legs.

"God must have been getting tired by the day He created donkeys," Jasper pronounced. "But I suppose we just helped the Lord out a little, right, Martin?"

"Right. Now all we have to do is keep Baby alive." Benjy's toothless grin faded. "Mama will know how."

Which reminded the others of the further consequence of Baby's purchase. "Now we'll never be able to buy Mama the velvet for Christmas."

Jasper sighed and expressed the thought none of them had wanted to put into words, for fear of jinxing the wondrous notion: "And the viscount is used to fancy ladies in satin and lace. That's what Molly said." They glumly marched on. Then Benjy asked, "Do you think he'll take up with Miss Viola?"

Martin squared his shoulders. "If he does, then he's not the man for Mama anyway."

They put Chocolate in her stall next to their mother's gelding, and tried to get the donkey to take some water. Soon they were all sopping wet. They gave up and sent Benjy to sneak the trim from the wreath Sabina had placed on the front gate. In a few minutes they all trooped in to the little parlor, three bedraggled, dripping boys and one ribbon-bedecked, dazed, and half-dead donkey.

"Here, Mama. Look what we bought you for Christmas. Her name is Velvet."

7

Sabina used to wish her husband's cottage wasn't so isolated, being nearer to the castle than the village. That evening she was relieved no neighbors were kept up long into the night the way she was, listening to the new arrival's complaints. Her own babies hadn't set up such a racket. They hadn't cried *ee-aw* either.

She'd done what she could for the poor thing, mixing up some mash and trying to teach Velvet to eat from a dish. More of the concoction was on her, Sabina knew, than in the donkey. Then, with the boys' help, she'd made a warm nest of straw in the corner of the little stable, with bales of hay to keep the creature penned. She'd tried barricading their old hound, Beau, in with Velvet, but after licking up the spilled mash, Beau headed back to his warm blanket next to the kitchen stove. Sabina couldn't blame him; she felt too old for this, too.

Now she lay awake, wondering how she was going to feed this new mouth—and clean up after it. In a few years, she supposed, she might teach Velvet to pull her light rig, so the boys could ride her gelding. Martin was ready for a full-size horse now, and Jasper would be by then. They should each have their own mount, she believed, angry all over again at the miserly trustees and her dead husband for not deeming her capable of knowing what was best for their sons. Connor Hamilton would never make his children share one old pony. Whatever else his faults, he was generous and kind, offering to take her sons skating as soon as the pond froze over, if he was still here. He remembered that childhood should be fun. He'd likely spoil his progeny dreadfully, Sabina thought, especially if he had a little girl, a dainty little charmer with dimples—and red hair.

Now that kind of thinking would never do, Sabina told herself. The donkey's plaintive braying was bad enough without her own maudlin musings. Then she realized that the noise from the barn had stopped. Velvet had exhausted herself, finally. Unless she was too weak to cry anymore. Perhaps she was sick, or worse. Good heavens, the boys would be distraught. Sabina put on her heavy robe, then her cloak over that. She pulled on her boots, awkwardly wrapped a scarf over her head with her bandaged hand, and lit the lantern by the kitchen door. She had no idea what she could do if the little jenny was expiring, nor what she could tell the boys. If ever there was a time she wished for another to share the burdens of life, this was it. Someone who knew about horses and such, and wouldn't mind leaving a warm bed to go traipsing across the yard in frigid December temperatures. Instead, old Beau wasn't even around to accompany her on the dire mission.

Sabina hurried to the barn as fast as she could without jeopardizing the lantern's light. She pushed open the door, dreading what she might find, and held the light aloft, so she could inspect the makeshift enclosure. She couldn't even see the donkey, surrounded as Velvet was by three sleeping boys, two barn cats, and one comfort-seeking hound. Her sons were tumbled together in the straw with quilts from their beds and, yes, that was her old shawl that she saved for cleaning stalls. She straightened the covers as best she could, feeling her throat tighten at the sight of her beautiful, big-hearted boys. They were perfect, no matter what anyone in the village said, or what certain toplofty aristocrats accused them of. She wouldn't change a hair on their red heads.

Beau lifted his muzzle from the pile of arms, legs, and donkey, then went back to snoring. All was right with the world.

*

Some women could stay up all night, worrying over donkeys and bank deposits, and still look beautiful in the morning. Sabina was not one of them. She looked haggard, in fact, with her complexion as dull and gray as the faded, shapeless gown she wore. A limp cap covered every inch of the red hair that would have enlivened her appearance, but she hadn't had the energy to brush it out and pin it up on her aching head. Her hand was paining her, and Benjamin was covered with a rash from the straw. At least she hoped it was a rash and not flea bites from the barn cats.

Since she did not have to work on the pageant costumes, Sabina had taken up her mending again this morning, trying to see what she could salvage of her sons' adventures yesterday. Not much. At this rate, they'd be running around like half-naked savages by spring. At least the weather would be warmer. Sabina moved her chair closer to the fire and huddled into her shawl, hoping she wasn't sickening for something. Who would look after the boys then, or the baby jenny? Her thoughts were as dismal as her dress.

Altogether, she was not pleased to see Viscount Royce that next morning. He was looking bang up to the mark, as Martin would say, with his Hessians shining brighter than any surface in her house. Not a dog hair clung to his burgundy coat, not a scratch or worn spot marred his buckskin breeches. Well, she thought, ten minutes here, and Connor would be embarrassed to be seen at his clubs, since that was about how long clean clothes seemed to last in her household.

Connor's first words were not what a female wanted to hear from an attractive, affluent, aristocratic gentleman. "Gads, you look like last week's laundry. What has you so blue-deviled?"

"The ass," she snapped back.

"Snavely? Is that bounder bothering you or the boys again? I warned the makebait that I'd toss him off the property next time. I hadn't wanted to evict him yet, because his wife seems a decent sort."

"No, Wilfred is not bothering me. It's Velvet, my ass."

She couldn't be saying what Connor thought he was hearing — or thinking. "Excuse me?"

"I own a donkey, you gudgeon. Her name is Velvet, and my sons gave her to me for Christmas."

He tried to hide his smile since she seemed so moped about it. "Odd, I always gave my mother a box of comfits."

"I don't like comfits," she said, lest he think poorly of the boys' choice.

"But you do like donkeys? I'll make a note of that for my Christmas list."

"Oh, stop teasing, do. They meant well."

Connor inspected his sleeve for lint. "I do believe I have heard that phrase before, in reference to the threesome. More harm has been done in the name of good intentions than Satan himself could imagine."

"So you are still blaming my sons for your arrival at Espinham? You are not faring so poorly, that I can see. You and the duke must be rubbing along well together, else you would have left days ago, once you saw he was not truly ailing."

"We manage. His Grace and I play games. Chess, backgammon, and pretend. He pretends all the silly young chits he invites to the castle are not there for my inspection. I pretend he is not an interfering old matchmaker."

"Then your coming was not such a bad thing, after all."

"I haven't decided yet." He didn't want to talk about it, either. "Tell me about the ass."

Sabina frowned. "She's an orphaned infant that won't eat properly and cries all night. She might have colic for all I know. I understand babies, not big-eared beasts!"

"I'll take it up to the castle, then. There's bound to be a mare in milk. Some will let another foal suckle. My grooms can stay up with it, otherwise. I don't know much about asses myself." He couldn't help grinning.

"No, I want to keep her here. The boys would be heartbroken, and they'd think I didn't like their gift."

"Then I'll send someone down to see what's needed."

"I cannot be so deeply in your debt. You have already done enough for us, Connor—my lord. Why, having Sophia Townsend to sew the costumes was a godsend. She's at the vicar's right now, taking measurements for new choir robes. It seems she always wanted to help, but could not feel comfortable offering her services whilst in your father's employ."

"She should have asked. Father would have let her—" He paused at her raised eyebrows. "Well, perhaps not. Still, he is mellowing, which is one of the other reasons for my call. I have actually come to beg a favor of you, so you need not feel indebted at all if I provide assistance with the donkey. Tit for tat, don't you know."

"What is the favor? If it involves the duke, I am not in good odor with him, you know. He always blamed me for your leaving, and has taken his ire out on my boys. I believe he referred to my sons as mannerless mongrels the last time we spoke."

"And you called him a stiff-rumped old stick. Yes, I've heard. But calling on you for aid was his idea. The thing is, he wishes to reinstate the old Christmas festivities at the castle, in honor of the bishop's visit. Remember how the Great Hall was thrown open to all the villagers and tenants and everyone else for miles around, with feasting and dancing? His Grace is afraid this will be his last Christmas, and wants to see it done up right."

"Nonsense, he wants to show his son off to the countryside, is all. He just won't admit it."

Connor laughed. "Either way, he's put me in charge. The problem is, I'm no hand at decorating and such, and no one at the castle remembers how it should be. The housekeeper is new since the last grand celebration, before my mother moved to Bath for her health."

"She moved to Bath to avoid His Grace, and everyone knows it."

He shrugged. "Theirs was an arranged marriage. Her Grace felt she'd done her duty by producing the heir. Of course, no one else would dare to mention the family's dirty linen, Sabina. I cannot tell you how refreshing it is to find a woman who speaks her mind, after the simpering debs my father keeps finding. But to return to my difficulty, the attics must be filled with all the old ornaments and stuff, but I have no idea where to begin. I am begging you to come help."

Sabina remembered how the hall was festooned with ribbons, and candles lit every corner. Tables had been spread along one wall, piled high with food, and there was still room for anyone who wanted to dance. She and Connor had watched many a fete from the minstrels' gallery before they were old enough to join the company. The servants had smuggled cakes and punch to them. Such sweet memories…

"You'll be staying, though?" she asked. "You don't mean I should decorate the castle so you can go back to London?"

"No, I am staying, through Twelfth Night, at least. After that, who knows? There are two factors that need to be decided. It's too soon to tell. For now, I want to stay to see how the duke goes on, and the party will give me a chance to meet the rest of the tenants and local gentry. I'm sure that was His Grace's plan, but how can I deny him when he claims to be hearing Gabriel's trumpet?"

"Shall you mind?' Sabina wanted to know.

"Mind? I've always loved the country. But Espinwall never let me *do* anything, not even hold an opinion of my own. Do you know that the first time I defeated His Grace at chess last week, and he complimented me on a good game, that was the first bit of praise I have ever heard from his lips? I was as useless here as the arrow slits on the castle turrets. That was one of the reasons I had to leave then, to find something to do with my life. I had thought the army might be it. Now I discover I am busy every moment with some estate matter or other, and I am enjoying it. Which is not to say that I would be content to spend every last one of my days immured in the countryside."

"Of course not. A gentleman cannot be without his tailor for long."

He flashed the dimple at her. "Must be à la mode for the milch cows, don't you know. Seriously, though, even if I do not stay year round, I won't be gone entirely again. I see nothing wrong with enjoying the theater, the galleries, and one's friends betwixt the beets and beef. Have you ever considered visiting the city?"

The opera, the shops, the book-lenders! She'd considered it many times, in her dreams. Sabina sighed. "London has always sounded marvelous, and the boys would be in alt to see Astley's Amphitheater and the Tower Menagerie, but can you imagine loosing my sons on the streets there? Why, I'd never have a moment's peace, worrying that they'd be kidnapped...or arrested."

"But if they had a competent tutor?"

"Ah, then London would be a delight. And educational, too. But if wishes were horses, my lord, I wouldn't have a baby donkey in my barn."

8

Sabina could not spend the necessary hours at the castle if it meant leaving her sons unsupervised. So the viscount had to do some hard bargaining.

Having heard about Snavely's dastardly extortion of their Christmas money, Connor offered the Greene boys a fair wage if they would come to the castle with their mother and assist her in decorating. They'd also have to help him gather the branches and such she'd want, and climb trees after the mistletoe required for the kissing boughs. In addition, they just might be drafted to help exercise the horses if the stable grooms were too busy to ride. In return, he promised them enough blunt to purchase the velvet for their mother's dress.

"And if you stick close by me, so I am never left alone with any of the young misses, I'll even get Sophia Townsend to sew the dress, so it will be a real surprise. Your mother might be too busy, and her hand is still bandaged. That way she'll have her new velvet gown to wear for the party."

"Red?" Benjy wanted to be sure. "It's got to be red."

With Sabina's hair? She'd look like a forest fire—or a wanton. "I'll try, but the shops just might be out of red, what with the holidays and all. How would you feel about a nice dark green, to match her eyes?" Martin and Jasper allowed how their mother would look beautiful in anything. Benjy wasn't so easy to convince, until his older brothers kicked him. "The viscount knows all about ladies' clothes," they whispered. "You heard Molly."

So they solemnly shook hands all around. "But, my lord," Martin felt compelled to tell Connor, "we would have helped for nothing, you know."

"I know, lad. And I would have bought the dress for your mother whether you helped or not, so we are even."

*

Sabina worked feverishly to transform the Great Hall from a great barracks to a grand ballroom. She also worked hard to keep her darlings out of mischief, which meant out of the duke's way. They wanted to play with the ancient weapons on the walls, slide down the banisters, try all the antique instruments. Coming to the castle was a mistake, she began to realize. Then the viscount came to help. He was all thumbs at braiding swags of pine boughs, but he was a marvel at entertaining small boys. He took them with him to fetch the mistletoe and the Yule log, to deliver hampers of foodstuffs to his tenants, to visit the stables and the kennels and the dovecotes. This was the best holiday her sons had ever had, and it wasn't even Christmas yet. What a good father Connor would make—to some other woman's children. Coming to the castle was a dreadful mistake.

But the place was beginning to take on a festive appearance. They'd found filigree candleholders and gilded pinecones in the attics, along with boxes of bows and bells and blown-glass icicles. Sabina found places for everything, as well as the forest of greenery Connor and the boys brought in for her to wrap around newel posts and knights in their dented armor. Soon each old warrior had a wreath around his neck, or a clove-studded orange skewered on his sword, or a red ribbon on his arm, like a lady's favor. The duke grumbled about the sacrilege to his ancestors' memories, but also reminded Sabina that at least four kissing boughs were needed.

"Four, Your Grace?"

"Aye, to ensure I get to kiss all the pretty ladies without having to walk too far."

So Sabina made four balls of twined vines and ribbons, with clusters of mistletoe hanging from each. The enormous chandelier was lowered so she could hang garlands of holly and ivy, with red and green and gold silk streamers trailing to the edges of the vast chamber. Between times, she looked over the menus with the chef, inspected the silver serving pieces with the butler, and assigned guest rooms with the housekeeper. All the servants were deferring to her opinion, and even the duke allowed as to how the place was beginning to look like Christmas the way he remembered it.

Sabina left the castle—in the viscount's carriage—only to rehearse the village children for the pageant. Then she went home to her cottage that was looking tinier and shabbier every day, by comparison, and fell into her bed without ever hanging one ribbon or sprig of holly in her own parlor. Ah well, she thought in the instant before falling asleep, the boys will have enough of Christmas at the castle. What more could they ask?

"What are you going to wish for on Christmas Eve, Martin?" Jasper inquired of his brother as they were making paper chains to decorate the little barn for Chocolate, Velvet, and her new foster mother, a placid bay mare. "A horse of your own?"

Martin knew that was an impossibility. As the eldest, he was more aware of their straitened circumstances. Besides, now that they could ride the viscount's cattle sometimes, having a horse of one's very own wasn't quite as important. Or so he told himself. "I suppose I'll wish for a book. That way I won't be disappointed. Mama always buys us books for Christmas. Then I can tell her my wish came true."

Jasper nodded. Their mother was working so hard, helping the duke get ready for his party, that she'd have no time to buy them toys, even if she could afford them. But Viscount Royce had given them the run of his old nursery, so they had tops and darts and balls aplenty, for once. "I s'pose I'll wish for new mittens, then. I saw her knitting them last month."

Perhaps Benjy was too young to understand nobility and sacrifice. Perhaps he was simply more honest, or more hopeful. "I'm going to wish for a castle!" he announced.

"Don't be a cake, Benjy. You might as well wish for a piece of the moon. You might get it sooner than a castle of your own."

"I didn't say it had to be my own, did I? I want the duke's castle. I want us to live there, forever."

"Maybe if we all wish for the same thing…"

*

Everything was as ready as it was going to be. The castle looked like an enchanted kingdom, waiting for a fairy princess. And Sabina almost felt like the eldritch being in her green velvet dress. The boys proudly presented it to her on the afternoon of Christmas Eve so she could wear it to church, and then to the duke's party. The gown was simple in style, with long sleeves and a slim skirt that fell from a fashionably high waist. But there was nothing simple about the fit, or the neckline. No little boy had selected this dress, she knew. It was the work of a man, a connoisseur of women.

Sabina felt indecently exposed. Decadent, in fact—deliciously so. Never had she worn so daring a décolletage. Never had she had more of her out of a dress than in it. Never had she felt more beautiful, more womanly. She spent almost an hour with her hair, gathering most of it onto her head with a coronet of ivy, but leaving a few long tendrils to trail down her nearly bare shoulders, against her pale skin. And she wore her locket. The gown needed some ornamentation, Sabina told herself, to distract the eye from the obvious evidence that she'd nursed three infants. She'd have her cloak over it anyway, during church at least. But she wouldn't feel like a country dowd later, at the castle, among Lord Royce's elegant friends. She'd feel almost...seductive, she thought, her hand rubbing against the soft nap, as if she'd dressed to please a man. Which she hadn't, of course. Furthermore, those were not proper thoughts for a widowed lady on her way to church for this holiest of times. She was a mother, for heaven's sake, not in the muslin-company. If she needed any reminder of her place, Sabina was brought back from her daydreams by Jasper's announcement that he was feeling poorly. He was anxious about his part in the play, and Lord only knew what they'd been feeding him at the duke's kitchens. Marzipan pigs for luncheon, most likely. "Mama, I am going to be sick."

"Not in the duke's carriage, you won't," she firmly ordered. "Not on my new gown."

The Espinham carriage was coming to fetch the entire Green ménage to church, then carry them on to the castle, where they were to spend the night. That way the boys could enjoy more of the festivities, and Sabina could stay till the end of the party, in case there was a problem with provisions or proceedings. Of course the duke's household had managed very well without her all these years. Sabina was certain the competent staff was well enough trained to cope with any difficulty. They'd been managing the irascible duke for years, hadn't they? Still, they seemed to be counting on her.

She was counting on seeing Connor's blue eyes light up when he saw her in, and partly out of, her new gown later, when they reached the castle and she removed her cloak. Then she'd see if her secret Christmas wish had any chance of coming true. No, she told herself, almost as firmly as she'd commanded Jasper not to be sick—she would limit her wish to one dance, one dance with him to remind her of the girl she once was, and how it had felt to be cherished. That ought to be enough for the long winter, without chasing after moonbeams.

The enormous coach, with the Hamilton family coat of arms emblazoned on the side panels, brought them to the church early, by design. Sabina and Molly joined with Sophia Townsend, the seamstress, to help the village children into their costumes, smooth ragged nerves, and repeat forgotten lines.

Then it was time for Sabina to take her seat in the church, as nervous as Jasper over the coming performance. The little chapel was so crowded with townspeople and farmers filling every pew and aisle that the rear doors had to be propped open, so those left outside could hear the service. Surely, the bishop would be impressed that Chipping Espy needed a new church. Mrs. Marsden slid closer to her husband, making a space for Sabina in the second row. The only other empty seats were in the first row, the Duke of Espinwall's family pew. All Sabina could see in front of her were two broad backs in midnight superfine. The bishop was seated at the altar, looking out of place in his fine robes. Sabina prayed for the vicar's sake that he approved their service.

The children's Nativity pageant went first, so the children did not have to wait on tenterhooks through the sermon and hymns. Martin walked in from the rear door first, moved to the lectern, and began to tell the story of the infant's birth. Sabina felt tears well in her eyes.

Next came Joseph and Mary, riding her ass into Bethlehem. Mary, Georginia Marsden with a pillow-stuffed stomach, was having a fit of the giggles because redheaded Joseph's spectacles kept sliding down his nose. And she wasn't actually riding the ass, either. Jasper was tugging on Velvet's lead, begging the little donkey to come along and stop embarrassing them all, between muttered threats to squire's youngest daughter. An angel, one of the tenants' girls, recited a short verse and danced across the altar with her paper star, urging everyone to come worship the newborn babe. The shepherd followed the star. Benjy led poor, patient Beau with a sheepskin tied around his neck up to the makeshift manger. The hound threw himself down on a bale of hay with an exhausted sigh and began snoring; Luckily, everyone was watching the three kings with their gilt-trimmed robes and crowns march in, their hands filled with gifts. Even Young Wilfred Snavely remembered to lay his chest at the foot of the manger. He'd refused to be an ox again this year.

When all the children, innkeeper, animals and angels, were present, they stood together to sing "Gather ye, Shepherds, Gather ye, Kings." Surely, Sabina thought, heaven was a little closer to all of them this evening, as the pure, sweet voices rejoiced.

While the children were singing, Mary was supposed to reach behind her and put the hidden infant Jesus in the hay-filled manger. But the manger was already occupied. Velvet had climbed into the soft crib and was half asleep there. Georgina was about to bash the little donkey over the head with her doll, while everyone, even the bishop, laughed. Jasper took the doll away and tucked it next to

Velvet in the creche. Martin improvised: "And the donkey made a pillow for the infant."

Sabina was weeping during the last children's hymn, and could barely see the handkerchief Connor handed over the back of the pew to her. Then the children all scurried to seats on the floor or on parents' laps, and it was time for Vicar Davenport's reading and sermon. He said all the right words, Sabina was certain, but she couldn't concentrate on the message. Was everything as it should be at the castle? Would the duke approve her efforts? Was her gown too coming? Perhaps she ought to change when they dropped Beau and Velvet back at the cottage.

Sabina wasn't the only member of the congregation paying scant attention. Benjy had his head in her lap, and Squire Marsden was sliding farther and farther down his seat, while his wife poked him awake. Even the bishop seemed to be nodding off. At last it was time for the choir, with their familiar hymns and traditional carols. The entire congregation joined in. This was the real Christmas, Sabina thought, wrapping Benjy in her cloak and smoothing back Jasper's hair, then touching Martin's cheek—not the food and gifts and decorations.

9

As soon as the last note of the last hymn was sung, the organ sounded. All eyes turned to Mrs. Greene. Yes, Sabina was still in the second row, her hand bandaged. Then who…? They all craned their necks to look into the organ recess, where exquisite music was being created that no one was listening to.

"By George, it's the Gaines woman," Squire exclaimed, slapping his knee. "In church. Ain't that a rare 'un!"

Such a performance was rare, indeed. Miss Viola Gaines was playing to perfection, and she knew it. She knew they were all whispering about her, and smiled over her shoulder at the congregation while her fingers found the correct keys.

Miss Viola's improbably blond hair was braided atop her head to resemble a halo, with enough feather plumes stuck in it to waft a small angel to heaven. Her gown was decorous, thank goodness, Sabina thought, not as daringly cut as her own and in the same dark plum-colored fabric as the choir's new robes. The woman sincerely seemed to be enjoying herself and the music. Sabina closed her eyes to enjoy the masterful performance, too.

"'Tain't right, I says," a voice from the rear of the church called out, "one such as her playing in our church on Christmas Eve. Sacrilege, that's what it is." Other whispers could be heard, along with foot shuffling. Reverend Davenport mopped at the sweat pouring down his forehead, and it was still cold in the chapel. Some of his congregants were gathering their children and their hymnals, preparing to leave. "This is Christmas, time of forgiveness," he reminded them, shouting to be heard over the continuing organ music, "as the Lord forgave us."

Still there were mutters, and one starched-up matron did leave.

"Such talent is a gift from God," the vicar called out, but he was losing them, he knew, and his hopes for a bigger church.

Then Sabina stood up. "Mama, you can't leave!" wailed Jasper.

"No, darling," she said, tucking her cloak more firmly around Benjy, asleep on the bench. "I am only going to help turn Miss Gaines's pages for her." Sabina forgot that her new gown—and her bosom—would now be exposed to all eyes. She remembered when she heard Connor's indrawn breath as she passed in front of him on her way to the organ niche, and when she heard Wilfred Snavely shout out, "And there's another of the straw sisterhood. I don't want my wife being exposed to such blasphemy. If you won't throw 'em out, Vicar, I'll be leaving. Come on, Mavis."

The duke got up, too, and shook his head. "The man's a maggot, but he's right. Can't have Chatworth's castoff playing the organ in church. And the Greene gel will be tarred with the same brush. Too bad, but that's the way of it. Come along then, Royce." As usual, he spoke loudly enough that most of the assembly could hear him over the organ.

The viscount stood, and Sabina held her breath, but Connor put his strong hand on his father's shoulder and pushed him back to his seat. "Sit, Father," he said. "We are staying. Or are you so righteous that you cannot bend a little on Christmas Eve?" The duke knew what his stubbornness had cost him in the past; he saw what he could lose in the future. He sat.

Connor turned to face the congregation. "Let him without sin cast the first stone," he told them, "and that goes doubly for you, Snavely. One more insult to either of these ladies and you'll have me to answer to. Miss Gaines has kindly offered to share her remarkable musical talent with us at the castle fete later, so let us permit her to finish here."

Everyone knew what he was saying—that if they walked out now, they weren't invited to the party.

"Oh, sit down and shut your trap, Wilfred," Mavis Snavely was heard to say. "There's already one jackass in church. Iffen I don't get my dance with our handsome lordship, you'll be eating cold porridge the rest of your days."

"And sleeping in a cold bed," another voice called out, laughing.

Sabina was grateful to the viscount, and proud of him for standing up to his father without a confrontation, but she had to worry about his reasons. He was a rake; his motives had to be suspect. He had to have known that her own standing in town could have stood the test, so Connor was really defending Viola Gaines, a beautiful, talented woman some five or six years younger than Sabina, and many years older in knowing how to please a man. Suddenly, Sabina felt that it wasn't fairy dust that had been sprinkled over her tonight, but the sands of time, running out.

Then Viscount Royce reached over the carved back of the pew and lifted sleeping Benjamin in his arms, her cloak and all, and sat with him next to the duke. With that one gesture he stated his intentions, made his claim. Sabina's heart soared with the music.

*

A huge candle-lit procession wended its way back to the castle, carriages and carts, farm wagons piled high with hay and drowsy children, sturdy village men carrying torches. They all sang carols as they went, and looked up to see if they could find the Christmas star, or a snowflake. They all fell silent when they caught sight of the castle, even Sabina, who'd known what to expect. The whole pile was lit by candles in every window, and Chinese lanterns strung from the battlements, and a bonfire in the front, where the moat used to be. Inside looked just as magical. The wassail bowls were filled, the tables were invisible under the platters of foods, and the hired musicians were tuning their instruments.

The duke led off the first dance, a stately minuet, with Lady Arbuthnot from the next shire. Then Connor shouted, "Now let the real dancing begin!" and ordered the orchestra to play reels and contra dances and fast, frenzied jigs everyone could join in, from the oldest grandmother to the youngest toddler. The swords on the walls rattled with the music and the pounding of hundreds of pairs of feet. The castle had never been merrier. Sabina had never been happier. Her sons were playing snapdragon, watched by a hundred doting castle servants, and Viola Gaines was being drooled over by Lord Arbuthnot. Sabina danced with the squire and had her feet stepped on by the blacksmith. She went down the lines with the baker and the banker and bald Lord Quigley. Then the orchestra struck the first chords of a waltz.

"This is my dance, I believe?" Connor was bowing before her.

"No, it's my Christmas wish," was all she could say. He laughed and led her onto the cleared area set aside for dancing. "You are beautiful tonight, in case none of the two thousand other men you've danced with haven't told you. And you are quite, quite tipsy, I believe. No more lamb's wool for you, my girl." And no more words as she floated in his arms, her eyes closed.

When she opened them, they stood in an alcove, partially hidden by tapestries. She was suddenly shy, afraid to ruin the moment with a wrong word. "The, ah, duke seems to be enjoying himself. Having you here has done wonders for his health."

"The old faker will live to be a hundred, I'd guess, just to spite the devil. He'll be fine."

"Then you are free to leave again?" She had always known he'd return to his pleasure-seeking ways, his gaming and opera-dancers.

She must have spoken aloud, for he answered, "I find that my pleasure is here, Sabina, and always has been. Besides, someone has to be around to look after the boys so you don't coddle them too much. Will you marry me, Sabina?"

"What, so you can have my sons? I know you've grown fond of them, and they of you, but surely—"

"Don't be a peagoose, my precious. You are all I want, all I've ever wanted. The boys are simply an added bonus."

Sabina waved her hand around at the room, the opulence, the wealth beyond measure. "It would still be an unequal match Everyone would talk."

"Very well, if you think your boys are worth more, I'll deed the London house to you, too."

"No, silly, you know very well what I mean. You have everything—"

"Except the one thing I need most. You can give it to me, Sabina, only you." His hands were stroking up and down her arms, setting fires in cold, dark places.

"You said there were two conditions to be met before you'd stay."

"You are the first. I wouldn't, couldn't stay here if you won't stay with me. I cannot see you without wanting you, don't you understand that, sweetheart?"

She was beginning to, as his hands reached higher, to the bare skin of her shoulders and the locket around her neck. "I never could, never will, no matter how hard I tried to forget you."

She sighed. "And I, too, never loved another."

She thought he'd kiss her then, but Connor wanted to explain more. "The other reason I could not swear to remain was the duke. I couldn't subject your sons to his choleric temper. That's why I wanted them around the castle so much this past sennight, to see if he could be livable with three boys in the house. If he couldn't, then I'd have done my damnedest to convince you—all of you—to run away with me. This time I would not have taken no for an answer, my girl."

"You wouldn't have had to." She gestured toward the nearby corner of the room, where the duke was holding court from his thronelike chair, his gouty foot propped on satin pillows. Martin and Jasper were leaning over his shoulders, rapt in the stud book he held. Benjamin was asleep in his lap, peppermint-sticky face pressed against the duke's previously pristine white waistcoat.

"So will you, my darling Sabina—will you finally be my wife after a very long engagement?"

"Of course I will, Connor. That's what I really wanted for Christmas, you know," she confessed with a tender smile. "Not one measly waltz. I wanted your love, for all time, as you've got mine."

"And I really want a red-haired choir of my own," he said, before finally sealing their vows with a kiss that had waited more than a decade.

*

The enormous clock in the hall started chiming the hour, and the church bells in the village started tolling. It was twelve o'clock, and Christmas had finally arrived. Everyone had collected their wraps and their children for the trek back home, as soon as one more toast was made. The wassail cups were all refilled as the duke signaled for the company to gather near the vast hearth.

"The name of Hamilton is an ancient one," he began, loudly enough to wake sleeping babies. "Handed down from generation to generation, from father to son since the time of the Normans. With the names goes the title, and with the title goes the land and the responsibility for everyone on it."

"Hear, hear!" was heard from one who'd already had too much of the heady brew.

"Now I hand it to my son," the duke continued, turning to Connor, "along with this sliver from last year's Yule log, to carry on the tradition, to carry on the family into a long and happy future." Among shouts and cheers, he set flame to the bit of wood. "Just make sure you have someone to pass it to, while I'm still around to see."

Connor looked at the burning stick in his hand, then turned to Martin, bending to his level. "I am not your father in name or in blood," he told the boy, "but I would be your father in heart. Will you and your brothers help light this fire, until your mama blesses us with a son of our own? And then you'll help him be the man he should be?"

Martin almost tripped in his hurry to light the Yule log before the match burned out, and all their luck with it. His hand in Connor's, together they lit the new log from the old. When it caught, Martin called out, "To the House of Hamilton, long may they prosper."

Jasper shouted to be heard over the cheers and clapping: "And all of us with them!"

And Benjy, from his mother's arms, mumbled, "And to good deeds."

Epilogue

So the church had its extension, and a new roof, to boot. The viscount had his choir, and the new viscountess a new green velvet dress every Christmas. The donkey was in many a Nativity pageant, with many a red-haired Joseph and a few redheaded Marys. The duke shouted at all of the children impartially, and the vicar wed Sophia Townsend, the seamstress. Oh, and Viola Gaines? She went home with the bishop.

Christmas Wish List

1

"Christmas is coming," proclaimed the vicar. "Rejoice." His voice rose in volume and in fervor as he expounded on the holiday season, the holy child, the princely gifts, the hope for mankind. "And we must not forget the less fortunate at this time of sharing," Reverend Buttons went on. And on, reminding his parishioners of the indigent, the ill, the orphans, and how much more blessed it was to give than to receive. As his voice rose, his eyes did too, directing the congregants' gazes to the water-stained ceiling of the old stone chapel. "Be generous, my friends."

Or be wet when the roof collapsed, Miss Geraldine Selden correctly interpreted the vicar's unspoken message. Well, she and her brother were having too hard a time keeping a roof over their own heads to contribute much to the church fund. While Reverend Buttons started to decry the selfish greed rampant in the world, his favorite theme, Gerry let her mind wander. She mentally counted the jars of jams already put up, the shirts she'd been sewing for months, the shillings she'd managed to set aside for the Christmas boxes. There were apples and tops and cornhusk dolls for the children, packets of sugar tied in pretty ribbons for their mothers, a twist of tobacco for Old Man Pingtree who lived behind the livery. The Seldens were doing what they could, despite their own meager finances. But Gerry would *not* think of their straitened circumstances, not now.

So what if she and her brother Eustace, or Stacey as everyone called him, were forced to live in their former gatekeeper's cottage? They had each other, didn't they? And the rents from Selden House went to pay the mortgage and their father's other debts, so Stacey's patrimony would not be lost entirely. They had their health, their friends, enough food to eat, and enough funds to celebrate the holiday season.

Without repining over what used to be, Gerry daydreamed about what was to come: the smells of fresh-baked gingerbread and fresh-cut evergreens, the red velvet ribbons she was going to wind around the bannister railing, and the red-berried holly she'd gather for the mantel. There would be caroling and wassail and the annual ball at Squire's, the children's Christmas pageant, the Christmas Eve lantern walk to church, and the Christmas pudding she and Mrs. Mamford would put up this afternoon, after everyone in the small household had made their wishes. Christmas was coming, what joy!

*

"And what are you going to wish for, Miss Gerry?" the cook-housekeeper asked. "You'd ought to be asking for another London Season, where some handsome nob will sweep you off your feet and carry you away to a life of luxury." Then Mrs. Mamford and her husband, who acted as butler, groom, and valet to Sir Eustace, could retire to a little cottage near her sister's, without regrets. That was Mrs. Mamford's wish, anyway, and her husband's.

Gerry looked up from the nuts she was chopping and laughed. "What, Mamie, you think some wealthy peer is going to fall madly in love with the dowerless daughter of an impoverished baronet who'd driven his wife to an early grave and his son's inheritance to the money-lenders? Not likely. No, I shan't waste my wishes that way. Besides, I like keeping busy. What would I do as a lady of leisure?"

"I know what I'd do," swore Annie, the maid, from next to the sink. "I'd never look at another pot or pan or potato peel again. I'm going to wish for a new dress, I am, to catch the eye of Rodney, over at the smithy's. He can afford to take a wife now, and I aim for it to be me, instead of that red-haired Kitty Trump."

Gerry made a note to purchase Annie a dress length of calico. She might have to forgo new gloves for her own Christmas outfit, but every young girl deserved to have her dreams come true. In years past, Gerry remembered wishing for a special doll, a new cape, and once wanting to be older, so she could attend the holiday parties with her parents, foolish chit that she was, trying to hurry her adulthood. She might as well ask for those years back, but at five and twenty, Miss Selden knew better than to wish for what could never be. Another Season? No, she never missed the silliness, the empty chatter, and the endless gossip. She did not miss the fancy clothes either, for who would see her in the country in her homemade dresses, to titter behind their fans? The money was better spent on new equipment for the Home Farm, to add to their paltry income.

"So what are you going to wish for, Miss Gerry?" Annie wanted to know.

Gerry tucked a long brown lock of hair back into its braid before attacking the bowl of raisins. "Oh, I suppose I shall wish for peace on earth, an end to war, an easy winter."

Mrs. Mamford clucked her tongue and tossed a sliver of fruit to the cat at her feet. "Go on with you, Ranee," she told the cat, "and you, too, missy. Them's for bedtime prayers. Pudding wishes are for something special, something for yourself."

Gerry stopped chopping to think. She might secretly dream of a house and family of her own, but that was as goosish as wishing for the pot at the end of the rainbow, and the past years had made her much more practical than that. She was actually hoping that this season of hope would bring her something far more substantial than a castle in the sky, something like a new student for pianoforte or painting lessons, something that would add to her small cache of coins, so that she could buy her brother a horse.

Gerry regretted the family's decline much more for Stacey's sake than for her own. They'd come about, he always declared when she worried aloud about their future, and she believed him, but how was he ever to find a bride or support a family? He swore he did not mind working the fields alongside his farmhands, nor tutoring Squire Remington's doltish sons for extra income, but Gerry saw him look out the window every time a rider went past, and knew he was missing the Selden House stables. The most promising filly to be auctioned off for their father's debts had been Jigtime, Stacey's favorite. Gerry smiled as she added her raisins to the batter. For today, she would not wish for the moon, only for a mare.

* * *

Christmas was coming, alas.

Sir Eustace Selden put off answering his sister's call to the kitchen as long as possible. He could hear the women's laughter and smell the scents of cooking, but he had to force himself to put on a smile when he entered the narrow, cluttered room. He knew what he'd find: his sister up to her elbows in flour, smudges on her apron, with her cheeks flushed from the oven's heat and her hair undone, looking no better than the maid, Annie. But his sister was no scullery maid, dash it. Gerry was a lady of quality, and every time Stacey saw her working at tasks his mother never dreamed of, he felt another pang of guilt. Christmas time was the worst, for he'd recall the celebrations at Selden House and know what she must be missing. Her merry grin only added to his remorse, for his sister was a regular Trojan, never complaining of her lack of opportunities buried in this tiny cottage, never whining over the life they'd lost. Gerry's many sacrifices deserved so much more, more than he feared he'd ever be able to give her. By the time he reclaimed Selden House, Stacey worried, his sister would be too old for a dowry to matter, if she wasn't worn to the bone with all her lessons and charities, the scrimping and saving they had to do for the simplest of celebrations. Deuce take it, she was five and twenty already. And he was a year older, and no closer to providing for his only kin than he'd been at nineteen.

"Come, Sir Eustace," Annie called when she saw him lingering in the doorway. "It's time to stir the pudding batter and make your Christmas wish. I wished for a new dress, I did, so now I'm sure to get it."

Gerry's wink told him the frock was as good as in Annie's trunk. "And did you wish for a new gown too, sis?" he asked. He could afford that for her, at least, so she wouldn't have to go to Squire's Christmas party in last year's dress.

"Oh no, I already have a length of green velvet that Mr. Cutler couldn't sell because of the water marks. Once I've embroidered flowers over the spots, no one will know the difference. And no, I will not tell you what I wished for. Go on, make your wish."

Stacey took the mixing spoon from Mrs. Mamford, stalling while he despaired over his sister making her own gown out of inferior goods. She should be dressed in moonbeams and dancing on clouds. Or at least dancing with some eligible *parti*, instead of the apothecary or the vicar's nephew at Squire's country ball. Wishing would not make it so, no matter how hard he stirred the confounded concoction. The rent money was not going to increase, nor the farm's income, not this year. But perhaps, just perhaps, someone new would attend the ball. In that case, the baronet wanted his sister to shine. So he wished for a necklace for her, but not just any bauble. Her own pearls with the diamond butterfly clasp were the one bit of finery their father hadn't managed to find to sell before his death. Gerry had put them on the auctioneer's block herself, to help pay off his debts. Their sometime neighbor, Lord Boughton, had purchased the pearls, likely for one of the licentious lord's London ladybirds. Nevertheless, Stacey wished the earl would come home for Christmas, bringing the necklace, and agreeing to permit Stacey to pay him back over time for their retrieval. Meanwhile, Sir Eustace decided to ask if he could add Latin lessons to Squire's sons' schooling, even though he thought he'd have better luck teaching Caesar to Squire's pigs.

* * *

Christmas was coming, thought Squire Remington. Botheration. No hunting, no fishing, and every man jack in the county coming to celebrate the season at the Manor, same as they had since his grandfather's time. Only his grandfather hadn't been a widower with three young sons to raise. This year, not only did Squire have no wife to handle all the details of the annual ball, but he had no housekeeper either. His hell-born brats had seen to that. Something about a fire in her apartment. No, that was the last one.

This one was the snake. And Vicar thought he'd ought to rejoice? Hah! As for charity, Squire swore he'd give everything he owned just for a little peace and quiet.

What he really wanted this Christmas was a competent chatelaine, someone to take his boys in hand until they were old enough to send away to school, if any institution was desperate enough to take them. Squire wanted someone to make sure his mutton was hot, his ale was cold, and his bed was warm. Was it too much to ask that his dogs were permitted in his house, and his sons' vermin weren't? He wished he had a loyal housekeeper, but he supposed he'd settle for another wife. A wife couldn't up and quit.

*

"So what do you think, Miss Selden? Can we make a match?"

Gerry twisted the ribbons of her sash between restless fingers. "This is so...sudden, Squire."

"Sudden? M'wife's been gone these three years. None of the old tabbies can find fault with that."

"That, ah, was not what I meant. It's just that I never thought to... You and I...? Not that I am not honored by your offer, of course," she hurried to add, offering the plate of tea biscuits. "Just that I need some time to consider your proposal."

"What's to consider?" Remington waved one beefy hand around the tiny parlor, taking in the threadbare carpet, the faded upholstery, the mended curtains. "I'm no Midas, but I'm no nipcheese either. You'd have the household allowance and your pin money. A house of your own, mayhaps children of your own, too, though I just know my boys'll take to you like their own ma." He also knew enough not to bring the brats along, not wanting to scare her off afore he'd said his piece. Squire was so determined to conclude what he saw as an advantageous arrangement for both of them that he didn't notice Gerry's shudder, whether at the thought of mothering his hellions or of begetting a babe with him. "I'll even throw in that mare you want for your brother, as a marriage settlement."

Now that was horse-trading. Gerry told him she needed a few days to decide, with which Squire had to be content. On his way home, though, he passed young Selden, who asked him for additional work.

"I'll tell you what, my boy. You convince your sister to accept my hand and I'll see you don't have to be giving lessons anymore. I'll make you my factor or something. With a horse of your own. You think on it."

Sir Eustace did think, about how his sister's future would be secure, how she'd never want for anything again.

"Anything but love," Gerry replied to his suggestion that she carefully consider Remington's offer, for she was not likely to receive a better one. "And you know we promised each other that neither of us would wed for mere expediency, no matter what other sacrifices we have to make. Our parents' unhappy marriage of convenience was lesson enough. Besides, Christmas is coming. Anything can happen."

2

Christmas was coming, blast it. The government was nearly shut down, most of his friends had decamped for their country seats, and even his secretary had taken a long vacation to visit with family. Bah! Now Albrett Wouk, Lord Boughton, was left with an alpine mound of correspondence, an awesome list of dependents, an ambitious mistress, and absolutely no inclination for any of the argle-bargle. Everyone wanted something at this time of year, confound it, from the social-climbing hostesses to the suddenly solicitous servants. What did Lord Boughton want for Christmas? He wanted it to be over. If he desired something, he'd have purchased it for himself, no matter how extravagant. If he wished to visit somewhere, he would have gone, no matter how far. And if he wanted to put on leg-shackles again, well, he would have shot himself.

There was not one deuced thing that Brett could think of to make this season the least bit enjoyable, much less endurable. Merry and bright? Mawkish sentimentality and base avarice. Comfort and joy? Forced conviviality and just plain gluttony. Jolly? Fah. Without the la-la-la.

The earl shuffled through the stack of mail, sorting out the invitations. He supposed he'd accept one fashionable house party or another, the same as he did every year, for lack of anything better to do. He'd find the same overabundance of food and drink, the same overripe widows, the same overwhelming tedium.

Gads, last year the Sherills had trotted out three unmarried nieces to serenade the company at the Yule log ritual. The chits had been as entertaining as the log, though less talented. Hell and damnation, none of the invites sounded in the least appealing.

Even his current mistress was growing less appealing by the day—or night. If he stayed in Town for the holidays, Charleen would take the opportunity to cling even tighter to him and his purse. She'd expect him to do the pretty, naturally, and Lud only knew what she'd expect after that. Brett did not intend to find out.

231

Lord Boughton flipped through a few letters until one caught his interest. "Presumptuous puppy," he muttered to himself, tapping the page on the edge of the desk. That Bartholomew babe Selden from Upper Ossing wanted to purchase back, at cost and over time, a necklace he'd sold at auction. What did the cabbage-head think the earl was, a money-lender? Father Christmas? Brett ripped the note in half and tossed the pieces on the floor with the rejected invitations. Let the bumpkin buy his own baubles.

His lordship frowned, remembering the sale at Selden House. He'd arrived too late to bid on the cattle, but the pearls had caught his fancy. As soon as he had the necklace home, though, the earl had realized it was a pretty trifle, but not extravagant or showy enough for the birds of paradise he usually decked in diamonds. Well, the confounded necklace must still be in his vault somewhere. He'd send it to Charleen, Lord Boughton decided, along with a check. That way, he'd be saved the aggravation of Christmas shopping and, with any luck, an emotional scene when Charleen realized that was all she was getting from him, ever.

Christmas was coming, by Heaven, and the New Year after. That meant another birthday in her dish, and the devil take them all! Charleen, Lady Trant, was getting old. It must have happened when she wasn't looking, for just yesterday she'd been an Incomparable, a Toast. Today she was a slice of toast, dry and hard. Charleen swept her diamond-braceleted arm along the top of her dressing table, knocking scores of bottles, jars, and tins to the carpet. What good were all the lotions and potions? They couldn't make her two and twenty again. One bottle had escaped her wrath, so she tossed it against the wall. Why not? She could barely read the label, anyway.

Charleen was not looking forward to another year of trying to cover the gray hairs, the fine lines, and her living expenses. If she didn't snabble herself a new husband soon, the men wearing a path to her door wouldn't be eager suitors, they'd be bailiffs and bill collectors. Maybe she could marry one of them. Lud knew she wasn't getting any closer to bringing Lord Boughton up to scratch. Hell, her bosoms would reach her waist before he reached the conclusion that he needed a new wife. Charleen, on the other, ruby-ringed hand, had decided she needed to be Countess Boughton ages ago. The earl was well-mannered, well-favored, and most important of all, well-breeched. What was in his well-tailored breeches was not half bad either.

Well, Christmas was coming, and she'd make deuced sure the earl did his gift selection at Rundell and Bridge's. Charleen really wanted a gold band and all that it entailed, but being well-versed in reality, the lady allowed as how she'd settle for a diamond necklace. She could always sell the sparklers and invest in the Funds. The future had to hold something besides stiff joints and swollen ankles, something that would last a lot longer than her looks.

*

Christmas was coming, at last! Lady Samantha Wouk sat up in bed and practiced her cough. She was not going to let such a golden opportunity get past her, not another year. This holiday, the earl's seven-year-old daughter vowed to herself, was going to be different. She and her governess were already at The Boughs, fortuitously deposited there a month ago when Aunt Jane came down with the influenza. That was the excuse given for packing her off, bag and baggage, anyway. Not that Lady Samantha wished the lady ill, but being sent off like a sack of dirty laundry suited her down to the ground, so long as the ground was her father's country estate in Ossing. Now all she had to do was get that elusive gentleman to come visit his own home.

According to the servants, Lord Boughton seldom rusticated, but seldom was better odds than never, in Samantha's book. He never came to Aunt Jane's at all, not once since Samantha had been taken there as an infant on her mother's death. Not that the earl's daughter blamed him. Oh no, Samantha knew how much Aunt Jane disapproved of Lord Boughton's extravagant lifestyle, with his clubs, his horse races, and his parties, all of which sounded perfectly delightful to the gentleman's offspring. Aunt Jane always clucked her tongue when his name was mentioned in the newspapers. That was how Samantha knew to sneak a look.

Samantha did not mean to interfere with what Aunt Jane called the earl's hedonistic pursuit of pleasure. She did not expect the stranger who happened to be her father to play at dolls' tea parties or know how to braid hair ribbons. She only wanted to remind him of her existence. What she really wished for this Christmas—and had, for all the ones that came before—was a mother, someone to whom she wouldn't merely be a responsibility or a paid chore. Someone who wouldn't pass her off to distant relatives or, worse, a boarding school. According to Aunt Jane and the servants, though, when they did not think she was listening, the earl did not like women. He never danced at coming-out balls, and he never escorted the same lady for very long. From what Samantha had gathered, Albrett Wouk hadn't much liked her mother, either. Theirs had been an arranged marriage, more for the begetting of heirs than for being life companions. In fact, and according to her old nursemaid who'd been left to help look after Aunt Jane, the earl had abandoned his countess in the country as soon as she was breeding. Most likely he'd have returned to try again for a son, but Lady Boughton had not long survived her daughter's birth. Nanny said they'd all heard the earl swear he'd never marry again, but would let one of his cousins succeed him. He hadn't changed his mind in seven years, and Samantha didn't think he'd change it for a girl-child he never bothered to visit, no matter how lonely she was.

Well, Christmas was coming, and if she couldn't have a mother, Samantha had decided, she'd settle for a cat.

In truth, Lady Samantha didn't mean to get truly sick. She coughed under the covers until her throat was sore, and she made sure her toes came out of the blankets, into the chill night air. She picked at her food, dragged her feet during walks, and rubbed her temples, the way she'd seen Aunt Jane do. Unfortunately, her charade thoroughly convinced Miss Musgrove, her governess, who immediately sent for the local physician. When Mr. Weeks found nothing wrong, Miss Musgrove ordered the cook to start brewing healing draughts from an old herbal tome in the library.

Either the recipe was in error, or the ingredients were mislabeled, or perhaps the proportions were simply not suitable for such a tiny mite of a miss, but Lady Samantha took a turn for the worse. Now she couldn't keep any food in her stomach, and could barely lift her head off the pillow. The physician shook his head and ordered her bled. One look at the leeches, and Lady Samantha started screaming for, of all persons, her father. Then she fainted. The doctor proceeded for five days after that, as the earl's daughter lay limp on her bed, growing paler and thinner and weaker.

*

Christmas was coming, dear Lord, and the child was dying. Miss Musgrove spooned another dose of the latest concoction down her charge's throat, then watched as the brownish liquid dribbled out of Lady Samantha's mouth. She scrubbed at the untidiness with a damp towel, wishing she could make the entire unpleasant situation disappear as easily.

Miss Musgrove smoothed out the skirts of her black bombazine gown, frowning. Now she'd never have that school of her own where her pupils did not outgrow her teaching or her discipline. Goodness, a person got tired of looking for new positions, of being relegated to the wasteland between the servants' hall and the family rooms. Was it too much to ask to wish for a bit of security, a touch of independence? Now she'd not even get a reference from the earl or his sister-in-law, not after letting their kin die in this godforsaken place with its one incompetent doctor.

The governess's hands trembled to think that they might even blame her. The earl was an influential man. He could have her sent to Botany Bay. But no, she'd followed the directions carefully, to the best of her ability. And the servants could tell him that she'd called for the doctor immediately. It was the old charlatan's fault that the disease had progressed so rapidly. If Weeks had treated the girl when they'd first sent for him, perhaps Miss Musgrove would not find herself in such a coil. No, they couldn't blame her. Besides, everyone knew the earl didn't much care what happened to the chit anyway. It wasn't as if she were his heir or anything. Miss Musgrove cared. Horrors, Christmas was coming and she could find herself out of a position.

After much hand-wringing, Miss Musgrove did what she'd been hired specifically never to do: she wrote to the earl. His sister-in-law Jane was too weak, and the earl was the one who paid her wages. Let him come take responsibility, and let him see what a good job of nursing the governess had done, certainly worthy of a bonus.

*

Brett finally reached the bottom of the pile of correspondence, vowing to raise his secretary's salary, if the chap ever returned from his vacation. The last letter was addressed in distinctly feminine, perfect copperplate. Brett held it to his nose, but the scent was indecipherable. The seal on the back was also unrecognizable, being common red household wax. The sender was definitely not Lady Trant, for Charleen could barely read the opera program, much less write such an elegant hand.

Unfolding the page, the earl let his eyes drop to the signature. He did not recognize that either. He almost tossed the letter to the floor with the rest of useless drivel, but the name "Samantha" caught his eye. As in "your daughter, Samantha." Brett read the letter, then read it again, swearing at the bone-headed woman, his missing secretary, his negligent sister-in-law, and his dead wife. Then he called for his carriage. No, his horse would be faster. The coach could follow with his bags, with his own Harley Street sawbones, with the contents of the nearest apothecary shop. While he was waiting, Brett scrawled a note to his solicitor, directing him to see to Charleen, the check, and the necklace. And to hire a temporary secretary to handle the rest of the mess.

Somewhere in the furor of his departure, whilst changing his clothes, gathering together money and his pistol and a hastily packed hamper for the journey, Lord Boughton discovered that he knew what he wanted for Christmas after all. He wanted to be a father.

3

"What does Mactavish want now?" Gerry asked her brother when she saw the note he was holding. Only one person of their acquaintance wrote with such a bold, sprawling hand. Besides, she'd seen the writing all too often enough in the past years. Mr. Euan Mactavish was the India nabob who was leasing Selden House. It suited the wealthy merchant to live in a gentleman's house. It did not suit him to live with falling tiles, smoking chimneys, or leaking drains. Sir Eustace was frequently summoned to their old home to listen to the latest disaster, and to renegotiate the terms of Mactavish's lease in recompense. Lud knew the Seldens could not afford the repairs and renovations Mactavish insisted upon. Gerry couldn't help her suspicions that the self-made mogul liked having a titled gentleman at his beck and call, even if Stacey was a mere baronet. "What does he want you to fix this time?"

"I have no idea. The message is addressed to you, sis."

"Goodness, what could Mr. Mactavish want with me?"

"Perhaps he wants to make an offer for your hand, too," Stacey teased. "Just think, you could move back to our old house and live like a princess. A much better bargain than Squire and his three imps of Satan."

Mr. Mactavish was short and bald and took snuff. He was loud, demanding, and used to giving orders. He was also old enough to be Gerry's father. "Don't be absurd," Gerry told her brother, taking the letter from him and slitting the seal on the back. "I cannot imagine what's on the man's mind now."

What was on the canny Cit's mind was a title. Christmas was coming, and he hadn't gotten rich by letting the grass grow under his feet, no sir. Who knew what bucks and beaus Squire might assemble for that annual ball of his? Mactavish meant for his little girl to meet all of them and marry the most elevated of the lot. If Squire couldn't produce anything better than young Sir Eustace, at least his Ginger would get her feet wet in the social waters. Mactavish meant to bring her out in London in the spring. Not all

239

doors would be open to a tradesman's daughter, of course, but enough would, an' he make her portion generous enough. The problem was, his little Ginger'd been at a fancy seminary for young females until now. With no wife and no permanent home, Mactavish hadn't been able to have the rearing of the chit. Now that he had her home, he realized he'd made one of his few miscalculations. Ginger was as pretty as she could stare, and well educated, for a female. The price of her wardrobe could have clothed entire Indian villages. But there was no getting around the fact that his little gal was no dasher. She was a shy, wispy thing who didn't know how to go on in company. So Mactavish wrote to Miss Geraldine Selden, who was one of the few ladies in the neighborhood, and the only one who gave lessons in the village. Pianoforte and such, Mactavish recalled. She'd even had a London Season before that ne'er-do-well father of hers popped off. Surely Miss Selden would know just what to do to put some life into the little puss.

*

"He wants me to be a kind of companion to his daughter, who is finally home from school," Gerry told her brother after reading her letter. "And listen to this: he is willing to pay me handsomely, just for showing her how to go on, introducing her around the neighborhood, that sort of thing so she won't feel such a stranger."

Gerry twirled around and kissed her brother's cheek. "Our luck is changing, Stacey, I just know it is! And right in time for Christmas!" Now she might even earn enough blunt to buy Stacey's horse back from Squire.

Stacey was not quite as excited. He was sincerely happy for Gerry's windfall, of course, and hoped she'd use her wages to purchase some luxury he couldn't afford for her. Still, he hated to see his sister going out to work as an upper servant. And a moody young miss who sat mumchance could be as difficult a pupil as Squire's threesome, who only sat when they were tied to their chairs. "The chit might be a hopeless antidote, you know, besides shy. She could be short and bald like her papa."

"Heiresses are never the wrong height or hair color, silly. And Mactavish can afford to purchase her a wig!" Gerry was not going to be discouraged. "I'll call on them this very afternoon. And I'll bring along a special gift, so Miss Mactavish understands that I wish to be her friend, not merely another instructor. The poor girl must be tired of lessons after all these years. Of course, I'll have to make sure she can do the country dances, and I know she'll be asked to entertain the company at some party or other. I'll have to see what she can perform on the pianoforte. And if she knows the proper way to pour tea, how low to curtsey, that type of thing. Goodness, there's not a moment to spare, with Christmas right around the corner."

Unfortunately, Christmas was not the only thing coming around the corner.

Sir Eustace went off about estate business, leaving Gerry to dither about which gown to wear for the visit, not that she had a great many to choose from. 'Twould never do to appear dowdy, not when Mr. Mactavish was counting on her—and paying her—to bring Miss Mactavish into style. In the end she selected her newest walking dress, a dainty sprigged muslin copied directly from the pages of *La Belle Assemblee.* The fact that the frock was more suited to a September stroll than to a winter's walk was irrelevant. What was warmth compared to making a good impression? Gerry pulled her heavy brown wool cape on over the gown, instead of her more fashionable but thin pelisse. The niffy-naffy butler who had taken Mamford's place at Selden House was the only one who would see such a plebeian article. Besides, the voluminous cape had pockets both inside and out to hold pencil and paper for making lists, the latest novel from the lending library, and the gift she was bringing to welcome Miss Virginia Mactavish to Upper Ossing.

Rather than trudge the entire two miles along the winding carriage drive, Gerry decided to walk the short distance along the high road to the gap in Selden's stone wall. From there the house was a mere stone's throw away. The high road, though, was in poor condition after the recent rains and yesterday's market day traffic. Gerry stepped through the gate and picked her way carefully between puddles and ruts and piles of horse droppings. The pair coming from the other direction took no such precautions.

The horse was huge and black, and covered yards with every pounding step. He wasn't at an all-out gallop, but a steady gait that could last for miles. The rider sat tall and straight, with his caped greatcoat billowing behind him like some dark angel's wings. He was bare-headed, with his black hair pulled back in a queue. Together they were a magnificent sight, one she was sorry Stacey would miss. Gerry stopped walking to admire the superb pairing of horse and rider as they neared, until she realized that they were going to pass altogether too near. She'd be pelted with the gobs of mire and muck tossed up by the stallion's hooves. She was going to arrive at Mactavish's looking like a wet, filthy mudhen. With a yelp, Gerry leaped backward. Only there was nothing beneath her feet, behind her. She screamed as she skidded to an ignominious seat in the roadway, almost under the stallion's feet.

The rider tried to stop, truly he did, shouting and pulling the horse back on its hind legs till it was a miracle he stayed aboard. But now a frightened, confused mass of black muscle was towering over her, with metal shoes about to descend. Scrabbling for purchase in the mud, Gerry heaved herself away and rolled to safety—in the ditch.

She was sopping wet, covered head to toe in filth, and stank like a midden heap. All because some London toff was in too much of a hurry to mind where he was going. Gerry had no doubt the rider was from the City, as full of himself and his importance to the world as her half boots were full of stagnant water. "Damn you to hell!" she shouted to his receding back, as she tried to pull herself out of the ditch.

Lord Boughton had ridden just far enough past the fallen female to let Riddles gain his footing, then he turned and sped back, leaping off the stallion, dreading what he might find. Thank God the woman was standing, not lying with her head against a rock, or her limbs twisted, or her neck broken. Brett did not even hear her curses over the pounding of his heart. He reached down to lift her from the knee-deep scum.

Gerry couldn't help but notice that the gentleman's boots, at her eye level, were still gleaming. And the hand he held out to her was gloved in immaculate York tan kid. She took great satisfaction in putting her own sodden mitt in his. And greater satisfaction in telling the arrogant bounder just what she thought of such reckless, irresponsible, cow-handed riding. "How dare you act as if you owned the very roadways! Are you so high-and-mighty that no one else is allowed to share the very air you breathe?"

The air surrounding the bedraggled female was none too aromatic, so Brett quickly released her hand, once she was back on the roadway. She did not even pause in her diatribe. "Don't you even bother to look where you are going, or are we lesser mortals supposed to anticipate your presence and run for safety?"

He'd seen the brown dab of a girl step through the little cottage's gate, of course, but naturally assumed she'd get out of the way, not stand and gape at him and Riddles like a bacon-brained booby. She'd cost him enough time already, though, so rather than stand arguing in the ill-kept road, Brett reached into his pocket and tossed the chit a coin. "For your inconvenience," he said.

"Inconvenient? You call this inconvenient?" Gerry gestured to her befouled cape, the bonnet that was floating, upside down, in the ditch water, her ruined shoes. Now she could not go to Mactavish's this afternoon at all, and this great gawk of a so-called gentleman thought it was an inconvenience! "You puffed-up popinjay! I could have been killed!"

"And still might be," Brett muttered under his breath. What a little shrew! Some poor fool might have been saved a lifetime of misery if the archwife had drowned in the ditch after all. He tossed her another coin so he could be on his way. The infuriated female caught the gold piece and tossed it back in his face, along with a dollop of mud. At least Brett hoped it was mud. He closed the distance between them and took her shoulders, growing angry himself at the delay. "You should learn to hold your temper, girl, before your betters."

"When I come upon someone better, I shall know precisely how to behave, sirrah! Unhand me, you dastard."

This close, Brett couldn't help noticing that her thick brown hair was fallen like a velvet shawl over her shoulders, and flame sparked from the depths of dark brown eyes. The petite country hoyden would be quite an attractive armful, he decided with a connoisseur's eye, except for her waspish tongue. Well, he knew how to still a woman's mouth, all right. He kissed her.

Her lips were cold and wet, but Lud, they sent a fire through him. There must be something about rustic wenches and their very earthiness, Brett thought, that moved him as no hothouse London beauty had in ages.

Miss Selden was stunned. She'd never experienced more than a timid peck or a chaste salute, hardly kisses at all when compared to this...this ravishment. Good Heavens, no wonder so many girls came to grief in the City! Of course, this devilishly handsome rogue, with his blue eyes and cleft chin, had to be an expert at the art. Why, she'd felt that kiss down to her toes—her waterlogged and frozen toes, the cad! How dare he take such unfair advantage of what he undoubtedly thought was some poor milkmaid or a farmer's ignorant daughter. So she slapped him.

Rubbing his cheek, and incidentally spreading dirt from his no longer pristine gloves, Brett drawled, "My apologies, miss." He was not about to tell this rag-mannered wench how affected he'd been by her innocent, unaware sensuality. "It was only a kiss, so you can stop sputtering now. Not a very proficient kiss, as these things go. Perhaps you'd like lessons, my dear?"

Not very proficient? That was more insulting than the stolen kiss! "How dare you bring your licentious ways to a decent neighborhood, you rakehell. You libertine, you immoral bas—"

So he kissed her again, longer and deeper. Then he stepped back to wait for the slap, knowing he deserved it, knowing the kiss had been worth it. Instead the girl gasped, patted her pockets, and shouted, "Bandit!" Brett glanced both ways along the road, searching for the danger, until he realized she meant him. "Dash it, I stole a kiss, nothing else. I admit I was riding too quickly, but I am no highwayman."

She wasn't paying him the least attention, rushing around in a frenzy. "Not you, you clunch. Bandit's a kitten. He was in my pocket." She bent over to peer into the ditch, leaving him with a draggle-tailed but delightful view.

Brett knew he should be on his way, but there was just something about this female that made him reluctant to leave. And he was, in truth, responsible for her difficulties, to say nothing of the liberties he'd taken with her person. So he stepped nearer, to help in the hunt, poking with his boot toe behind fallen branches, echoing the chit's "Here, kitty, kitty." And feeling like a prize fool on all counts.

"There you are!" she exclaimed, tearing her befouled mittens off to lift something out from behind a rock.

"That?" Brett asked, staring at the handful of lint she held. "That's no cat, that's what's left in the currying comb after I brush my horse." But she was cooing to the palm-sized dustball with blue eyes and a pushed-in face like a pug dog's. "Great Scot, did it get squashed in the fall?"

Without taking her eyes off the ridiculous creature, Gerry told him, "No, that's the way he's supposed to look. It's a rare type of long-haired cat from Malukistan, along the Silk Route. My uncle sent a pair back from his travels, and now I and a few other cat fanciers are trying to establish them as a special breed, without weakening the strain through too-close matings."

Brett believed he now knew more about long-haired cats than he ever needed to. He also believed that he might have made an error. A serious error. His little rustic beauty was not quite as young as he'd thought, and he noticed that her accent, now that she was not shrieking like a banshee, was educated and refined. And her fingers bore no rings. Bloody hell.

"Yes, well, I am glad to see that the animal has not come to any harm. Now I really must continue my journey, Miss...ah, Miss...?"

She had already turned her back to him and gone through the gate toward the cottage. She was the first woman to cut him in his memory. Brett shrugged and remounted. He wasn't here for any country dalliance, he told himself. Nor duels with irate fathers.

4

The earl was in Ossing, in time, thank goodness.

The child looked as pathetic as any undernourished, disease-ridden scrap of humanity he'd seen in London's stews and kennels. Lud, how many times had he tossed such a creature a coin? And how much good had that done? he wondered now, for surely this ashen, enervated child was past praying for.

Brett prayed anyway, using words and phrases from his childhood, making bargains he didn't know if he could keep, with forces he didn't know if he believed. She couldn't die, this black-haired piece of himself, she simply could not. "Do you hear me, Samantha?" he whispered, fearing a shout might still the shallow breaths altogether. "You cannot die. I forbid it! I have come all the way to see you, miss, and see you I shall. Don't you dare leave me before I have even discovered the color of your eyes. Dash it, Samantha, wake up and look at me."

Her eyes were blue, the same as his. But they were vacant, unfocused, as though she were staring at a light he couldn't see.

"No, you can do better than that, Samantha. Try, sweetheart. You've got to get better, you know, because...because it's almost Christmas. Come on, Sammy, you can do it. Wake up. Please."

Butterfly lashes fluttered, then opened wider. "No one ever calls me Sammy," she whispered back.

He leaned closer to hear. "No? Not your aunt or Miss Musgrove?"

"Oh, no. They say that would be common. I am a lady, you know."

He nodded. "Yes, I did know that, Lady Samantha Wouk. Is that what you wish me to call you?"

Her brows knit in confusion. "I think you must, sir, as we have not been introduced. That's one of the rules, you know." She sighed. "There are so many I cannot remember them all. But you won't tell Aunt Jane, will you, sir?"

"What, tattle on a new friend? Never. Besides, sometimes I forget some of those silly rules, too."

"You do?"

"Of course. Word of a gentleman. No, word of a Wouk. That's even better, you know, for we might forget a few plaguey manners, but we never forget a promise."

Her blue eyes widened. "Are you really my father, then? You really came?"

"I came."

"Then I suppose you can call me Sammy." She smiled, showing a missing tooth and a dimple.

Lud, Brett thought, she was going to break a hundred hearts in a few years. "And I would be proud if you would call me Papa."

"Not 'my lord'?"

That's how Brett had always addressed his sire, with proper respect for the cold, sanctimonious stranger. "Definitely not 'my lord.' Now you rest and get better, my girl, all right?"

"Word of a Wouk," she murmured contentedly before drifting back to sleep.

*

The earl was in Ossing, thank heaven, thought a much relieved Miss Musgrove. At least she was relieved until Lord Boughton dismissed the doctor, tossed out the tonics, and announced that he would sit by Lady Samantha's bedside from now on. How was she supposed to prove her dedication and devotion to the brat? How was she supposed to get a reference from him, or a Christmas bonus? Drat.

*

The earl really was in Ossing, for her! The next time Samantha awoke, he was asleep in the chair next to her bedside, with his bare feet on a stool and a dark shadow on his chin. He was her father, in

248

truth, not a fever dream, because he looked just like his portrait in the library downstairs, only much handsomer. How absolutely, positively glorious! Her plan was working even better than she'd expected. Samantha almost clapped her hands in excitement.

Her slight movement was enough to startle Lord Boughton awake. "Sammy? Are you thirsty, sweetheart? Would you like some fresh lemonade? I've been keeping it cool near the window. Or perhaps some hot broth?"

She wrinkled her nose. "Not one of Miss Musgrove's potions?"

He'd thrown them out the window, after one smell of the noxious brews. The nearby hedges were already withered. "No, you don't need them anymore, now that you are doing so much better."

She wasn't well enough for him to leave yet! Samantha shook her head and whimpered, "I do not feel like anything right now, thank you. I'll just lie here awhile."

"Well, don't plan on staying abed for too long, for we've a lot to do if we're going to be ready for Christmas."

"We do?"

"Of course. We need to gather greenery to decorate, and ribbons to tie around everything. We'll have to search through the attics for my mother's ornaments and such, and we'll have to find us the biggest Yule log in Upper Ossing." What he used to disdain at friends' house parties now seemed eminently desirable, if he could tempt the child from her sickbed. The rituals and rigamarole of the season might even be pleasurable, if seen through those blue eyes, raised to him so trustingly. Why, once she was recovered— and he refused to consider that she might not—he could take the poppet skating and sledding, if the weather were not too cold, and if she were bundled tightly enough. And if they got snow. He found himself wishing for a blizzard like the veriest schoolboy, for his daughter's sake, of course. Perhaps sledding was too rough a sport for such a delicate little sprite, though. How should he know? At least he could teach her to make snow angels, something he was certain neither his starched-up sister-in-law nor the proper Miss

Musgrove would have taught her. How much else had she missed because he was such a wretched parent? He thought of all the other activities his hosts and their families had delighted in through all those interminable holiday gatherings, to his aggravation. "Oh, and we'll have to make at least one kissing bough, if you promise not to get up any flirtations with the footmen."

"Papa! I am only seven years old!"

"Ah, then I suppose it's safe to have mistletoe in the house. And candles in every window. And caroling. We definitely must have caroling. You'll like that, won't you, poppet, all the trappings and trimmings?"

In her dreams, Samantha could not have imagined a more perfect holiday. She'd never even seen anything like what he described, not at her puritanical aunt's house. They'd prayed on Christmas and had a goose for dinner; that was all. She thought she'd like this celebration much better, if he was there with her. "You'll stay?"

He wouldn't lie to her, not after boasting that a Wouk's word was his bond. "I cannot stay forever, Sammy, for I have business in London and other properties to oversee." Deuce take it, he was a conscientious landlord; how could he have ignored his own child for so long? But she'd been an infant when his wife died. Sending the babe to her aunt had seemed the best solution. Now remorse made him say, "But I will be here as long as you need me."

Samantha sighed and the earl grabbed up her tiny hand, as if to keep her from drifting off again, whence she might not return. Desperate to focus her attention on the future, so that she'd fight to have one, he asked, "Surely there is something special you want to do for Christmas, some magical gift you are looking forward to? Perhaps a new doll? A pony?"

She had a closet full of dolls. His secretary sent her one for each birthday and holiday. She had a pony, Jessie, because Aunt Jane considered equestrian skills to be part of a proper female's education. But she'd never had a pet of her own. "I've always wanted a kitten, but Aunt Jane says they are dirty, sneaky creatures."

"Your aunt's opinions do not matter here, Sammy. This is my house, and yours."

"But Miss Musgrove would never permit an animal in the nursery."

"If Miss Musgrove disapproves"—and the poker-backed governess seemed to disapprove of everything!—"she will have to leave."

"You can do that, Papa?"

"Of course I can. I'm an earl, remember. I cannot toss her out in the cold, for that would be ungentlemanly, but if you don't care for her, and she does not care for your pet, then we'll find her another position or something. What do you think about that?"

"Would I have to go away to a school?"

"Eventually, so you'll meet other girls your age. You'll like making new friends."

"I've never had a playmate. Aunt Jane says the village children are too vulgar for an earl's daughter."

Brett was growing heartily sick of Jane's dictates. And feeling guilty as hell for leaving the little mite with Miss Prunes and Prisms for so long. No pets, no friends, nothing but lessons and prayers? The earl might know tuppence about being a parent, but he'd wager he could do better than that. Medea could do better than that! He patted his daughter's hand. "You'll just have to make a speedier recuperation, then, so we can go pick out your kitten. I'm sure the tenants will have any number for you to choose from if there is no kitchen cat with a litter here. And I'll ask the grooms about the barn mousers. We'll find the prettiest one in the bunch. Maybe a white one, so you can call it Snowball. How would that be?" He vowed he'd find her a purple one, if that was what she wanted.

"Oh, no, Papa, I don't want just any old kind of cat." Suddenly Brett was feeling a draft on the back of his neck. Or was that a prickling of doom? "No? You wanted a lion cub or a tiger, perhaps?"

"No, silly. I want a special, *special* cat."

Oh, Lud, he was about to be punished for all his sins. "And I suppose you know exactly where to find this doubly special feline?"

Samantha sat up in bed, showing more energy than she had since he'd come. "Of course I do! Miss Selden raises them, you see, at the old gatekeeper's cottage."

"Miss Selden from Selden House lives at the gatehouse?" He'd been too concerned with his daughter's health to ask about anything else. "The baronet's sister?" Let there be another Miss Selden, he prayed, almost as fervently as he'd prayed for his daughter's return to health.

"And Sir Eustace, also. Mr. Mactavish rents the big house. Miss Musgrove thinks he is common, but Miss Selden and Sir Eustace are Quality, she says, so we went to call on them once, when we first arrived. And I saw the most adorable kitties in the whole wide world. I want one of those kittens, Papa."

Once, when he was swimming, the earl had stepped on an eel. That almost described what he was feeling now.

*

The earl was in Upper Ossing? Confound his craven heart, fumed Charleen, Lady Trant, as she peered again at the letter from Brett's solicitor. Where the deuce was that anyway? And could the message really say that Boughton was going to be indefinitely detained in the country on account of a sick girl child? Her vision must be worse than she'd thought. By all that was holy, though, Charleen would *not* purchase spectacles. And she would not be cast aside like yesterday's mutton. A skimpy string of pearls, that's what he thought she deserved after she'd served his needs for all these months? Never mind his generosity at the dressmakers, the milliners, and the wine merchant, she was entitled to more. To his title, in fact.

Blast! Even with the diamond butterfly clasp, the necklace wouldn't bring enough blunt to keep her in candles for a month. Her eyesight was good enough to count the diamond chips, but not to notice the folded bank draft that was tucked beneath the pearls. Perhaps he'd meant the necklace as a token of his esteem, until he could purchase a more worthy gift, Charleen decided. Yes, that was it: he'd left in such a hurry he'd delegated his fusty old man of affairs to send her a trifle, to show his regrets at being away from her over Christmas.

Of course, there was no good reason for them to be apart. The earl was certain to grow bored in the country. Lonely. He'd need a companion, perhaps a lady to act as hostess to the local gentry. Why, Charleen would be doing him a favor by traveling to... Where the devil was that place? Osier? Orange? And she could help with the sick child, too. She could, ah, read to her. No, that wouldn't work. Charleen could play at dolls. Well, her maid could sew up some doll clothes, at any rate. Boughton would see what a good mother she'd make, what a good wife, what a good countess. What a good idea!

5

The earl was in Ossing, drat the man. Miss Selden had slapped one of the foremost members of the beau monde. She knew it even before the rumor mills started to grinding. After all, she'd heard the little girl was ailing, and what kind of unnatural father would leave a child alone on Christmas anyway?

Aside from the logic of Lord Boughton's appearing at this time, there simply could not be many other such nonpareils as her highway accoster. But if by some chance there should ever happen to be a more handsome, more virile, more commanding gentleman—not that she thought he was gentlemanly, not by half— well, he wouldn't be riding through Upper Ossing.

The libertine from the lane was the earl, all right, from his famous elegant tailoring to his fabled standing among the demimonde. And now he was standing in Gerry's shabby parlor with a bouquet of flowers in one hand. Roses, no less, and this December. If his clothes or his confidence did not proclaim the rogue's worth, the roses would have. And there she was, in a faded gown, likely with stains and spots from the ivy she'd been braiding for the mantel. At least she'd managed to wash away the stink of yesterday's dousing; now if she could only get rid of his lordship so easily. He was everything she disliked in a man: arrogant and immoral. Like others she'd met during her London Season, the earl thought his wealth and title could buy him respect and affection. Likely they did. Then he'd gamble it all away on the turn of a card or a turned-down sheet, while others did his work, his worrying. No, Gerry did not admire his lordship's ilk at all. Of course the earl's dark good looks were another matter altogether.

She made him her best curtsey without offering her hand, which was all scratched from the holly's prickers. Then she indicated the best chair. No, Ranee had been sleeping there this morning and the pillows were covered with tawny cat hair, just the color to show well on his midnight blue superfine coat. She sat in it herself before her knees gave way, nodding him toward the uncushioned wooden desk chair.

The earl didn't sit, but took to pacing back and forth in front of the fireplace. What, the rug wasn't threadbare enough? But Gerry felt reassured by this sign of his lordship's unease. So the care-for-no-one nobleman had a conscience after all. Feeling generous, she began: "Lord Boughton, there was no need for you to come here. I assure you our previous encounter is better forgotten by both of us."

"No," he said. "I had to come, Miss Selden, to ascertain your well-being and that of your, ah, small companion."

"We are both unharmed by the incident, my lord, thank you." She was not about to tell him how stiff and sore she was, nor how half the scratches on her arms were from Bandit's bath.

"Yes, well, I am pleased to hear that. I most sincerely apologize, both for my careless riding and…and the other."

"The other?" Generosity only went so far.

"For, ah, mistaking you for a country lass, Miss Selden."

"You 'mistook' me for one of your light-skirts, my lord."

"I can only beg you to excuse my behavior on the grounds that I am not used to ladies wandering around by themselves or dressed with such practicality."

He must mean frumpish, Gerry thought, frowning, and ignorant of polite behavior. "Your so gracious apology is accepted, my lord," she snapped at him. "And my conduct was less than genteel in return. There, now we are quits, and you do not have to keep looking at the doorway to see if my brother is going to rush in and challenge you to a duel over my honor. I would not be so nonsensical as to mention the contretemps to anyone, and I trust you will do the same." She stood, declaring the visit at an end. "Will that be all?"

"Not precisely." Boughton started to shred one of the roses he still held in his hand, so Gerry took the bouquet away before he damaged the perfect blooms. "Oh, yes, quite. With my regards."

Taking pity on his discomposure at last—truly she'd thought a nonesuch would have better address—she asked after his daughter. "A charming child. I was sorry to hear she was ill. I trust she is improving, else you'd not be out making calls."

"Yes, Sammy. Thank you. Quite a remarkable recovery, actually. That's why I've come, you see."

Gerry frowned. "Not to tender an apology?"

Devil take the woman, Brett thought. Must she make everything so deuced difficult? "Of course that was first in my mind. But I did have another mission also. I should like to purchase one of your kittens for my daughter."

"No."

"No? Just like that? Come now, you cannot hold my behavior against an innocent child. Sammy has her heart set on a kitten." And he had his heart set on seeing the last of this plain-speaking pocket-venus who seemed to rob him of his manners, his morals, and his masterful way with women. "Surely you'll reconsider, for a price."

So now he thought she was mercenary! Gerry strode toward the door, leaving him to follow. "For one thing, my lord, my kittens are not for sale. I *give* them to those who will love them and care for them, and not let them breed with the kitchen Tom or a stray. You do not fulfill my requirements, my lord, with your hedonistic, pleasure-seeking way of life. Look how you cared for your own child."

He chose not to. "Then think of that child. You cannot be so heartless as to deny a dying girl her wish, can you?"

"You said yourself she is recovering nicely. And if she were not, the last thing she'd need is a helpless creature to take care of."

"I have a battalion of servants, Miss Selden. Surely you do not have to worry that the kitten will not be cared for."

"What, after Lady Samantha returns to her aunt's and you return to your travels, do you really think those servants are going to brush the cat daily, and make sure it never gets lost? My cats are used to a great deal of affection. Can you swear that your servants will provide that, too?"

Brett countered with the one argument he was sure of: "Sam will not be returning to her aunt's. She'll be lonely here in Ossing."

"Then she needs playmates, sisters and brothers, a parent's love. No, you shall not use one of my cats to make up for your own failings. Good day, my lord."

Lud, how had such a simple thing as purchasing a cat become so involved? Since when did a fellow have to pass a court-martial to be deemed worthy of a rat-catcher? And how the devil was he going to tell Sam there would be no pug-faced furball for her on Christmas? "I beg you to reconsider, Miss Selden, for Sammy's sake."

"And I beg you to leave, my lord. I don't like you and you don't like cats."

"Of course I do." He couldn't recall being in the same room with one of the creatures, but saw no reason to mention the fact. He couldn't recall being in the room with a woman who disliked him, either, but that was a problem for a different day. "The little bugger, ah, baby in the ditch surprised me, is all."

"If you liked cats, you'd have one."

Her smug tone was grating on Brett's temper. And her pursed lips were crying out for kisses, which would not help his cause in the least, he was sure. He took a deep breath and said, "I like giraffes, Miss Selden, and I do not have one of those either. Try me with a cat. That's the only fair test."

Gerry nodded, and went into the hall, making odd bird-call noises. In a moment, a large, extremely fluffy black cat with a plume of a tail and a nub of a nose strolled into the room, wrapping itself around Miss Selden's legs. "This is Mizra Khan, the sire of most of the kittens I breed. If you sit down, he will come to you."

He sat on the sofa, and sure enough, Mizra Khan leaped up alongside him, butting his head against the earl's sleeve. The earl tried to school his features into not showing distaste at the innumerable cat hairs left on the fine wool. "There, it likes me."

"He wants his ears scratched."

So Brett scratched the cat's silky ears, and was rewarded with a loud rumbling purr. Then he took out his quizzing glass on its ribbon and let the cat bat at it awhile. He grinned up at his hostess, his puss-prowess proven, when Mizra Khan stepped closer, onto his lap, in fact, and began to knead the earl's thigh with his front paws. The claws dug in, catching on the fawn-colored breeches, catching on the earl's skin beneath. Brett gingerly lifted the cat down to the floor in a controlled hurry, then glanced at Miss Selden to see if she disapproved. The cat, meanwhile, had discovered the tassels on Lord Boughton's Hessians and was swatting at them. "Playful chap, isn't he?" the earl asked, bending to pat the cat and subtly push him away from the mirror-surfaced boots. Mizra Khan had other ideas. He stood on his back legs and started to use those unblemished boots as a scratching post. "I say!" Brett said, giving the cat a firmer shove, at which Mizra Khan sank his teeth into Lord Boughton's thumb.

"Bloody hell!" he shouted, clutching his bloodied finger. "Now I suppose I'll have to worry about contracting some dread disease!"

Gerry was already cuddling the cat. "Silly kitty, now we'll have to worry about you contracting some dread disease. Good day, my lord."

*

The earl was in a taking when he rode back to The Boughs. He did not even visit the nursery until he'd had half a bottle of brandy, and soaked his thumb in the other half.

"Did you get it, Papa? Did you get my kitten?"

"Hush, poppet. You wouldn't want to ruin your Christmas surprise, would you?"

*

The earl was in Ossing, thought Eustace. How fortunate. Now he could go ask about Gerry's necklace in person.

Interrupted amid the new stack of correspondence that had been delivered from London, Brett did not believe young Selden wanted the necklace for his sister. The handsome young baronet likely had a ladybird somewhere and was too embarrassed to admit it, the mooncalf. For sure the woman Sir Eustace was describing bore no relation to the harridan Lord Boughton had twice encountered. Good-natured and giving? Hah! She hadn't given him one of the blasted cats, had she?

And the necklace was undoubtedly in Charleen's grasping hands by now. He could easily get it back, the earl knew, by promising a more expensive bauble, but the lad had no money and no claim to the pearls. He did, however, have something the earl wanted very badly.

"You'll trade me the pearls for one of m'sister's kittens?" Sir Eustace scratched his head. "I don't know, she's that particular about where they go. If she turned you down, she must have had good reason." He paused, but the earl was not about to discuss Miss Selden's mutton-headed motives. "Technically, the cats are half mine, as our uncle meant the first pair for both of us. But I would never go against m'sister's wishes in the matter." From what he'd seen of the earl's grand estate, though, Stacey could hardly imagine a better home for anyone, feline or otherwise. And he realized how foolish his attempt to purchase the pearls had been. Why, the earl had more blunt than Golden Ball. "I'll have to think on it, my lord."

"You do that," Boughton told him, going back to his paperwork. Damn, what he wouldn't give for a secretary! "I say, you wouldn't perchance be interested in a position, would you?"

* * *

The earl was in Ossing, what an opportunity! Euan Mactavish was not one to let an opportunity slip by, b'gad. He hadn't made his fortune by waiting for it to fall into his lap, by Jupiter, and he wasn't going to let this chance, or this earl, pass him by. The chap just might be looking for a sweet young thing to mother his little girl, an unspoiled beauty who wouldn't mind being left in the country while the earl pursued his own pleasures. Boughton might be above his Ginger's touch, but Mactavish had nothing to lose by trying, and a title to gain. So the merchant decided he'd throw a fancy dinner to welcome his nibs back to the neighborhood. Ginger would have a new gown, and sparklers enough to dazzle even a London buck, and she'd impress the nob with her ladylike ways and her ability to run a gentleman's household. The only problem was, his Ginger could barely order herself a cup of tea, much less a dinner for a top-of-the-trees toff. He sent for Miss Geraldine Selden.

Gerry did not mind in the least being hired on to plan a lavish entertainment at her old home, in addition to her sessions with Miss Virginia, and she was pleased with the extra income. She was that much closer to being able to make Squire a respectable offer for the mare. What Gerry could not approve, however, were the plans Mr. Mactavish confided in her for his daughter's future. Miss Virginia was a sweet child, and Boughton would eat her for breakfast. Whatever poise Gerry had managed to instill in the lovely innocent would be drained away by one of the earl's dark scowls. And if he kissed her, as the rake was wont to do with every female who crossed his path, Gerry supposed Miss Mactavish would dissolve in a puddle of tears. She was already red-eyed and swollen-faced, likely from crying over her father's ambitions to throw her at the neighborhood's most eligible and elevated gentleman. Fortunately, in Gerry's mind, Ginger now had the kitten Bandit to console her.

*

The earl was in Upper Ossing, and what a pawky little village it was, too, with barely a decent shop. But if Boughton was at The Boughs, that's where Charleen, Lady Trant, was bound.

The earl was not pleased to see her. He didn't used to be so stuffy, she told him, but he didn't used to think of himself as a parent, either. A gentleman simply did not stable his convenient alongside his family. Charleen was deuced inconvenient, in fact, even if she had brought her old auntie along as chaperone to satisfy the conventions. That wouldn't satisfy one brown-eyed beldam who already thought he was a womanizer. Besides, the aunt was stone deaf, and twice as short of sight as Charleen. Damn. And he couldn't throw them out until he had the blasted necklace. Young Selden had turned out to be an excellent secretary, for one thing, and Brett still had hopes of trading for the kitten, for another. But Charleen was not parting with the gewgaw, not even when he said that his solicitor must have made an error, that he'd meant the pearls as a gift for his daughter. Not even when he said a diamond and ruby necklace would be waiting for Charleen in London. No, now she wanted more before she'd leave him in peace. Now she wanted one of the blasted exotic cats Sammy was raving about. Double damn.

*

The earl was in Ossing, good heavens, and his mistress was there with him! Miss Musgrove found the situation unpalatable, unprincipled, and untenable. Even if she could not tell from her bedroom in the nursery wing if the earl was winging toward his paramour's suite every night, Miss Musgrove was mortally offended. In fact, if Miss Musgrove had somewhere else to go, she'd be out of this house of licentious depravity in an instant. The idea of a cat in the house was bad enough, but a courtesan?

6

The earl was in Ossing, by George! Squire Remington was delighted. At last, a decent hand of cards! Boughton accepted the invite—he never had been high in the instep, Squire reflected—and arrived one evening after his daughter was asleep. Squire politely inquired into the little miss's health and raised his glass to her continued recovery.

"And your fine family?" Brett asked, savoring the cognac and cigars, away from the disapproving Miss Musgrove or the clinging Lady Trant or her old deaf auntie. Conditions at The Boughs were not precisely congenial. "What is it, three boys?"

Squire sighed. "Aye, my good wife Rose blessed me with three healthy sons: Tibold, Corcoran, and Diogenes. She bore 'em and gave 'em jumped-up names, then had the good sense to shuffle off this mortal coil afore she had to raise the limbs of Satan. No matter, I call 'em all Sonny, on account of they never sit still long enough for me to figure which is which." He sighed again and refilled his glass.

"It sounds as if they need a firm disciplinarian," Brett suggested from a superior position. *His* daughter would never cause a groat of trouble.

"Aye, but the village schoolmaster won't have them back, even after the school is rebuilt, the vicar refuses to let them come near him except on Sundays, and young Selden is too tenderhearted. I tried to convince his sister to take them in hand, but it 'pears Miss Gerry knows them too well."

"You tried to hire the baronet's sister as governess?" He knew they were fallen on hard times, but never thought things had come to such a pass. He could not envision the proud little beauty in some menial post.

"Governess? Hell, no. Offered to marry her, don't you know. Governesses can up and quit; wives can't. Fine gel, Miss Gerry.

Everyone hereabouts adores her. She helps run the orphanage and the Ladies' Aid Society, besides assisting vicar with the parish."

"A veritable paragon." Brett was having to revise his opinions of Miss Selden in light of his own daughter's near veneration of the female. The servants, the tradesmen, the local shopkeepers, all sang her praises. Unfortunately, the lady showed charity to everyone but him.

Squire sighed yet again. "Aye, she is that. Would have suited me to a cow's thumb, having her around. She turned me down, though, even when I offered to pay some of the brother's expenses."

"Why? Was she holding out for a better offer?"

Squire scowled at him. "Miss Gerry? The gel ain't greedy, if that's what you're hinting at. Said she wouldn't feel right marrying without her heart coming along."

Brett raised his glass, and his estimation of the lady. "To an honest woman."

After a few more hands of piquet, which mostly went in the earl's favor, Brett reintroduced the topic. "You say you are looking for a governess, then?"

"More like a warden, till the lads are ready for boarding school." Remington put his cards down and looked at Brett like an eager puppy. "D'you know of any?"

"I just might know a respectable woman in need of a position. Not in the first blush of youth, mind, but she has high standards, and will not tolerate any nonsense in her house."

"Just the thing! I'd be mightily obliged if you'd give me her direction. Obliged enough to lose another fifty pounds to you."

Brett waved aside the money. "Would you be obliged enough to beg a favor from Miss Selden? I want one of her kittens, but don't seem to pass muster."

"Sorry, Boughton, but she won't part with them for an abbey." He rubbed his chin. "Happens though that I do have something she wants, a horse her brother raised up from a foal. Jigtime ought to be racing, but I'm more interested in hunters, don't you know. I figured to let my oldest have her when he's ready. Seems Miss Gerry's been giving lessons and such just to pay the price. It's a shame really. She's a game little mare."

Jigtime or Miss Selden? Brett wondered. It seemed that the hard-working brother and sister really were that devoted that they would make such sacrifices toward the other's happiness. Damn, and he'd given her pearls to his particular! He made a mental note to send to London for an even costlier necklace for Charleen. "And you say Miss Selden wants to get the horse back for her brother?"

"Aye, a Christmas present. If you're serious about finding me a caretaker for the cubs, I'll trade you the horse for m'gaming vouchers, when your woman takes the job. If you offer the horse, mayhaps Miss Gerry will look on you more kindly." He shrugged. "Didn't work for me, but you might have better luck. After all, you only want a cat. I wanted a keeper for my boys."

*

Miss Selden was not seeing the earl in a better light. Oh, the light was better, thanks to the new chandeliers Mr. Mactavish had installed at Selden House, and the countless oil lamps on every surface. And the earl was looking bang up to the mark, as her brother would say, in his formal evening dress, with his black hair combed back, except for one dark lock that fell on his forehead. That forehead might as well have sprouted horns when she heard his latest offer.

"A kitten for the horse, that Squire owns, but might trade for your daughter's governess? That's...that's diabolical!"

The earl studied his manicured fingers. If Miss Selden thought this negotiation was demon-spawned, he prayed she never heard the rest of the bargain. Charleen had agreed to give up the pearls if he produced an expensive bracelet, a new protector, and a kitten. So he had to get the horse from Squire, so he could trade Miss Selden for a kitten, which he would give to Charleen, in order to get the pearls for Sir Eustace, who was then supposed to get another kitten for Samantha. And everything hinged on musty Miss Musgrove surviving a week of Squire's sons. Deuce take it, why couldn't Miss Selden just give him the blasted cat before his wits went begging altogether? And why did she have to look so deuced pretty with her hair done up in a crown-like coil atop her head, held by a ribbon that almost begged a man to tug loose, so he could see the brown locks flow down across her shoulders, across his pillow. Lud, where had that come from? He was supposed to be thinking of exchanging livestock with the woman, not heated kisses!

"It's a trifling matter," Brett lied. "I have something you want; you have something I want. A simple transaction among friends."

They weren't friends and nothing was simple. Except perhaps her brother, for acting the mooncalf over Miss Ginger. Mactavish was furious, dinner was a disaster, and Gerry had the headache.

The first catastrophe was the cook's tantrum in the drawing room where the company was taking sherry before dinner. No, that wasn't even the first crisis. The first calamity was Boughton bringing his mistress to Selden House for supper! Ginger was tongue-tied, Stacey's eyes never strayed above Lady Trant's inadequate neckline, and Gerry was outraged. How dare he! Then the old auntie tripped over the kitten, which by rights should not have been in the parlor and for which Mactavish loudly berated his daughter and Gerry both, in front of the company. The shout sent Lady Trant's aunt careening into the end table, spilling the sherry.

Ginger started to cry, naturally, clutching Bandit to her— compared to Lady Trant's expanse—girlish bosom. Her eyes, already red, started to overflow. Stacey went to her, out of kindness, and removed the kitten from her grip to make sure it had taken no harm, handing over his own handkerchief. Whether it was his gentle smile, despite her being quite out of looks, or the way he held the kitten without the least regard for his dark coat, Miss Mactavish was smitten. Anyone listening hard enough could have heard Ginger's heart fall at Stacey's feet, which were five feet off the ground by this time. He'd received a timid smile from an angel, and he was lost. He never even looked at Lady Trant's bosom again.

And Ginger never thought to send for a servant to clean up the mess, so Gerry had to, and asked that dinner be set forward, which caused the irate chef to appear, which sent Ginger into strong hysterics, which led Stacey into putting his arms around her, which led Mactavish to turn even redder in the face than his daughter. And which caused the dastardly earl to wink at her!

A downy one such as Lord Boughton had to have known Mactavish's ambitions to snabble him for a son-in-law, just as he had to notice his mistress eyeing the lavish appointments—added to Selden House by Mactavish—with an appraiser's eye. He found it amusing! He even smiled at her throughout the longest dinner of Gerry's life, as if asking her to share the joke. Some joke, when she would lose her prize pupil at the best, and they might lose Mactavish as a tenant at worst. There was no way he would tolerate an alliance between his princess and a pockets-to-let baronet. Gerry would not have been surprised if he'd ordered them from the house, instead of ordering the next course, when Ginger neglected to do so.

Seated at the foot of the table as hostess, Ginger had eyes—and words—for Stacey only. Heaven knew what they found to talk about, as Gerry hadn't wrung more than a few sentences out of the girl all week, unless they spoke of cats. Perhaps that's what Stacey had found to amuse the heiress, tales of the family pets. Either way, the girl ignored her other, intended dinner partner, the earl. Gerry was too far away to kick her under the table, so could only pray Mactavish did not notice his daughter's rag manners.

She needn't have worried. At the other end of the mahogany table, Lady Trant was serving up a generous display of bare flesh for the merchant's delectation, and Mactavish was seasoning his conversation with talk of investments, when he wasn't pouring the butter boat over the dashing widow. Across from Gerry, the aunt dipped her hand in the soup instead of the finger bowl. Gerry prayed for dessert.

When the ladies finally withdrew, after the butler had to remind Miss Mactavish to lead the women from the room, Lady Trant made much of the kitten, who hadn't ought to be in the Green Salon, either, sharpening its claws on the Aubusson carpet, and asked Gerry for one of her own.

"For it's sure to make a splash in London, don't you know. I'd like to be the first to have one of the newest breeds."

Gerry wasn't sure about the kind of home the kitten would have, or what would happen when Lady Trant grew tired of the latest fancy.

"And don't think the little darling would be left alone. Auntie is home most of the time. She would love a kitty on her lap. Wouldn't you, Aunt Forbish?"

"Eh?"

"Cats, I said. You love cats, don't you?" Charleen shouted.

"Eh?"

Lady Trant then offered to do Gerry a favor in exchange: "I'll convince our host that his chit is never going to do better than a baronet, not even with all his blunt greasing her way, and that he'll never find a lad who'll treat the gal better. Just seeing the pair of them makes me want to weep."

Gerry, too. "You'll never convince Mr. Mactavish. He has his heart set on a viscountcy at least." Charleen pulled up a dangling curl, and pulled down the lace at her bodice. "You just watch, my dear. At the least I can distract him for a bit. Otherwise he's liable to toss you and your delightful brother out before the tea tray is brought in."

When the men returned, Stacey went straight to the heiress, the nodcock, leading her and the kitten to the pianoforte. Giving Gerry a grin, Charleen draped herself over Mactavish's arm and begged him to show her the collection of carvings he'd brought back from

India, in the other direction. The aunt was snoring. And Gerry was alone with the earl.

Rather than permit him to bring up the issue of the cats again, she waved toward Lady Trant's departing trills of laughter. "Your, ah, friend seems to have abandoned you." Then she felt her cheeks flush with her impertinence.

"Greener fields, don't you know." The earl brushed her embarrassment aside, as if he made a practice of speaking about his ladybirds to ladies of quality. Or as if Gerry were a mature, intelligent female who understood the ways of the world. She understood nothing, except that his broad shoulders were close to hers on the sofa, and his well-muscled thigh was almost touching her leg. Good grief, she could not be attracted to such a here-and-thereian! Although her opinion of him was changing with each report Stacey brought home from The Boughs about the number of worthy charities that his lordship supported, and how he was having Stacey make lists of needed improvements to his tenants' holdings. And how his daughter thought he'd hung the moon.

"I did not invite Lady Trant to The Boughs," he was saying. "I encouraged her to leave, in fact." He wasn't sure why he felt he had to explain away his onetime inamorata, present-time houseguest, but he'd given over wondering why he'd wish to look better in this woman's eyes. Big, beautiful brown eyes they were, eyes a man could get lost in. He caught himself leaning closer, bending lower, breathing in the scent of her. Roses and something else, perhaps evergreen, from all the garlands around the room. He put another inch of distance between them, for safety's sake. "I just gave my blessings for Mactavish to hunt on my coverts anyway."

"Hunt on your...? Oh."

"I had thought she'd be more eager to return to London if she had one of your kittens to show off." Along with the diamond and ruby bracelet he'd ordered. "But now I doubt if she'd go, until she's got her claws firmly into the wealthy Cit."

"You don't mind?"

"What, that she's finding a new protector? That's why I asked to bring her tonight. It was either Mactavish or Remington. I am relieved."

So was Gerry.

"Oh, and I put in a good word with Mactavish about your brother. Told him I thought the lad would do well in politics, with the right backing. And that Prinny was handing out titles like tea cakes, to those who made significant contributions to the regent's coffers. No reason a baronet couldn't be elevated to baron or some such. I agreed to use my influence in Town."

He hadn't only hung the moon, but the stars along with it. "You did all that? For Stacey?"

"No, for a Christmas kitten for my daughter." And one for Charleen.

7

Miss Geraldine Selden wished she had more time, alas. With Christmas right around the corner, there were never enough hours for all the shopping, sewing, baking, and decorating, much less choir rehearsals, children's parties at the orphanage and the school, and informal gatherings at the neighbors'. Every year she vowed to start earlier, and every year she enjoyed every minute of the frantic rush. This year, however, she truly needed a few more weeks to try to earn enough money to reclaim Stacey's horse. He would be so disappointed when Mactavish banned him from Selden House as a suitor for the heiress, he'd need cheering more than ever. The mare couldn't take the place of Miss Mactavish's hand in marriage, of course; then again, Jigtime wouldn't soak his shirtfront with constant tears, as Miss Ginger seemed wont to do.

Gerry decided to make one more attempt to bargain with Squire Remington. Sadly, he no longer owned the horse, but he did want a kitten. Under no conditions would Gerry give one of her darlings to a house full of unruly, uncivilized little heathens, to say nothing of the hard-drinking squire and his flea-bitten hounds. He said he wanted the kitten for his sister in Bath, however, a poor invalid who could never travel. That was the excuse she gave for never visiting Remington Manor, at any rate. Gerry said she'd think about it.

*

Squire wished he had more time, blast it. With that confounded ball coming faster than a bull with a burr up his nose, Remington needed help. He put on his Sunday clothes, having washed his hands and face and behind his ears, and took himself off to Boughton's place. At The Boughs, he made Miss Musgrove a handsome offer, which she handily accepted. The governess moved into the manor; Jigtime moved to the earl's stables. Suddenly there was peace and quiet.

Suddenly the servants were not threatening to leave. Suddenly Squire could take a nap in his own book room without barricading the door and hiding the key to his gun cabinet or his wine cellar. Glory! And the woman had done it all in…jig time. Squire slapped his knee. Damn, things were looking up. He was feeling so in charity with the world, in fact, that when Miss Selden called, he asked for one of her infernal cats. Silly creatures, they were, all hair and no nose, with enough airs to shame a duchess, but if she was too stubborn to trade with the earl, Squire decided, he'd see they both got what they wanted. They might even get a bit more than they bargained for. He slapped his knee again, which a mangy brindle dog named Squeaky took as invitation to join him on the couch.

*

Miss Musgrove wished she had more time, by heaven. The whole county was invited to Squire's ball and she'd barely begun to get the little savages in hand—a hand which incidentally held a birch rod—much less the servants, the sty of a manor, and Squire himself. The dogs had to go, as soon as she had a firmer grip on the reins, but at least Miss Musgrove was only sharing her quarters with unmannered mongrels, not mistresses.

*

Charleen, Lady Trant, wished, once again, that she had more time. But there was another wrinkle in her mirror every day, so she dare not wait much longer. She was no closer to melting Boughton's heart, if he had one to melt, and her bills were no closer to being paid. Most likely she'd never had a chance of bringing the top-sawyer up to scratch, no, not even if she'd managed to get one of those curtain-climbing cats for his sickly little brat. His gratitude would extend only so far. So far he had presented her with a necklace she wouldn't be ashamed to walk into a pawn shop with, and the promise of a check waiting for her in London—if she left, and left him the pearls. His patience was growing as thin as

Charleen's hair, from all the bleaching. Aunt Forbisher's kissing the antique armored knights, hoping for one of the footmen under the mistletoe, wasn't helping. So Charleen powdered her nose and rouged her cheeks, and went to see Mr. Mactavish. The bald old man couldn't hold a candle to the earl, but he did hold a king's ransom in Consols.

*

Mactavish wished he had more time, by George, time to show his little girl off in London and time to make a noble match for her. But she was getting her heart set on young Selden more every day. And turning into a blotch-faced watering pot, besides. With her looks so off, it was a wonder even the baronet came to call. Mactavish wanted her married, he wanted her a lady, but more and more, he wanted his mewling daughter and her meowing cat off his hands. Especially now, when he could wrap his hands around the tidiest bit of willing woman he'd encountered in years—if his daughter were not underfoot. That was why he got so excited when Lord Boughton came to make an offer. Unfortunately, the offer was for Ginger's cat, not Ginger.

"What, part those two? Be easier to part the Red Sea, my lord. The widgeon ain't been the same since she got the puss, but I've got enough woe trying to get her mind off young Selden without sending her into a decline. But happens I might be able to persuade Miss Selden to give me another, to sweeten me toward the family, like. I could say I got so used to having the little blighter underfoot that I want one of my own, for when Ginger goes off on her wedding trip."

"You get the cat for me, Mactavish, and I'll get Selden a higher title, even if I have to give him one of mine."

*

The earl wished he had more time, by Jupiter. Christmas was just days away and he was no nearer to getting one of the wretched little beasts for his daughter than he was to flying. He'd even inspected every litter of kittens in the shire, it seemed, in hopes of finding one that looked peculiar enough to pass for one of Miss Selden's misfits. He had his London solicitor make inquiries at the Royal Feline Fanciers Society, with no luck. Drat the woman for being a pig-headed prude when it came to giving away the Malukistan mousers. And drat her for intruding on his dreams, too. She was not mistress material, and she sure as the devil would not make a comfortable wife, if he were in the Marriage Market, which he was assuredly not. Therefore, she had no business in his thoughts, his imaginings, his Christmas wishing. Brett vowed to put Miss Selden entirely out of his mind—as soon as he'd gone to the gatekeeper's cottage one more time.

*

Sir Eustace wished he had more time, hang it. At first he worried that Mactavish would scoop Ginger off to London for presentation to every fortune hunter in town, or arrange a marriage for her with some ancient aristocrat. He didn't think the merchant could outright ban him from the doorstep of Selden House, since Stacey still owned the pile, but he could make sure Ginger wasn't home to receive him. The old man seemed to be leaning toward favoring his suit, though, with the earl's influence, Stacey didn't doubt. At least he'd stopped slamming doors and throwing things, according to Ginger, who was adorably ablush as she offered him tea. Before the old crab could change his mind again, Stacey meant to make a formal offer for his darling Ginger. He was fairly certain she'd accept, too, if her father gave permission. She'd whispered to him after church that she missed him. What joy! Stacey had walked into a tree, waving goodbye. Lud, he wanted his sister to know such happiness. Furthermore, he wanted her to have a comfortable future, without having to share the cottage with him and Ginger. Even if Mactavish let them all move back to Selden House, the baronet knew Gerry would not be content as a poor relation in another woman's home.

Sir Eustace desperately wanted his sister to shine at Squire's ball, his last hope that a particular nobleman would take notice. He wanted her pearls.

Gerry was out delivering baskets to the needy when Boughton called, but Sir Eustace was glad to see his employer, even if he was a shade embarrassed to have to wipe cat hairs off the chair before he could invite the earl to sit. Once he'd poured a glass of brandy, he put forth his new offer. As he explained to the earl, if Stacey could gain Mactavish's blessing, then the bank would surely make him a loan against future expectations, with which he could pay Lord Boughton back for his sister's necklace. Not that he was interested in Miss Mactavish for her father's money, he made sure the earl knew.

"I never supposed such a thing, not with the two of you making sheep's eyes at each other across the church aisle all through vicar's sermon." He reached into his coat pocket and withdrew a velvet pouch. "No, the pearls should never have been sold. I understand the need at the time, and I only blame your father for that, not you. But they belong to Miss Selden. So, here, take them, for her. You've worked hard enough to earn them. They're yours, no strings attached. The only thing is, if you could see your way clear…"

"You still need a kitten for your daughter."

So Stacey asked his sister for one of the cats as soon as she returned home. "You just have to trust me on this, Gerry. You know I'd never do anything to hurt one of them."

Since he was sitting on the sofa with Ranee on his shoulder and Mizra Khan playing with his watch fob, and kittens tumbling in his lap, she could not refute his love for the creatures. Nor how happy and carefree he seemed, for the first time in ages. "I'll think about it," was all she said.

"Don't think for too long. I mean it for a Christmas present."

Gerry wished she had more time. And more kittens.

*

Lady Samantha Wouk wished she had more time, but she was not giving up hope. Her father was here, Miss Musgrove was not, and Sammy needed only one more miracle.

"Papa, why don't you ask Miss Selden to call, so she can see what a nice home we'll give the kitten?"

"You know I cannot invite an unmarried woman to my house, poppet. That must have been one of Aunt Jane's rules you forgot."

"You could if we invited Sir Eustace and Miss Mactavish to tea, also, couldn't you?"

"I suppose that might suit, if you are sure you are well enough for it."

"Papa, I am feeling fine!"

She was looking less peaked every day, and had, to his mind, an inordinate amount of energy for a sickly child. One more game of Hide and Seek would have him taking to his bed. Company tea sounded lovely. The invitations went out, were accepted, and Lady Samantha threw herself into planning her first party.

First to arrive, Gerry and her brother were met at the door by two footmen who took their wraps, and a bewigged butler who escorted them to the nursery parlor, where another footman threw open the door, so the butler could announce their names with every ounce of pomposity he could muster. Lady Samantha giggled. So did Gerry.

A gentleman playing with his son was always an affecting sight, but a lord presiding at his daughter's dolls' tea party was sheer magic. The earl was seated at a child-sized table, his knees almost touching his chest, balancing a tiny teacup. How had Gerry ever thought him stiff and careless of others, arrogant and unloving? His affection for the little girl shone through the embarrassed flush at being caught in such an undignified pose. "We, ah, that is, Sammy thought you should see where the kitten would reside, before taking tea downstairs. Perhaps you would care to wait below, Sir Eustace, in case Miss Mactavish arrives soon and wonders where her host and hostess have disappeared to."

Stacey was down the stairs before the hoped-for cat could lick its ear. Gerry did not have time to feel the awkwardness in the situation—although she did note that there was no impropriety, with the young housemaid mending one of Lady Samantha's pinafores in the corner—before the child took her hand and led her to the nursery bedroom. Gerry was encouraged to inspect the wicker basket, lined with the softest flannel, that was to be the kitten's bed. Pretty porcelain bowls were already set out on an embroidered table runner, waiting food and water.

"And behind the screen in the schoolroom is where its earth box will go. Jed Groom is building it. What do you think?"

"I think you and your father have thought of everything," Gerry noted, except, of course, how devastated the child would be if no kitten appeared on Christmas morn. Now this was blackmail in the worst degree. Gerry glowered at the earl, who merely shrugged his shoulders, but he couldn't hide the dimpled grin, the same one Samantha wore. Gerry conceded, as they all knew she must.

"I can see you will make an admirable cat keeper, my dear. I am sure one of Ranee's kittens will be happy to come live with you."

The child threw her thin arms around Gerry's legs, almost toppling her, in her excitement. "Oh, but Papa said it's to be a surprise."

"I'll wager he did," Gerry said dryly, trying not to smile at the shamefaced earl. "Have you decided on a name for this Christmas surprise?"

"Why, I—Papa! Mistletoe!"

"That's a lovely name for a—" Gerry started, until she noticed the little girl was pointing upward. There, above her head in the doorway of the room, was a lopsided ball of crudely woven vines, with a ribbon-tied spray of mistletoe dangling from one twig.

"Gentleman's duty, don't you know," the earl teased, taking her by the shoulders. He meant for the kiss to be a quick touching. It wasn't. Gerry meant to offer her cheek for the ritual. She didn't. They both intended to remain unaffected by the forced contact. They weren't. Warmth and wanting mingled with their breaths, tenderness and unspoken yearnings.

The kiss went on and on, touching eternity, touching paradise. Then Samantha was touching them. "Papa, won't Miss Mactavish and Sir Eustace think we are rude if we don't go down soon?"

8

Christmas wishes did come true. Just ask anyone at Squire's country ball. Why, there was hardly a dry eye in the place.

Squire wiped away tears of pride to see his three boys polished up like bright new apples, and his house gleaming. Even his hounds had had baths. Almost bursting his buttons, he welcomed his friends and neighbors, and bade them share a toast to his forthcoming nuptials to dear Ermintrude.

"Who the deuce is Ermintrude?" murmured more than one of the company. Then Remington brought forth Miss Musgrove, her black bombazine exchanged for a dove-gray merino that made her look more like a pouter pigeon than an old crow. Not that the ex-governess would be guilty of showing such emotion in public, but she nobly restrained tears of satisfaction, that she would never have to seek another position.

After a few more toasts, Mr. Mactavish cleared his throat and, despite tears of chagrin, announced the betrothal of his daughter Virginia, to Sir Eustace. Ginger was as damp-eyed and sniffly as usual, but no one doubted her happiness, the way she beamed at the young baronet through her tears. She never left her fiancé's side.

At Mactavish's side, Charleen, Lady Trant, sported a new ruby bracelet besides the new diamond necklace, with stones so big she didn't need spectacles to be dazzled. She kept bottled up inside the tears of relief that she wouldn't end her days in the poor house. Nothing ruined a woman's looks faster than weeping, she'd always believed, or made a man more uncomfortable. Charleen was going to make sure that Mr. Mactavish stayed very comfortable indeed.

Her aunt kept dabbing at tears of mirth. That old uncle of the squire's was more shortsighted than she was, and the two were having a high old time under the mistletoe boughs. At least she told the old coot it was mistletoe.

Sir Eustace was also enjoying the kissing balls, and the congratulations of all his friends and neighbors. He'd actually gone and won the hand of the sweetest, most adorable girl in all of England. By sheer luck, she'd turned out to be one of the wealthiest heiresses. Now he'd never have to worry about losing his heritage, his family home. And he'd be able to look after his dear sister, too. Why, just seeing Gerry in her green velvet gown, with the string of pearls at her throat, made him almost as watery-eyed as his beloved. To add to his joy, Gerry had made him shut his eyes that afternoon, as Jigtime had been brought round by the earl's groom, with red bows woven in the mare's mane, and bells on her bridle. Truly this was the finest Christmas in memory.

It was positively Lady Samantha's best yuletide ever. Her first real party, held in her father's arms as Squire lit the Yule log in the manor's huge fireplace and blessed all the company. She was so tired, though, that she nearly fell asleep there on her father's shoulder during the caroling, almost weeping that she'd be sent home with Maggie and the footmen, without seeing Papa dance with Miss Selden. Her only consolation was that when she awoke in the morning, she'd have a cat of her own.

Everyone would have a cat of their own. Gerry had seen to it. Mr. Mactavish was getting Tiffany, the gold-colored kitten. Squire was to have placid Coco, for his sister in Bath. Gerry thought her brother should have Speedwell, the kitten with the bluest eyes, for they almost matched his Ginger's eyes, when they weren't swollen shut. Lady Trant was a perfect match for Sheree, the prettiest kitten, the one that Gerry had thought to keep for herself. And the smallest, Mistletoe, of course, was asleep in her lidded basket, waiting for Lady Samantha. Gerry wished she could see the look on the child's face on Christmas morning. But this evening would be enough, if she didn't take to blubbering with gladness over her brother's bliss.

The Earl of Boughton was not crying, of course. If his eyes were moist, it was likely due to the game of snapdragon he'd played earlier, trying to win Samantha a raisin from the flaming bowl. Brett could not deny, though, that his heart was overflowing. Never had he known such contentment over such simple pleasures as he was finding among friends and family. He'd never felt such satisfaction, not without being castaway, winning a fortune at wagering, or being sexually satiated.

He could make this joy last, Brett knew, longer than this one night, longer even than the Twelve Days of Christmas. All he had to do was give up his freedom, place himself and his child at the mercy of a managing female he barely knew—and could barely keep his hands off, in her green velvet gown. *Now* he felt like crying.

But he'd do it, humble himself, for Sam's sake. That Miss Geraldine Selden fit perfectly beneath his chin, or that she had the softest skin in the kingdom and the most generous nature on earth, had little to do with the fact that she doted on his little girl and Sam adored her. Like hell it didn't.

"Would you care to look at Remington's portrait gallery?" he asked sometime later, when she was resting between vigorous country reels.

"Oh, Squire doesn't have a formal gallery. He keeps a few ancestors in the book room, where the card tables are set out."

"A trip to the refreshments room, then?"

"No, thank you, my lord. Mr. Heron just brought me a glass of lemonade."

"A walk outside?" Lud, he was getting desperate. It was colder out than Charleen's heart. Gerry just smiled, handed him her lemonade, and went off to dance with the curate. Brett's patience came to an end altogether when the party ended and he hadn't had one minute alone with Gerry. He suggested, therefore, that Sir Eustace escort his betrothed home. He would see to Miss Selden's return to the cottage.

Too enamored to question the propriety of such a happy notion, Stacey went off with Ginger. How much could happen between Remington Manor and the cottage, anyway?

One kiss. One kiss lasted the entire journey, with infrequent pauses for breathing, for shifting Gerry onto Brett's lap. One kiss, and her hair and bodice were both disarranged.

"Oh, dear, I cannot go home like this."

"Good." Brett rapped on the carriage roof and instructed the driver to stop by The Boughs first. "To deliver the kitten," he added for the driver's benefit. "I gave the servants the night off," he added for Gerry's. The earl waited in his library, counting his blessings, while Gerry tidied herself in one of the spare bedrooms. They went up to the nursery together, the kitten complaining at being in the basket so long.

Gerry spoke softly: "Hush, Mistletoe. It's not every cat that gets to be a Christmas wish come true."

By the light of the oil lamp left burning, they could see that Samantha was fast asleep. Gerry tucked one hand under the covers, and then she tucked the kitten under the child's chin.

Brett raised an eyebrow. "What about the cat bed, on the floor?"

"Don't be a gudgeon," was all she said. "Mistletoe will end up here anyway." She kissed the kitten on the nose, and the child on the forehead, and stepped back. "There, that's done."

"And what about your Christmas wishes, my dear?" Brett asked.

"Did you see how pleased my brother was? He intends to start a racing stud, so he won't be so dependent on Mactavish's money forever." She touched the necklace at her throat. "And I got my pearls, something I never expected at all. It's a perfect holiday already. And you? What did you wish for?"

Brett looked at his sleeping daughter, and the beautiful woman at her bedside. "I was too blind to know what to wish for. I couldn't have described it or given it a name in words. But it seems fate knew what I needed for my happiness, far more than I. Now there is only one thing missing from my perfect holiday."

"Goodness, what could that be? You can have anything you want."

"Can I?" He took a ring from his pocket, a huge diamond set with emeralds. "Will you accept?"

Gerry had never seen a diamond so big, not even on Lady Trant. "Heavens, you aren't offering me *carte blanche,* are you?"

"With the Boughton engagement ring? I'll find something more to your taste if you don't like it."

"Oh, no, I love it." She was already admiring the ring on her finger.

"And me?"

Now she turned to admire the anticipation she saw burning in his eyes. "Oh, I must have loved you from the moment your horse pushed me into the mud. My wits have gone begging ever since, don't you know."

He knew very well, having suffered the same condition without the excuse of a knock on the head. "And I love you, my precious Miss Selden. Will you do me the honor of becoming my wife, my countess, my happily-ever-after?"

Despite the absence of nearby mistletoe—the berries, not the cat—they sealed their engagement with a kiss. Sometime later, Gerry heard the hall clock chime. "Gracious. I must be getting home. It's almost time for church. And I'll have to fix my hair again."

He was searching the carpet for her missing hairpins. "Before you go, I have a problem that requires your expertise."

"A problem?"

He nodded as he led her downstairs to the library. "A person can have too many, ah, blessings, it seems." There in the corner of the room, barricaded behind hastily rearranged chairs, pillows from the couch, and piles of books, was a laundry basket, filled with kittens. Long-haired, short-nosed, blue-eyed kittens. "But...?"

He bent to put one of the kittens back in the basket. "But Squire had no sister in Bath, and Mactavish doesn't even like cats. Lady Trant has no need to make a splash in London, now that she's got her nabob. Your brother only wanted to exchange one for the pearls." He held up Bandit. "And Miss Mactavish has concluded that she'd rather not spend the rest of her days sneezing and wheezing."

"It was the cat all along?"

He nodded. "It seems all of our friends wanted Sam to have her kitten. More than that, I'd guess half were playing at matchmaker. And they were right. I can't do without you. I could manage to raise my daughter, and I could even survive the emptiness I knew before you." He gestured toward the wriggling kittens. "But this? Only you can help."

She knelt by his side. "Will you mind?"

"What, that your brother gets to raise prime horseflesh and I get to raise push-faced hairballs? Not at all, sweetings."

Gerry knew he was teasing by the way he was rubbing a kitten's belly, with one gentle finger. "I wish…"

"Anything, my love."

"I wish you would kiss me again."

So he did, because Christmas wishes really do come true.

Little Miracles

1

They were as poor as church mice. No, they were the church mice. It was the little stone church that was so poor it could barely sustain a resident family of Rodentia religiosa. St. Cecilia's in the Trees was so poor it could have been called St. Cecilia's in the Twigs, for all the nearby oaks had been cut long ago for firewood. The church was so poor that when Portio Mea Domine, named for the page from the Book of Common Prayers she was given for bedding, decided to use the alms box for a nursery, nothing disturbed her nestlings. Not a shilling, not a farthing, nary a ha'penny interrupted the infants' rest, not even hungry fingers seeking aid. The parishioners knew better, for they were as poor as the church. Prices were high, incomes were low. Wars and enclosures, bad weather and bad management, influenza and indifference had taken their toll on the entire region of Lower Winfrey. Whole families had moved, seeking better lives in the New World, or in the factory cities of the north.

Whole families of the Churchmouse clan had to move, too. Without the Sunday worshipers, no pockets were filled with crumbled muffins from hurried breakfasts, no childish hands clutched sacks of peppermint drops. The Communion bread barely stretched as far as the few poor congregants who still attended services. Nothing was left for the mice. The gleanings were not enough to fill a flea, much less a family of *Mus ministerus.*

The mice could not even raid the vicarage's paltry pantry, not while the sexton's tomcat, Dread Fred, was on patrol. They lost both little Hope of Redemption and one-eared Abiding Hope to Dread Fred in one week. All hope of continuing the clan, in fact, was nearly gone. What the family had left, though, was a burning, inborn need to propagate their species, and an old secret. The secret of St. Cecilia's hidden wealth had been passed down from father to furry son for generations past counting. Now all they had to do was tell someone about it.

The church clansmice were true believers, of course, and one of their enduring beliefs was in the vow that God had made to the animals one Christmas Eve so long ago. He promised that on every succeeding Christmas Eve, the animals could talk, donkey to dung beetle, hen to horse. Peace would reign among them for that night, the lion lying down with the lamb; they could communicate with one another then, and be understood. This was the Lord's reward to the beasts who shared their humble shelter with the Holy Child.

One Christmas Eve, therefore, the head of the remaining Churchmouse clan, Uncle Nunc Dimittis, begged the nearby creatures to come to the little church. Dread Fred came, and Mrs. Sexton Cotter's chickens, along with the vicar's old horse, a passing fox, an owl, a rabbit, and some sleepy sparrows from the vicarage eaves.

"Why should we help you pesky vermin?" mumbled the horse, unused to speaking since he'd had no stablemates after the vicar sold his carriage pair.

No one wanted to be the one to explain that the richer the church, the fatter the mice, and the more mice, the easier the hunting. The more food for the cat and the fox and the owl, the less they would prey on the chickens and the sparrows. Everyone but the hay-eating horse saw the advantages, but in the blessed spirit of brotherhood, the fox merely said, "Because we are all God's children."

So the creatures agreed to help. Climbing past fallen stones in the walls or under the rotten floorboards or through the holes in the roof, they took up places around the little church and waited for the vicar to come. The horse poked his grizzled muzzle through a broken window.

As was his wont, Vicar Althorpe came to pray after ringing the bells for twelve o'clock. Now the vicar was an old man who had seen his parish and his income decimated, despite his prayers. Tonight they were going to be answered. "Lord, is that you?" he

288

cried in disbelief or awe. "Look to St. Francis," he heard again from every corner of the dilapidated church. "Look to St. Francis."

He spun around to see where the voices were coming from, and to find the statue of the saint in its niche. Before he could take a step in that direction, though, he clutched his chest, fell to the floor, and breathed his last, with a smile upon his lips.

The new vicar was a bitter young man, forced by his family into a profession clearly at odds with his predilection for gaming, wenching, and wine. Mr. Rudd was even more incensed when he realized what a meager living his family had found for him. His salary did not half cover his expenses, so he took to selling off the remaining stained glass windows, the last gold offering plate, and even an old hymnal or two. As was his wont, he entered the church one Christmas Eve after making sure the sexton rang the midnight bells, since they could be heard by his superior in Upper Winfrey. Rudd was not there to pray, but to see if by some chance some fool of a passerby had left a donation.

"Look to St. Francis," the animals called. The old horse was not among them, since Rudd would rather walk than be seen on such a decrepit beast, nor the rabbit, for Rudd had a rifle. "Look to St. Francis," they all tried to shout louder.

In their eagerness, the animals had forgotten a small technicality of the Christmas miracle: only a righteous man could hear and comprehend their speech. Rudd was so far from righteous he couldn't have heard Gabriel's trumpet.

"Bugger this," Dread Fred muttered. He leaped from the back of a pew onto the molding under St. Francis's niche. Using his well-honed claws, he climbed to the base of the statue and arched his back, making sure the other animals had seen his prowess. "Now watch."

When the vicar turned from the empty poor box, considering whether he could fence the gold chalice, and for how much, Dread Fred nudged the statue so it fell. St. Francis did not, however, land at Rudd's feet. The heavy statue hit the vicar on the head.

"He'd have stolen the thing anyway," the cat hissed as he slinked away.

In the morning the sexton replaced the statue in its niche, then he sent to replace the vicar.

Now the stone church was considered cursed, and was emptier than ever. Every one of the parishioners who could walk, ride, or drive the extra miles traveled to Most Holy Church in Upper Winfrey, with its choir loft and organ, its padded pews and charcoal braziers in winter. Only a few ancient villagers and farm folk came to St. Cecilia's on a Sunday, and then more to visit with one another than to pay homage.

Only two of the Churchmouse clan remained, old Exultemus Domine, who was too old to attract a mate, and young Passeth-All-Understanding, who had nothing to offer a wife, no rich cache of grains, no warm nest. Their prayer book was empty of pages to make a bridal bower, and they were reduced to eating the leather covers. They were out of paper, out of names, and nearly out of time. This would be the last Christmas for the clan, unless a miracle occurred. The other animals refused to help anymore, lest they be persecuted worse than they already were, so Pass and Ed could only huddle together and pray.

"...Give us this day our daily bread crumbs."

*

"And lead us not into temptation," the Reverend Mr. Evan Merriweather prayed, with little hope of success. How, by all that was holy and a few things that were not, was he to avoid temptation at Squire Prescott's Sunday dinner? He could easily resist second helpings, although the weekly meal was the only decent food he'd see all week. Compared to what he was served at the vicarage, Squire's mutton was manna. According to Ned Cotter, Mrs. Sexton Cotter had trouble seeing the labels on the spice jars. Evan believed she must have trouble seeing the spice jars at all. Complaining did no good, since Mrs. Cotter heard as well as she saw. The old sexton and his wife had come with the vicarage, and Evan did not have the heart to replace them. He did not have the funds to replace them with more competent help, either.

Still, he was easily able to refuse additional portions at Squire's, knowing the leftovers would be bundled into baskets for him to take round to the parish poor. There were so many poor, and so few baskets, not a single belly would be full, less so if the new vicar stuffed himself at Squire's board.

Mr. Merriweather was not remotely tempted to blow a cloud with Squire after the meal—filthy habit that it was—nor partake of the cognac Prescott pressed on him. Spirits gave Evan the headache, for one, and he did not deem them quite proper for a parson, on a Sunday. He had to set an example for his parishioners, didn't he? What if they saw him staggering back to the vicarage after an afternoon of imbibing?

Lud, how much worse if they saw him lusting after Squire's daughter? Evan ran his hands through his sandy hair and prayed harder, knowing how futile his efforts to avoid her attraction. He simply could not resist Alice Prescott. He was a man, by Heaven, not a monk, nor in his dotage, and she was a beautiful young woman, all rounded and soft, with silky golden curls. Beyond that, Miss Prescott was the sweetest, kindest creature ever put on God's green earth. Evan knew it was she who packed the foodstuffs for the poor, and she who added jams and apples and eggs from Squire's larder. She was the one who insisted the squire and his family attend little St. Cecilia's, rather than join the other gentry at Most Holy, thus putting their pence on the collection plate where they would do most good. Of course the rector at Most Holy still demanded his share of the tithes, likely to gild the baptismal font there, while St. Cecilia's used a chipped porcelain bowl.

Alice—for that's how Evan thought of Miss Prescott, although he would never presume to use her given name—brought flowers and greenery to the church, and embroidered new altar cloths. She visited the sick with broth and restoratives, and she helped teach the village girls skills and letters, so they might better themselves. Her mind and her morals everything admirable, Miss Prescott was as beautiful inside as out.

In other words, words Evan tried not to admit, even to himself, Alice Prescott was everything he could ever want in a wife—a helpmate, the perfect mother to his children, and yes, an alluring lover. She was everything he wanted, and nothing he would ever have. He could never make her an honorable offer, for he honestly had nothing to offer her but a rundown vicarage, an impoverished parish, and a pittance of a salary. Miss Prescott deserved so much more, and her father would insist upon it.

Mr. Merriweather had spent many hours since coming to Lower Winfrey and St. Cecilia's in the Trees three months ago in thinking how he could improve the conditions for his congregation. He'd spent endless hours more once he'd met Miss Prescott in wondering how he could improve his own position enough to be considered an eligible *parti.* His birth was decent, with connections to the current Lord Whittendale, titleholder of note in this area of Sussex, but that would not count with the squire or his wife. It barely counted with Lord Whittendale, who had ignored all of Evan's letters and all the messages sent through his land steward.

Evan could shore up the fallen roof of his church, and he could share his meager rations with the poor, but he could not change a blessed thing for his parishioners. He could tutor the few boys whose parents could afford Latin lessons, and he could scribe letters for the occasional traveler, but he could never afford to take a wife, not while he stayed on at St. Cecilia's.

Sometimes, in the dark of night, Evan thought of leaving. Not of leaving the Church, for unlike many others in orders, he'd never wished to be anything but a cleric, like his own father, may he rest in peace. But he could find another, better post somewhere, he was sure. Evan had taken honors at university, and had recommendations from the archbishop himself. Surely some wealthy parish needed a reverend ready to serve, although none could need him as much as St. Cecilia's. Being needed, Mr. Merriweather was sadly finding, was not the same as being useful. Yet how could he leave, and leave Alice Prescott?

Still on his knees there on the cold floor, making sure his trousers did not snag on any loose boards, for who knew how long before he could replace them, both the boards and the trousers, Evan pondered not going to Squire's for dinner, thus sparing himself the pain of seeing what he could not have. That would mean denying the needy the baskets of food, though, and denying himself the joy of one of Alice's smiles. He could no more stay away than the moth could stay away from the candle, but he could pray for inner peace and acceptance of his place in God's Greater Plan. If He meant His minister to be celibate and sorrowful, well, Evan would do his best, despite pangs for a hunger no mutton could satisfy.

2

The Reverend Mr. Merriweather dressed with care for dinner at the Manor. One did, he told himself, to honor one's hosts, to befit one's position, and to make a good impression on any guests Squire might also have invited. He was not fussing like a belle at her first ball on account of hoping to find favor in a pair of heavenly blue eyes. Of course not. He might be a poor vicar, but he had his dignity.

He had his pride, too. Evan could not help preening a bit in the mirror in the vicarage parlor, noting that all his work resetting the stone walls and sawing boards for the church roof had gained him muscles, as well as calluses. No scholarly stoop for this servant of the Lord. He smoothed his good coat over broader shoulders, and tried to flatten the cowlick at the back of his head.

"What's the lad doing, then, Ned?" Mrs. Cotter called to her husband. "Spitting on his hands?"

"He's trying to fix his hair, Emma, I think. I've got some pig grease I used on the church door, Reverend. Want I should fetch that? That's what I used when I was a-courtin' my Emma." Ned guffawed, then repeated his offer loudly enough for Emma to hear, and the neighbors next door.

"I am not going courting, and I do not wish to arrive at Squire's smelling of bacon, thank you."

"Aye, smelling of April and May is enough." Ned and Emma chuckled again.

So much for his pride and his dignity and his prayers that no one knew of his impossible affection for Miss Alice Prescott. Evan crammed his beaver hat over the offending curl and set off to walk the two miles to Prescott Manor, forlorn hope his only companion.

Squire, at least, was in a jovial mood, welcoming Evan with a glass of sherry before dinner. From his high color and booming voice, it appeared that Prescott had already welcomed the Naysmiths and Colonel Halsey, all of whom attended services at

Most Holy Church, with similar glasses of spirits. Evan made his bows, pretending to sip at his wine, pretending not to be watching the door. Then she was there.

Miss Prescott was wearing a blue gown embroidered with tiny flowers. Evan did not think it was the dress she'd worn to church that morning, but he could not be certain, since no one in St. Cecilia's removed their cloaks, not in December. He thought he would have noticed if her eyes were even bluer than usual, though, reflecting the color of her frock. He certainly would have noticed the silk flowers twined in her neatly coiled hair, matching the sprigs on her skirt. Reverend Merriweather decided he did not need dinner if he could feast his eyes on such a delicacy. For sure he'd never manage to swallow, not past the foolish grin on his face. Alice smiled at him and held out her hand. Evan put his glass of sherry in it.

His cheeks redder than Squire's, the vicar took the glass back, recalling courtesy and the company. He bowed to Mrs. Prescott, thanking her for the kind invitation, and inquired after the health of Squire's ancient auntie. Gratified, the antique relative latched onto his sleeve, which was already straining from his newly acquired muscles, and enumerated every ache and pain a person could suffer and still survive. Evan wondered whether his coat or his patience would expire first. Seated between Aunt Minerva and Mrs. Naysmith, whose husband owned the Winfrey Mercantile, Mr. Merriweather could look directly across the table, over a bowl of fruit, at Alice. He blessed Aunt Minerva and her megrims. Then he blessed the food, after Squire cleared his throat a few times and Alice kicked Evan's ankle, under the table.

As soon as grace was spoken, Squire raised his glass in a toast, to good food, good friends, and good news. "For Colonel Halsey has brought tidings of great import to our little neighborhood. Yes, and the Naysmiths have confirmed it. Lord Whittendale is coming home to White Oaks for Christmas."

"And about time," Aunt Minerva seconded, taking a healthy swig of her wine for such a febrile female.

Viscount Whittendale being Mr. Merriweather's patron, as well as a distant cousin, Evan would never say anything derogatory about the man. There was, however, no denying that Randolph Whitmore was a feckless, reckless here-and-thereian. Bad enough he callously let St. Cecilia's collapse, and the neighboring economy with it, but the viscount was a libertine, a known womanizer, an extravagant gambler, a devil-may-care chaser after the moment's pleasure. For the life of him, Evan could not think why anyone would be in alt to have such a one in their midst.

Sensing Evan's disapproval, the squire explained, "Good for business, don't you see? White Oaks is already ordering goods from the Mercantile, for the house party he'll be bringing with him."

More like an orgy, from what Evan knew of the viscount, but he refrained from comment as Mr. Naysmith raised his own glass. "Linens and toweling, soaps and candles. And his steward is adding on staff."

"And we heard he might hold a ball." Mrs. Naysmith beamed at the Prescott ladies, visions of dress lengths and lace dancing in her eyes.

"Yes, I can see where that can help put some money in local pockets," Evan admitted, "but Lower Winfrey needs more than a fortnight of revelry."

Squire slurped at his soup. "Who's to say Whittendale will be gone after Twelfth Night?"

"Lord Whittendale himself. He told me he despised ruralizing, the one time I met him when I interviewed for this position. He said he hadn't been here in a donkey's age, and didn't intend to visit any time soon." He had not bothered to reply to Evan's pleas for him to visit, to see conditions for himself. "I confess I should like a few moments of my lord's time, but doubt he'll stay even that long."

Prescott waved his spoon in the air, sending droplets of soup toward the centerpiece. Evan decided to forgo the fruit. "Idle

297

chitchat," Squire said, dismissing the vicar's misgivings. "No, word is that Lord Whittendale is ready to settle down."

"About time," Aunt Minerva repeated.

Even Squire's wife looked dubious. She read the London gossip columns as often as her husband. The *on dits* reached Sussex a few days late, but not *that* late.

"Just think," Prescott said around a slab of meat. "The man is thirty if he is a day. Long past time he starts setting up his nursery. He's sown his wild oats, aye, more than his fair share, but he knows what's due his name and his title. *Noblesse oblige* and all that. Asides, all that rushing from party to party and staying out all night grows tiresome. Mark my words, our viscount is coming to look over the country seat, with an eye toward rusticating."

"I hope you may be right, for St. Cecilia's sake, as well as for the rest of the community." Perhaps Evan would even get to ask the viscount for a raise in his salary. While the others speculated on the size and social standing of the viscount's house party, Reverend Merriweather let his mind wander to the size of increase he'd request. His thoughts traveled further afield on paths of gold and landed, as usual, on Alice Prescott—who was looking right at him.

She smiled as if she could see inside his mind and said, "I think we must all benefit from Lord Whittendale's visit, no matter how short."

"Quite right, puss. And I daresay if you play your cards right, you can be a viscountess one day."

Everyone turned to stare at Mr. Merriweather as his fork clattered onto his plate, then skittered to the floor. Mortified, Evan bent to pick it up, bumping his head on the mahogany table. Alice caught her father's attention to cover the vicar's awkwardness. "What fustian nonsense, Papa. As if I ever aspired to such lofty estate."

"And why not, I want to know?" her doting father asked. "You're wellborn enough. Wasn't your mama's grandfather a duke? And I paid enough for that fancy finishing academy to please the highest sticklers. Besides, you're a devilishly pretty chit, if I have to say so myself who shouldn't. Image of your mother at that age, don't you know. And she had beaux swarming at her feet. Could have had an earl, by George, but she chose me." Squire gazed fondly at his wife, the tender sentiments marred only by the gravy dripping down his chin.

"Yes, dearest," Mrs. Prescott said. "But the viscount is so...so sophisticated."

"So? Our gal had her London Season. I turned down plenty of offers on her behalf, too. Not like she's some chit fresh out of the schoolroom. Puss mightn't be a dasher, but she'll do, if Whittendale knows what's good for him."

"Doing it too brown, Papa. You know the viscount would never look at me when he has all those elegant females to choose from."

"Now who's talking gammon? A man don't want some pretty wigeon to be mother to his children and to run his household. When he's ready to take on leg shackles, he wants a sensible female, not an ornament. You're a good girl, my Alice, and Whittendale is bound to see that. If he doesn't, I'll bring it to his attention."

Blushing rosily, Alice took a hasty sip of wine. "You'll do nothing of the kind, Papa. Didn't you say that Lady Farnham was to be of the party? Her name was linked with that of the viscount last spring, when we went to London."

"Aye, Farnham's widow is coming along, for all the good it'll do her. A man don't marry his mistress, puss." Now Evan was blushing, as well as Mrs. Prescott and Mrs. Naysmith. Only Aunt Minerva, used to the freer morals of an earlier age, was unaffected by Squire's bluntness. The colonel harumphed. "Ladies present, I say."

Ladies were supposed to be conveniently deaf, dumb, and blind to the existence of such creatures, Evan knew, even when their husbands paraded their convenients through the park or at the

Opera. That was the kind of marriage Squire wished for his daughter?

It appeared so. "Tender sensibilities be blasted," Squire Prescott said, reaching across the table with his knife to spear another boiled potato. "Everyone knows it's due. A fellow might light on any number of full-blown roses, but he's going to wed the unopened bud."

A virgin, Evan thought. Squire was back to sacrificing virgins on the altar of ambition, like some pot-valiant pagan.

Aunt Minerva was nodding her agreement. "Unless he's dicked in the nob, and no one ever called little Randy Whitmore a slowtop."

Squire passed her the dish of eels in aspic, as reward for agreeing with him. "Right. A chap don't want to worry over his wife's morals, or what cuckoo bird is landing in his nest, especially not the toffs with their generations of blue blood to preserve. He don't want his sons' noses bloodied defending their mum, and he don't want to be forever dueling over rumors of her misconduct, either. There has never been a shred of gossip about my girl, and never will be, do you hear?"

Evan heard the warning, and could only wonder. Did Squire Prescott think *he* would cast dishonor on Alice's name? He'd sooner see his own tongue pickled in that aspic. "Of course not. Miss Prescott is the embodiment of virtue. A perfect lady. More so than many with the title before their names, I daresay."

"Just think, our dear Miss Prescott will be Lady Whittendale." Mrs. Naysmith was already calculating the cachet of having a titled lady as patron.

"My little girl, a viscountess," Mrs. Prescott said with a contented sigh.

Alice was sputtering, trying to topple her parents' air castles before they collapsed around her. She might as well have tried to hold back the tide, for Mrs. Prescott was already wondering where they should hold the wedding ceremony. "Not at St. Cecilia's, that's for certain, not with half the county and all those elegant London guests coming. Perhaps the viscount would prefer to be married in the City after all. I'm sure his town house can easily accommodate the wedding breakfast."

"Mama, there will be no—"

Squire turned to Evan. "So what do you think, eh, Reverend?"

Evan thought the mutton in his mouth tasted like masonry.

3

"I wish you would reconsider your notion to approach Lord Whittendale about a match with Miss Prescott, sir."

"I'll just bet you do, Merriweather. I'll just bet you do." Squire puffed on his cigar, filling the dining room with a blue haze. The ladies had departed for the withdrawing room, and Mr. Naysmith and the colonel had stepped out to use the necessary.

Evan did not want to think of the meaning behind Squire's words. Did everyone know of his calf-love for Alice? Had he been that obvious in his admiration? Evan brushed that dreadful thought aside with a sweep of his hand to clear the smoke. Maybe he could sweep away the fog in his brain box, too, for it was imperative that he think clearly now. Alice's entire future depended on him.

"As...as spiritual advisor to your family, I beg you to reexamine your heart. Do you truly think that Lord Whittendale will make your daughter a good husband?"

Squire blew a smoke ring. "As good as any. I never heard of Whittendale being the brutal sort. He'll not lay a hand on her, not with her papa next door."

"Good grief, I never meant to imply otherwise. I was thinking of her happiness."

"Of course she'll be happy as Viscountess Whittendale. She can have all the pretty dresses she desires, and she can enjoy herself in Town now and again, with invites that would never come her way as some country gentleman's offspring. She'll want for nothing. Rest assured I'll make sure the settlements are generous."

"Those are material things. What of peace of mind? Miss Prescott and my lord have neither interests, experiences, nor friends in common. Heavens, what will they even talk about?"

"The weather, for all I care." Squire's cheeks were getting red again, behind the blue smoke. "Dash it, they'll make friends, learn new interests, same as every married couple. That's what leg shackles are all about, don't you know. No, of course you don't."

Evan bravely persevered. "I know that a couple needs more than a license to make a go of a marriage, sir. You and Mrs. Prescott share a fine affection. Would you wish less for your daughter?"

The squire thought for a moment, swirling his brandy in its glass. "They can ride together, that's what. It's a start. Alice is a notable horsewoman, and Whittendale is renowned for his prowess."

The viscount was known for his neck-or-nothing style of riding. Surely Mr. Prescott did not intend for Alice to take up Lord Whittendale's daredevil ways. Evan's stomach lurched at the thought of gentle Alice riding hell-for-leather through the woods of White Oaks. She'd be tossed, or left behind at the first too-high hedge. He gulped a swallow of the brandy, knowing he'd have a headache later. He already had a heartache, so what was the difference? "He'll abandon her here in the country as soon as she is breeding. You know Lord Whittendale will not give up the pleasures of the City."

"Aye, and her mother will be thrilled to have the infants nearby to spoil. I won't mind dandling a little lordling on my knee either. Wonder if Whittendale has any courtesy titles lying around for his firstborn? Aunt Minerva will know."

Evan almost shouted in desperation. "But what of Alice?"

"She loves children. Always has. Says she wants a bunch of the little blighters. What comes of being an only child, I suppose. Not that Mrs. Prescott and I didn't try, a'course."

"No, I mean, what of Alice's wants and desires?"

"As lady of White Oaks, my gal will be the first female of the neighborhood. She can do all the good deeds she wants. Why, she might just be able to put in a word for you with his lordship, get you a raise in living and fix up the church so folks won't be afraid the roof'll collapse on them."

Evan gave up. "Perhaps his lordship will not be interested," he muttered under his breath. Perhaps pigs would fly, too.

Squire's hearing must have been better than his comprehension. "He'll be interested, by Jupiter. He's not fool enough to turn down the chance to get Prescott Manor when I toddle off."

"Lord Whittendale does not seem terribly concerned with increasing his holdings. He could make White Oaks a more profitable estate, with better management."

"No matter. Once he takes a gander at my Alice, he'll see all the advantages."

That's what Evan feared, too. How could any man resist her sweet charms? He sighed.

The squire heard that, too. "It's not as though her heart is given to another eligible gentleman, you know. I wouldn't stand in the way if Alice showed a partiality, long as the chap was in a position to make her a decent offer. I don't aim to see my puss living hand to mouth in some ramshackle cottage, you understand."

Evan understood all too well.

"Take a bloke like yourself, hard-working and with a good head on your shoulders. Nice, steady fellow, righteous, even. But you haven't got a pot to piss in, have you?" Only a chipped, battered bowl, which was how Evan was feeling at this moment.

"No, I've got to look out for my little chick, I do. Asides, you mightn't live past Christmas Eve, what with the day being a tad unhealthy for the vicars of St. Cecilia's, you might say."

*

With less than a month to live—not that Evan believed in curses or such, of course—the vicar decided to relish what few pleasures came his way. He accepted Miss Prescott's invitation to survey the conservatory. She thought they might decide how best to decorate St. Cecilia's, in case the tonnish guests chose to attend services there. Pine boughs could cover the expanses of missing mortar, and perhaps one of her mother's potted palms or flowering plants could hide that gaping hole in the rear corner.

Evan agreed with whatever Alice suggested, although he doubted that the London party would step foot in his little church, or any church for that matter, sinners that they were. No, he told himself, he should not condemn them without evidence, certainly not while he himself was having impious thoughts of Miss Prescott as she bent over this fern and that flower. Perhaps Lord Whittendale was not a rake, after all, and perhaps Lady Farnham was not his mistress. Victims of vicious tongues, that's what they might be, not villains. Surely they'd attend a few parties, let the locals gawk and gossip, then return to their butterfly lives in London—without Alice.

Before Whittendale left, Evan did mean to show him the disrepair, even if he had to drag his lordship into the church by the silly tassels on the high-polished boots he was sure to be wearing. Once the viscount had made provisions for St. Cecilia's, then Evan would speed him on his way with his blessings. As long as he left without Alice.

The vicar trailed behind Miss Prescott, moving a pot for her, fetching the watering can when she noticed a thirsty plant. Now his head was filled with the scents of warm earth and Alice, instead of Squire's cigar. He still could not think properly.

"There, I think these will do," she finally said. "I'll see that they are brought to the church on Saturday, along with more greens and a ribbon or two. You don't think bows would be too frivolous for church, do you?"

The only bow Evan could think of was the one tied beneath the high waist of Alice's blue gown, right beneath her delectable décolletage. He took a deep breath and blurted: "What do you think of your father's plan?"

She did not pretend to misunderstand. "Oh, I think Papa is happy in his plotting, but nothing will come of it. Lord Whittendale could have married any number of wellborn beauties with dowries far greater than mine if he wished to be wed at all, which I doubt." She plucked a dead leaf off an ivy.

"But your father is correct; the viscount will have to wed sometime."

"Yes, and I fear Papa will do his best to remind the unfortunate gentleman, as if his own family was not ragging at him enough. But so many snares have been set for Lord Whittendale that by now he must be too downy a bird to fall into any ambitious parent's net."

"If he is ready to start his nursery, however, how can you be so certain he won't be smitten with you?"

Alice chuckled. "Lord Whittendale is not interested in country misses. He was polite enough to attend my come-out ball at Lady Henesley's. That's Mama's godmother, you know. He must have felt duty-bound to come, since our families have known each other for ages, of course, although not on such familiar terms. The viscount brought a crowd of his friends, all gentlemen who rarely accepted such insipid invitations, which quite puffed up Lady Henesley. Whittendale took the floor with me for one set, which inflated my own consequence. Mama was *au anges.* Two days later, when we passed in the park, he did not recognize me as an acquaintance. So no, I do not fear he will be interested in making me an offer."

"Your father is convinced otherwise."

She shrugged and removed another spent bloom. "Papa will have no one to blame but himself when he is disappointed."

Evan had to persist, because he had to know. "What if he does manage to convince the viscount? Would you be tempted to accept? Your father can be very persuasive." So could the viscount's worldly assets.

"I should hate to go against Papa's wishes, but no, I would never accept an arranged match with Lord Whittendale, no matter the advantages. That is simply not the kind of marriage I want. I would rather remain unwed, in fact, than give myself into the keeping of a man who does not care for me, nor I him."

"Good." Convinced, Evan could breathe again. "You deserve a husband who will cherish and adore you, not merely require a mother for his heirs. You will find such a man, I know it."

She stopped fussing with the flowers and turned to him. "Will I? Where?"

"Where? Um, the assemblies in Upper Winfrey? London in the spring?"

"I have been there. What about here?"

The vicar swallowed. "Here?" He looked around. Here was a dark room that smelled of growing things. The only thing she could find in a place like this was trouble. "Oh, Lord. We really should not be alone like this."

"Nonsense. You are the family's spiritual advisor. Who better to discuss such an important decision?" She turned, and would have tripped on her skirts but for the arm Evan put out to steady her. Then her hand was on his shoulder as she looked up into his eyes. "I think we have both come to the same conclusion, haven't we?"

"Concerning Lord Whittendale?"

"Bother Lord Whittendale." Alice stepped closer still, and licked her lips.

Evan Merriweather was a man of honor, a man of principles, a man of the cloth, by heaven. Hell, he was merely a man. He kissed her. Her lips were as sweet as he'd known they would be; her body as soft in his arms as he'd dreamed it would be; her tiny mews of pleasure as heady as a choir of angels. "The Devil!" He dropped his arms, and nearly dropped Alice. "Good grief, what am I doing?"

"You are kissing me, and about time, sir."

"No, no. I cannot kiss you!"

"But you do it so well," she teased, a tender smile on her pinkened lips.

"No, I mean I cannot compromise you. Your father's trust...my calling. This is wrong, my dear."

"Oh, then you do not love me? That would make it wrong indeed. I thought... That is, forgive me if I was wrong." A tear trailed down her silky cheek.

"Oh, Lord," he cried, kissing the tear away. "Of course I love you, my angel, more than life. I have from the first minute I saw you. But do you...? That is, could you...?"

"Love you? Of course, silly. Or did you think I kiss every gentleman of my acquaintance in Mama's conservatory?"

So he had to kiss her again, until his conscience pricked him. No, this time it was a cactus. "Thunderation, Alice, you deserve so much better than I can give you."

"Do you mean I deserve a cold and empty marriage, as I would have with Lord Whittendale?"

"Never. But you know it will take an act of divine intervention before your father gives us his blessing."

Alice stood on tiptoe and kissed his cheek. "Well, you are on good terms with the Lord, aren't you?"

4

Evan could speak to God, but he couldn't speak to Squire until he'd spoken to the viscount. Without an improvement in his condition, Mr. Merriweather would not, could not, subject his beloved to life in the vicarage. Alice thought her father would relent and support them, but Evan could not bear to take both Prescott's daughter and his charity. What kind of man battens on his in-laws? Rather he batten on his distant cousin, who could well afford to pay an honest wage.

Dressing with care once more, Evan set out for White Oaks, Lord Whittendale's estate. By the time he got there, though, a cold, windy rain had set in, so he was damp and disheveled, chilled to the bone. The viscount's niffy-naffy London butler made him wait in the unheated hall, dripping on the marble entry, while he inquired if his lordship was receiving. Evan could hear laughter from down the corridor, men's and women's both, so the viscount was already entertaining. Surely a lord's pleasures could be interrupted a moment for the Lord's work?

Feeling more wretched and clumsy with every step, Evan followed the starched-up butler down the hall. If the servant was so top-lofty, he thought, how accommodating could the master be? The majordomo snapped his fingers at a footman to take Merriweather's coat and hat, rather than soil his own immaculate white gloves. Perhaps in similar manner Whittendale would try to relegate Evan to his secretary's care, rather than disturb his revelries. Not this time, the vicar swore to himself.

The company was arrayed as if for portraits, in elegant groupings of twos and threes. Posed most becomingly, dressed in silks and satins, with jewels sparkling from necks, wrists, and cravats, they all had drinks or cards or each other in hand, and the clock not yet gone on noon. A few looked up from their conversations, then went back to their pastimes, dismissing the rumpled rustic as of no account. One or two of the woman smiled at him speculatively, as if watching his coat stretch across his shoulders. Lud, he thought in panic, what if the seams were finally giving out? He'd be half-naked in the *haute monde*. Evan almost turned and fled back the muddy way he had come. No, he had to speak his piece. For St. Cecilia's. For Alice.

The viscount strode forward, his hand extended. Surprised, Evan shook it, noting his lordship's firm grip. Whittendale was a noted sportsman, after all, so Merriweather should not have been unready, yet he'd been recalling the dissipated, debauched, and drink-sodden spawn of the devil from their previous interview. Instead, the viscount was the picture of good health and good grooming, some few years older than Evan's own six-and-twenty, with black hair that fell in deliberate tousles. Evan was sure the viscount did not have a cowlick, just as he was sure the gentleman's well-fitting, securely stitched coat cost more than his own yearly stipend.

The viscount was about Evan's height, but he seemed of sturdier build, and his brown eyes were laughing at the vicar's inspection. "Do I pass muster, old chap? Or were you expecting that I'd grown horns and a tail since we met last? A bad day, if I recall, after a good night. Never mind. Come stand by the fire and warm yourself. Bea, fetch the good vicar some cognac, will you? No, better make that hot tea, from our visitor's disapproving looks. One of the early martyrs must have worn such an expression on his face just before meeting the lion."

A tall, stunning, auburn-haired woman in a flowing green velvet gown brought Evan a cup of tea. Her smile was enough to warm him to his damp toes, even without the blessedly hot brew. Whittendale's introduction confirmed that this vision was Beatrice, Lady Farnham. The sultry looks that passed between them and the seemingly accidental brushing of her skirts against Whittendale's thighs confirmed that they were lovers.

Embarrassed all over again, Evan stammered, "I...I did not mean to intrude, my lord, just to beg a moment of your time."

Whittendale sipped his cognac, his eyes watching Lady Farnham as she joined a pair of Tulips at the pianoforte. "Yes, yes, you are going to shame me into looking over your little church, aren't you? I did read your letters, you know."

He had not answered a one. "The living is in your keeping, my lord," Evan said. "No one else will see to the repairs, and I cannot afford to do more than patchwork with my income."

"Very well, I shall make an inspection. Perhaps I'll bring my guests this Sunday. Heaven knows they could use some religion."

Evan thought he'd start with the seven deadly sins. More than a few were in practice this morning: lust, sloth, avarice, and adultery, unless he missed his guess and a wedding ring or two. "There was another matter, my lord, if we could be private? I could return later if this is not a convenient time?" Evan hated having to make an appointment like some importunate tradesman, and he hated worse the idea of trekking home on such a miserable day and then back again. Still, he would not get the viscount's back up. The reverend realized, belatedly, that he should have sent round a note asking the viscount to name a time for their meeting. Of course, he had no handy footman to carry the message, and he doubted Lord Whittendale would have replied at all.

To Evan's relief, the viscount shook his head. "Nonsense. You are already here. Since my guests and I are forced indoors by the poor weather, this is an opportune moment, although I cannot imagine what's important enough to bring you out in the rain." He pulled a quizzing glass on a ribbon from his pocket and surveyed Evan's wet, muddy boots. "Gads, did you walk the distance?"

"The vicarage has no mount, my lord." In case the not-so-gentle hint irritated his host, Evan added, "Exercise is good for the soul, my lord."

"So is a hot fire on a cold day, dash it. Well, come along, then. We can be private in my book room."

Evan regretfully put down his tea, which he had been letting cool. Thank goodness his hands were no longer numb from holding the fragile cup, he thought. Thank goodness he hadn't dropped the dainty thing. He followed his patron back to the hallway, past the poker-backed butler. Before they could be seated, a footman brought in another tray. "Lady Farnham thought your guest might wish refreshments, my lord."

"How kind of her," Evan said as he accepted a mug of hot lambswool punch, for its warmth and its encouragement. He cleared his throat and began his memorized speech: "You see, my lord, there is more wrong with St. Cecilia's than a rotted roof and loose floorboards. The whole neighborhood is in difficulties, and I cannot make your steward understand that it is in your interest to meet those needs."

"I'm not sure I understand myself how emptying my coffers to fix highways and drainage ditches is of any benefit to me, but I will look into it. You're late, you see. The squire was already at me about the parish, too, as if I was in short pants again, needing a lecture on my responsibilities. I suppose I can check if my steward is doing a competent job."

"I am sure you will make a fair judgment once you visit the tenant farmers and the villagers."

"Deuce take it, I said I'd look at your church, not spend my time inspecting pig pens and cow byres. That other is my steward's job, and if he is not doing it, I'll find another." His handsome dark eyes narrowed. "You and Squire didn't discuss this between you, did you?"

"No, my lord. Well, yes, but not in so many words, just that we were both pleased to see you in Sussex. We are glad of the opportunity to bring injustices to your notice." He had to add, in all honesty, "Squire did mention he was hoping you'd decide to stay on in the country."

"Not bloody—pardon, not blessed likely. I will see what's to be done, though, just to stop the flow of mail. I'm not Golden Ball, you understand. I cannot fix all the woes of the world with my bank checks."

"Of course not. No one expects that." Evan took another sip of his toddy, feeling the spirits warm him from the inside out. "Simply put, we are hoping that, once you are aware of the deplorable conditions, you will see fit to make an increase in the living wages of those who are dependent upon you." He tacked on a "my lord."

"Like yourself, you mean?"

Evan felt his cheeks growing warm now. "I...ah... Whittendale laughed. "Squire mentioned your plight, too. He sang your praises for what you've tried to do for the people, said you needed some support. I'll look into it." The viscount was being so reasonable, not at all condescending, that the vicar couldn't help raising his estimation of the man. Why, Evan thought he might even like the gentleman. Until Lord Whittendale said, "Squire mentioned his daughter, too."

Evan detested the dastard. He also dropped his napkin. When he bent to retrieve it, the sound of ripping stitches reverberated through the room.

The viscount had his obnoxious quizzing glass out again. "You are in a sad way, aren't you?"

May he never know how sad, Evan silently prayed around a forced smile.

Whittendale sat back in his chair. "But tell me about Squire's daughter. Little Alice used to be a charmer. Is she still? I know I saw her at some ball or other, but all those chits in their white gowns look alike."

"That would have been Miss Prescott's come-out at Lady Henesley's. And yes, Miss Prescott is still everything pleasing. A fine young woman. A blessing to the neighborhood, in fact."

"I suppose she'd make some chap an admirable wife, then?" His lordship stared into his cup of cheer, without any. "As Prescott and my innumerable female relations keep reminding me, it is past time I considered setting up my nursery. I do not relish shopping the Marriage Mart." He swallowed the contents of his cup and poured another, shuddering. "Almack's, by Hades. Be simpler to take one who's to hand."

Evan felt compelled to defend his Alice as more than just a convenient solution to a pesky problem. "Miss Prescott would make any man an excellent wife. She is kind and intelligent, compassionate to those less fortunate."

Whittendale winced. "A veritable paragon of virtue. Lud, that I've come to this. I suppose that's what parson's mousetrap is all about."

"Not in this parson's book, my lord. What about affection, loyalty, shared interests?" Evan was repeating what he'd told Alice's father, hoping to be heeded this time. "What about love and passion? Do you not want those things from the woman with whom you will spend the rest of your life?"

Whittendale grimaced at the "rest of your life" part. "Hell, no. That's why they make mistresses, don't you know? A chap wouldn't want a wife enacting Cheltenham tragedies every time he decided to attend a mill instead of another blasted musicale, or when he let his eye wander, if you know what I mean." He noted Evan's frown. "No, of course you don't. Forgot your calling. Trust me, Vicar, a well-brought-up miss makes a comfortable wife, and a comfortable life, without all those other entanglements."

Knowing he was stepping beyond the line, even for a supposed spiritual advisor, Evan felt he had to say, "Lady Farnham is a beautiful woman who shares your way of life."

Lord Whittendale nodded his agreement, then raised one dark eyebrow. "So?"

"So she would make you a more suitable bride than Alice...Miss Prescott."

The viscount threw his head back and laughed. "You really are a green 'un, Merriweather, trying to legitimize a liaison. A man don't marry his mistress. Oh, Prinny might have tried, but the scandal sheets made a laughingstock out of him. Lady Whittendale, when I finally take a bride, will be unsullied, with a spotless reputation, as befits my station in life." He held up a manicured hand with a flashing ruby in his signet ring. "Not that Bea is a lightskirt, mind, or would play me false while we have an understanding. She's a good sort, Beatrice is. Married off to the old wind-bag at an early age, and never strayed from his side that I ever heard. The thing is, Reverend, with no bark on it, Bea is used goods."

"What, like a carriage discarded for a newer model?" Evan was appalled. "She is a woman, my lord, not an old shoe."

The viscount's eyebrow raised again. "I think you forget who pays your salary, sirrah. The salary you wish increased. Or perhaps you think those clerical collars give you license to poke your nose where it don't belong."

Where he didn't belong was in the profligate's parlor, trying to impart a smidgeon of a scruple. Evan set his cup down and stood. "I have taken enough of your time, my lord. I appreciate your promise to address the needs of our little community."

"Yes, yes. I shall be at the chapel on Sunday, as promised. I suppose the squire's chit will attend, so I can take a look at her then, too." Walking the vicar to the door, Lord Whittendale added, "You know, Merriweather, you ought to consider taking a wife yourself. Find a homely woman with a handsome dowry, and you will be set for life. You won't need to be hanging on my sleeve for every little thing like the carriage I'll send you home in."

Missing windows and rotted pews were no little thing. The viscount would see for himself, so Evan had to be satisfied for now. He bowed his head. "Too kind, my lord. As a matter of fact, I am also considering matrimony."

With the same woman.

*

They were supposed to be putting flowers in urns, instead of roses in Alice's cheeks. The placement of the wreaths and boughs for Whittendale's impending visit had deteriorated to placing not so chaste kisses. Evan Merriweather was a devilish kisser, for a holy man. In fact, 'twas a good thing mistletoe was considered too pagan for the church, or Heaven alone knew where such goings-on would lead.

The mice knew.

"You see, everyone understands the rules about 'Be fruitful and multiply.' Even human people."

"Aye, and these two need our help, too, so keep gnawing. They can't mate until we rescue the church, no more than we can."

The last remaining St. Cecilia Churchmice were in St. Francis's niche, grinding away at the layers of paint coating their favorite golden statue.

"But we're getting nowhere," Passeth-All-Understanding complained. "My teeth are worn to nubbins, and we'll never have St. Francis shiny enough by Christmas Eve for anyone to notice."

"We will if you stop staring out the crack in the wall at that little field mouse." Exultemus Domine flicked his whiskers clear of paint chips. "Besides, as soon as the vicar and that nice Miss Alice leave, we can go nibble on the meal she brought for us."

"Those are flowers and greens, Ed."

"They call it salad. Not filling, but better than nothing. Keep gnawing."

5

They did not want the church to look shabby and unloved for the London visitors, but Evan and Alice did not want St. Cecilia's to look so festive that Lord Whittendale could ignore the disrepair.

The mice helped. They ate the decorations.

Balancing on that same thin line, Evan spent hours on a sermon that would gently nudge his congregation toward the path of righteousness, without being either censorious of the sinners or accepting of the sins.

The mice helped. They ate his notes.

Reciting from memory, the Reverend Mr. Merriweather first had to master a nearly uncontrollable urge to stare at Alice, who looked enchanting to him in a blue bonnet and a warm red wool cloak. Sitting between her mother and her great-aunt Minerva in the third row, Alice kept her eyes on her prayer book, but a tender smile played upon her lips—the lips he'd been kissing. Evan lost his place and had to start over.

This time he forced his eyes to the rest of the congregation. The few faithful worshipers from the village were sitting in the last rows as usual, ready to bolt if the roof collapsed. They were all wrapped in shawls and mufflers, for the church was as cold as Lord Whittendale's heart this mid-December morning. The White Oaks house party occupied the first two pews, dressed in all their finery, with Lady Farnham at the viscount's side, in a gaily decorated bonnet and fur-lined mantle. Whittendale looked bored, but the beautiful young widow nodded encouragingly, so Evan cleared his throat and began again, trying to inject a bit more fervor, a touch of fire and brimstone along with the—

"Cherries! I see cherries!" Passeth-All-Understanding was jumping up and down on St. Francis's right side.

White-muzzled Exultemus Domine frowned from the statue's other side. "Can't be cherries. Cherries are in summer. This is winter, you catbait."

"Your eyesight is as dull as your teeth, Ed. I tell you, I see cherries on that lady's hat." The younger mouse wrinkled his nose. "It even smells like cherries."

"No, the human people roll in flowers so they don't smell so bad. That's what has you confused."

"I know cherries when I see them!" And Passeth-All-Understanding was going to get himself some. He leaped from the statue's niche to the mildewed molding, then scurried down a warped wall panel and under an equally flawed floorboard, coming up again at the correct crumbling pew. He climbed nimbly up the back of the wooden seat and jumped from there onto Lady Farnham's shoulder, thence to her high collar, just inches away from the cherries on her bonnet. He was just about to reach up for one of the tender delicacies when he realized he was standing on the enemy—an ermine. A jumped-up weasel, to be sure, but still a mouse-menace. So he screamed.

No one heard him, of course, nor the rest of Mr. Merriweather's sermon, for all the ladies were shrieking, the ones who were not swooning, at any rate. Thinking the roof must be falling in, the villagers fled for the door, clogging the exit, only to be shoved aside by the Londoners. Squire Prescott had to half carry his wife out, and Alice, white-faced, supported Aunt Minerva behind him. Shouting "Tallyho," Lord Whittendale and one of his sporting friends took up the hunt after the tiny, terrified culprit, up the aisles and down the pews, until Passeth-All-Understanding passed between the fallen stones in the far corner, and bolted for the out-of-doors. The gentlemen charged out the side door, still on the chase.

"...So go forth and sin no more," Evan concluded to the echoing stones and plaster saints. If the mouse hole were big enough, he'd crawl through it himself.

Then he realized that the church was not entirely evacuated. Lady Farnham remained huddled in her seat, abandoned, ashen, trembling, clutching her Bible as if for defense. He approached her cautiously, lest he frighten the poor woman worse. "My lady, are you injured or unwell? Shall I fetch your maid? Lord Whittendale?"

She shook her head no.

"A glass of water, then? Wine?" He'd give her the sacramental wine, if that would help.

"No. Thank you."

"A vinaigrette?" He dubiously eyed the tiny beaded reticule dangling from her arm. "Smelling salts?"

"No. Please do not concern yourself, Mr. Merriweather. I will recover in a moment."

But Evan could see tears coursing down the widow's high cheekbones. He fumbled in his pocket to find his handkerchief, then debated handing such a plebeian linen square to her, aware that Lady Farnham was used to far finer fabrics. Then again, she was not used to being attacked by maniacal mice.

She accepted his handkerchief with a nod, then clasped it to her mouth in a wad, as if trying to stifle her sobs. Evan had nothing else to offer but comfort. He awkwardly patted her shoulder. "There, there, my dear. You'll feel better in a moment."

"No, I won't," she wailed, flinging herself into the vicar's arms. She clung there, weeping on his chest.

Giving solace to the sorrowful was one thing; holding his patron's mistress was quite another. Mr. Merriweather tried to loosen her arms from around his neck, but Lady Farnham was latched on like a limpet. Lud, how could he explain this to Lord Whittendale? How could he explain it to Alice? He cleared his throat. "My dear lady, I know you were startled, but it was only a mouse."

She laughed, a pitiful keening sound, but sat back, blotting at her eyes and nose. "No, it's not only a mouse. It's a baby."

"A baby? You're...? His? Of course it is. I should not have asked. Have you told him?"

"What for?"

"So he can do the honorable thing, of course."

"Oh, he would do what the polite world considers proper—give me a check and a deed to a little cottage somewhere. He might even come visit now and again when London grew too hot or too cold or too thin of company."

"I meant that he would marry you if he knew about the baby."

She made an unladylike sound. "In your prayers, Reverend. In the real world, a man does not marry his mistress, no matter how much she loves him."

"So everyone keeps telling me. Who makes these wretched rules anyway? An enceinte mistress is precisely whom a man should marry, to give his child a name, to restore his lady's reputation. Especially if he loves her in return."

"I suppose Randolph does love me, in his way. Not enough, however, to risk society's censure." She started to shred Evan's best handkerchief, adding to his misery.

"What shall you do, then?'

Beatrice shrugged. "I cannot go to my family, or the Farnham Dower House, for the shame. I suppose I could travel abroad with the bit of money I inherited from my husband's estate, and I can always sell my jewelry. Randy has been very generous, you know." She choked back a sob. "So I will be able to take up my life anew, after the child is born." She began to weep again. "But without my baby. Only without my child. How can I do that, give up my own flesh and blood?"

Evan could not even fix the church's roof. How could he fix Lady Farnham's troubles? "Perhaps you can convince another man to marry you. A beautiful woman with a bank account ought to have no difficulty finding a husband." Evan knew he was suggesting just the sort of coldblooded, business-arrangement type of marriage that he deplored, but needs must when the devil drove. No child should be born a bastard.

"Do you think I have not considered such a course? How can I find an eligible *parti* while I am in Randy's keeping? There is not one man in London brave enough to poach on his preserves. Besides, how can I give myself to another man, knowing that I only want Whittendale, hard as that may be to believe? How unfair to this hypothetical husband, a wife lacking both her virginity and her heart. I could not be that dishonest to any man I cared for enough to marry."

Now she discovered a sense of honor? Evan thought. He shook his head, wishing he had his handkerchief to mop his damp brow. Fornication was acceptable but fabrication was not? He would never understand the *beau monde* and its morality, or lack thereof.

Lady Farnham, meanwhile, had regained some of her composure and was regarding Mr. Merriweather with a speculative eye. She noted that he was thin but nicely muscled, with a full head of sandy hair in need of a trimming. "It seems to me that you could do with a helpmeet, too. Especially one with a bit of blunt. I don't suppose…?"

"M-me?" His voice came out like the bleating of a goat "That is, I could not offer you the life you are used to, the style you enjoy, not even with your money. I am a simple country vicar, and content to remain as such. I am honored—nay, I am confounded—that you could consider me in your dilemma, but I wish my wife to love me, as I would love her, and no others."

She nodded. "It was a moment's thought, nothing more, but I'd wager you would make a good father."

Evan thought of that quiverful of children Alice wanted, all blue-eyed, blond-haired cherubim. He would love them, every one of them, but he could not feed them or clothe them or send them to school. He sighed. "I fear I might never know, for it is going to take a power greater than mine to see such a thing come to pass. I cannot afford a dog, much less a wife and children."

Now she sighed. "Life seems so unfair sometimes."

"But never hopeless. We'll both come about, I swear. The Lord will provide."

Lady Farnham looked around, noting the angled pole supporting the roof, the boarded-over windows. "It seems the Lord is having troubles enough providing for His own house."

*

The young church mouse had doubled back through another hole in the stone wall of St. Cecilia's. He was hiding under the floorboards, quivering, catching his breath, and getting lectured.

"For certain you were named rightly." Exultemus Domine was also quivering, in outrage. "For it passes all understanding how you can be as greedy as a fox cub and as stupid as a duck. What if the lady had hit you with her Bible, or one of those panicked fools had stepped on you? What if Dread Fred were on patrol outside? Then what would happen? Our whole line would die out, that's what. Not one Churchmouse would remain to pass on our ancient heritage. Don't you understand responsibility, destiny, Noah-blessed oblige?"

"Oh, stop nattering at me and listen. They're talking about Viscount Whittendale."

After hearing Lady Farnham's tale of woe, Ed wrinkled his nose as if he smelled a ferret. "His lordship is a wicked, wicked man."

"Aye, but he's the one getting to sow his seed."

6

"The devil!" Arriving back inside the church, the viscount was not best pleased to find his mistress nearly in Merriweather's lap.

Misinterpreting his lordship's exclamation, Evan jumped to his feet, explaining, "Lady Farnham is not injured, merely frightened."

Belatedly, Whittendale noticed Beatrice's tear-streaked cheeks and reddened eyes. "Dash it, Bea, it ain't like you to be hen-hearted. You drive with me in my phaeton, don't you?" When she gave him a teary smile, he held out his hand. "There's my girl. Come on now, the others are waiting in the carriages to return to White Oaks."

Instead of mounting his chestnut gelding to ride back alongside the carriage, Whittendale motioned the driver to proceed. He returned to the church, tapping his crop against his leg.

"Blast it, Merriweather, were you trying to make a fool out of me in front of my friends?"

Evan was trying to restore the trampled greenery. "What, do you think I arranged for a mouse to run amok in my church?"

"I am not speaking about your deuced resident rodents. I'm referring to your arms around my *chère ami*. I can just imagine all the talk if any of the fellows had seen that tender little episode. They'd laugh that I was being supplanted in the lady's affections by an impoverished cleric in ill-fitting clothes."

Evan would not be cowed. "She was startled, and you were not here to soothe her, that was all."

"You were holding her hand, by George!" The viscount slapped his crop against the first pew, disturbing the dry rot "I saw the way you were looking at the little Prescott chit, and you might get away with that until I come to terms with her father, but you have no right to be looking at Bea Farnham, much less touching her."

"As a man of the cloth I have every right to stand as spiritual advisor to whomever needs my comfort and my counsel."

Lord Whittendale recalled Bea's wistful farewell to the vicar, and her promise to visit St. Cecilia's again. "No one comforts my woman but me, do you hear me?"

Evan frowned. "I heard a troubled woman not getting solace from those who should support her in her hour of need."

"Need? Need? Bea wants for nothing. She wouldn't have any need for you if your cheese-paring church wasn't overridden by rats!"

The vicar was a forgiving man, but an insult to his church was a slap in the face. Being accused of dalliance with a demi-rep was bad enough; being charged with bad housekeeping in the home of the Lord was too much. Evan squared his shoulders, glad for the extra heft. "What do you know about need? You have never wanted for anything in your life, except for a conscience, perhaps. If you met your responsibilities, the church wouldn't be infested and your lady wouldn't be weeping."

"How dare you lecture me on my duties, you impertinent clod. If you weren't in orders, I'd order you horsewhipped."

Evan snapped back to the man who thought his wealth and title could purchase Alice, "If I weren't in orders, I'd pop your cork for your treatment of those around you, especially women."

"Hah! I'd like to see you try."

Things might have progressed to a bloody, schoolboyish conclusion, but one of the floorboards suddenly shifted with a loud squeak.

Recalled to their location—and their respective dignities—the vicar and the viscount both nodded and stepped back. The reverend knelt to inspect the faulty board, while the lord paced toward the rear door. Before he left, however, Whittendale warned Evan: "I will brook no interference with my females, not the ones I bed nor the one I'll wed. Stay away from Bea Farnham and the Prescott chit or I'll tear this place down with my bare hands."

Evan shifted the board back into alignment with its fellows and straightened up. "You'll never marry Alice Prescott," he told his supposed benefactor, "not after I inform Squire that you intend to litter the countryside with your butter stamps."

"Butter stamps? I have never left a by-blow any—Bea? She is increasing?" Lord Whittendale sat down abruptly in the last row.

Evan blanched. "She did not want to tell you."

"Of course not, the peagoose. She knows I'll send her into the countryside somewhere, and she can't bear to miss a ball. She'll have to forgo the spring Season, I suppose. Can't have a breeding female on my arm."

"That's all you can think of, parties and appearances? What about the child? Have you thought about the child for one instant?"

"I only just heard about the brat this minute, by Jupiter. I suppose I can find a decent family to take it in. Give it all the best, that kind of thing."

"The best? You'd buy your son a pony and send him to an expensive school. You'd offer your daughter a china doll and a dowry. That's your best. But what about love, what about Lady Farnham's heartache to hold her own babe to her breast?"

"Thunderation, this is none of your concern." Whittendale stood to leave, but was stopped at the door by the reverend's words: "Can you bear to see another man raise your child? What if he drinks or grows violent? What if the mother tells the poor babe that his own parents did not want him? Is that what you want for your son? Can you truly live with such a decision?"

Whittendale hesitated at the threshold, almost as if he was considering the vicar's questions. Then he straightened his caped riding coat around his shoulders and turned with a sneer. "Stay out of affairs that are beyond your ken, Merriweather. You have a small church and a small mind."

*

The viscount brushed right past Alice on the church steps without recognizing her. He tipped his hat automatically, but was concentrating too hard on his own thoughts, and on the rickety stairs, to notice that this was the woman he intended to marry.

Alice dropped a curtsey and a murmured "My lord," before hurrying inside. She had seen her mother dosed with the laudanum bottle, her father ensconced with the brandy bottle, and her great-aunt closeted with the ink bottle. Aunt Minerva was writing all of her friends about the debacle, how all those fancified London swells went sprinting for their lives as if the Hounds of Hell were snapping at their heels, instead of a wee bit of whiskers. This was the most entertainment she'd seen in Lower Winfrey in years. Alice, of course, had not shared her relative's delight. Using the usual Sunday food baskets as an excuse, she'd driven her pony cart to the church, and Mr. Merriweather, as soon as she could, just in time to overhear the last of the viscount's conversation.

"Heavens," was all she could say, sinking onto a pew next to Evan, under the statue of St. Francis.

Evan had his head bowed, his hands clenched on the back of the seat in front of him, the picture of despair. He couldn't look at his beloved. "Now I have torn it for sure. I've gone and offended Lord Whittendale so badly that he'll never help us."

Alice put her gloved hand over one of his. "You cannot know that for certain. When he gets over his shock and his anger, perhaps your words will have some better effect on him."

"No. If he thinks about what I said at all, he's liable to replace me as vicar here altogether. Ah, Alice, I am so sorry."

"He's the one who should be sorry, Evan, for planning to abandon his child and its mother."

"You heard, then?"

"Yes, and I think all the less of Lord Whittendale for his cold heart. No matter what happens, if Papa never gives us permission to wed, I would never marry a man who could leave his baby for strangers to rear."

He grasped her hand. "Good, for seeing you as another man's bride would be bad enough, but to think of you going to an arrogant jackass who would not appreciate you as you deserve would break my own heart all over again. If I cannot have you, I can at least pray for your happiness with an admirable man."

"You are kinder than I, my dearest, for if I cannot marry you, I would despise the woman who did. Nor do I think I could bear to see you happy in such a union, whilst I was steeped in misery. No, I would have to leave, go somewhere I would not be reminded every day of my own loss, if such a place exists."

He had to bring her hand to his lips, he simply had to. "I will have no other woman to wife, I swear." Evan would do nothing more than kiss her gloved fingers, despite the invitation in her blue eyes. In fact, he regretted the kisses they had already shared. No, he did not rue the dishonorable kisses, he regretted that there could never be any more. And that he'd sent Lord Whittendale away in anger.

"I pity the poor female the viscount does marry," he said now, turning the subject from his dismal thoughts. "Such a one as Lord Whittendale would make a wretched husband for any woman."

"And a dreadful father, I should think, even to his legitimate offspring. Why, he'd likely forget his children's names."

"And their birthdays, unless his secretary reminded him," Evan added.

"Or if they threw spots from strawberries, or were afraid of thunder."

"He'd never take his sons fishing, nor share dolls' tea parties with his daughters."

"What, and chance soiling his boots or having his friends see him? Never." Alice squeezed Evan's hand and said, "You, however, would make an excellent father, my dear Mr. Merriweather."

Evan laughed, but without humor. "So everyone seems to think, for all the good anyone's opinions will do. I am afraid it will take a miracle for sure now for me to afford a wife and children."

"We have to have faith, Evan."

"Oh, I do, my dear," he said, brushing flakes of paint off her shoulder. "I do, even with the church falling down around our ears. Nor do I intend to sit around waiting for Lord Whittendale to develop Christmas cheer and a generous spirit. After we deliver your bundles of food, I can start splitting wood for new stair treads this very afternoon, and I can get rid of the mice, at least. I'm sure Mrs. Cotter won't mind if I close her cat in here for a bit."

*

"Now see what you've done, fleas-for-brains?"

7

Lady Farnham returned to St. Cecilia's as promised, with a basket of food from the White Oaks kitchen for the needy. She managed to get Lord Whittendale to drive her, to carry the hamper inside, and to apologize for any insult he may inadvertently have given Mr. Merriweather.

Inadvertent? The man had nearly threatened to have Evan boiled in oil for merely speaking to this woman. Or to Alice. Still, the vicar graciously accepted the basket and the new opportunity to win the viscount to St. Cecilia's side. A reprieve, thank the Lord. He gladly shook the peer's hand, then felt a coin pressed into his own palm. The viscount might merely be trying to appease his conscience, Evan thought, but St. Cecilia's would be grateful nevertheless. He put the coin in his pocket.

When his lordship left to wait outside while the beautiful young widow prayed, Evan softly vowed, "Never again will I doubt the power of prayers."

Lady Farnham smiled. "And never doubt the effect of a woman's weeping. When Randolph told me what he had said to you, I confess I turned into a watering pot again. I understand women become highly emotional at such times."

"He must love you very much, then, to care about your tears."

She shrugged in her fur-lined cloak as she sat in one of the far pews, indicating that Evan should sit with her. "I suppose he does, in his way."

"But not enough to...?"

Bea dabbed at her eyes with a scrap of lace-edged linen. Evan reached for his own, more adequate, handkerchief, but Lady Farnham shook her head. "No, I have used up all my tears. In fact, I must return the handkerchief you so kindly lent me."

Evan took the freshly laundered square she held out, feeling the coins in its folds. "This is not necessary, my lady."

"No, but you and your little church need it far more than I do. A few shillings will not make a difference in my condition, but they might mean the difference between an empty larder and a full one for some of your parishioners."

"I thank you, madam, but surely you are going to need every groat for when—"

"No, Randy is being very generous. Shortly after Christmas he is going to purchase a little cottage not far from London, so that he can come visit frequently. He will make sure I have the best of care and want for nothing. I...I have hopes that he will let me stay on there with the baby, although he says he will have his solicitor look for a likely family. Perhaps if I cry enough, he will relent. Who knows? I understand that such an unsanctioned arrangement cannot find acceptance in the eyes of the Church, but will you pray with me, Vicar?"

"Of course, my lady. Surely our Lord will hear your prayers, so close to Christmas and the birth of His own son."

*

While the vicar and the widow prayed, the mice eyed the wicker basket of food sitting so invitingly in the aisle.

"Got to be something better than paint chips in there, don't you think?"

Ed licked his lips. "And better than the pine needles from the decorations. I say we are as needy as anyone in the parish, and charity does begin at home."

"Let's go."

So the last remaining hopes of the Churchmouse clan took a break from their gnawing and scurried across St. Francis's niche, down the molding, under the loose floorboards, surfacing inches away from the basket.

The sexton's wife's cat was also speculating about the contents of Lady Farnham's basket, and his chances of helping himself to a chicken leg or a bit of cheese or an apple tart. He was deserving of a reward, wasn't he, keeping watch in this cold, drafty, dusty church, instead of sitting by Mrs. Cotter's nice warm cookstove? Fred cocked one scarred ear toward the praying pair and stealthily stalked toward supper. Instead he saw...dessert!

"Well, bless my soul if Christmas isn't coming a week early!" With a loud meow he leaped at the two mousekins.

Passeth-All-Understanding made it back to the gaping floorboard, with Dread Fred's fetid cat-breath on his shoulder, but elder Exultemus Domine was too slow. Now the marauding mouser was between him and the hole. The people were between him and the crumbling stone wall. Ed froze in place, as still and stiff as the statue of St. Francis.

"Run, Ed. Run for the roof! You'll be safe there."

So Ed fled, up the post that the vicar had propped in the corner to support one of the sagging roof beams. Dread Fred followed.

The pole collapsed under the weight of the well-fed Fred. With the sudden loss of the upright, the rotted roof beam groaned, shifted, and cracked. Cat, mouse, post, beam, and a good portion of the roof fell onto the floor of the church, scant feet away from Lady Farnham and Reverend Merriweather. She screamed, he screamed, and Mrs. Cotter, who was coming to fetch her precious puss for a spot of tea, screamed. Viscount Whittendale screamed from the outside, tearing into the church and shoving rubble out of his way as he raced to reach Beatrice's side.

Ed screamed, but no one heard him. He burrowed deeper in the debris.

Mrs. Cotter reached her pet first, not that anyone else was trying to rescue the feline.

A board had fallen on Dread Fred's head.

He bled, but he hung on by a thread, not quite dead.

Mrs. Potter scooped him up in her apron, sobbing that the church must truly be bedeviled, picking on innocent pusses now, instead of preachers. Still screaming, she carried him away to safety and his blanket-bed near the cook-stove.

Evan was choking on the cloud of disturbed dust, but he went to look at the damage as soon as he made sure Lady Farnham was uninjured. She was uninjured so far, but the way Lord Whittendale was clutching her to his chest, Evan worried that she'd soon have broken ribs.

"Are you all right, Bea?" the viscount was desperately asking. "Are you sure? God, when I heard that awful noise, I thought for a moment I had lost you."

Lady Farnham caught her breath and nodded. "I am fine, truly. Mr. Merriweather pushed me aside when he realized what was happening."

"And the baby? What about the baby?"

Lady Farnham reached up to wipe a smudge of dirt from his cheek, a smudge that had a suspiciously moist track through it. "We are both fine, I swear. But do you really care about the baby?"

"Lud, Bea, more than I thought possible. Losing the child now would have been the perfect solution, but I couldn't bear the idea of not seeing my son or daughter at your breast. Ah, Bea, I don't want any milk-and-water miss in my bed or sitting across the breakfast table or beside me at the Opera. I want you, none other. Perhaps I am a fool for needing such a near-tragedy to show me what I value most in this world, but will you marry me anyway, my dearest?"

"But what of Society?"

"Society be damned." The viscount noticed Merriweather standing nearby, the remnants of the wicker basket in his hands. "Sorry, Reverend." Then he turned back to Bea. "Say you will, darling, and make me the happiest of men."

"Oh, do, Lady Farnham," Evan put in, "before he changes his mind. That is, excuse me. The excitement, don't you know."

"You can give me your answer in the carriage, my love." The viscount scowled over her head. "As for you, Merriweather, rest assured I shall not change my mind. I owe you for protecting my lady, and for your plain speaking on Sunday, so I will raise your wages. That doesn't mean that I am willing to throw good money after bad, though. If no one will come to this church, cursed or not, I see no reason to repair it. I will make you a bargain, Merriweather. You fill this church for Christmas morning service, and I will make the repairs and endow your charities. Yes, and I'll make the vicarage more habitable, too. If the church is not used, especially on Christmas morning, it is not worth fixing, so I will let the living lapse. I'll ask the bishop to find you another post, and have Most Holy take over the parish duties.

"But Christmas is next week. I cannot—"

They were gone, their eyes only on each other.

"Watch out for the rotten stairs!" Evan called.

The viscount waved a casual acknowledgment with the hand that was not around Lady Farnham. "Next week."

*

As soon as word reached the Manor, Alice hurried to the church to assess the latest damage and disaster.

Evan was standing behind the lectern, using his handkerchief to wipe dirt from the ceiling off the large Bible there. A small collection of coins, two of them golden, rested beside the Book.

Alice picked her way over the debris, careful not to snag her cloak, and joined him at the front of the church. She looked up at the grayish-blue sky visible above and said, "At least it is not raining."

"Ah, my heart, trust you to find the silver lining in this cloud of dust." Then he went on to describe Lord Whittendale's ultimatum.

"How dare he make a game out of people's lives. That worm!"

"That worm is going to marry Lady Farnham after all, thank goodness, despite the censure of his friends and acquaintances."

"Then they will go back to London and not give another thought to St. Cecilia's or Lower Winfrey."

"No, I think he will keep his word about supporting the parish, if we meet his conditions."

Alice looked up, not to seek divine guidance, but to watch a passing cloud. "How can we satisfy him, Evan? The church has not been filled since the viscount's mother's funeral. There are not enough people in the village to fill the pews, even if no one goes to Most Holy instead." Evan stacked the coins. "I've been thinking. I can use these contributions and the rest of my quarter's salary to fix the ceiling. Then our people might not be so anxious about attending St. Cecilia's."

Alice did not want to worry Evan further by reminding him that the villagers feared the bad luck of the previous vicars' deaths, not the bad roof. She nodded encouragingly.

"Or else," Evan reflected, "I could use the blunt to buy foodstuffs. If I promise the poor souls in the almshouse a Christmas dinner, maybe they will come to services. Unfortunately, I cannot do both. It's either the roof and the villagers, or the food and the unfortunate. Either way, the church will be half empty."

"No, it won't, for I have some pin money of my own put by. We can fix the church and have a feast to celebrate. And I can help with the repairs, and the baking, too." He shook his head, sending dust from his hair back onto the Bible. "I cannot take your money, Alice."

Alice brushed a smudge from his cheek, her fingers lingering there. "It's not for you. It's for St. Cecilia's."

"But you know that without Lord Whittendale's money, we'll never have enough brass to make the church really safe for anyone to worship here, not even you. Especially you, my dear."

"I'll be here. And I will make sure everyone I know is here, to help save St. Cecilia's."

Evan kissed her fingers, so near his lips. "Poor Lord Whittendale."

"Poor, that makebait?"

"Aye. He doesn't get to marry the finest woman in the kingdom."

"I thought you liked Lady Farnham. She is certainly beautiful enough."

"She isn't you."

8

White Oaks had not opened its vast doors to the community in ages. Not since the viscount's mother's time had the huge ancient pile hosted what used to be an annual Christmas Eve ball. Tonight the party was twice as joyous, twice as lavish as any Lady Whittendale had ever thrown, for tonight the current titleholder was going to announce his engagement.

Money had flowed through village hands from the influx of travelers and traders. The restored fortress needed to be refurbished, restocked, and restaffed, and what could not be ordered in time from London was purchased nearby. Since everyone in the vicinity was also invited to the lively party in the barn if not the formal dance in the ballroom, spirits were high, and not just because spirits were flowing as well as Lord Whittendale's blunt.

One person was not enjoying himself. The Reverend Mr. Merriweather could not share in the joy of the occasion. Oh, he'd made a sincere blessing over the happy couple and, indeed, wished them well. He'd also blessed the meal, both at the long oak table and at the trestles set up for the common folk. He was pleased to see his neighbors so carefree, so happy in the moment, yet he could not join in their merriment. Here it was, Christmas Eve, perhaps his first, last, and only Christmas Eve as vicar of St. Cecilia's, and here he was, watching Alice dance with all the London bucks and blades. She was beautiful in her new gown of ivory lace over emerald-green satin, with holly twined in her upswept hair, and every man there knew it. All those wealthy, titled, landed gentlemen were waiting in line for her hand, to dazzle her with their diamond stickpins and polished manners, to shower her with flowery compliments and flirtatious conversation. Evan could no more turn a pretty phrase than he could turn into a Town Beau.

He'd had one dance with his beloved, a stately minuet as befitted his station, and their relationship as minister and congregant. Whittendale was getting to have nearly every dance with his affianced bride, the lucky dog. No one would think any the less of Lady Farnham, not in light of her betrothal, and the light of adoration in the viscount's eyes. No one would dare slight her, or bring up old gossip, not once the engagement was announced. Beatrice was going to be Lady Whittendale, a blanket of respectability that could ward off all but the chilliest of disapproval.

Envy sat heavily in Evan's heart, along with uncertainty over his own future.

Another gentleman was also less than delighted with the occasion. Mr. Prescott found Evan leaning against a pillar, half hidden by a potted palm tree. "Wretched thing, balls," Squire complained. "How they expect a fellow to cavort around on his toes after feeding him six courses, I'll never know." He accepted another glass of punch from a passing footman, and leaned on the other side of the pillar. "Much rather have a nap or a quiet game of cards. M'wife insists I stay right here, though, keeping an eye on Alice, what with all those randy, ramshackle rakes Whittendale calls friends around. As if one of those loose screws is going to drag the gal behind a drapery to steal a kiss when there's all this mistletoe in plain sight."

Botheration, Evan hadn't noticed the mistletoe. He could have— No, he could not have. He was the vicar—the impoverished vicar. He sighed.

Squire sighed louder, watching Alice float by in a cloud of lace, in the same set as Lord Whittendale and his radiant wife-to-be. Lady Farnham was wearing the Whittendale heirloom engagement ring, the enormous diamond reflecting the hundreds of candles around the room. "Deuce take it, I suppose now I'll have to take Alice back to London in the spring. I was hoping to be done with all those folderols and furbelows, especially at planting season." Mr. Merriweather could only nod in commiseration. The thought of Alice going to London to find a *parti* to wed stuck in his throat like a piece of Mrs. Cotter's Christmas pudding.

"I don't suppose she mentioned an interest in any of these coxcombs when you were as close as inkle weavers all week, did she?" Squire asked hopefully. "I could get a ring on her finger by New Year's. Not the size of Lady Farnham's, of course. None of the popinjays can touch Whittendale's deep pockets. Not that I mean to sell my gal to the highest bidder or anything. Won't even hold out for a title if the chap is a decent sort."

The pain in Evan's chest grew with each of Squire's words. He swallowed and said, "No, she never mentioned any of Lord Whittendale's company by name, although I know she dined with them a time or two, and entertained some of the gentlemen at tea."

"Hmpf. She could have fixed any number of the toffs' attention if she'd set her mind to it and stayed home instead of spending every minute at St. Cecilia's. Her mother had to tie her down, nearly, to be at home in the afternoon."

"Miss Prescott was a great help this week. She lent her hand to mending the altar cloth and helping Mrs. Cotter prepare Christmas dinner for the needy. She taught the children their lines for the Nativity pageant, and she sewed their costumes. I don't know what I would have done without her." Yes, he did. He would have given up and handed in his resignation before Lord Whittendale could dismiss him from his post.

"Aye, she's a good girl, my Alice."

"There is none finer." Evan raised his own cup of wassail in a toast to the only woman he could ever love. Then he made his farewells, citing exhaustion and last-minute work on his sermon for the morning.

He was certainly tired from all the work he had done this week, and anxious about the morrow, but mostly he could not bear to wait for midnight and the lighting of the Yule log in White Oaks's cavernous hearth. All of the revelers would come into the Great Hall for the ceremony, where a sliver of last year's log would be used to start the new mammoth one, thus ensuring the prosperity of the house and its inhabitants. Evan did not know what they would use as last year's kindling, since Lord Whittendale hadn't been in the county, but he did know that everyone would lift their glasses and cheer the viscount and his lady, toasting the health of his unborn sons, the continuance of his line, the hope of the community.

Evan was pleased for Lady Farnham, and more relieved that that firstborn child would bear his father's name. Still, he could not stay to watch.

Besides, he told himself, his sexton could not be trusted to leave the party in the barn in time to ring the church bell at midnight, or to be sober enough to pull the rope. If this was to be St. Cecilia's last Christmas, the bells had to ring.

He'd done his best to save the church, Evan reflected. He'd used his money to hire carpenters and buy lumber, and he'd been sawing and nailing alongside the workmen. The roof was secured, albeit temporarily. The new stairs would not collapse under the weight of the heaviest worshiper. A few broken pews were shored up, a few more stones were remortared. All the dust and dirt was swept out, fresh pine boughs, holly, and ivy were brought in.

Evan had not stopped there. He'd helped roll out the gingerbread for the children, and found parts in the Nativity pageant for every child he could bribe, knowing their parents would then attend, if only to see their offspring as Magi and shepherds.

Now it was up to the Lord to see if His servant's best was good enough.

On his way home in the gig Alice had convinced the squire to put at his disposal, Evan counted. He did not count the miles back to the vicarage, nor the stars overhead, nor the number of smiles Alice had bestowed on her various dancing partners. No, he counted seats, empty seats.

The poor from the almshouse. The loyal villagers. The sheep farmers whose children were sheep in the pageant. Alice and her reluctant family. Those were all he could count on. And they were not enough. He doubted if any of the White Oaks guests would attend, not after the revelries of this evening. The rest of the gentry at the Christmas ball would undoubtedly go to Most Holy, with its gleaming stained glass windows and its choir's voices raised on high.

In despair, Evan knew the only thing to be raised at St. Cecilia's was more dust. He had too many seats, and too few sitters.

*

The mice had toiled mightily that week also. With Fred holding on to the last of his nine lives, and firmly intending to spend that one safely alongside Mrs. Cotter's nice warm stove, the desperate, determined duo worked all the harder, not having to look over their shoulders. They were invigorated by the crusts of bread and apple cores the carpenters left behind, too, as well as the vicar's efforts to save their home.

They had St. Francis polished to a fare-thee-well. His back side still had patches of paint and plaster, but his front shone as lustrous as soft fur and mouse spit could burnish it. His robes showed a few extra folds, and his face a few more wrinkles, where the gnawing had been a tad too enthusiastic, and one of his fingers was sadly missing altogether, but his smile seemed all the sweeter to the weary rodents. Surely now, after all of their work, one of the worshipers would notice the golden gleam.

Unfortunately, they realized St. Cecilia's had too many dark corners and not enough candles.

"What if no one sees the statue?" Pass fretted.

"They have to," Ed insisted. To a mouse's eyes, the gold was as unmistakable and beckoning as a ripening ear of corn.

"I don't know, Ed. These human people aren't all that bright. They forgot about hiding the golden statue when the bad men were coming, didn't they? We've got to do something."

So when Vicar Merriweather came to his church to pray for a miracle, he heard Cotter ring the bells for midnight. He heard the answering chorus of Most Holy's pair of bells chime back. And he heard another pair of tiny, tiny voices.

"Look to St Francis," Evan thought he heard.

"Fine," he muttered. "Now I am hearing things. It is not enough that I shall lose my church and lose the woman I love; now I am to lose my mind as well."

"Look to St. Francis," floated again across the empty church.

Evan supposed it wouldn't hurt to pray to each and every one of the plaster saints in their niches, though he rather thought he'd do better starting with St. Jude, patron of lost causes. Still, he would not deny the little voice in his ear. Lifting his candle the better to pick out the correct niche, Evan walked to the side of the church.

There was St. Francis, one arm extended to an alighting sparrow, the other cradling a...bear? Another creature sat by his feet. Odd, Evan could not recall any such animals surrounding the saint when last he'd dusted the statue. He stepped closer, holding his candle higher.

"You see, you see!" Ed was hopping up and down, and Pass had to wrap his tail around St. Francis's neck to keep from falling off in his excitement.

"I see," Evan murmured, and he had eyes for nothing but the statue, gleaming golden in its niche, as bright as the Christmas star leading the Wise Men to Bethlehem, as bright as the love he had for Alice. "I see."

After the shortest prayer of thanks in Christendom, Evan ran for the door and shouted, "Ring that bell, Mr. Cotter. Keep ringing it. Tell everyone. We've got our miracle."

9

Most Holy Church was almost empty that Christmas morning. Everyone came to St. Cecilia's to see the golden statue, treasure lost since the times of Cromwell, found, by everything holy, on Christmas Eve.

The pews were filled, and the aisles, too. So many people crowded into the little building that the heat from their breaths warmed their bodies and their souls and the old stones of the church.

The collection plate was filled. Evan would not have to petition the bishop to sell the statue in order to finish the repairs, but would even have some money left to feed the hungry. There would not be so many needy mouths, not once Lord Whittendale kept his promise to better conditions for his dependents.

Alice's eyes were filled with tears of happiness.

Mr. Merriweather's heart was filled with joy and hope.

The mice's bellies were filled, too, with the slice of Christmas pudding the vicar had hidden behind the lectern where no one could see.

Never had there been a more glorious Christmas service. The children all remembered their parts, and so many voices joined in the hymns and carols that no choir could have sounded sweeter. Evan was so elated that his words, for once, flowed smoothly, movingly, in benediction. No souls burnt in eternal damnation in this sermon; he spoke only of the love of God for His children. Feeling the vicar's sincere spirituality, knowing he cared for their well-being as well as their redemption, the congregants vowed not to miss a single one of his Sunday services.

Evan knew that would take another miracle, but he smiled as he shook hands with everyone leaving the church. Some were on their way to the feast at the vicarage, while others were on their way home to share Christmas dinner with family and friends. Some were headed toward White Oaks and another elegant repast.

"My man of affairs will call on you in the morning, Merriweather, to see what's to be done and in what order," Lord Whittendale told him.

"I have some of the ready in the church funds now, my lord, so St. Cecilia's can get by on its own for a bit."

"Nonsense, the sooner the church is fully repaired, the better."

Lady Farnham, stunning in her white furs, laughed. "I told him I wanted to be wed in St. Cecilia's, that's why Randolph is in such a rush. A special license would only give rise to more talk, so we would prefer starting to call the banns this Sunday, if you will."

"I would be honored, my lady. And St. Cecilia's will be glistening for the wedding in three weeks, I swear it."

The viscount nodded. "And not a moment too soon, lest people start counting months. I'll come by later, after my guests have left, to discuss what changes we can bring to the parish. Perhaps we can establish a pottery or a brickworks, to employ some of our people, so they don't have to leave for positions in the factories and mines."

"Don't forget the school," Lady Farnham reminded him.

"That's right, we'll set up a proper school for the children, boys and girls, so they can better their lot in life. That's if you are willing to oversee its operation, at a raise in pay, of course, in addition to the increase I already promised."

"I...I..."

"Can't expect you to do more work without recompense. Yes, and I intend to recommend that the bishop consider you for rector of Most Holy, when old Bramblethorpe there retires. No reason you cannot hold two livings, earn a decent wage. That ought to make your days brighter, by Jupiter."

"You are too generous, my lord. That was never part of our bargain, nor a school nor a pottery."

"Nonsense, my son is going to be born here, isn't he? Can't have him living in some beggar's backwater."

"Your daughter Cecily will be born here," Lady Farnham corrected. "Then your son Francis."

"Francis?"

As the two left, arm in arm and bickering over the sex of their firstborn, Squire Prescott took their place, with his womenfolk behind him stopping to greet some of the neighbors.

The squire pumped Evan's hand. "Good show, lad, good show, I say. Didn't know you had it in you. Alice said you did, of course, but she always had a soft spot for this church. I heard what Lord Whittendale said about when Bramblethorpe retires, and I'll second his recommendation. Meantime you've got a respectable livelihood, eh?"

"More than respectable. In fact now I can—"

"And I suppose now that you're come into your own you'll be looking around you for a wife."

"Why no, I don't need to—"

The squire shook his head in regret. "You'll be off to London, I'd wager, before the cat can lick its ear."

Since the cat could barely lick its foot currently, Evan would not be leaving any time soon. He tried to tell Squire he had no intention of seeking a bride in London, or anywhere else, for that matter, but Prescott was bemoaning his fate. "Dash it, just when I find an eligible match for m'daughter, one that will keep her in style but close to home, he up and marries a dashing widow. Now you'll be looking over the crop of heiresses in Town, the devil take them, and I'll have to traipse off to Bath or some outlandish place to find puss a proper match."

"I am not going to London, Squire, and I am not looking for a bride. I already found one, if Alice will have me, and if we have your blessing. We do, don't we?"

"Love her, do you?"

"With all my heart, till my dying day."

"Good, for I fear she'll have no other. Just like her mother, she is, knows her own mind and won't settle for less. You're a lucky man, Vicar."

"She hasn't said yes yet."

Squire laughed. "She will."

She did, after the rest of the worshipers left the churchyard.

"You are sure, Alice? Life won't be all parties and pretty gowns and trips to Town."

"Such a life would be pointless, without you in it. But are you sure, Evan? You could find a woman with a larger dowry."

"But none I could love more. Will you marry me, my Alice, now that I am a man of means and can make you an honorable offer? I promise to fix the vicarage roof and windows first, of course, so you are not frozen by the drafts."

"I would marry you if we had to take up residence in the barn, my love. And I refuse to wait until all of the renovations are completed. You will just have to keep me warm until then."

As Alice and Evan went to help serve Christmas dinner in the vicarage, they made a detour around the back of the church, to seal their pledge with a kiss. They were out of sight of everyone but two very small observers.

"I told you they weren't very smart," said Pass, rubbing at his ear.

"How so? These two seem to be catching on to the really important business of life. I'd wager there's the patter of little feet in the nursery before next Christmas."

"What, are those barn mice moving in now that Dread Fred stays in the kitchen?"

"No, you dunderhead, a baby."

"Oh. Well, I might be a dunderhead, but how long do you figure before those human people think to look at the rest of the statues?"

*

The parishioners uncovered the rest of the gold before Twelfth Night. St Cecilia's didn't need half as many candles, with all the gleaming. It just needed an extension, to hold everyone who came to see.

And Exultemus Domine was right: The Merriweathers had a daughter within the year, named Faith. She arrived not too many months after the somewhat premature birth of the viscount's heir, Randolph Francis Pemburton Whitmore.

Long before that, young Passeth-All-Understanding had a mate of his own, and her mother and sisters moved in, too, with a cousin or three, and an old auntie to keep Ed company. Together they managed to drag a new book behind the altar, for bedding and names for the next generation.

The firstborn, the biggest and strongest and smartest mousekin, was the cub chosen to be the leader, the one destined to guard the clan's perpetuation. They named him after the vicar who made sure they were well fed, and after the new book.

His name was Merriweather Christian Hymnal Churchmouse.

They called him Merry Christmouse, for short.

CPSIA information can be obtained
at www.ICGtesting.com
Printed in the USA
LVHW111452130821
695242LV00012B/217